FIC
DUERIG

MW01125169

8-14

STAN'S LEAP

— † —

Tom Duerig

FIC
DUERIG

iUniverse, Inc.
Bloomington

Stan's Leap

Copyright © 2011 Tom Duerig

This is a work of fiction. All of the characters, names, incidents, organizations, and dialogue in this novel are either the products of the author's imagination or are used fictitiously.

iUniverse books may be ordered through booksellers or by contacting:

iUniverse
1663 Liberty Drive
Bloomington, IN 47403
www.iuniverse.com
1-800-Authors (1-800-288-4677)

Because of the dynamic nature of the Internet, any Web addresses or links contained in this book may have changed since publication and may no longer be valid. The views expressed in this work are solely those of the author and do not necessarily reflect the views of the publisher, and the publisher hereby disclaims any responsibility for them.

Any people depicted in stock imagery provided by Thinkstock are models, and such images are being used for illustrative purposes only.

Certain stock imagery © Thinkstock.

ISBN: 978-0-595-50848-8 (sc)
ISBN: 978-0-595-50106-9 (hc)
ISBN: 978-0-59-561675-6 (e)

Printed in the United States of America

iUniverse rev. date: 9/14/2011

PART I

✝

Henderson Island

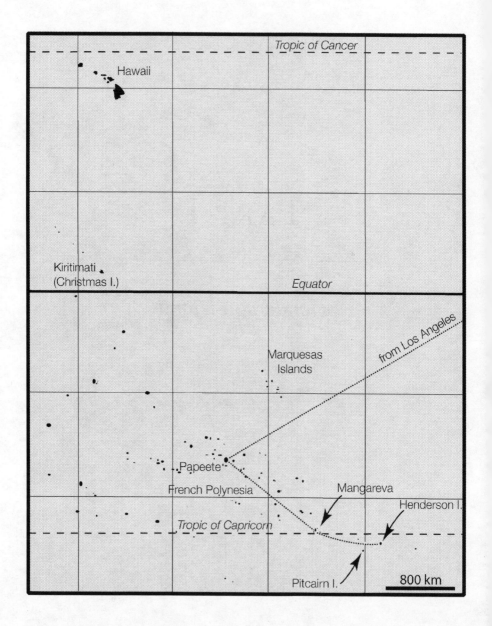

Tropic of Cancer

Hawaii

Kiritimati
(Christmas I.)

Equator

from Los Angeles

Marquesas
Islands

Papeete
French Polynesia

Mangareva

Henderson I.

Tropic of Capricorn

Pitcairn I.

800 km

Chapter 1

STAN CLUTCHED HIS STOMACH and groaned. "What the hell was that?"

Before Jenny could reply, the pilot turned his head and shouted over the drone of the engines. "Sorry about that. There was a goat on the runway, but I think we scared him off. We'll just circle around and try again. No worries. We'll be on the ground in just a few minutes."

Jenny shook her head in disbelief. "A goat? Is he serious?"

"He's serious all right. I can see it down there, just watching us," Stan said, peering out his window. "Probably waiting for just the right moment to come back. But I'm not so sure I'd call it a runway—it looks more like a beach—it's not even paved. He glanced behind him at the other six passengers, somewhat reassured that they were taking the aborted landing in stride.

Still, as their tiny plane dipped its left wing to begin a tight turn, Stan couldn't help but feel a bit uneasy with just how far they were from home. Neither Jenny nor Stan were big travelers. Their honeymoon in Kona, on the Big Island of Hawaii, was the first time either of them had seen an ocean—strange, given their mutual penchant for reading Pacific Island adventures and Jenny's competitive swimming experience. Now here they were, dodging goats in the middle of the Pacific Ocean, and tomorrow, there would be yet another flight, from Mangareva to New Eden, wherever that was.

Stan stared down at the small daypack crammed under the seat in front of him. That was all they had for their two-week stay on New Eden. Their instructions had been clear, "We'll provide everything you need, just bring what you need for the trip out—no personal belongings will be allowed on the island."

Stan reached across and squeezed his wife's hand. "Having second thoughts?"

"No way!" Jenny jerked upright. "Are you?" She seemed almost combative.

Stan shrugged.

Jenny squeezed his hand reassuringly. "My grandfather always said his only regrets in life were regrets of omission—the stuff we don't do—never the things we do."

The trip had been Jenny's idea: a last fling before parenthood. They had learned about New Eden from an airline magazine on their flight back from Kona three months earlier. It was a short article, almost an advertisement, about a unique resort just about ready to open, run by an outfit calling itself "Polynesian Retrospectives." New Eden promised to create an authentic ancient Polynesian experience for its twenty guests. To Jenny and Stan, returning from an idyllic Hawaiian honeymoon to a particularly wet and gray winter in Pittsburgh, it seemed like paradise.

Jenny's pregnancy had been a surprise—a welcome surprise, but one that immediately changed their life. Jenny quickly decided to dump her plans to go to medical school, at least for now, and focus on parenthood. She had enthusiastically but lovingly bullied Stan into taking time off work without pay so they could take a "babymoon." Stan was receptive to the idea until Jenny reminded him of the article on New Eden. They had the rest of their lives for working and taking ordinary vacations, she argued, but an adventure like that was something they might not ever be able to do again.

Stan's counter, that they hadn't the money for such an extravagant trip, lost traction when Jenny learned that during the first few months of operation there were no fees from the resort, they simply had to get themselves to some place called Mangareva.

Fortunately, the goat made no attempt to intercept the plane on its next landing attempt. The moment they bounced to a stop, the pilot, who was also the acting flight attendant and ground crew, jumped out and opened the main door for his passengers. Stan slung his daypack over his shoulder and followed the others onto the runway. As soon as he stepped into Mangareva's warm, tropical air, his flagging optimism returned. Opening a flap at the top of his daypack, he retrieved a small map. Holding it between them, Stan and Jenny silently took their bearings.

Jenny pointed to a hill off to their left. "Must be up there."

"Looks like it. Feel like walking through town a bit before heading up to the hotel—or guest house, or whatever it is?"

"Sure. I really need to stretch my legs."

There were no signs to indicate which direction the "town" was, but all the other passengers had unhesitatingly turned left in front of the airport, so Stan and Jenny decided to go with the flow. Within a few minutes, it was clear that they had found their way to Mangareva's main town of Rikitea. Their small map indicated a loop walk: a tour that included the island's seven stores and the small, dank, and ambitiously-named St. Michael's Cathedral. An hour later, they concluded that they had seen just about all there was to see of Mangareva's bustling downtown and started up the hill they had spotted from the airport. They easily found their tiny bed and breakfast, ate an authentic, family-style Polynesian dinner, and finally enjoyed a much-needed and well-earned sleep.

When they returned to the airport the next morning, they noticed another couple, looking as out of place and lost as they themselves felt. Knowing that there were to be two others joining them on the next leg to New Eden, they wandered over to introduce themselves. Stan stood just over six feet tall, but this guy was several inches taller still and built like a linebacker, oversized in all respects except his neck, which was notably absent. The fit of his black and silver Oakland Raiders T-shirt was obviously intended to show off the results of his weightlifting efforts. The girl on his arm appeared to be of about the same age, slim, average height, brilliantly blonde, and buxom enough to leave no doubt that she wasn't entirely the work of nature.

"You heading to New Eden?" asked Stan.

The man threw up his hands, brushing the girl off to the side. "Well, that's the idea, but nobody's even here. What the fuck kind of an airport is this anyhow?" He barely glanced at Stan, instead directing his reply to his companion.

Jenny and Stan looked at each other for a moment before Jenny tried to pick up the conversation with the giant's blonde companion. "I'm Jenny and this is Stan. We're headed to New Eden too."

"Hi!" The girl laughed and held out her hand to Jenny, and then Stan. "I'm Claire and this is my fiancé, Bob. We're from LA. What about you guys?"

"Pennsylvania. You seen the pilot yet?"

Their struggling conversation was interrupted by an ageless, scruffy man of average height and build walking through the back door. In his cut-off jeans and baseball cap, Jenny thought he looked as though he'd been lifted right out of a Hemingway novel. He studied the small group for a moment and then asked in a slow drawl, "I suppose you're the group headed out to Henderson?"

Stan stepped forward. "No, we're going to New Eden. Do you know who we're supposed to talk to?"

"Me. I'm Alan, your pilot. Looks like you're all here, so let's get going. I don't suppose anybody will care if we leave a little early." Alan turned and walked toward the back door leading out onto the runway, then suddenly stopped, turned, and pointed to an unmarked door on the left wall. "The trip will be three hours or so, depending upon winds, and there aren't any bathrooms on board, so use 'em now if you can."

The four passengers looked at one another, leaving a moment of silence that Alan took as their answer. "No? Well, then let's get going. The plane's all checked out and ready, and the weather's not getting any better."

While Jenny and Stan were still recovering from their confusion,

Bob boomed, "Three hours? I thought this was a short flight! Where is this New Eden place anyway?"

Alan shook his head. "New Eden! The island's called Henderson Island, and yeah, it's about three hours away. The last people I took out said the same thing. They somehow thought the island was nearby. Well, it's not." He turned to the main entrance, toward an attractive black-haired Caucasian girl just walking through the front door. "Janice, I thought you were going to take care of that."

The girl, obviously not a native of the island, ignored Alan and smiled to the others. "Hi, I'm Janice, the office manager for Polynesian Retrospectives. I'm guessing you're Stan and Jenny. We spoke on the phone a couple of weeks ago." Jenny nodded. "And you two must be Bob and Claire." Bob rolled his eyes, somehow acknowledging that she had guessed correctly.

Janice glaring briefly at Alan then turned back to the guests. "Sorry about the name. We don't like to tell people the real name of the island because we don't want curious yachters coming around—it would make it hard to create an authentic atmosphere if we had yachts circling the island day and night. It's not that long a flight really; you'll be there before you know it."

"I don't understand," Jenny said. "Where is this New Eden then?"

"It's south and east of here. Kimo will explain it all—he runs the operation on the island." She hesitated before continuing, "You'll love it. It's really an incredibly beautiful place."

"Are we the only ones going?"

Alan pulled open the back door. "Today, yes. The plane only carries six passengers, seven in a jam. I take four every Saturday, six on Sundays. Ten coming and ten going every weekend, all staying for two weeks—that's pretty much the run."

As Alan and Jenny led them through the back door onto the airstrip, they noticed three small planes, none of which looked particularly airworthy. They had seen the planes the day before when they'd landed but had assumed they were relics that had nothing to do with their trip. Stan's angst mounted sharply as Alan led them past the first two aircraft toward the oldest-looking: a boxy, single-engine plane, with two cracked passenger windows and a heavy streak of soot on the tail complementing an impressive array of rust-covered dents. Stan, who had always been a bit troubled by flying, flashed a concerned sideward glance at Jenny, who tried to smile reassuringly. Stan shrugged back and climbed in.

Bob was not as subtle. "What the hell is this, some kind of fucking joke?"

Alan laughed. "Well, at least you're honest. Don't be fooled by her looks, she's very safe—an Otter DHC-3, one of the most reliable planes ever made—and she's been flying without an accident a fair bit longer than any of you have been alive. I do all the maintenance myself, and I've got every bit as much interest in her safety as you do."

Bob looked at the plane and then turned back to Janice, "Look, this isn't exactly what we were expecting. Claire's afraid of small planes. This just isn't going to—"

"No, it's all right, I'm not scared," Claire said, stepping through the plane's hatchway. Bob's frown deepened, but he slowly followed. For a moment, Stan thought they were all going to have to push to squeeze him through the doorway.

Inside, they met torn, threadbare seats and frayed seat belts. The cockpit instruments, however, appeared to have been updated to digital standards.

Just before Alan closed the door, Janice called up to him, "Hey, I almost forgot what I came down to tell you. I just heard that Mr. Stetson is going to be here tomorrow morning."

"On that famous yacht of his?"

"Yep. I guess they're sailing in the area and want to stop by and meet us."

Alan sarcastically replied, "Super. I'm sure we'll have a lot to talk about."

"No, really, he wants to take us out on his yacht to see New Eden. He's never even seen it. He wants you to fly tomorrow's clients out early so we can join him on his boat in the afternoon."

"I fly, I don't sail. Boats sink. Besides, it would take at least a couple of days to get there by boat," Alan grumbled.

"Oh, come on, it'll be fun. How often do you get to meet a billionaire?"

"Just as often as I want to."

"Boy, you're sure in a grumpy mood." Janice turned to the guests and waved good-bye, "Anyway, see you guys in two weeks, or maybe sooner if Mr. Stetson really decides to sail out there. Have a great time and say hi to Kimo and Nani for me."

Jenny leaned forward toward Alan. "Is that *Chris* Stetson you were talking about?"

"That's the one. He owns this whole operation. His idea. Guess he got tired of his airline and wants to try screwing up something else."

Alan closed the door, and almost immediately after he took his seat in the cockpit, the engine started.

The three-hour flight seemed endless given the small, hard seats and Bob's loud, persistent complaining. Alan remained silent except for about two hours into the flight when he turned and informed everyone that Pitcairn Island was visible off to the right.

Stan leaned forward and asked Alan, "*The* Pitcairn Island? Where Fletcher Christian settled after the mutiny on the Bounty?"

"There's only one."

"Isn't that the Mel Gibson movie?" asked Claire from behind.

Stan and Jenny locked eyes in silence. The book, *Mutiny on the Bounty*, was a childhood favorite of Stan's, and he had shared it with Jenny shortly after they had first met. While not so interested in the two hundred year old mutiny itself, Jenny had become enthralled with its aftermath: nine of the *Bounty* mutineers kidnapped twelve Tahitian women, a three-month-old girl, and six men as servants, then set sail looking for someplace to hide from the omnipresent wrath of the British admiralty. After months of searching, they stumbled onto Pitcairn Island, which had been incorrectly positioned on all the maritime charts of the day. They decided a misplaced island in the most remote and isolated part of the world was as good a place as any to hide, so they unloaded their stores, dismantled the ship, then deliberately sunk the *Bounty*'s hull so that none of them would be tempted to ever leave.

It was eighteen years before another ship spotted the misplaced island, and another seven before somebody finally set foot there and spoke with its settlers. Fifteen men, twelve women and a baby were left completely alone for twenty-five years on a postage stamp of an island no more than a couple of square miles in size. Within a just a few years, all the men, both English and Tahitian, were dead save one of the mutineers. Exactly what happened isn't clear, but the bloodshed began with a war between the races and concluded with a war between the sexes—a war that was won, Jenny often pointed, by the women. Sensibly, the women decided to keep one man—a common seaman named John Adams—alive. The instigator of the mutiny, the infamous but now remorseful Fletcher Christian, had been one of the earliest casualties of the violence.

By the time an American whaling ship finally stumbled across the tiny island, the one surviving mutineer was still alive, happily living among a thriving, English speaking population of Tahitian women and teenagers. Though Adams and the surviving Tahitian women were extensively interviewed by later visitors, there is no consistent record of what happened on the island, a fact that led to extensive speculation during the following two centuries, mostly in the form of novels and pseudo-histories.

Stan leaned across Jenny's lap and together they stared down onto what appeared to be little more than a rock, accidentally plopped down into the middle of the ocean. "It's really unbelievable isn't it?" he said. "Can you imagine knowing that you were going to live the rest of your life on that little rock out there?"

"No," replied Jenny. "But it's even harder to understand how they could systematically murder each other until there was just one man left on the entire island. What if he had died too? Not a great testament to mankind. Sometimes I wonder if we're better than that today."

Chapter 2

STAN AND JENNY GOT their first view of New Eden just seconds before touching down. The dirt airstrip was even smaller and bumpier than Mangareva's, but at least there were no goats to greet them. As the foursome deplaned, Stan surveyed the island that was to be their home for the next two weeks. Just as the Polynesian Retrospectives website had promised, it was green and lush, with palm trees swaying in a warm, brisk, perfumed breeze set against a brilliant blue sky. The only structure within sight was an ugly white concrete cube off to the north, some ten feet on a side. A couple was walking toward the runway, she wearing an ivory-colored cloth wrap with black pattern, and he wearing the mirror image: a black cloth with a white pattern. The man was on the tall side of average, well-muscled but lean—almost wiry—with sun-bleached blond hair flowing in ragged curls to his shoulders, a scraggily blond beard, and a weathered complexion darkened by constant exposure to the sun. Most striking were his intense, deep brown eyes that drew Stan's attention because of the incongruity with his blonde hair.

"Welcome to New Eden!" the man boomed with a wide smile. "My name is Kimo, and this is Nanihi, or Nani if you prefer." He gestured to his companion, who stood slightly behind him glancing up through slightly downcast eyes. Nani had silky black hair and the most perfect complexion Stan had ever seen, copper-colored and flawless, giving a translucent impression. She had a lean but curvaceous body and almost unnaturally large, warm brown eyes that Jenny noticed lingered for a moment on Stan. Whereas Kimo's weather-worn face made his age difficult to determine, Nani's age was masked by the perfect texture of her skin—her skin and eyes were those of child, but her body that of

11

a woman. Stan thought she might be of Polynesian descent, but it was difficult to tell—she was racially ambiguous, with features that made her impossible to label.

"We'll be your hosts while you're here," Kimo continued. "I'm sure it's been a hassle getting here, but now you have nothing to do but relax. I know you've already read all about our project here, and I promise it'll be all that you read about and more." Kimo's speech gave him away as an American, likely from the West Coast. "We've got just a few things to go over before we head to the village, but let's start with refreshments and introductions."

Stan stepped forward and extended his hand to Kimo. "Hi, I'm Stan Brown and this is my wife Jenny."

"Whoa!" Kimo said, raising his hands and stepping back from Stan's proffered hand as if it were red hot. "Hey, life is complicated enough without two names to remember. One will do fine here, so take your pick: is it Brown or Stan?"

Stan smiled. "Well, then, I guess I'll be Stan, and this is my wife Jenny."

"Much better. Welcome, Stan and Jenny!" Kimo grasped Stan's hand and then firmly pressed a kiss against each of Jenny's cheeks. His enthusiasm was effusive and contagious, making Stan and Jenny instantly comfortable.

Nani stepped forward and kissed Jenny on both cheeks and then turned to Stan. Lifting herself slightly to her toes and holding his shoulders to steady herself, she leaned forward to welcome him the same way. Unsure which cheek was first, Stan turned his head the same way she did and clunked his head against hers. Nani giggled and tried again, this time landing a soft kiss on both blushing cheeks.

Their hosts then introduced themselves to Bob and Claire receiving a grunt from Bob in reply. The six made small talk while enjoying slices of fresh mango Nani had brought with her. Kimo did most of the talking and when Nani did speak, it was with a lilt that was difficult to place, but just enough so that a listener would know English wasn't her native language.

Kimo turned to Stan. "So, what brings you and Jenny here? Why the interest in ancient Polynesian ways?"

Stan shrugged. " I guess it was really Jenny's idea. Kind of a last fling before..." A sharp elbow from Jenny brought Stan to an abrupt stop. The release forms they had signed had listed a host of medical conditions that would have disqualified them, including pregnancy. The wording wasn't exactly ambiguous, with bold capital letters making it clear there were no medical facilities on the island. To drive home the point, the release form required witnessed signatures.

Jenny was quick to the rescue. "What Stan means is that I'm about to start medical school and it'll be a long time before we're going to be able to take a long vacation again." Kimo frowned, confused. "We read about New Eden in an article in an airline magazine, and it sounded like a real adventure." She reached for Stan's hand. "We've both always been interested in Polynesia and thought this would be a way to really find out what it's really like."

Kimo's smile returned. "What are you hoping to do while you're here?"

"Swim!" replied Jenny.

"Jenny's a great swimmer. She was on the swimming team at Pitt."

Kimo turned to Stan. "And what do you do back in the real world, Stan?"

"I'm a software engineer."

"Well, swimming we have, software we don't." Kimo turned away with an unmistakable look of distain. "Okay, let's get started. This is where we ask everybody to leave the modern world and completely immerse themselves in the Polynesian way of life. It may be a bit more awkward than you'd like at first, but in a couple days, you'll never want to go back. I see you all have small travel bags, but now that you're here, you won't need them. The white building over there ..." Kimo pointed at the cube-like structure to his right, "is what we call the bunker. We'll store your things there."

"Wait a minute," Bob interrupted. "We weren't told anything about giving up our luggage—just that we shouldn't bring electronics or modern shit. I've got my clothes, bathing suits, razor... we need that stuff!"

"Bob, I hope that's not true," Kimo replied with a condescending smile, "the release forms you signed made all that very clear. I promise the island will provide everything you need. I'll bet just about everything in your bags would have been foreign to the Polynesian way of life. Claire, how 'bout you? Is there anything in there that you think you need? Things that you think would have been part of the Polynesian lifestyle?"

They all turned to Claire's bright floral carry-on. She hesitated, turning toward Bob.

Kimo continued. "Think about the bag itself. What's it made of?"

"Well ..." she started, as if answering a trick question. "I've just got some clothes and make-up and stuff like that ... and really, I have no idea what it's made of. Whatever they make suitcases from, probably Nylon or Dacron, something like that?"

Kimo replied as if trying to maintain his patience with a child. "Are those things that the Polynesians would have had hundreds of years ago? Toothpaste? Razors? Nylon? Remember what you came here for: to experience a paradise unaltered by man."

Bob looked away in apparent disgust, but Kimo continued. "Look, what we're asking is pretty simple—take no man-made things beyond the airstrip, and that includes anything metal or plastic, any toiletries, and any modern clothes. Everything you need is already here. We only make exceptions for the things that were listed in the paperwork: a pair of sandals, so long as they're not plastic, corrective eyeglasses or contact lenses, and medications if they're absolutely essential—and I don't mean aspirin. Let's stick to that, okay? If you don't have appropriate sandals, we can loan you some, though I see you're all wearing sandals as it is. It's not—"

"This is bullshit!" Bob interrupted. "You mean I can't even take pictures while I'm here? Or shave? Come on, you can't be serious. This is supposed to be a vacation. I need my stuff."

Jenny and Stan stepped back, terrified by a man the size of Bob so animated. Kimo, however, didn't flinch. For a second, anger flickered across his face, but just as quickly, he softened. He stepped directly in front of Bob and asked, "Bob, why'd you come here? Why not Maui or Cancun? You could have taken all your *stuff* there. And if I'm not mistaken, you're signed up for four weeks."

Bob shrugged and stared at the ground, but Kimo pressed on, "No really, Bob, why here? You knew what we're about didn't you?"

Claire finally answered for him. "It really wasn't our choice, or at least not completely. My dad—"

"Hey!" Bob screamed. "That's none of his damn business, Claire, so just shut up, okay?"

Claire stepped back cowering while an uneasy silence settled over the group. Kimo softly but firmly broke in. "Look, if you want, you can go back with Alan when he brings the new guests tomorrow morning. He'll have a couple of extra seats. Spend the night here; decide in the morning, okay? One way or the other, though, your clothes and the rest of your gear are not going beyond this landing strip. I'm afraid that's just not negotiable. Your belongings will be perfectly safe inside the bunker. Please understand, if any of our guests violates our code, it compromises the experience for everyone."

"How about books?" Jenny asked, trying to deflect the confrontation. "I'd really hoped to catch up on some reading."

Kimo sighed. "Books don't belong on a Polynesian island, but it was decided to allow them if you feel it's necessary. Really, though, I'd encourage you to play it straight. You said yourself you wanted to learn how it was on the islands hundreds of years ago when men and women were part of nature rather than its enemy."

Bob wasn't mollified by the concession. "I want to talk to whoever's in charge here. We've been traveling for nearly three days trying to get here, and the hell if I'm going to just go back tomorrow morning. I want to at least bring my fishing gear. And you're telling me I can't even bring sunglasses?" To make the point, Bob held out his sunglasses.

A fiery look crossed Kimo's eyes. "First of all, I *am* the guy in charge.

Second, there are no phones on the island, so my word is final. You can complain as much as you want when you get home, but you'll find that the release form you signed before coming makes our policies clear… and yes, that includes leaving behind your overpriced Oakley's. If you're afraid of the sun, find a tree to sit under."

Kimo smoothly reached out and took the sunglasses from Bob's hands. Before Bob could react, Kimo turned to the rest of the group. "Listen, I admit the first few minutes or even hours here can be a shock—people don't always realize just how much their lives have become dependent upon modern technology. Lots of people talk about living as nature intended, but they don't really know what it means. Do any of you go backpacking?"

Stan and Jenny nodded.

"Well, imagine camping without nylon tents or sleeping bags—no stove or freeze-dried food or even matches. Wouldn't be the same, would it? These next two weeks will change you. Just go with the flow, so to speak. Trust the island to take care of everything you need and trust us as your guides. Explore a new way of living." He smiled and then added, "Or maybe I should say an old way of living."

When Kimo's passionate delivery stopped, the group stood silent—even Bob. Apparently relieved that he had a consensus, Kimo donned a huge smile.

"Good, then first thing's first: clothing. On all the Polynesian islands, clothing was simple, and so it is here. Nani and I are wearing what are called *pareos*—simple rectangular pieces of cloth made from natural fibers. Polynesians made them from *tutu* bark, or *ti* leaves. Different islands had different names for these simple wraps and they wore them differently, but they were the essence of all Polynesian dress. So, let's get rid of your modern clothing and get you into some pareos. If you prefer, you can go the way of many islands and wear nothing, but you'll still need a pareo; they serve many purposes other than just protecting your modesty.

"Ladies, if you follow Nani, she'll show you some pareos to choose from—we've got a bunch. I confess ours are made of cotton, not tutu bark, but it's a compromise that you'd appreciate if you felt the real thing. They'll be yours while you're here and to take with you when you go. And if you want to try to make your own pareo from real tutu bark while you're here, Nani will show you how. Right now, she'll give you a quick lesson on how to wrap yourselves to fit various occasions—I think you'll be surprised how elegant they can be. Stan and Bob, follow me, and we'll head over there behind the bunker. We can change there. Then we'll all meet back here and pack the clothes you're wearing now in your bags and put everything in the bunker. So, ready to become islanders?" With Bob grumbling, the group split up. As Stan walked off, he heard Alan's plane start and take off.

After about a half-hour, the new arrivals gathered again on the airstrip dressed in their pareos. The women were wrapped from just above the knees to just above their breasts, Claire in red and Jenny in light blue; the men wore their pareos as simple skirts to just above their knees, Bob in black, and Stan in ivory.

The pareos did look elegant, Jenny thought, though she felt a bit uncomfortable with nothing underneath her wrap, which was held in place by a tenuous bit of tucked cloth; a small slip or tug and she would be naked to the world. But at the same time, it excited her a bit and gave her a sense of freedom.

Stan walked up to Jenny and whispered, "He wouldn't even let us keep our underwear."

Jenny looked down at his pareo and giggled. "I can see that."

Stan peered down at himself. One thing for sure, he thought, sexual excitement would be hard to hide here. Jenny's playfulness was somewhat quieted when she saw Stan's gaze shift to her own pareo and realized that the details of her own anatomy weren't completely hidden either.

Kimo led the group to the bunker, which appeared to be aptly-named with a tightly fitting steel door secured with a heavy combination lock. He opened the door and then turned to address the group. "The bunker is our only connection to the twenty-first century. It and the stuff inside are the only things that weren't part of ancient Polynesian culture. We built it to keep emergency food, water, medical supplies, radios, and extra fuel for the airplane, in case Alan has to turn around halfway due to unexpected bad weather. There are also no mountains on the island, so the bunker is nearly air and water-tight and can act as shelter in case of typhoons or tsunamis—at least that's the idea, but there's really no history of either, so no worries."

Refusing Stan's offer to help, Kimo carried the bags into the bunker and reappeared in the doorway seconds later, empty handed. He reached for the door to swing it closed but abruptly stopped and nodded toward Bob's wrist. "Oops, we missed one thing, I see."

Bob either didn't notice, or chose to ignore Kimo.

"Your watch," Kimo persisted. "Probably more than anything else, watches or clocks would destroy the atmosphere we're trying to create. You'll be amazed what a difference that—"

"I'll be *amazed*?" Bob exploded. "Is that what you said? How's my damn Rolex going to affect anybody's experience here? And how am I supposed to know when it's time to wake up or eat?"

Kimo laughed and mimicked a thoughtful expression. "Hmm, let's see if I can answer that. Well, it's time to eat when you're hungry and there's food to eat, and it's time to wake up when you feel you've had enough rest and want to get up. Come on, Bob, I'll put it in your case with the rest of your stuff."

The two men stared at each other for several tense seconds that dragged on like minutes. Stan glanced at Nani, who was grinning broadly as if it were all just a game.

Jenny tried to defuse the situation with a joke, but when her voice came out, it was quiet and shaky. "Well, I could sure use a bit of time away from time—sounds relaxing."

Her play on words seemed to break the tension, giving Bob an excuse to back down without losing face. Cursing under his breath, he removed his watch and angrily tossed it to Kimo who briefly disappeared inside the bunker. After locking up, Kimo turned to lead the group down a well-worn trail to the north, away from the landing strip.

"So why the heavy lock?" Stan asked.

Kimo shrugged. "No real reason, just what we happened to have around. Besides, it's kind of symbolic in a way—you know, completely locking out the outside world? Anyway, if you need something, just come and see me."

Kimo continued to talk as he led the group. "The village is just a few minutes' walk to the north, on the northeast corner of the island. It's near what we call the Point. It can get hot and humid inland, but the steady breeze near the Point really makes it comfortable year round. Just as it gets to the hottest part of the day, the wind kicks in, then dies down again as the sun sets. Kinda like built-in air-conditioning. It never gets warmer than about eighty-five or colder than seventy, and as I say, the hot side of that always comes with the big fan."

"How 'bout rain?" asked Stan.

"There's a light rain about every other day, but it usually doesn't last long, and you'll find it refreshing. In fact, you'll probably look forward to the afternoon showers, especially inland where it's hotter." Gesturing behind him as he walked, he continued. "To the south, there's a farm where we grow our food, but we'll go through all that tomorrow afternoon when Sunday's guests arrive. We'll do a full orientation then; and tomorrow night, we'll have a welcome celebration. Right now, I'll show you to your huts, and then you can take it easy until dinner. Go for a swim if you want, or sit on the beach, or just get to know the other guests. For your safety, though, please don't roam too far until tomorrow's orientation; after that, the island's yours to explore."

They walked through what was obviously the center of the village, a large clearing covered with soft, comfortable sand, which was a distinct contrast to the surrounding rough rocky areas. There was a central cooking fire surrounded by several piles of stones that might be ovens, a large wooden eating table with several benches, and a large lean-to shelter. Scattered palm trees cast fluttering shadows on about a dozen huts—sturdy bamboo frames covered with tightly woven yellow-green palms. The huts were clustered around the village in a *V*, which seemed to point to a thirty-foot-high ridge protruding into the ocean, obviously what Kimo meant by the Point. Each hut was about a hundred feet from its neighbor, and about fifty feet from either the east or north beach, with a door facing the clearing and a window, with an improvised roll-down wind block, facing the ocean.

Kimo led Jenny and Stan to their hut on the north beach first. Inside, was a single room, no more than fifteen feet to a side, with two thick grass mats, each covered with a simple sheet and a woven grass pillow. There were two bamboo-and-reed chairs against a wall, and a large clay pot of water on a small table. Certainly less romantic was the bathroom—a hole dug behind the hut covered by a bamboo seat and surrounded by two woven reed walls. There was a pile of leaves next to the hole. The rules, Kimo explained, were to follow each use with a fistful of leaves and a few scoops of sand. The combination, he claimed, promoted decomposition and reduced odor.

Simple and rough, but Kimo assured them they would seldom be in their huts anyway.

Chapter 3

"WELL, SHALL WE UNPACK?" joked Stan as soon as they were alone.

Before Jenny could reply, they heard a booming "You've gotta be kidding!" off in the distance, followed by a muffled argument they couldn't really make out.

"Wow, I'm glad we're on the other side of the village," Jenny said. After a moment she reconsidered, "Though it does promise to provide some entertainment in case things get boring. Kimo's got a lot of guts standing up to that monster—I think he could break Kimo over his knee if he wanted to. He may be the biggest human being I've ever seen."

"And mean too. He scares me."

With nothing to do inside the hut, Jenny and Stan decided to check out the beach. It was as idyllic as the website had shown: fine, uniform, pink sand surrounded by a quiet lagoon so transparent that it was difficult to even see where the water started and the sand ended. A reef some hundred yards from shore protected the lagoon and provided a steady background roar, evidence of the huge waves built up by the vast unbroken expanse of the South Pacific, relentlessly trying to battle its way through the reef. The wide beach was scattered with palm and coconut trees, offering generous areas of both sun and shade.

Jenny and Stan noticed two couples sitting in a group about a hundred yards to the west. They started to walk in their direction to introduce themselves, but stopped short when they simultaneously realized that the foursome was completely naked, sitting on their pareos rather than wearing them. They started to turn and walk the other way when one of the women waved them over. Stan and Jenny looked at each other for a moment before Jenny shrugged and began walking toward the group. Stan held back for just a second, but then tentatively followed her.

Instead of covering up, all four stood to greet them. An attractive dark-haired woman that looked to be in her early thirties broke the ice. "Hey, you must be the new recruits! I'm Sue, this is my husband George, and this is Wayne and Allison. Welcome."

Trying to avert her eyes without making her discomfort noticeable, Jenny said, "Hi. I'm Jenny and this is Stan. Sorry, we didn't mean to spy on you."

Sue looked confused, but then looked down at herself and laughed. "Oh, this. Sorry, I didn't even realize ... well, never mind, you'll get used to it." Nevertheless, the foursome picked up their pareos and covered themselves.

"We weren't so sure in the beginning either," Allison said. "Things are ... I don't know ... just different here, I guess. Besides, we thought it can't be a sin if God put us all here like this in the beginning." She glanced at Wayne, who nodded slightly in approval.

They spent the next hour or so getting to know one another. George and Sue were from New York, in their midthirties. They both worked on Wall Street for different investment banks—lovers at home, competitors at work. Wayne and Allison were also from New York and had been best friends with George and Sue when they had all gone to Columbia University together. Wayne had majored in electrical engineering and now worked for General Electric. Allison, a nutrition major, was trying to make a go of it starting a health food store. Allison and Wayne were perhaps a bit less enthusiastic than George and Sue about their stay on the island so far, but it was clear they were all happy after their first week on New Eden, which was a relief to Jenny and Stan.

"So, what'd you think of Kimo?" Sue asked.

"A bit of a control freak, maybe, but he sure is passionate about his mission. And he seems competent enough, I suppose," Stan said. "Why, is there more to the story?"

George shrugged. "No, not really. You've read him pretty well. He takes this thing pretty seriously, but as long as you let him put on his little show, he's really great. I think this whole place would fall apart without him. You'll see what I mean tomorrow. What'd you think of his playmate?"

Stan paused for a minute until he got it. "You mean Nani? I don't really know, she didn't say much. Pretty girl though."

"Yeah, well, wait till you see the rest of her!" George said under his breath.

Sue nudged him. "Hey, come on, that's not fair to us mere mortals. Why are all you guys so enthralled with her anyway?"

"It would be hard not to be," George said. "Even you have to admit she's pretty spectacular."

With the sun still a couple of hours above the horizon, the two couples excused themselves, explaining that they had volunteered to help with dinner preparations. They politely declined Jenny and Stan's offer to help, saying there wasn't much to do, and that there'd be plenty of time to help tomorrow. Left alone with nothing but endless beach in sight, Stan smiled, then tugged on the knot that secured Jenny's pareo. Without a fight, Jenny let it fall to the sand and then, laughing, did the same to Stan's. Without the privacy to continue in the direction they wanted, however, they both abruptly sat up on their pareos and looked out over the ocean at the sun just beginning cast a pink hue across the horizon.

"You know," Stan said, "I could get used to this." He lay on his back, closed his eyes, and stretched his arms above his head. Jenny looked around to make sure nobody was watching and then surprised him with a quick kiss.

"Hey, no fair kissing below the belt!"

"You're not wearing a belt. And besides, it doesn't look to me like all of you is objecting."

Nervous about his rapidly changing anatomy and their lack of privacy, Stan folded his pareo over his waist. "Hmm, why do I think that you're not going to have any trouble adjusting to island life?"

Dinner began just as the sun set. The nearly full moon shed ample light on their meals of vegetables, grilled fish, and fire-roasted yams. The website had warned that the food would be simple, and so it was, but it was also nothing short of excellent.

When Stan and Jenny finished eating, Kimo approached them and said he wanted to introduce them to the remaining three couples, who were all now a week into their two-week stays. He began by leading them to an attractive dark-haired couple in their early forties.

"Stan, Jenny, this is Marco and Francesca from Italy. Marco's proven to be quite the fisherman—you'll come to appreciate his efforts while you're here. And let's see if I remember this right, Marco, you design clothing back home?"

"Yes, for sports. We both do."

"Where are you from in Italy?" asked Stan.

"Udine, in the northeast," Marco said. "Do you know it?"

Stan shook his head and then asked whether they were enjoying the island. Marco and Francesca seemed even more at home on New Eden than the foursome they had met earlier. Quiet and polite, both spoke English well, only occasionally searching for words that resulted in phrasing that, while perfectly understandable, was unusual. They had three children, all either off on their own or in college.

Next, Kimo took them to meet a blond couple huddled in close conversation. The couple stood to unusually tall heights as the trio approached, and extended their hands to Stan and Jenny.

Kimo spoke before they had a chance to introduce themselves. "This is Stefani, and this is Erik. They're from Frankfurt, but I can't remember exactly what you guys do there."

"We both work for Lufthansa," Erik said. "I am a mechanic and Stefani is a travel organizer for large groups. Where are you from?"

"From Pittsburgh, in Pennsylvania."

Erik lit up. "Yes, we were there. Last year we rented a camper and took a long tour of the United States—six weeks. I remember the three rivers and a fort where they come together. We had bad weather when we drove through, but I think it was a very friendly place."

"It is very friendly. You two travel a lot then?"

"We love travel. It is why we work for Lufthansa. I think we go next to Nepal trekking for a few weeks."

Jenny perked up. "Cool, I always wanted to do that! When are you going?"

Erik laughed. "Don't ask me. Stefani is the planner. I only follow orders. I think sometimes she has the rest of our lives planned."

Stefani joined the conversation. "We leave on September fourth." Her voice was quiet and formal, but polite.

Jenny was enthralled by how many places the young German couple had been. With the conversation obviously self-sustaining, Kimo excused himself. About a half hour later, the final pair wandered over to introduce themselves.

"Hi, you must be Jenny and Stan," said a tall, lean African America woman perhaps in her midthirties. "I'm Lynda."

"And I'm Linda." The other woman giggled and covered her mouth like a child keeping a secret. She appeared to be the same age as her partner, but her pale skin, light blonde hair, and short, stocky figure cast her as a complete contrast.

Stan and Jenny were taken aback, unsure whether they were joking. After an awkward few seconds, Jenny stepped forward and extended her hand. "Hi, I'm Jenny and this is Stan."

"Oh, I thought you were Stan and he was Jenny," Lynda came back quickly, laughing. "Sorry, we have too much fun introducing ourselves—it's really not fair. I'm Lynda, spelled with a *y*, and this my partner, Linda, spelled with an *i*."

Both successful businesswomen working for the same large medical company, they explained that they enjoyed the confusion their names caused. Any comment or question directed toward one was inadvertently redirected to both, so they could always choose who would respond. It gave them a sense of control, Linda said. Despite their differences in personality and appearance, they somehow merged into one person. Like a pair of shoes, each of them by herself seemed incomplete.

After dinner, couples began to drift back to their huts. The newcomers were the last to depart, and Kimo called after them. "Hey, listen for the plane tomorrow. It usually arrives around midmorning, but you'll hear it. Let's meet at the village center just after that for an island orientation—say, about half an hour after it lands."

"How the fuck are we supposed to know when a half hour is up?" Bob shouted back.

Kimo smiled. "Guess. We'll wait for you."

Polynesian Retrospectives
PO Box 39 – Rikitea
Mangareva 98755
+689 97 55 55

Kimo,

Here's your guest list for the next two weeks – looks like an interesting bunch!

Arrival on June 2nd:
　Wayne & Allison Selkirk (New York)
　George & Sue Simpson (New York) – traveling with Wayne & Allison

Arrival on June 3rd:
　Erik & Stefanie Schneider (Germany) – both in the travel industry so treat them _well_!
　Marco & Francesca Liera (Italy) – ok English skills, but they should be fine
　Linda Callaway & Lynda Curtis (New Jersey) – don't ask!

Arrival on June 7th:
　Stan & Jenny Brown (Pennsylvania) – replacing the couple that dropped out last week...
　Bob James & Claire Johnson (California) – signed up for 4 weeks – I _hope_ you get along with them

Arrival on June 10th:
　Don & Mary Olsen (Colorado) – a bit older, but insist they like rugged vacations
　Russ & Jules Lindeman (Australia) – Russ is a real crack-up, you'll like him
　David Shukov & Michelle Frey (Maine) – on their honeymoon believe it or not also, Michelle is a nurse so if anything comes up...

Say hi to Nani for me!

　　　　Ciao,
　　　　Janice

Chapter 4

WITH JUNE CLOSING IN on winter in the southern hemisphere, daylight arrived late the next morning. As they awoke, Jenny and Stan found themselves looking at their wrists only to find pale bands that refused to tell the time. After washing their faces in their clay water pot and visiting the back of the hut, they wandered out to the north beach. They were greeted by a magnificent sky with endless rows of brilliant red-orange clouds. The sound of the waves crashing on the reef and the invigorating salt breeze created the impression that the clouds were rolling waves of an inverted ocean—and that somewhere off in infinity, the two oceans had collided, producing the growing, orange half-disk of the sun.

"Wow!" Jenny put her arm around Stan's waist and rested her head on his shoulder. They stood watching nature's theater until the sun climbed high enough to finally dissolve the hues of sunrise. Finally, as the last tint of orange disappeared, Jenny uncoupled from their embrace and wandered down to the water. For the first time since she'd been here, she really appreciated the incredibly soft texture of the sand, the variety of tiny shells strewn along the beach, and the cleanliness of an ocean uncluttered by the debris of civilization. Looking around, she unwrapped her pareo and headed toward the water.

"Are you sure that's a good idea?" Stan had snuck up behind her. "Kimo said we should be careful until the orientation. Why don't you wait and see what he says about swimming?"

Jenny was about to remind Stan that Kimo had already told them the lagoon was safe for swimming when they heard the aircraft.

Stan turned toward the sound and then looked at Jenny. "Seems like Alan's a bit early."

Jenny rewrapped her pareo. "All right, let's go meet the new guests and hear what Kimo has to tell us about the island."

Reluctantly, they turned their backs to the sea and headed toward the village center. Bob and Claire were there rummaging through a wooden bowl of fruit on the main eating table. They looked bedraggled, as if they hadn't slept. *Claire looks a bit less imposing without her make up*, Jenny thought. Bob looked beaten and resigned, and not particularly pleased with the selection he was finding in the bowl.

Stan almost decided to share their religious encounter with the sunrise but reconsidered, figuring that it probably wouldn't impress them anyway. And in a way, he liked their defeated personalities more than yesterday's combative arrogance. *No*, he thought, *better we keep the sunrise for ourselves.*

"Any sign of the others?" asked Stan cautiously.

"Yeah," Bob said, his face flat. "They just left for the *farm*, whatever the hell that is—something about getting there before it got too hot." Bob still didn't bother to look at Stan as he spoke.

After an uncomfortable few moments trying to communicate with Bob and Claire, Jenny and Stan were relieved to see Kimo approaching with three new couples in tow, freshly stripped of their possessions and noticeably uncomfortable in their new pareos. As they spent the next half hour in introductions, Jenny was surprised that the newcomers seemed to be looking to them for encouragement. The pair that appeared most comfortable with their new surroundings was Don and Mary, the oldest of the new arrivals. Don was built on a small frame, balding, but exceptionally fit with the sun-baked complexion of a true outdoorsman. If Kimo was almost wiry, Don was the very definition of wiry. He was a materials scientist at the Colorado School of Mines, and Mary was a housewife and part-time social worker. The trip was to be their celebration of independence, as the last of their three children had just left home for college.

"It's short-lived independence, though," Don said.

Mary laughed. "Yep. Our oldest is due with our first grandson next month. And guess who's taking care of the baby?" she said, directing her thumb back at herself. Don raised his eyebrows, apparently uncertain that his wife's new role was the best option.

David and Michelle—a physicist in his midthirties and a nurse in her late twenties—were honeymooners from Maine. She was somewhat fidgety and nervous, and he seemed quiet and cerebral, often disengaging from idle conversation. Like Bob and Claire, David and Michelle gave the distinct impression they didn't belong here, but she relayed that her parents had been only too happy to care for her five-year-old daughter and two-year-old son from a prior marriage; they had been so happy, in fact, that they'd paid the airfare as a wedding present. Something in the way they spoke, however, led Stan to believe the trip wasn't entirely a shared passion.

The final pair was from Melbourne, Australia: Russ and Jules. A petite, attractive, and perfectly matched pair, they were lively, wore broad smiles, and broadcast an infectious and uplifting effervescence. When Stan asked Russ what he did for a living, he said, "I'm Australian. What do you think I do? I drink beer." Only after a few minutes of probing, did they finally find out how close to the truth that was—Russ was an advertising executive for Fosters. Jules worked in sales for an American drug company. They had no children, and often went on unusual and adventurous vacations. Getting to know this couple made Jenny and Stan more optimistic about the two weeks ahead. As before, Nani was quiet throughout the introductions: always elegant, smiling, and observant, dispensing words as if they were rare orchids.

After the conversation started to wane, Kimo stepped out and addressed the group. "Again, welcome, everybody. Now comes my favorite part of the job: to introduce you to *our* island. I emphasize *our*, because we want you to treat it as your island while you're here. Enjoy it, love it, and take care of it as if it were yours. It's a fragile island, but it will take good care of all of us if we treat it with just a little respect and care."

The group edged closer around Kimo, clearly enamored by his compelling, magnetic ardor.

"I'm going to take you on a walking tour that'll take most of the morning. We'll do a loop around the northern half or so of the island, which is really all that's useable."

"So we're on the north part now?" asked Claire. "But the sun … oh, that's right, we're in the southern hemisphere, aren't we?"

"That's right," Kimo continued, amusement crossing his face. "We're on the north-facing shore, and yes, the sun is to the north, not the south."

Though Kimo made Claire's question seem silly, Stan realized that he hadn't even questioned why the sun was to the north. *Not bad for a blonde ditz from LA*, he thought.

Kimo gestured straight ahead. "That's the north beach over there." And then pointing to his right, he continued, "And that's the east beach, where your hut is, Claire."

Kimo grabbed a stick off the ground and drew an oblong shape in the sand. "Our island is shaped kind of like a rectangle, about six miles by three miles, with the long sides running north-south. Right now we're up here, at the northeast corner."

Tapping his stick on far end of his sand drawing, he said, "The southern part of the island is exposed to heavy surf and strong winds that blow up a lot of salt spray, so the vegetation is sparse and the ground is much rockier. It's really not of any use. If you want to explore it anyway, go ahead, but there are no trails to speak of, so please walk carefully. A good rule of thumb is that if there's vegetation covering the ground and you can't see rock underneath, then don't step there. In fact, that's a good rule of thumb for the whole island: don't just assume you're about to step onto solid ground—make sure. It's really not a life-threatening issue, but it'd be pretty easy to ruin your vacation by stepping into a hole and twisting an ankle. And in case you haven't noticed by now, the rock around here is pretty sharp and irregular, so please be careful."

He pointed to a little bump on the other end of his drawing. "Right there is the Point. You can see it out there." He pointed up to the rocky ridge separating the north and east beaches. "The Point extends out into the open ocean, beyond the reef, like a needle piercing right through the lagoon. There can be some pretty impressive waves out there, so be careful. You don't want to be surprised by a rogue wave and washed out to sea.

"Both the north and east beaches are some of the best you'll see anywhere, protected by reefs a couple hundred yards from shore. The sand's made from coral ground by the waves and parrotfish; that's what gives it its pink color. Swimming is perfectly safe within the protected lagoon, and the water's pretty shallow—generally less than six feet. During low tide, you can wade almost all the way out to the breakwater itself, but be careful where you step. It's mostly a sand bottom, but there are plenty of coral heads as you approach the main reef. There are no sea urchins to worry about, at least."

"There are a couple of deep water channels through the reef into the lagoon, one on either side of the point. You've probably noticed that the waves beyond the reef are pretty serious stuff, so I guess it's obvious that swimming through the channels isn't exactly advisable. But in case you're tempted, don't. There are always strong currents running from east to west. It would be suicide to try to swim over the reef, so if you get swept to the west of the two channels, there's no way back. Might as well keep swimming west—Australia is just a few thousand miles away, unless you get really lucky and hit Pitcairn Island first."

He then pointed back to the Point. "The fishing from the Point is excellent—the really cool thing is that because the tip of the Point extends all the way past the reef, you can fish in deep water right off the tip, or reef fish off the sides. Inside the protected waters, by the way, there are tons of lobsters. I'm not sure why, but it's gotta be about the highest density of lobsters on the planet, so I hope you like lobster. Oh, by the way, these are the spiny variety, so they don't have claws—no worries for swimmers or waders. I should have mentioned, too, that the beaches are so beautiful that we have to share them with sea turtles that come annually to lay their eggs. You may see a couple while you're here, but the real invasion comes during the summer months—January and February. It's really something to see in case you decide to come back again."

Kimo waved over his shoulder toward a small pool of water. "Also, over there is a spring that's our main source of fresh water. You can drink from it right from the ground without any concern. Fresh water is limited on the island, though, so if you go off exploring, make sure to bring some water with you. There's usually some standing water near the farm; we use it for irrigation, but I wouldn't drink it if I were you."

Kimo stopped and looked at Nani. "So what am I missing?"

Nani, shrugged with a smile.

"Then I guess that's about it for the main village area, so let's start our walk." Kimo turned to his right and walked toward a well-worn, narrow path just above the east beach. "We're going to walk south, along the cliff above the east beach for about a mile, and then we'll head inland to the farm—that's where all the other guests are right now. The east beach is great during the hot hours of the day, because it's the windward side of the island."

He led the group at a brisk pace, continuing his orientation of the island.

During a lull in Kimo's discourse, Stan asked, "So what's this island called anyway? The brochures we saw called it New Eden, but on the way over, Alan called it Henderson. Neither one seems like much of a Polynesian name."

Kimo laughed. "That's a bit of a can of worms. At first, the New Eden Resort was supposed to be on a small island in the Mangareva group, but then Stetson—I guess you guys know he's the owner and founder of this place—bought Henderson Island, which was much larger and more remote, so he shifted his plans and put it here. He always hated the name *Henderson*—he said it wasn't marketable. So since the resort is the only thing on the island, he decided to just call the whole island New Eden, but the official name is still Henderson Island. You're certainly not going to find New Eden on any map. Anyway, New

Eden or Henderson, I really don't care what you call it. I guess I'm like Alan and tend to use its official name."

"So where'd the name Henderson come from?" asked Stan.

"That's another interesting question. It's named after Captain James Henderson who discovered it in 1819—actually I should say rediscovered because it was discovered in the early 1600s by the Spanish. They called it San Juan Bautista Island, but that's even worse than Henderson Island.

"But even though the Spanish were the first recorded outsiders to set foot on the island, there's a lot of evidence that it was inhabited for a couple of hundred years by Polynesians, probably sometime between 1000 and 1500 AD. Our best guess is that the population reached about a hundred or so at its peak. We don't know where they came from, where they went, or why they left, though people speculate that the civilization died off because they couldn't trade with nearby islands. Sociologists believe that without active trade, long-term survival requires a population of at least a thousand people, much more than this island can support on its own. Who knows, maybe while you're here, you'll discover some key clue to the island's history."

The trail took them along the steep cliff overlooking the east beach, providing spectacular views and occasionally veering off onto steep side-trails that extended down to the beach. After thirty minutes or so, the beach and crystal-clear shallows below were suddenly replaced by waves breaking onto jagged limestone cliffs. There the trail then turned inland. Kimo explained that everything to the south was just more of the same, with no safe way to get down to the water. The waves were indeed spectacular. Watching them pound onto the rock for a few moments drove home the dangers of trying to cross the reef itself.

As they walked on, Kimo continued to describe the native geology and flora. He explained that the island, made entirely of limestone, was technically called a "raised atoll." Millions of years ago, a volcano had erupted leaving a rim just below the ocean surface. Over the millennia, the rim and crater became a coral reef, which was then lifted by further volcanic action to a fairly uniform hundred feet above the surface. The beautiful beaches had been formed by the surf pulverizing the coral into sand and then washing it onto still-raised coral. There were no mountains or even hills on Henderson, and no permanent streams, but a slight general depression in the middle of the island hinted of the original volcanic crater.

The thick covering of vegetation lay among stunted trees, the tallest of which were only about thirty feet high. Kimo pointed out some of the edible flora that was rumored to be indigenous to the island—taro root and trees bearing coconuts, bananas, guavas, and mangos—although, he said that some speculated they'd actually been introduced by Polynesian settlers.

"But no matter," he said, "they now flourish all over the northern part of the island, and we encourage you to help yourselves whenever you want."

He did admit, however that when constructing the village, some effort had been made to transplant additional fruit varieties such as limes, oranges, and papaya.

Kimo told them about other vegetation useful to island life, as well, including candlenut trees, which had nut husks that made excellent torches and ink; hibiscus, which could be used to make rope; the ti plant, which had a great number of uses, from wrapping food for cooking to making a kind of fabric, to concocting a crude sort of sugar; and the tutu tree, which was used by ancient islanders to make pareos and other cloth.

As they followed the trail inland they noticed an extraordinary variety of birds, some with stunning plumage. Kimo pointed out that many were flightless, made so by an unthreatening environment that rendered flight unnecessary. He added that the birds provided a plentiful supply of fresh eggs, as well as tough but tasty meat.

The sandy soil soon gave way to a rockier, increasingly irregular, sharp surface. Nani, who had started the walk in bare feet, soon donned a pair of sandals she had been carrying. Even in their sandals, the guests were forced to slow their pace, yet Kimo, in bare feet, walked briskly on, showing no discomfort at all. The temperature also steadily rose as the increasingly dense vegetation screened the ocean wind. After about twenty minutes, the trail opened up to a large clearing that must have been almost a half a mile across. The other guests were there working.

Kimo continued his narrative. "So this is the farm—the main source of food on the island. I suppose you could survive on the native flora, but I think you'd get pretty tired of the diet after a while. This is the best soil on the island, and we've brought in crops from other local Polynesian islands. You'll be spending a fair bit of time here; it's almost a second village."

Kimo walked them through the vegetable fields, obviously proud of the well-organized, healthy, and weed-free crops: peas, corn, soybeans, pineapples, tomatoes, peppers, squash, and pumpkins, as well as several others they didn't recognize until Kimo identified them, and still others with completely unfamiliar names. On the western end of the clearing were several trees planted at regular intervals, including breadfruit, limes, grapefruits, peaches, and pears.

On the south end of the clearing were a few thatched lean-to's and three crudely fenced pens, one containing a dozen or so goats, the second a half dozen pigs, and the last, a bunch of chickens industriously pecking the ground. The goats, Kimo explained, produced milk (with the exception of two rather mean billy-goats which must have been there for either food or reproductive purposes). Kimo explained that his goal was to cultivate a large enough population of pigs so that within a year he could release them into the wild, where, if all went as planned, they'd develop into a self-sustaining species that could provide much-needed variety to their diet. The chickens produced both eggs and meat, of course, but Kimo said their quality was inferior to what the wild bird population had to offer.

"What's this?" Bob asked from behind.

Surprised to hear him show any interest at all, the whole group turned to see him fondling a pointed leaf on a tall plant.

Kimo walked over to him. "That's hemp. It's one of the most useful plants on the island. We use it to make rope, primarily, but it is also a source of food and can produce several useful drugs … and no, it's not what you're thinking. It's closely related to marijuana, but this is just hemp. Smoke as much as you like, but it won't do a thing for you."

Then Kimo pointed out a trail heading directly north from the farm. "That's the shortest way between the village and the farm. It'll take you to the airstrip first, and from there, straight back to the village—about a twenty minute walk. You'll get to know that trail well by the end of your stay. But now we'll keep going across the island, over to the west beach."

After a hot and uninteresting fifteen minutes or so, they were greeted with yet another magnificent view of the coast, perhaps even more spectacular than that along the east beach trail. They had arrived at the west beach, right at the point where the sand dissolved into rocky cliffs and the protective reef finally gave way, allowing the punishing surf through to the island. As on the east coast, Kimo explained, there was again nothing but rugged limestone cliffs to the south, unprotected by the reef.

The trail turned north along the coast, tracing the top of the cliff, about fifty feet above the beach. Kimo pointed to a steep rock scramble on the beach. "That leads to the Lone Frigate Cave, where much archeological evidence of ancient Polynesian settlement has been discovered, although to call it a cave is a bit of an overstatement. It really isn't much more than a hollow in the limestone cliff, barely above the waterline."

After following the coast to the north for a few kilometers, the path reached the northwestern corner of the island, then gently veered right to follow the north beach. Whereas the east beach was separated from the north beach by the distinct rocky Point, the west beach swept gently to the right to become the north beach. Kimo took the opportunity to tell them about the brown rats that were the only native mammal life on the island, the abundant *miro* wood that Pitcairn Islanders treasured for carving, and the history of castaways from various shipwrecks on the island, including the whaling ship *Essex*, whose crew opted to face starvation at sea, and even cannibalism, rather than staying on Henderson Island. He also told of a most mysterious adventurer named

Rob Tomarchin, who unsuccessfully tried to settle on the island with his chimpanzee companion Moko in the early 1960s—though his escape (or rescue) from Henderson was well-chronicled, Kimo said, the subsequent whereabouts of this mystery-man were still completely unknown.

As they approached the village, Kimo stopped and turned to address the group. "Really, there aren't any rules or obligations here. If you want, you can simply hang out. It would be nice if some of you wanted to learn some of the ways of Polynesian life, but it isn't required. Jobs that we appreciate help with are things like collecting wood for the cooking fire, working at the farm, and harvesting food for our meals each day. You're going to love the fresh food, by the way. I guarantee you'll never eat better than you will here. But harvested plants need to be replanted, and there's always weeding, feeding the animals, milking the goats—things like that."

"Milking the goats?" Jenny said. "I'd like to learn how to do that."

"We'll teach you whatever you want to learn, including plucking chickens if you want."

In apparent contradiction to his earlier claim that nobody needed to work, he added, "But, bottom line, it'd be really helpful if everybody could wander down to the farm each morning and put in an hour or so of work. Best while it's still early, before it gets too hot. You'll find it fun, really."

Kimo glanced at Nani and then added, "Oh, and in the evenings, there's also cooking to be done. You'll find it interesting to see how the Polynesians cooked without the use of any metal. Anybody like to fish?"

Bob begrudgingly nodded.

"Fishing is fantastic here, and I'd be happy to show you how the Polynesians fished. Some of you already met Marco—he can help you too. Fishing can be anything from just checking the fish and lobster traps in the lagoon, line fishing for tuna from the Point, or spear fishing in the lagoon. Spear fishing is a real blast. Try it while you're here, you'll enjoy it.

We do have one important rule: please don't touch the main fire unless it's to cook. If the fire goes out, whoever put it out will have to start a new one—and trust me, that's no easy task."

A final highlight of the tour was a small, nondescript pile of rocks on the western end of the village. This, Kimo said in near reverence, was the entire island's supply of decent rock.

"For making tools and such," he said. "The soft limestone on the island is all but worthless, so we decided to supplement the island's raw materials by bringing in some basalt from Pitcairn Island nearby. In fact, the quality of the rock was so critical to the Stone Age Polynesian way of life, it may well have been one of the reasons they couldn't keep the island populated. There's evidence that during the years of Polynesian settlement, they had imported rock from nearby Pitcairn Island, maybe trading it for things that were common on Henderson but hard to find on Pitcairn."

Kimo picked up a stone knife blade and handed it to Russ, who was nearest him. "Feel how sharp this is."

Russ ran his finger gingerly over the edge and nodded in amazement. "Christ, it's as sharp as a friggin' razor."

Kimo laughed and took back the knife. "Actually it's probably sharper than a razor. Stone Age tools were very functional … and, yes, sharp. Some of the islanders actually shunned steel tools for decades after Captain Cook introduced steel to the islands. The only problem with stone tools is that they broke easily, and that's what eventually led to iron and steel—but it wasn't because they weren't sharp."

"But you forgot about the Bronze Age," Stan said. "It was bronze tools that displaced stone tools. The Iron Age came much later."

"Actually, that, too, is a common misconception. Bronze was rare and only available to the rich, so most common folk in Europe and Asia continued to use stone tools throughout the Bronze Age. Copper is rare and precious throughout the world, whereas iron ore can be found almost everywhere. Well, everywhere but on the islands. Anyway, since the poor people did most of the real work, and they couldn't afford bronze, bronze tools were really only for show. It wasn't until we figured out how to win iron from ore that metal tools really took over. In any case, the other problem with stone tools is that they're hard to make. I'll show you how next week."

By that time, the others had begun to prepare a lunch of boiled vegetables and some snapper that Marco had caught that morning. The meal was a leisurely, social affair with everybody serving themselves on wooden plates that they, afterwards, cleaned themselves. Kimo introduced that day's newcomers to the five couples beginning their second week. As they were all trying to find intersection points in their lives, Stan particularly enjoyed watching Linda and Lynda introduce themselves to Russ and Jules, who lit up at the idea of a couple named Linda and Lynda.

As the sun continued its westward journey, people began to scatter, some to rest in the shade, others to swim, work, explore, or fish. George announced that he felt like lobster for dinner and asked if anybody was interested in helping him gather some. Somewhat bored and curious, Don and Stan quickly volunteered. Nani, meanwhile, asked if anybody wanted to help her make bread—several women volunteered, including Jenny.

Lobster hunting hardly turned out to be as challenging or manly as the name might suggest. It was really nothing more than checking traps that had been previously placed in waist-deep water. The traps were made of sticks lashed together with hemp twine, each marked by a floating coconut and weighted down with a few stones. All they had to do was wade out in the crystal clear lagoon to the markers, haul up the traps, remove crabs, lobsters, and strays from the traps, inspect and repair any damage to the traps, and then place them in a new location. As promised, the lobsters were of the spiny variety and could be handled with complete safety.

It took about two hours to finish, but that was largely because they had no desire to work quickly; it was light work and refreshing to be in the water. They also stopped working often—each time one of them found some interesting fish, sea turtle, or coral head, he would call out to the others to come see it. In all, the traps yielded nineteen lobsters and a bunch of small crabs, not including four additional lobsters they grabbed straight from the water while wading out to the traps and back. At first, Stan felt a bit weird working naked in the water, but by the time he finished, he found himself starting back to camp in the buff before remembering to put on his pareo.

If catching lobsters was cool and refreshing work, making bread was just the opposite. Various grains (mostly wheat) had to be ground into flour before anything could begin. Yeast wasn't exactly available in little foil packages on supermarket shelves, so the dough was fermented using a bit of moldy dough set aside just for that purpose. The women took turns kneading the dough, until finally the loaves were ready to bake in one of the clay ovens. With no way to measure the oven temperature and only limited experience among them, the resulting bread was heavy, hard, and had an irregularly colored thick crust.

Though baking and lobster hunting took much of the afternoon, Stan and Jenny had time to for a quick swim and rest on the east beach, which they felt afforded them the most privacy. Stan dozed off for just a moment, and woke to find Jenny missing from her pareo. Sitting up, he scanned the horizon, and spotted her swimming out through the narrow channel in the reef into the open ocean. He donned his pareo and walked along the coast, helplessly following her progress as she swam outside the reef, around the Point and back through the channel to the north beach. When she finally reentered the safety of the lagoon, he retrieved her sandals and pareo, then stood on the shore waiting for her.

When she finally stepped ashore, Stan angrily tossed her her pareo. "What were you thinking? Didn't you listen to anything Kimo said? You know, if you got into trouble out there, there would have been no way to get to you."

She was surprised by his anger. "Sorry. I wasn't trying to worry you. I didn't mean to go through the reef when I started, but there's a big opening through the reef, and the currents aren't nearly as strong as Kimo made them sound. It really wasn't a problem at all. I'm not sure it would be so much fun to swim the other direction, but—"

"And what if I hadn't seen you go around the Point and brought your pareo and sandals to you? Would you have just wandered through the village buck naked and barefoot to get back to the north beach?"

Jenny suddenly stopped drying herself. "You know, I didn't even think about it. Sue was right the other day, you just lose track." She hugged Stan and whispered, "I'm sorry. Thanks for watching. Next time, I'll be more careful."

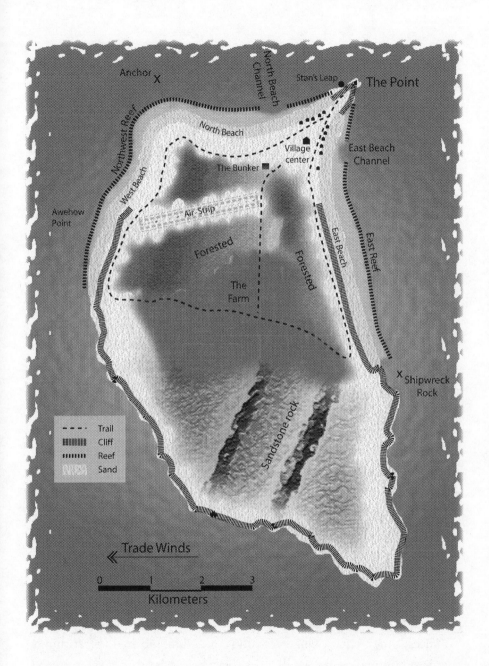

Anchor ✗

North Beach Channel

Stan's Leap

The Point

Northwest Reef

North Beach

Village center

East Beach Channel

West Beach

The Bunker

Awehow Point

Air-Strip

Forested

Forested

East Beach

East Reef

The Farm

✗ Shipwreck Rock

- - - - Trail

|||||||| Cliff

꘏꘏꘏꘏ Reef

Sand

Sandstone rock

Trade Winds

0   1   2   3

Kilometers

Chapter 5

DINNER WAS AN EXTRAVAGANT affair, and everybody participated in the preparation. Kimo and some of the men took on the task of cooking yams, taro root, and sweet potatoes in an underground pit, which itself was quite a production—heating rocks in a blazing fire, burying the rocks with the vegetables, covering the pit with banana leaves, and then topping off everything with a thick layer of sand. Kimo explained that underground cooking is really steaming, so the trick was to make sure the space under the banana leaves didn't go dry. Whenever a wisp of steam chirped up from the pit, he resealed it by shoveling on more sand.

The lobsters were cooked live on hot coals and were served with freshly picked lemons. A variety of green vegetables were prepared, as well, including a fantastic taro-leaf salad. The end result was enough even to stop Bob from complaining.

After dinner, Kimo lit the several candlenut torches surrounding the main cooking fire, and asked everyone to sit in a wide circle. He took a few shrubs he had stashed behind a tree and threw them into the fire, which immediately flared brightly and began to produce a seductive, aromatic smoke. Then he pronounced it entertainment time.

"Everybody's invited to contribute something," he said. "Jokes, dances, songs, tricks, whatever you want. Nani and I will start things out." He pulled out a small drum and began beating a slow, steady rhythm, like a heart beat. The newcomers looked toward the second-weekers for some clue as to what might be next or what they were supposed to do, but their attention was riveted on Nani. Almost immediately, Nani stood and moved slowly toward the fire. She began to sway with the beat, subtly at first, but with time, in larger movements, her hips seemingly disconnected from her upper body. Her arms and hands traced fluid patterns in the air. Her dance movements were neither amateur nor improvised, seemingly choreographed to convey a story, even if undecipherable to her audience.

The beating hastened. Her movements picked up energy until she was absorbed in the rhythm, as if in a trance. She began to dance to the group rather than for them, slowly moving from person to person around the fire, but focusing her attention on the male members, staring directly into their eyes as she gyrated in the sand in front of them. As she passed Kimo, he missed a single drumbeat as his hand darted up to grab the bottom of her pareo and pulled it away. Nani continued, oblivious to her exposed state. Her long dark hair danced across the front of her naked form, highlighted by flickering shadows.

Jenny scanned the men in the group. They watched her undulating form like tigers stalking a gazelle. Even the women couldn't take their eyes away from her lithe, fluid movements. As she progressed around the circle, she soon arrived in front of Stan. To Jenny's dismay, Stan appeared to be just as enthralled as the others had been, if not more so. In turn, Nani seemed to enjoy the effect she had on Stan, edging slowly closer to him.

Stan's trance deepened as the scent of coconut oil perfumed the narrowing gap between them. Nani began to wrap her form around him, bringing her body as close as she could to his without actually touching. Then she deliberately swept her waist-length hair behind her back, revealing herself in full to Stan. Though Jenny had always been sympathetic of the male hormonal drives, it soon became too much for her territorial instincts. She leaned into the fray and nudged him. "What do you think?"

The gentle reminder of her presence was enough to shatter his trance. He fidgeted, forced a small laugh, and deliberately looked away from Nani. For just a few seconds, Nani tried to reconnect with him, but when she realized the moment had passed, she continued gliding around the circle, making hormonal slaves of all the rest of the men.

After a few minutes, the beat accelerated yet again and the dance to lost its sensuality and morphed into a demonstration of raw energy, with Nani's hips moving in violent vibrations. She began to glisten with sweat, until the pace was finally too much for her to keep up. She suddenly broke into laughter, ran to Kimo, and took away his drum. The group applauded as Nani nodded her thanks to everybody, obviously enjoying the attention and admiration. Then, as if just realizing that she was naked, she abruptly turned away, picked up her pareo and wrapped herself.

Kimo explained that dances like this were common in old Tahiti, startling early visitors to the island. Both men and women participated. The hula dances one sees today are just a distant shadow of what they were. Nani then invited the others to learn the dance movements. With no volunteers, Nani took Jenny by both hands and pulled her to center stage. Jenny tried to sit down again, but as Kimo began his drumming, Nani grabbed Jenny's arm, prompting her to stay and at least try. It was quickly obvious that Jenny was unable to move the way Nani had, despite Nani's earnest coaching. The same dance that had created such sensuality just moments ago, now just invoked sympathetic laughter. Jenny made a point of steering well clear of Kimo, unsure of what she'd do should her own pareo suddenly slip away. After making a brief but diligent effort, she raised her hands in resignation. Nani gave her a brief hug and led her by the hand back to Stan.

Nani went back to center stage and, one by one, invited the others to try. Finally Lynda gamely joined her. Unlike Jenny, she quickly shed her inhibitions and made a genuine effort to imitate Nani's movements. And while not remotely comparable to Nani, she was energetic and enjoyed being the center of attention.

Before the end, Nani managed to convince Linda, Sue, and Jules to try. After Jules had made a feeble attempt, she grabbed Russ and forced Nani to teach him some of the hip movements. Before long, the group was roaring in laughter.

After the dancing lessons, Kimo asked for other volunteers to sing, dance, tell jokes, or whatever else they wanted. Francesca and Marco did a credible job of singing some Italian folk songs—Francesca, in particular, had an excellent voice. Inspired by the Italians, Erik and Stefani offered up a German drinking song and then challenged Jules and Russ to counter with an Australian drinking song. The camaraderie and the flickering torchlight created an environment that was uninhibited and free.

As Stan and Jenny walked back to their hut, Jenny laughed. "It's like getting drunk without the hangover." *And without risk to the baby*, she thought.

Chapter 6

JENNY AND STAN HEADED directly to the beach the next morning to bask in another spectacular sunrise. Then while the sun was still low, they headed for the farm, taking the well-worn trail through the airstrip. Passing the concrete bunker, however, sparked their curiosity enough to prompt a slight detour. As they walked around the concrete obelisk, inspecting it from all sides, Don and Mary joined them.

"Hey, good morning!" Don said. "You guys catch sunrise this morning?"

"How could we not?" Stan said. "We didn't see you out on the beach though. Were you watching from the village?"

"No, I had trouble sleeping and got up early for a quick run around the loop trail Kimo took us on yesterday. I only caught the end as I was running through the farm out to the—what is it? —I guess the east beach. Spectacular, though."

"You run a lot?" asked Jenny, herself also an avid runner.

"A little. I—"

"Hah!" interrupted Mary. "What a liar. He runs *all* the time. At least five miles a day, and marathons most weekends."

Don shook his head in denial while reaching out to touch the concrete Bunker wall. "So what d'ya think this bunker is all about anyway? Kimo locked it up like Fort Knox."

"Yeah, we were just talking about the same thing," Stan said. "It does seem weird, like Kimo's personal treasure trove or something. I don't see what kind of emergency supplies would be so secret. You know he didn't even want us to carry our backpacks inside? He insisted we leave them outside and he carried them in himself. I mean, what's that all about?"

"Who knows? He did the same with us." Don studied the sturdy combination lock and heavy steel hasp. "Well, I guess we all have our quirks."

The foursome continued to wander slowly to the farm. The temperature was ideal, accompanied by a wispy morning breeze. Kimo was already there, feeding the animals. He greeted them with a broad smile, thanked them for coming, and gave them each a few chores. He showed Jenny how to milk the goats while Stan collected eggs and helped Nani plant vegetables. Kimo had been right: it was less work than it was simple fun.

Kimo's pride in the farm was even more obvious than it had been the previous day—not only were all the plants uniformly spaced and the garden free of weeds, he also meticulously studied each crop's progress. He dug small holes in various places around the farm to test the water content of the soil, and carefully planned what should be planted in order to keep a constant, varied production of food. While polite, he was also precise in his instructions, explaining just where and how deep seeds should be planted, pointing out an occasional offending weed they may have missed, and so on. It seemed somewhat contradictory to Stan: Kimo espoused such a carefree existence, yet when it came to the farm, he seemed obsessive-compulsive.

Everybody showed up at some point during the morning except Bob and Claire. They weren't really missed, though, as there really wasn't all that much work to do anyway. It was more of a social affair than anything. And as Kimo had promised, just as the morning heat began to get uncomfortable, a light rainsquall moved in that was both beautiful and refreshing. It was at this point that the group headed back to the village for lunch.

After lunch, Jenny and Stan decided to explore the west beach to find the cave Kimo had told them about. Upon learning of their plans, Kimo gave them a skin of water, and told them to look for bones, purportedly from the ancient Polynesian settlers. They wandered south along the beach rather than taking the trail above the cliff. The variety of shells strewn along the sand far exceeded anything they had ever seen, giving them the feeling that they were the first humans to have ever walked there. Finally, with difficulty, they managed to find the cave—but it was little more than a nook in the rock wall. And the famous bones were hardly impressive either, unrecognizable as either human or ancient.

They then scrambled up to the loop trail that ran along the top of the cliff and explored inland, even heading a bit south of the farm. The going became difficult and treacherous as the trail gradually dissolved, with little to reward their effort and risk; the island simply became ever more unfriendly. The bird population increased as one went south, but not in variety. There were simply more of them. They noticed, too, that the birds had no fear of humans, allowing them to wander right up to their nests, squawking only if they reached out to actually touch them. Many of the larger birds even allowed them to touch and pick up their eggs without complaining. Humans were not, apparently, frequent company.

They arrived back at the village by what they judged to be a few hours before sunset. Dinner preparations were just beginning, though obviously it was to be a much simpler meal than the previous night's: vegetables and some small poultry that Kimo had plucked from the wild. Stan watched Kimo braise the fowl in some coconut milk. He was surprised when Kimo dumped the water from the green coconut and started to vigorously pound the husks with an elongated stone to produce the milk—he had always thought coconut milk *was* the liquid inside the coconut.

When they sat down to eat, some of the new guests were a bit hesitant to eat such small birds, but after digging in, the consensus was they tasted better than any chicken they'd ever eaten. The meal ended in quiet conversation and an early bedtime that was readily accepted—a full day in the sun and fresh breeze had taken a lot out of everyone.

Well into the night, after only a little restless dozing, Jenny sat up and turned to Stan. "Hey, you awake?"

"Yeah. It's so hot and muggy I can't sleep. I'm completely covered in sweat."

"Good. I was thinking it was just me and hoping there wasn't something wrong with … well, I was hoping it wasn't just me. Feel like a quick dip to cool off?"

"Great idea. Looks like a nearly a full moon too."

They slid into their sandals, grabbed their pareos, and made their way by moonlight to the north beach.

"Wow, this is spooky!" Jenny said. "Feel how warm the wind is! It's almost like we're standing in front of a huge hair dryer. I've never felt anything like it. I thought Kimo said the weather was always mild here."

"Yeah, and that the wind always cools things down in the evening." Stan slipped out of his sandals and pareo.

Hand-in-hand, they waded slowly into the lagoon, giving any creatures below plenty of time to move away.

"This is really cool—*neat* cool, not *cold* cool," Stan said. "Look at the way the moon's reflecting off the water. And the water feels great, doesn't it?"

Jenny wrapped her legs around Stan. "And I know how to make it feel even better."

They danced in chest-deep water to a silent rhythm that their bodies naturally found, enjoying the sensation of the weightless touch of each other's bodies. Their pace quickened in unison until they climaxed together. But as their senses returned, they became aware they weren't alone. Another couple stood in the water only a hundred feet away.

"Oh my God, do you think they saw us?" Jenny laughed quietly.

"I have no idea. Let's just act normal and go say *hi*. I can't even see who it is, can you?"

They untangled themselves and swam a slow breaststroke over to the couple. It turned out to be Linda and Lynda.

"Well, hello! How're you feeling?" Linda's mischievous tone left no doubt that they knew perfectly well what was going on.

Stan ignored the innuendo. "Fine, except for the heat. You couldn't sleep either?"

"No, and it looks like Allison and Wayne couldn't either," Lynda replied, nodding over her shoulder. Sure enough, there was another couple, a hundred or so feet away, bobbing around in about five feet of water.

"It's the first time we've had heat like this," Linda said. "The nights so far have all been just perfect for sleeping. I really wonder what Kimo's going to say about it tomorrow."

As she was talking, Stan noticed the dark figures of yet another couple walking down the beach. "I wonder who that is."

"I'll bet on Don and Mary," Linda replied. All four couples soon converged and began talking. Not long afterward, they were joined by Sue and George.

"Well, that's everyone with huts on the north beach. How much you want to bet that all the others are in the east beach lagoon right now?" Lynda asked.

Mary pointed off to the west. "What's that?" she asked. "Sunrise already?" An eerie reddish glow filled the sky.

"No way—the moon's still up," Don said. "And tonight, the moon should set before sunrise. Wrong direction for sunrise anyway."

Over the next ten minutes or so, the couples watched as the strange red glow pulsated, repeatedly growing and fading behind a heavy cloud cover, sometimes spreading halfway across the sky.

"Maybe it's like the northern lights," George said. "Do they have southern lights, too?"

"Beats me," Stan replied, "but I think you can only see them near the earth's poles anyway, and we're not exactly near either pole. Besides I thought they were usually blue or green."

"No, they can be red," said David, "but you're right about being too far from the pole. We're way too close to the equator for any kind of lights."

Jenny sighed. "It's beautiful, though, isn't it? Look how the edges of the clouds are lit up."

The lights soon faded and, shortly afterward, the moon dropped below the horizon, enveloping them in total darkness. The temperature also seemed to drop just a bit, or perhaps the water had just chilled them. Regardless, they waded out of the water.

"Okay, where are my sandals?" asked Lynda.

"Where's the village for that matter?" asked Linda. "I can't see anything."

Stan said, "It's almost a full moon, so it can't be that long until sunrise. I think we should stay right here on the sand. I don't feel like shredding my bare feet on the rock around here."

Lynda chimed, "So, it's a vacation. Let's just wait here until sunrise." She giggled mischievously. "I can think of some things to do on the beach in the dark."

Less than an hour passed before the first morning light danced on the rippling water, promising a sunrise not far behind. As dim as it was, with their eyes conditioned by darkness, they were easily able to find their belongings. A breeze began to blow, dulling the unbearable heat and, within minutes, giving way to a wind that raised foam from the ocean and bombarded them with a fine shower of seawater. The feel of warm wind and fine ocean spray was exhilarating, but the sky remained a leaden gray—there was nothing to see of sunrise behind the heavy cloud cover that had moved in. The exhausted group wandered into the village center, where they were joined by the east beach dwellers. Kimo arrived last.

Don was the first to ask Kimo about the strange weather which, although less intense, was still oppressive.

Kimo replied, "Don't really know. I've never seen it like this. But no big deal, it's already cooling down, and now it looks like we've got some rain on the way." Sitting on the central eating table, he nodded toward the sky behind them. Dark gray diagonal sheets streaked across the sky and ocean. Then, as if to underscore Kimo's forecast, they heard the distant roll of thunder. "Should be fun. Storms don't usually last too long on the island."

Kimo jumped up and grabbed the edge of the table. "C'mon, let's carry this over and put it under the lean-to. We can watch the storm from there while we eat breakfast. There's still bread from the other night, and some bananas and grapefruit. I'm sure the weather will be fine by the time we finish eating."

They sat around the table under the shelter, fascinated by the slowly advancing black sheets of rain lit occasionally by fierce strikes of lightning. When the rain finally arrived, it was a wall of water, unlike anything Jenny or Stan had ever experienced. It fell so heavily that the rocky soil couldn't drain the water fast enough. In no time, the ground became a pool of water, and the growing winds seemed to blow as much water up from the ground as was falling from the sky. Soon they could only see a few feet from the shelter as the island vanished behind a featureless, gray curtain of water.

Stan and Jenny cowered in each other's arms. The lean-to was both well-made and open to the leeward rather than the windward direction, so there was no risk of it being lifted and blown away. Still, it was ineffective at keeping out the wind and rain. Stan tried to provide words of comfort, but had to shout directly into Jenny's ear to make himself heard over the pounding rain. Her expression, however, convinced him it was he, not she, who needed the comfort.

The main front passed after about half an hour. The wind dropped and the rain tapered from torrential to heavy, making visible the fringes of the forest behind the village. Lynda ventured out of the shelter to rinse off in the rain. "Come on out! It's really nice. Like a warm shower."

One by one, the others cautiously ventured out, each remarking how warm it was.

Disbelieving, Kimo finally went out himself. The temperature of the rain seemed to surprise him even more than the previous night's heat. He frowned. "Rain this time of year is always cool, driven up by the southeasterly winds." Apparently, he wasn't happy that nature wasn't conforming to his expectations.

As the morning wore on, they saw yet again that Kimo was fallible: the rain didn't stop as he had promised, but continued steadily and heavily. Stan wondered how the sky could hold so much water. By late morning, tired of waiting for the rain to stop, Kimo announced he was heading out to the farm and asked if anybody wanted to help him feed the animals and bring back food for lunch. Always restless, Don volunteered, faithfully followed by Mary.

About thirty minutes later, Don came running back. He stopped under the lean-to, bent at the waist, hands on his knees, and spoke to the group between gasping breaths. "Listen ... the crops are getting washed away ... Kimo wants everybody to give him a hand up there ... digging some drainage trenches. He said on our way out there ... we should grab some digging sticks from the front of his hut."

The group rose from the table in near unison. Even Bob made a subdued show of cooperation. But after retrieving the digging sticks, they had trouble finding the trail. Bushes and leaves covered the path, and water still pooled over much of the grounds. Don showed them how to feel the trail with their feet and told them it cleared up a bit once outside the village itself. Approaching the farm, Stan could see that neatly staked rows were now a chaotic swamp. Plants had been washed away, bent, or crushed to the ground. Leaves and branches had blown over everything. A figure they could only assume was Kimo was caked in brown muck and working feverishly trying to cover exposed roots with mud.

It was at this point that Stan realized the storm was no longer fun and games—especially for Kimo. First it had had the nerve to disprove Kimo's predictions, and then it had launched a devastating attack on his pride and joy. For the guests, this was only a two-week vacation, which meant in their worst-case scenario, the bunker's emergency food supply bunker would get them through. But for Kimo and Nani, the destruction meant shutting down the resort until crops could be replanted or, the unthinkable, bringing in supplies from the outside. It was hard not to sympathize.

The guests immediately began to work with flattened digging sticks and bare hands. Some helped dig drainage trenches between the few rows of plants that remained. Others helped Kimo push mud back onto the roots of plants that looked salvageable. The plants that were beyond salvation were pulled out and their vegetables piled to the side to be carried back to the village later.

Their work continued well past lunchtime, and although the rain remained warm, the work was exhausting and frustrating. Their trenches became clogged and had to be cleared again. Their recovered roots were continually re-exposed by erosion. Faces were mired in mud, and the relentless downpour made it nearly impossible to tell others apart from more than ten feet away.

As darkness moved in, Kimo finally relented. Exhausted and depressed, he called out, "Hey, everybody, let's call it a day." Then surveying the area, he added, as if to convince himself, "I think it'll be okay from here. Let's carry some of this stuff back to the village for dinner and clean up."

By the time they arrived at the village, the rain had washed the mud off, but even under the lean-to, their situation didn't improve much: it was still raining and uncomfortably warm, and their pareos were still sopping wet and uncomfortable.

"Damn it!" shouted Kimo. "Who let the fire go out?"

Bob replied, "Well, let's see, who could that have been? Hmm, I'm trying to remember whose job you said the fire was."

Kimo glared at him. Finally, he replied to the entire group. "There's no way to start a fire with everything so wet, so we're going to have a cold dinner tonight. There're plenty of fresh vegetables and fruit. I'll start another fire in the morning."

"Aw, come on," Bob said. "You mean to tell me there are no matches in that stupid white building? Look, I got some in my stuff for sure, and I know there's gasoline in there—you told us there's extra fuel for the airplane. We've been working our asses off today to save that stupid garden of yours; the least you can do is bend your silly rules a little. This is supposed to be a vacation."

Stan couldn't help but note that Bob was the only person that hadn't really helped. He had gone to the farm, but had remained a spectator nearly the entire time.

At first, Kimo had seemed to yield to Bob's appeal, but then he visibly stiffened when Bob turned the verbal attack on the farm. He walked directly up to Bob and stared at him for a few moments.

"Thank you for the help, Bob, I appreciate it. Now let me explain a couple of things to you. First of all, the bunker is here for emergencies only. Rain is not an emergency—not even close. Are you really such a wimp? Tomorrow, I'll light the fire. One cold meal is not going to kill any of us. And that *garden* that you all helped me with is not just a hobby—it's the main source of food for the island, and it's critical to our survival here. If you want to live on fish and coconuts, go ahead, be my guest."

Kimo shook his head, as if trying to shake out his anger. "Look everyone, I know today wasn't the best of days, but I'll bet you'll look back on it as a great adventure. Hang with it till tomorrow. If things aren't any better then, well—" Seemingly on the verge of making a promise, he finished with a vague "then we'll see what we can do." He hesitated a moment, and then moped off toward his hut, leaving Nani to shrug and follow a few steps behind.

As darkness fell, Stan and Jenny sat with the others under the lean-to without talking, nibbling at their raw food. In light of their exhaustion, however, even eating seemed forced. Soon, one by one, they fumbled their way through the rain and darkness to their huts.

As Stan and Jenny made their way to their hut, Stan said, "I don't even know who's right and wrong any more. I have to admit I'd feel more comfortable if Kimo bent a little on the rules and let us into the bunker."

"I don't care," Jenny replied. "Bob's either an idiot or an asshole. Just a little tact and I'm sure Kimo would have opened it, but he seems more interested in pissing people off."

Stan turned to Jenny and took her hands. "Jenny, maybe we should tell Kimo about … about you. Don't you think?"

Jenny pulled her hands away from Stan. "About me? What about me? Stan, I'm pregnant. I don't have cancer. I keep telling you, I'm completely fine."

They stared at each other for a moment, prompting Jenny to put her hands back in Stan's. "I really am fine, Stan. Okay, a warm meal and fire might be nice, but like Kimo said, it's just a rainstorm." *Besides,* she thought, *something tells me Kimo wouldn't be too happy about my condition.*

Chapter 7

ANOTHER RESTLESS NIGHT. ALTHOUGH the heat wasn't as stifling, the air was stale, the humidity overwhelming, and their beds saturated—along with everything else on the island. Jenny and Stan lay awake, covered in an oppressive, sticky sheen of sweat. They considered another dip in the lagoon, but in their downtrodden moods, they opted to whittle away the hours tossing and turning in a futile attempt to get at least a few moments of decent sleep. For the first time, they found themselves looking forward to the end of their trip, and not because of the rain so much as the tension. The altercation between Kimo and Bob and the flood at the farm had quenched Kimo's fiery optimism, leaving everybody on edge.

By early morning, the rain had weakened to a depressing drizzle and the temperature had returned to normal, but the thick cloud cover showed no hint of an opening. Dazed, Jenny and Stan wandered into the central village, finding only Kimo there. With the winds quiet, the trees and bushes no longer danced and the excitement of yesterday's storm was gone. The whole island—trees, huts, even people—seemed to sag under the weight of the water. Kimo was kneeling under the lean-to, spinning a sharpened stick, its point buried into a split in a second stick. Without looking up, he gave the slightest nod, and continued his work. After a few minutes, he threw the sticks to the sand and made something of a growl.

"There won't be a fire today. Everything's still too wet." He stood and walked toward the trail. "I'm going to the farm to get food."

"Want some help?" Stan offered.

"No!"

As Kimo left, Bob wandered into the village center. Stan wished he were somewhere else, or that he and Jenny weren't the only others there.

"No fire?" Bob asked.

"Kimo couldn't light it," Stan replied. "He said everything was just too wet."

"Great! At least now we'll be able to get to our shit. I've got a bottle of Jack in my bag too. Man, that would be good right now."

About an hour later, with everybody now huddled again under the lean-to, Kimo returned, carrying a basket of muddy vegetables. Judging by the look on his face, the devastation at the farm must have continued. He slammed his load onto the table and stormed off toward the east beach.

"Hey, wait up," Bob called. Kimo kept walking. Bob jogged out in front of him and planted his feet directly across Kimo's path. "So, what about your damn bunker now? It's the other way, as I remember."

"I told you before, this is not an emergency. I'm not about to jeopardize the … the sanctity of this island because of a damn rain storm."

As Kimo walked around him, Bob shouted, "Well, this may be your idea of how to treat guests, but it isn't mine … and don't you dare walk away from me when I'm talking to you." Bob grabbed Kimo by the shoulder and spun him around. With Kimo off balance, Bob unloaded a powerful punch into Kimo's gut, knocking him back a couple of feet. Everybody froze. Calmly, Kimo squared right up to the immense man and stared at him, as rain streamed off their faces. Bob stood motionless, dumbfounded by Kimo's reaction.

Finally, in an even tone, Kimo said, "Consider that your free pass. You only get one." He smoothly turned and walked away, leaving Bob stunned and speechless. With downcast eyes and flushed cheeks, Bob slowly walked back to the others.

"Well, that sure helped," Claire said in pure sarcasm.

"Shut up, will ya?" He shoved her viciously to the ground. "I don't see you trying to do anything." Bob started toward their hut, but then turned to look at Claire, still on the ground in obvious pain. "You know, I'm outta here on Saturday when the plane comes. I don't care anymore about your damn father—it's finished."

Jenny immediately went to Claire and helped her up. Stan looked at Don, who was standing next to him, silently appealing for help should Bob move closer to Claire and Jenny. Instead, Bob quickly turned and left. Claire winced as Jenny lifted her slowly to her feet.

"Are you all right?" Jenny asked.

"Yeah, I guess. It's my fault. I shouldn't have said that. He's had some rough times recently." She seemed about to offer more, but then thought better of it. She started after Bob, stopped after a couple of steps, and then turned and wandered off toward the north beach.

Jenny walked back to Stan. "Well, that was … interesting? God, what an asshole." Then realizing that Nani was right beside her, she quickly added, "Sorry, I didn't mean Kimo. I meant Bob."

Nani smiled. "Don't worry, I knew what you meant." She locked eyes with Jenny for a moment. "It'll be okay. Really, don't worry." Then she left to catch up with Claire.

Stan and Jenny saw no more of either Kimo or Bob that day. The rain continued, fluctuating only slightly in intensity, which meant their meals were again cold and limp—mostly uprooted vegetables—but enough to quell their hunger. Without much to do to pass the time or even a glimpse of the sun to mark its passage, the couples sat around the village center talking and enduring their boredom. By afternoon they had become so accustomed to the rain, they were able to disregard it, going for short, wet walks just to break the monotony.

As the sun began to set, everybody but Kimo had returned to the close confines of the lean-to, prompting Stan to ask Nani, "Where's Kimo? Is he okay? Do you think we should we look for him?"

Without a trace of concern in her voice, she replied, "He's fine, don't worry. If he doesn't want to be found, you won't find him anyway—he's just by himself."

Night was again sticky and damp, bringing sleep in short, fitful intervals. Wednesday was a simple replay of Tuesday—no fire, not a moment free of rain, and Kimo nowhere in sight. Around midday, Stan organized a group trip to the farm. When they arrived, they found it in shambles, but with neither the energy nor the desire to resume their war with nature, they decided just to head back to camp and let the water have its way. The animals, however, had already been fed, so although Kimo was scarce around the village, he had evidently made his way to the farm. On the way back they took a short detour to the bunker and were disturbed to find a pool of water a good foot above the bottom of the door.

"Who's the flippin genius that decided to build the bunker in a depression?" Russ stared at the water. "I guess everything in there is sopping wet by now, including all our bags."

Early Thursday afternoon, the rain finally stopped. There was still no hope of starting a fire, however, partly because everything was saturated, but mostly because Kimo hadn't returned. Even Nani said she didn't have a chance of starting a fire without Kimo.

At one point, Bob grabbed a stone ax and announced that he had had enough, that he was going to break into the bunker to get his so oft-mentioned "stuff." He returned not long after, absent the ax, and stewing in anger. Apparently, a cold dinner and a miserable evening awaited them yet again. Their only glimpse of hope came in the form of a few stars occasionally peeking out between the clouds. Stan and Jenny spent the evening counting how many days they had left on Henderson, and dreaming of sitting in front of their TV in their bathrobes, feasting on take-out pizza.

Friday morning, endless waves of perfectly spaced pillows spanned the sky in bright oranges, reds, and yellows. A warm, fresh breeze immediately kicked up and began drying the island. As Stan and Jenny made their way to the village center, they were relieved to find several of the others surrounding Kimo, already on his knees nurturing a small fire.

He greeted Jenny and Stan as they joined the circle. "Good morning!

Looks like we're back in business. As soon as this thing's going, I'll make some hot tea. Then I'd really like some help over at the farm. We've got a lot of work to do."

"Sure," Stan said. And then encouraged by Kimo's optimism, he ventured further. "So what was all this rain about? I thought there were only supposed to be light sprinkles here?"

"Don't know, really. I've never seen anything like it. The heat, too. Very unusual. But come on, it's a little excitement—that's what life's about, isn't it?" He gestured to the eastern horizon. "And what a beautiful day. Makes it all worth it, doesn't it?"

Taking a deep breath of the fresh, clean ocean breeze, Stan had to agree.

Bob was hanging well back, when Kimo called to him. "So, Bob, you up for some fishing today? I'd like to try for a really special dinner tonight, and some snapper would be pretty nice. Shall I set you up with a line off the Point?"

Bob hesitated, obviously surprised but relieved that Kimo had even spoken to him. "Uh, sure. Hey, listen, about the other day …."

Kimo turned and raised his hand. "Hey, I already told you one free pass, okay? No problem, so long as you don't expect another. And look, if you want to go on tomorrow's plane or if you want to stay, either way, doesn't matter to me. Just let me know in the morning. Now, how 'bout a fish or two for tonight?"

A rare, but tight smile crossed Bob's face. "Not the best equipment in the world, but I guess I can try."

"C'mon, let me help you rig a line. Wayne, could you feed the fire a bit? Not too quickly. Lay the wood cross-wise so it gets plenty of air, and not too much at a time; you gotta give the fire time to dry out the wood." Then like best buddies, Kimo and Bob walked to the small hut that housed the fishing equipment and tools.

As soon as the fire was ablaze, Kimo led the others to the farm. As they passed the flooded bunker, Kimo just smiled and shook his head.

The devastation at the farm was even worse than it'd been just two days earlier, when Stan had led the group there. Probably three-quarters of the plants had been lost. Kimo's mood seemed to sink as quickly as it had been buoyed by the sunrise that morning, but he started working straight away, dourly staking the ground for new rows of crops. He then asked his volunteers to form raised beds between the stakes while he went back to his hut for seeds.

While he was gone, Stan and Jenny wandered about, taking stock of the changes to the landscape. Most impressive was a lake that had appeared just south of the farm, probably some five feet deep and encompassing perhaps five acres. The entire central depression had filled with water and showed no sign of draining. Another day or so of showers, and it would have engulfed the farm itself. The animals, however, had weathered the rains well—the pigs seemed particularly pleased with all the mud.

When Kimo returned, he divided the group into teams to plant various crops. They put in a full morning of muddy work and, by early afternoon, had planted everything that Kimo had set out. With that, Kimo called an end to the workday and had everyone carry as many uprooted vegetables as they could back to camp.

After lunch, Kimo demonstrated how to remove a wall from the huts to allow the warm breeze to dry the inside. Meanwhile, Bob had returned from the Point, proudly showing off two large fish.

Later, while most of the camp rested in their huts, Jenny and Stan went to the beach and enjoyed an afternoon nap in the shade of a palm tree. Kimo and Nani worked through the afternoon preparing a spectacular early dinner, which, with the distinct eat-it-before-it-rots attitude around camp, came with more than an abundance of food— and best of all, hot, cooked food.

After dinner, despite Kimo's encouragement, everybody was too tired and bloated for entertainment. They sat in small groups around the fire that Kimo had stoked up to a blaze, talking about their lives back home. Claire and Bob stayed to themselves, well away from the others, engaged in quiet argument most of the evening. Their discussion suddenly erupted in loud swearing as Bob stood and screamed threateningly at Claire before briskly walking off toward their hut.

Claire looked around at the others through downcast eyes. Noticing everybody's attention was focused on her, she fidgeted a bit, then stood and followed at Bob's heels.

Both Stan and Jenny automatically looked over to Kimo, sitting silently, shaking his head. It wasn't long before exhaustion and the lure of their cool, dry beds began to attract the others to their huts. For Stan and Jenny, it was the first good rest they'd had since they'd arrived.

Chapter 8

Saturday morning was ushered in by a light rain that, to Stan and Jenny's great relief, soon gave way to sunshine. They walked to the village center to say good-bye to George, Wayne, Allison, and Sue. The storm, although it had robbed them of a few days' vacation, had allowed them to forge tight bonds with one another. U sing graphite pencils, the only writing utensils allowed on the island, and some rough paper Kimo claimed was made from hemp, they exchanged e-mail addresses along with promises to write as soon as they got back.

Bob and Claire had decided to leave early after all. Or, more accurately, it was Bob who had decided, for Claire was still pleading to stay. As they joined the group that morning, it became suddenly evident to Jenny how much Claire had changed after just one week of island life. The outdoors had replaced her make-up-caked skin with natural tones and shadows that highlighted and enhanced her facial features. And perhaps in was only Jenny's perception, but it seemed that the sun had painted streaks of platinum in her hair, which, from the wind and rain, now framed her face with wild abandon. But more than just her appearance had changed. For the last week, while Bob had stood off to the side watching, she had worked side-by-side with the others and been rewarded with a sense of honest physical accomplishment. Though she still couldn't stand up to Bob's unyielding presence, not to mention his insistence on leaving, she no longer seemed merely a shadow of his will. The very fact that she'd expressed her opposition to leaving was a marked change.

Waiting for the plane, the group played impromptu games of bocce ball with coconuts then prepared a lunch. After eating, Kimo stayed at the village center, keeping food and drink at the ready for the new arrivals. It soon became evident, however, that Alan was late, and some voiced concern. Kimo told them not to worry, that it was probably just a late passenger—apparently late arrivals were not unexpected. Still, the next few hours passed uncomfortably. Jenny and Stan felt obligated to wait with the departing couples, but at the same time, felt bored and anxious to take to the beach or go for a walk.

With the sun well on its way across the afternoon sky, Kimo announced he was headed to the farm to check on things. The plane would be easy to hear from there, he said, and he would return as soon as it arrived. Taking his cue, the others scattered, going fishing, swimming, walking, or in the case of Linda and Lynda, napping in the shade.

By dinnertime, they concluded the plane wouldn't arrive at all that day. They speculated about weather, flooded airstrips, mechanical problems, even Alan's health, but Kimo managed to dispel each theory— the weather had been great for over a day now, Alan would fly in almost any weather and he always had a back-up pilot or plane he could call. As he headed off to his hut, he promised that no matter what the cause for the delay, Alan would surely make two trips on Sunday.

Sunday morning came and went, but still no plane appeared. Now twelve guests were in limbo, including Bob and Claire, who had apparently had another heated debate during the night, likely punctuated by a slap across Claire's face—or so Jenny believed based on the reddish hue of her left cheek.

For the first time since the storm broke, Kimo avoided the guests for much of the morning—unless he was cornered by a direct question, at which point he'd dole out a single-word response. Then just before noon, he disappeared completely. It was late afternoon when he finally reappeared, and Bob immediately approached him, pressing for answers.

"How 'bout using the radio? You said there was some kind of radio in that secret hideaway of yours."

Kimo glared at Bob for a moment, but didn't reply.

Don, who was in earshot of Bob, walked up to the men. "If you don't mind my saying so, Kimo, this *is* a bit concerning. Can't we just give the radio a try?"

Kimo closed his eyes and was silent for a moment. "I already did."

Bob clenched his fists. "You already did? You already called? Well, what'd they say?"

"I said I *tried* the radio." Kimo's voice was terse. "I never said I got through. I tried it just after lunch, but it's not working. It may have been damaged by the water—I'm not sure."

"Doesn't work? What do you mean, *doesn't work*? I don't believe you even tried it. Bring it here, I want to try it myself."

Kimo took a deep breath, and then raised his voice. "Okay, listen up everybody." Kimo waited until everyone had gathered. "Look, I don't know what's going on. I tried to call Mangareva early this morning, but the radio doesn't work. All I get is static. There was water in the bunker, so maybe it got wet—it's dry now, but it may have been damaged. I'll try again tomorrow. If anybody's an electronics or radio expert, your help would be appreciated. Meanwhile, relax. I'm sure whatever's going on, they'll get here as soon as they can—almost certainly tomorrow. I'm sure they haven't forgotten about us. We've got plenty of food, but I would ask that you refrain from picking anything from the garden. We need to ration our harvests until the new plants grow back. Any questions?" He looked around at the group.

"Yeah, can we get at our stuff now? How 'bout it?" Bob asked.

Kimo sighed. "Just what is it that you need so badly anyway? What is this obsession with your *stuff*? Tell me something you need."

"Well, for one thing, I could use a drink. I think we all could."

Stan didn't say anything, but he hoped Kimo would hold his ground, if for no other reason than to keep Bob away from his oft-mentioned Jack Daniels. The specter of a drunken Bob was not a pleasant one.

Kimo rolled eyes. "A drink. You want a drink. That's it? You think booze is going to help us?" He turned to the others. "What else?"

Bob wasn't about to give up. "Not just my Jack, all my stuff. My sunglasses, my watch, my clothes—real clothes, not this crappy Halloween costume."

"None of that is going to bring the plane any sooner. Seriously, if there's anybody that has something in the bunker that's going to help our situation, let me know and we'll get it, but I just don't see any reason to go in there just to … just to spoil the island." Again, he turned to the others. "Anyone?"

Wayne raised his hand halfway, which Kimo acknowledged with a hesitant nod.

"I'd like to get a book out, if I could," Wayne said.

"What book? What book could possibly help us?"

"My Bible."

Kimo sighed and turned away from Wayne. "Any other questions?"

"Yeah, I have one," Don said. "Just out of curiosity, how far is the nearest island? I mean, just how remote is this place?"

"The nearest island is Pitcairn, about a hundred miles to the west, or maybe a little south of west." Kimo pointed to his right. "There's another island called *Il Ducie* to the northwest, but it's uninhabited and uninhabitable—barely more than a spit of sand, famous only for its sharks. Why, thinking of swimming home?"

"No, just curious, that's all. Are there boats that stop by here?"

"The short answer is no. We're nowhere near any shipping lanes, nor are we near any vacation destinations. In fact, there aren't even any air routes nearby. Used to be a private sailboat would stop by a couple of times a year on its way to Pitcairn, but now Pitcairn is uninhabited, so that's not very likely either. There was also a *National Geographic* cruise ship called the *Endeavor* that stopped here every few years or so, but that was just because it was on the way to Pitcairn, so same thing, probably not going to happen any more… look, what difference does all that make? We're safe and happy, and Alan will get here soon. Don't worry and just relax, okay?"

George suddenly piped in, "Hey, I have a Blackberry in my bag. Maybe we could e-mail… " He grimaced, and contritely added, "I actually was thinking of renting a satellite phone, too."

A few others asked similar questions, but every inquiry seemed to make Kimo more hostile, bringing the questions to a quick end.

Chapter 9

Six days later, on the morning of their second Saturday on the island, Stan and Jenny wandered to the village center at first light, just as they—and everyone else—had done every day since the rain, the comfort of routine helping to stave off panic. Michelle was sitting alone by the fire—no matter how early Stan and Jenny arrived at the village center, Kimo had already been there to stoke up the coals from the night before.

"Good morning," Jenny said.

Michelle looked up at Jenny. She was disheveled and nervous but happy to have company. "Hey, good morning."

Jenny grabbed a clay pot. "Want some tea?"

"Sure, I guess. Thanks." Jenny filled the pot with water from the nearby spring and rested it on some coals at the edge of the fire. She sat down next to Stan to wait for the water to warm. As she studied Michelle, she noticed how much weight Michelle had lost. Except for the occasional nibbling of fruit, Jenny hadn't seen her eat all week.

After a moment she wandered over to Michelle and sat close beside her. "Hey listen, Michelle. You'll make it back for your daughter's birthday. I'm sure of it. How old will Tina be?"

Michelle smiled wanly. "Six. We're supposed to get back about midnight the night before her birthday. I promised her when she woke up, I'd be there next to her bed. I bought a bike for her—her first one."

"And I'm sure you'll be there to give it to her."

"I know, I know," Michelle said. "And I know it doesn't make sense, but I just feel so guilty for leaving them." She hesitated. "I guess I'm being completely silly, but ... I just keep wondering why I'm here."

"Where's David?" Jenny asked.

"I don't know. He went for a walk, I guess."

Stan sat down on the other side of Michelle. "Remember what Kimo's been saying all week. Even if the airfield or planes at Mangareva were completely destroyed by the storm and they had to send a boat from another island, somebody should still arrive today. He said there was no way it would take any longer than that." Even as Stan said it, he regretted it. Indeed this was the day they had identified as worst-case for help to arrive, and there was an unsaid agreement that they would begin to worry in earnest if nobody showed by the end of the day. But still, they had all become so conditioned by disappointment that he somehow didn't really believe it would happen.

As Stan thought about how to prepare Michelle for disappointment, Russ and Jules wandered over with their ever-present smiles. "Morning all," he said. "What's up?"

Russ immediately saw how upset Michelle was. "Listen, no worries, Michelle. I'm sure your kids are fine with your parents—maybe getting spoiled, but that's about all. There'll be a boat or plane today or tomorrow. It's going to be fine."

Though Russ intended well, his admission that their departure might not come today just made Michelle feel worse.

"Tomorrow never comes," she said. Then she walked off to be on her own.

Russ turned to Jules. "Well, I thought I handled that rather well, didn't you?" Jules just looked askance at him.

Just then, George arrived, with Sue close behind. "I don't understand how you can be so accepting of all this, Russ. I mean, how do you manage to stay so positive all the time?"

Russ shrugged. "I don't know. I guess there's nothing we can do to change our situation anyway, and we're not exactly in the worst place in the world. It'll sort itself out. What's the worry?"

"Well, you're probably not about to lose your job. Sue and I are already a week late, and I can tell you, excuses don't cut it in investment banking. It's all about results, and in this economy, results aren't so good. Even if a plane comes today, we're probably already out of a job. If it's a boat and we're another week late, forget about it!" As he was finishing, Don, Mary, Linda and Lynda wandered into the village center. George continued, "What about you, Don, you're in a pretty high-stress job, aren't you? Aren't you worried?"

Don shrugged. "I'm not sure I'd say *worried*, but maybe *concerned*? And not because of work, but because we're about to become grandparents." He looked at Mary. Stan noticed that they, unlike David and Michelle, were able to support each other and draw strength from their relationship. Marco and Francesca, who also had older children, seemed to become closer during the week, as well.

Lynda piped in. "Well, our jobs are in the same boat as yours, George, but careers aren't everything. If we lose our jobs, we'll find new ones. So will you. It's not the end of the world."

Jenny turned to them. "You two seem the happiest of everybody here. How come?"

Linda and Lynda looked at each other before Linda replied, "I guess because we can really be who we are."

"Exactly," Lynda said. "It's not like we keep our relationship a secret back home, but it's different here. We're totally open and it's completely okay. Nobody cares."

"So for the first time," Linda added, "we can be who we want and do what we want. And we really have time for each other, too."

They all paused, reflecting. Then Jenny looked at Erik and Stefani, just had just arrived at the main eating table. "What about you two? You don't seem particularly bothered by the situation either."

"Like Russ said, there is nothing to do." Erik spoke slowly and deliberately. "So we just try to enjoy the island and time here. We have no problem with our jobs, and we have no children back in Germany, so it think for us it is easier. What about you and Stan? You ask always about other people, but talk not so much about yourselves. How is it with you to be stuck here?"

Jenny and Stan looked at each other. Jenny had no job to go back to, and Stan knew he'd be taken back no matter how long he was gone. Their families also trusted them enough to know they would be fine wherever they were. Still, as that critical second weekend approached, Jenny had developed some amorphous anxieties about her fledgling pregnancy. She still felt fine physically, but was starting to wish she were closer to medical care, just in case. And she wasn't ready to share their secret with the others. She searched Stan's face, as if looking for help.

Seeing in Jenny's face that this wasn't the time for revelations, he answered, "It's not a problem for us either. We like it here too. But it's just difficult not knowing what's going on. I think if somebody flew over and dropped a note that said, "A boat is on the way but will take two weeks to arrive," we'd be completely fine. It's just the not knowing that's hard. And remember, we're not late either. This is only our second week anyway—when we're supposed to leave for home." The others nodded.

"Well, fuck you guys." Apparently Bob had arrived at some point in their exchange. "I don't understand how any of you can put up with this shit." He pinched his forefinger and thumb to within a fraction of an inch. "I'm about this close to seriously fucking up that Kimo guy."

It was hard not to have at least some sympathy for Bob's point of view. Kimo had become increasingly intransigent with each day. If anybody dared ask about the bunker or emergency supplies, he became immediately abrupt and flatly refused to discuss it. The only concession he'd made was to bring out the radio for Wayne and David to fix, but they said it was a bit like expecting an auto mechanic to rebuild a modern car engine using sticks and stones.

"I don't understand what you have against Kimo," Claire said, raising a few eyebrows in the group. "He's doing the best he can. And besides, I like it here." Claire was sitting on the other side of the table from Bob, about as far away as she could get—a situation that was more and more common of late.

Bob lifted himself to his feet, staring directly at Claire, muscles tense. Until now, Bob had been ambivalent to Claire's snubs, as if what she did or thought were completely irrelevant. This time, however, Stan sensed Bob needed an outlet for his anger and that Claire had just set herself up for the role.

Just then, Nani approached Bob from behind, a basket of fresh fruit under one arm, and placed a hand on his shoulder. In an unnaturally tranquil voice, she said, "Good morning, everybody. I brought some fruit."

Bob's shoulders visibly relaxed under her touch, the tension rippling through his muscles melting. He looked distracted for a moment, and then much to Stan's relief sat down.

Nobody wanted to just sit and wait around for a plane or boat. They'd learned that it was better just to engage the day and hope for the best. Stan and Jenny went for a walk around the island. Others went fishing or swimming, or played bocce ball—anything to keep their minds off of their situation and expectations. Still, they invariably found themselves reacting to the slightest shadow of a bird or crash of a wave, turning their heads toward the sky or sea in the hopes of finding a savior.

By dinnertime, it was apparent that their self-defined rescue day would end in disappointment. For the most part they accepted the outcome, because it had been so well presaged by the previous week. Stan and Jenny had now joined the group of overdue vacationers.

With Kimo's frequent absence, meals had become almost foraging exercises. Lobsters and crabs were easy enough to obtain, a variety of fruit was readily available from nearby trees, and fishing was a common afternoon pastime for several of the men. Nani would also bring back eggs and vegetables from the farm, though it was never clear whether it was with Kimo's permission. There was always enough food about the camp, but Nani was a provider, not an organizer, so meals were disorganized and poorly prepared. Saturday evening's meal was no exception. And again like every other night, after scrounging as much food as appealed to their limited appetites, the group began to discuss their situation.

"I just don't get it," Jenny asked, "how can they all have forgotten about us? Okay, I can understand a day or so late, but a week? It just doesn't make any sense."

"All I can figure," said David, "is that what we caught was the tail end of a really massive storm, a typhoon or something, that badly damaged Mangareva's boats, planes, and radio towers, and put them completely out of commission."

"Yeah, but come on," Sue replied, "it's been a full week now. This is the twenty-first century. Everyone back home would know about a storm that big, and they'd have sent help by now."

"Exactly. It's the twenty-first century," David said. "Satellite images and the Internet: they'd know the storm center missed us. They'd know we're safe. So I'm not sure we'd be on anybody's priority list. What could they do anyway? It's not as if they can land a jet here. There was barely enough runway for Alan's little Otter to land. It would take time to get to us."

"Okay, so then when will somebody get here?" asked Wayne.

"I don't know," David replied. "If Mangareva is really out of commission, I suppose there's nothing they could do but divert ships from nearby shipping routes or from some other island. Kimo said Pitcairn is uninhabited now, and that's the only other island nearby. Isn't Easter Island somewhere off to the east?"

"Yes, we stopped there on the way to Mangareva," Erik said. "It's to the east and a bit south, but I think it is more than a thousand kilometers away; maybe too far for a plane small enough to land here."

"Then what we should do is watch for ships and maybe get a signal fire ready so they know we need help," David said. "We can take turns at the Point, maybe a couple of hours each, watching for ships. I think if Mangareva is out of commission, our rescue will have to be by boat, not by plane."

Jenny interjected. "But we've been through this a million times. Even if they took a boat from Easter Island, it would be here by now. Kimo said they could get a boat here from Tahiti in a week. It still doesn't make sense."

Taking advantage of a slight lull in the conversation, Claire interjected, her voice low and unsure. "Soooo …what if the storm isn't the reason for the delay? Like, what if … I don't know … like if something caused the storm?"

Jenny, happy to have Claire engaged for a change, prompted her to continue. "What do you mean *something caused the storm*? I'm not sure I understand."

Claire hesitated and looked around, as if hoping someone would jump in and answer, but the others just looked at her and waited. "Well, remember how hot it was before the storm? Can't a lot of heat like that cause water to evaporate, and can't that cause heavy rains? Like the Monsoons or hurricanes?"

Looking surprised, David said, "Yes, that's right, it can. Why does that matter? You mean the heat could be causing the delay rather than the rain? How could a heat wave cause a delay?"

"I was just thinking, that's all." Nervous now, Claire turned to see how far away Michelle was, then lowered her voice so she wouldn't hear. "Remember how strange the heat wave was that night? I was just wondering, maybe the question we should be asking is, what could have made it so hot that night? Maybe we shouldn't always be thinking that the rainstorm is the problem, that's all. Maybe there was something else. Something that caused the heat, and then that caused the rain. But maybe it was whatever caused the heat wave that's somehow causing … I don't know … the delays."

David looked intently at Claire, as if to determine whether this was the same airhead that had come to the island two weeks ago. She was right—they had been focusing on the storm, and maybe that wasn't the answer. At least they should consider other possibilities.

"So what are you thinking," David asked. "Like a volcano on Mangareva? Something like that?"

"No, I don't think so. I read about Krakatoa, and they say people could hear the noise thousands of miles away, and there were huge clouds of ash going all around the world, and tidal waves, but nothing about heat. It just doesn't seem right that we'd feel heat from a volcano and nothing else. No sound, no ash, no tidal waves—know what I mean?"

She looked about, now embarrassed that everybody was listening so intently to her.

Stan added, "Same goes for meteors and asteroids, especially here. Anything like that within thousands of miles would be right in the middle of the ocean. It would have to create a huge tidal wave, right? I mean that's not exactly something we could have missed."

All eyes turned to David. Though it was as far from David's experience and knowledge as it was from everyone else's, they all seemed to test their thoughts on David, believing somehow that his physics background made him an expert on all natural phenomena.

"I agree," he said. "That makes sense. Same thing with an explosion: for us to feel the heat, it would have to be close enough to have other more obvious effects."

Jenny erupted in disbelief. "My God, you guys are really upbeat, aren't you? Listen to what you're saying! Some cranky old guy on a ratty old airplane is a little late picking us up and you're talking about nuclear Armageddon. Come on, be serious!"

"Yeah, I'm sure you're right." Claire looked down at her feet. "It is silly, I suppose."

A rustling sound turned everybody's heads. Kimo. He raised his hands, palms turned outward. "No, I don't know what's going on, so don't even ask. What I do know is that it's time you guys stop sitting around hoping for rescue and start taking care of yourselves. They'll get here when they get here."

He was interrupted by Michelle, who began sobbing. As Linda walked over and put her hand on Michelle's back. When Michelle quieted down, Kimo continued. "Look, we have everything we need on this island to comfortably survive indefinitely. We only need to organize things a bit and be a bit more disciplined."

At the word *indefinitely,* Michelle again broke into tears. Bob stood up and walked up to within a couple inches of Kimo and, arms on hips, glared down at him. He towered over Kimo, but Kimo held his ground. Bob didn't waste any time. "What d'ya mean *discipline*? We've had enough of your fucking discipline! It's over; you're not in charge any more, as far as I'm concerned … and let's start by you opening the damn bunker so we can get to our stuff. Like, right now!"

"Bob, I've had about enough your goddamned attitude. We need to all work together here, and I've already explained there's nothing in the bunker that'll help our situation. Is that clear?"

Bob reached out to shove Kimo, but before anyone could see what happened, Kimo grabbed Bob's outstretched hand and, using his opponent's momentum, spun him around and threw him on his back. Kimo stood over him, glowering. Bob jumped up and threw a wild punch at Kimo's face, but Kimo deftly sidestepped the blow and grabbed Bob by his fist, twisting it sharply, again forcing Bob to the ground.

Kimo released his grip and stepped back. "I told you only one free pass, and you've already used it. Quit now!" There was an urgency in Kimo's voice that was nothing short of terrifying.

Bob smiled tentatively as he got up, rubbing his wrist. "So, you really want to fight? Well that's okay by me. Let's go."

Claire pleaded with Bob to stop, but he was completely focused on Kimo, warily circling him, teasing him with feigned charges. In no more than fifteen seconds, Bob's patience ran out, and he charged like a raging bull, arms spread wide, this time determined not to let Kimo slip past. At the last second, Kimo darted forward just under Bob's approaching grasp, and yet again, Bob's inertia carried him past. By the time Bob had spun around to face Kimo, Kimo was locked and loaded: he landed a punch square into Bob's solar plexus.

With Bob doubled over, unable to breathe, Kimo wound up and drove an uppercut to his jaw. Miraculously, Bob managed to stay on his feet, so Kimo walked calmly behind him, leaped high into the air, and kicked him in the back of the neck. Bob was unconscious before he hit the ground, but Kimo continued. He methodically kicked him twice in the stomach and was rearing his foot back, aiming his heel to Bob's face, when Stan grabbed him from behind.

Kimo flipped Stan around and cast him to the side like a rag doll, then turned back to continue his demolition of Bob. Stan's diversion, however, had given Nani enough time to insert herself between Bob and Kimo. Not saying anything, she looked into Kimo's eyes, leaned her head against his chest, and tightened her arms around his waist.

Frozen, but with eyes ablaze in anger, Kimo looked over Nani's shoulders at Bob, still prone and motionless on the ground. Then slowly, his eyes softened as if recovering from a trance, he turned his gaze to the onlookers, surveying their frightened reactions. Finally, he very gently pushed away from Nani, turned, and slowly jogged off down the trail.

Claire and Michelle knelt next to Bob and rolled him over on his back. He was breathing evenly, but appeared otherwise lifeless, blood freely flowing from his nose. After a few minutes, he emitted a soft groan and turned on his side, curling his legs into his chest.

"Jeez, that was scary," George mumbled to nobody in particular.

"Bob's very lucky," Nani said quietly. She walked over to Stan who was sitting on the ground, nursing a bruise. She kneeled and extended a hand toward him. "Thank you, Stan. That was very brave." She pulled him to his feet.

As soon as Bob stirred, Claire stood and walked away, leaving Michelle to determine the extent of Bob's injuries.

"I've never seen anything like that," Stan said. "Where did Kimo learn to fight like that?"

Nani had already begun walking away, but stopped and thought for a moment. "Maybe it's best to tell you a bit about Kimo. Kimo is kind of the Hawaiian version of *Jim*—his name used to be Jim Ellis. I don't really know all the details because he hates talking about his past, but I know he was in some kind of special military organization. I'm not sure which one exactly, but he was trained to be some kind of super fighter or something. Anyway, he eventually killed another soldier from his own platoon or whatever it's called. It was in a training exercise for some mission they were planning. Kimo, or Jim back then, lost his temper. He said he just couldn't stop hitting the guy.

"The army or marines or whoever it was, decided they couldn't really punish him since they had trained him to act like that—at least that's what he told me. Maybe they just didn't want the publicity.

Anyway, they kicked him out and he changed his name and went to live by himself on the Na Pali coast of Kauai. He lived there in the wild for almost two years, living off the land—fishing, hunting goats now and then, gathering fruits and nuts and stuff.

"He really is a good person, but he's very passionate about things, like what he's doing here. He's learned to know when he's losing control of his temper. He said it's like another person taking over his body—like he's just watching from the outside. But now he just goes away when he feels it happening, so nobody's around. So when he needs to be alone, just give him some ... I guess ... *space*. Don't push him too hard, that's all." A flash of guilt crossed her face. "Maybe I should have warned Bob."

"Somehow I don't think that would have helped," Jenny offered. "Warning him probably would have only encouraged him."

"So how'd you meet Kimo?" Lynda asked Nani. "Did you guys meet here then?"

"No, we met when I was on a backpacking trip with some friends to the Na Pali coast—that's in Hawaii, on Kauai. I went for a hike inland, got lost, and ran into his camp. He ... well, anyway, we fell in love." She muffled a laugh. "I kind of shocked my friends because I just stayed there with him. At the end of the trip, when they were all ready to leave, I just told them I wasn't coming. I asked them to call my dad to let him know I was safe and happy. We lived on the coast for another few months, then eventually I talked him into coming back to Lihue with me."

"Is that when you came here?" asked Jenny.

"No, not right away, but soon. He didn't adjust well to civilization in Lihue. It was okay at first ... he even got a job as an island guide, organizing hikes and things. But he would get angry with the tourists, traffic, and even just reading the newspaper. I loved him, and when we were alone, he was wonderful, but sometimes he just lost control. So about two months after we returned from Na Pali, I saw an ad in the paper for this new project. We applied and that was that. We've been here ever since." She looked around, as if suddenly afraid that she had said too much, then abruptly knelt beside Bob, asking Michelle what she thought of his injuries.

Michelle said she guessed Bob had suffered two or three badly bruised or fractured ribs and a mild concussion, but nothing that wouldn't heal with rest. As Michelle was speaking, Jenny noticed she was looking across at her, as if expecting some kind confirmation. "Sorry, Michelle, it sounds right, but I'm sure you know a lot more about it than I do. I was just a medical student, not a doctor—I haven't even started real medical school. I'm sure you have much more experience with things like this."

After about thirty minutes, Stan and Don were able to help Bob back to his feet and back to his hut to rest. The others talked late into the night—about Kimo, about the travel delay, about Claire's ideas, about possible rescue and what they should do next. But in the end, they all concluded that Kimo was right about one thing: it was time to take their situation into their own hands.

Kimo never returned to the village that night. And when the camp finally retired, it was to a light and restless sleep.

The next morning, Jenny and Stan walked out of their hut to find only Kimo in the village center. He had tea boiling, eggs cooking, and fruit set out on the table. Kimo greeted them with a deadpan nod. Others began wandering out of their huts, but Kimo maintained his silence until finally Claire arrived, alone.

"How's Bob?" he asked softly.

"All right. He's in a lot of pain. I don't think he'll get out of bed today, but he'll be fine in a few days. Michelle already stopped by this morning to check on him. She's with him now."

"I'm sorry about what happened. I ..."

As he fished for more to say, Claire broke in. "No, he deserved it." She rubbed her still-bruised shoulder. "I wish I could have done that to him when he pushed me down last week. I should thank you for teaching him a lesson. Maybe for a change he'll understand what it's like to be the one picked up off the ground."

After breakfast, Kimo stood to address the group. "As I started to say yesterday, we have everything we need on this island. You guys keep talking about being *rescued*. We don't need to be rescued, but we do need to work together. I don't mean to be rude, but as of today, things have changed: you are no longer guests. Technically you're trespassers. If you want to stay in the village and harvest from the farm, then you'll all need to contribute—everyone—and we need to be more organized."

He looked around to gauge their reactions. Not only did they not object, they seemed happy that somebody had stepped forward to take control. Kimo's absence and the resulting lack of organization had taken a toll on their quality of life during this last week, and they were ready to return to the way things had been.

"All right then," Kimo started in. "First, the farm. With all the damage to the crops, I'm worried about the pigs. We can't grow enough food for them and us, and a couple of the sows are about to give birth, so it's only going to get harder. I want to set them free to forage the island, but in order to do that, we need to finish building the wall around the farm, so they don't come back and destroy all the crops. We started it a long time ago, but it's nowhere near done. I'd like to ask Erik, George, and Russ to work on building it up to waist height at least. Okay?"

All three nodded.

"Good. Then we need to plant some more crops. There are some seeds that we brought to the island that we haven't planted yet. Cotton and sugar beets, for example." He looked around the group. "Stan, Jenny, Linda, and Lynda, I'd like to ask you to take care of that."

They, too, nodded.

"Marco, you're in charge of fishing. That means spear fishing, line fishing, net fishing, traps, everything. In a few days, when the wall's finished, we'll get you some help, but for now, you're the man.

"Don, Wayne, and David, you're supposed to be the techies in the group. I don't know how we ended up with so many engineers, but you guys do whatever it is you do."

The three men looked blankly at one other.

"Look," Kimo said, "there's a lot for you guys to figure out: how to make fishing hooks, cooking utensils, oil. In fact, you should probably start with pottery—bowls, plates, cooking pots, things like that. All of those types of things that we had were brought here from outside the island, and a lot of it was destroyed in the storm. Put your PhD's or whatever degrees you have to good use for a change and figure it out."

The threesome continued to look baffled.

"Come on, it'll be a challenge," Kimo said. "Just do whatever you can with what's around on the island."

Don suggested, "Maybe we can try to build a boat."

Kimo sighed. "And just how would you propose doing that?"

Don shrugged.

"We don't have saws or any way to make boards," Kimo said. "Even if we had boards, we have nothing to make nails or screws with. And the trees are way too small to dig out a canoe, even if we knew how. So how're you going to build a boat?"

"We could build a raft or something by tying logs together."

"And then what? Where would you go in a raft? How would you steer? How would you know where to go, or even where you were? Do you have any idea how far we are from anywhere? Let me make it perfectly clear: there's nowhere to go, and no way to get there."

"But we could at least try, couldn't we?"

"No! I'm not about to let you cut down all the trees on the island just so you can engage in some crazy fantasy. Someday I'll tell you what happened on Easter Island." He paused. "Anything else?"

"Uh …" George hesitated, "we thought we should have a look-out for boats. Maybe set up a lookout at the Point, with a signal fire to let any boats that go by know we need help." He wanted to ask about the bunker, as well, but decided to wait for another time.

Kimo was quiet for a moment. "All right, go ahead. But to keep a full-time watch will take a lot of time. I'd suggest we combine it with the fishing responsibilities, okay?"

There was quiet.

"Okay then, the rest of you collect firewood, eggs, milk, fruit from the trees—and prepare meals, okay? It'll be a while before we can really rely on the farm, so we're going to be hunter-gatherers for a while."

Work on the wall was straightforward, but hot and hard on the hands. The indigenous limestone was light and gripped well when stacked. Kimo had deliberately chosen his teams so that there was one natural leader in each group. On the wall team, that was clearly Erik, who worked hard and steadily. Russ was upbeat, but preferred talking to working, and George simply preferred complaining to working. Based on their first day's progress, Erik thought it would take about two weeks to finish their project.

Planting was also easy in a physical sense, although it took much longer with their digging sticks than it would have with proper shovels. Stan wondered why Kimo picked him for this team, but had no complaints. He was happy to be with Jenny in case the heat or work started bothering her. During the last several days, he'd suggested to Jenny that they tell Kimo about her pregnancy, but still concerned about how he'd react, she preferred to keep it secret as long as possible.

The techies—or more precisely, Don, in his usual energetic fashion—started their duties with a discussion of how to make pottery.

"Well, I know we need clay and a furnace, but it has to be a really hot furnace. Any ideas?"

David and Wayne looked at each other and shrugged.

"Well, one thing I know," Don said, "is that they used to use the trade winds to generate heat; I mean in the old days, like in the Middle Ages or Roman times." Realizing that Wayne and David weren't following him, he continued. "I visited some place in England where they built furnaces that opened into the air like funnels to capture the wind. The tour guide explained how the wind provided the energy to heat the furnaces enough to smelt iron. Now, I don't know if that's how they made pottery, but if it's hot enough for iron, it's probably hot enough to fire clay."

"What'd they use for fuel?" asked David.

"Coal, probably, but I guess we're not going to find coal on the island. We can try wood, I suppose. Not sure there's a choice."

"Charcoal would be better. It burns hotter," suggested David.

"Yeah, that's right," Don recalled. "I also remember reading something about how they used to make charcoal by burning wood in underground pits. I guess starving the wood of oxygen makes it into charcoal. We'll have to play around with it unless somebody else knows how. We can ask tonight."

"Okay, fine," Wayne said. "So what if we can build a furnace. Then what? What are we going to melt—sand? In case you haven't noticed, there's not much else on this island."

David perked up. "Actually, I guess we could. I think sand is mostly silicon dioxide, same as glass. Maybe we could make glass."

"In what? Coconut shells?"

David sighed. "Come on, Wayne, what else is there to do? It'll be fun. If the Greeks and Romans figured it out thousands of years ago, so can we."

"It's just that I don't know why Kimo thinks we can do this. Does he really think they taught us stuff like this in college? Sure, I remember I aced advanced charcoal-making—it was a required course for EE's."

"So? What would you rather do, just sit around and do nothing?" David threw his hands up. "Isn't it better to work on something, even if we don't know what we're doing?"

Wayne crossed his arms and shrugged. "Maybe we should work on the radio again, and see if we can fix that."

Encouraged, David asked, "You're the electrical engineer. Do you think there's any hope?"

Wayne hung his head a bit. "No, I guess not. Even if we had tools to take it apart, there would be no way to fix it here."

Don continued. "So we might as well at least try to do what Kimo suggested, even if it's a wild goose chase."

"Where do you want to begin?" David said. "Looking for clay or building a furnace or making tools?"

The three continued in this way, without any clear insight or ambition, grumbling and debating about things of which they knew little to nothing. The only consensus was that whatever they did work on first, it would be just to kill the time.

By late Sunday afternoon, there was still no airplane or boat. Bob was either unable or unwilling to join them for dinner, and Claire refused to take him food, saying that if he were really hungry, he'd come out and get it himself. In the end, Michelle gave in and served him his meal bedside.

Dinner discussions revolved around thoughts of rescue, despite Kimo's persistent attempts to steer it toward making the island more livable. And unarguably, the term *rescue* had crept into their vocabulary without any identifiable turning point, and it was being used more and more in their daily conversations, making it all the more clear that, regardless of Kimo's objections, they now considered themselves stranded and in need of rescue.

Chapter 10

Three months passed. Despite Kimo's repeated reminders that Henderson Island was well off of the shipping and commercial flight paths, Stan thought it extraordinary that there'd been no trace of the outside world—not even a jet contrail. Each day brought less hope as well as an uncomfortable awareness of how strange their situation was, inviting further speculation and firmly cementing the concept of *rescue*.

By now, Claire's theory had gained an increased following, but by itself, it was still vague and incomplete—even conceding that there might have been some worldwide catastrophe, nothing made sense. And, worse, even if it did, thinking the outside world might be incapable of rescuing them was even more disturbing than having been forgotten.

Kimo had become increasingly demanding, with fewer pleases sprinkled in his requests and more reprimands for work not done to his satisfaction, but with good effect: the island was becoming more livable and days passed more comfortably. The new crops were flourishing, making their diet varied and fresh again, and just as Kimo had promised when they'd arrived: the best they'd ever had. In fact, in the rare moments they could forget they'd been abandoned, the island seemed almost a paradise.

Bob, after recovering, appeared to have developed a peculiar sort of loyalty to Kimo—almost like a beta dog acknowledging the leadership of the alpha. He remained intransigent, even mean, to the others, but was respectful and obedient to Kimo—although tension continued to surround the two.

Bob and Marco were becoming adroit at spearing fish in the shallow reef. In addition to contributing to the food supply, spear fishing had become a much-needed source of sport and entertainment.

Kimo had let the pigs loose as soon as the wall was built and, having no reason to fear humans, they were often seen foraging around the island. The two sows had given birth, so there were also ten piglets on the loose. Though their population appeared sustainable, Kimo remained adamant that pork would not appear on the menu for quite some time.

Kimo also remained resolute with respect to the bunker—he didn't even want anybody loitering around it. There was little objection, since it was difficult to imagine anything in the bunker that would help their situation, especially since most it had likely been ruined in the flood. Still, it annoyed them that Kimo wouldn't let them have their own belongings.

Wayne, David, and Don eventually crafted stone tools that allowed them to open the outer casing of the radio and look at the electronics. As they had suspected, however, the real guts of it was a bunch of integrated circuits that they had no hope of identifying, much less diagnosing or repairing. There was no apparent water damage, but they said that meant little in modern electronics. They knew the radio's solar cells were providing power because the radio emitted a steady static, but the static was steady, without even an occasional break to indicate it was picking up the faintest signal.

The tech team also succeeded in making charcoal and building a stone furnace that funneled the easterly trade winds from the ocean into a dome-shaped stone furnace that, by appearances, achieved very high temperatures. They hadn't found anything they could identify as clay on the island, so they tried every type of soil they could find in the furnace, each of which yielded nothing more than a blackened version of itself. Two other substances were only slightly transformed by the heat: sand, which produced cracked, amorphous, glassy-looking lumps of no apparent use and the omnipresent sandstone, which softened and turned stark white. Pulverizing the baked sandstone produced something Don pronounced to be lime, which they used to make a reasonably sound form of cement. Soon after, they celebrated the delivery of some cement chairs to the village. The chairs weren't terribly comfortable, and it was a small victory for science, but at least it kept them entertained.

Over time, David and Don worked well together, enjoying the exploration and experimentation. Wayne became more withdrawn, almost hostile, insisting it was all a waste of time. At least once a week they turned their minds toward building a boat but invariably concluded that Kimo was right: their raw materials were inadequate and they had no place to go anyway.

Kimo had also been right about the stone tools. While they were functional, they degraded quickly. Kimo showed them how to make new tools, but as he'd promised, it was a time-consuming art that required a great deal of practice. Blades and points were not ground into the stone, but rather flaked by smashing rocks together at grazing angles. Such controlled fractures created facets and thus sharp edges, he told them; however, a single inaccurate fracture would set them back to the beginning. With time they became more skilled, but none could match Kimo's speed and quality. Unfortunately, it was increasingly rare that Kimo worked instead of directing others to work.

Another success was making soap. The idea began one evening as they were talking about what they missed from home.

"What I think I miss most is just plain soap," Claire said. "I just feel sticky and dirty all the time, and a bucket of fresh water doesn't feel like it gets the salt off after swimming."

"It'd be nice to try shaving, too," added George. "I don't know how well it would work with the stone knives, but without soap there's just no way. I tried a few times, and it was horrible."

"Can't we make soap?" Linda asked. "Kimo, you know how?"

"Go ahead and try," Kimo said. "I know you need to boil fat and lye together, but that's about it. I do admit, though, it would be nice to have some soap." He turned to David and Don, who were sitting together. "How 'bout it guys, any ideas?"

David replied, "Fat's easy enough, and I know lye is a strong alkaline liquid that's used in oven cleaners, but I have no idea where we'd find lye around here."

Lynda jumped in. "I read a historical novel once where they talked about leaching ash to make lye, but I don't really know what that means. Maybe it's just soaking ash in water, I don't know. That's what *leaching* sounds like anyway."

Don shrugged. "We'll try tomorrow and see what happens. We can make a cement barrel and fill it with ash from the fire and some fresh water."

"How will you know if something's happening to the water?" asked Claire. "I mean whether it's becoming … alkaline, or whatever you call it?"

"Well," replied David, "if there's a chemical change in the water, its density should change. Like adding salt to water makes it denser. That's why you can float better in salt water."

"So you think the water will increase in density as the ash dissolves?" asked Jenny.

"I'm not sure if it will increase or decrease, just that it should change. But if we can't check its density, we should be able to taste it. Lye's got to taste pretty bad, I would think. Or we can hang a stone from a vertical stick and float it in the barrel. If the water gets heavier, the stick should float more and lift the stone higher out of the water; if it sinks down further, then the density is decreasing."

They checked the water every day, and sure enough, after a few days, the stick rode a bit higher in the water and the taste was becoming bitterer. After weeks of adding ash, they figured out how to filter the alkaline water from their cement barrel, combine it with chicken fat, and then boil it to form a crude but surprisingly effective soap.

That type of learning process became typical: start with some "I wish we had," add tidbits from someone's reading or experience, test the principles over the next couple of days, discuss the results during the evenings, and iterate until achieving something resembling success.

What really fascinated Stan was that anybody could ever have discovered these things in the first place, with no advance knowledge of the end point. What, he wondered, would have motivated somebody in the first place to add ash to water, leave it for several days, filter the ash from the water, boil it for hours on end with animal fat, and then try to wash with it, finally discovering that one had accidentally invented soap?

Kimo also taught them to make rope by soaking hemp stalks in water for a day or two, unraveling the strong, naturally woven fibers from the soft center core, and then spinning the bundles of fibers between sticks to build up the length and girth to whatever was needed.

Nani taught them to make *tapa* cloth using bark from the island's prolific tutu trees. It was an extremely time-consuming task, involving stripping the bark, drying it, soaking it in water overnight, and then hammering it with wooden mallets to make it thin—and then repeating the cycle over and over again until the cloth was thin and soft enough to be used for pareos or sleeping mats. Kimo had dispensed several extra pareos after the storm, so there was no practical need for the bark cloth except to offer something constructive to do to pass the days.

Yet another endeavor was brewing beer, an entrepreneurial project championed by Russ and Erik, with neither disapproval nor approval from Kimo. Erik had made beer at home and Russ had toured the plants at his company, Fosters, so both knew some basic principles, but making beer without brewer's yeast and glass or stainless steel containers was an entirely different matter. They had so much fun with their experiments, it was hardly a serious endeavor. Their early efforts were dramatic failures, producing the most foul-tasting substances imaginable. Over time, they experienced something resembling success, though it was unclear whether the brew was getting better or their expectations were just diminishing. Russ and Erik, both fun-loving, open people, became fast friends, constantly teasing each other that his own country had the better beer and the greater thirst for it.

Kimo's semiweekly feasts, or *gatherings* as they began to call them, were islands of celebration surrounded by oceans of worry, most other evenings being whiled away by speculating about the world beyond the reef and why it had apparently abandoned them. The typical discussion began with a rogue theory from one person, which the group built upon for an hour until someone presented an argument to disprove it. Participation traveled in waves, the leader of one night's session staying silent the next. Since introducing her theory, Claire had all but retreated from the discussions, speaking only when someone asked her a question. Kimo never participated in the speculations, while Michelle seldom made it through without breaking into tears and going off to her hut. It didn't help that her husband, David, was always so enthusiastically engaged, probably a result of his scientific curiosity. Michelle's outbreaks weren't reserved for evening discussions; whereas the group as a whole had adjusted and learned to cope with their situation on a day-to-day basis, Michelle often broke into tears at random times during the day.

At a gathering two months after the storm, as soon as Kimo announced it time for post-dinner entertainment, Stan stood, and the camp fell silent. Jenny stood up next to him, put her arm around his waist, and smiled nervously.

"We have an announcement to make." Stan smiled back at Jenny. "We're expecting."

Several of the women turned to their partners with an "I told you so" expression, and there were murmurs of congratulations. Linda asked Jenny when she thought the baby was due. At Jenny's answer, Kimo jumped up and stormed over to her. Stan immediately stepped between them, but Kimo spoke to her as if he didn't exist.

"You knew when you came, didn't you?"

Jenny's silence was answer enough.

"You must have! Weren't the rules clear enough for you? What the hell were you thinking? Do you think we have facilities to deal with this here?" He paced in a small circle, and again turned on her. "What do you expect us to do now? You're on your own with this one, girl."

After a tense moment of silence he started to walk away.

"Wait a minute!" Jenny had had enough. As if Kimo hadn't been enough of a pain over the last several weeks, now he had poisoned what should have been a joyous announcement. "How were we supposed to know we'd be stranded here for so long? I mean, if this Polynesian

Retrospectives bit was what you guys said it would be, this wouldn't be an issue at all, would it? If you had even reasonable back-ups and safety equipment, we'd be off the island by now. Don't try to blame me for all this shit."

Kimo turned and bore his eyes into her.

"Look," she continued more calmly, "I'm scared. Really scared. I know the risks. But it is what it is and we have to deal with it—at least I have to deal with it."

"*We* have to deal with," corrected Stan.

Stan recognized Kimo's fierce look as the one he'd laid into Bob the day he'd attacked him. Nani must have seen it too, as she walked over and embraced Jenny in congratulations, obviously deliberate in keeping Kimo away.

Kimo looked around at the others, and started to say something, but then suddenly turned and walked off. Freed from Kimo's intimidation and buoyed by Jenny's news, the group's spirits suddenly lifted.

"So, time for a toast," Russ said. As he scurried off to fetch his latest foul brew, there were groans of objection. Though Erik's and Russ's methods had evolved to the point that their brew contained some alcohol, it was only enough to inebriate a person just before drowning in the foul stuff. When he returned, they celebrated late into the night, enjoying songs and jokes and lighthearted conversation for the first time since the storm.

Chapter 11 _____

"BOAT! THERE IS A boat!"

Marco's shouts drew everybody into a tight circle, but Marco ignored them. He grabbed a torch, lit it from the cooking fire, and raced off again. Without hesitation, everybody dropped what they were doing and followed him toward the Point. Once there, Marco tossed the torch onto a pile of leaves and wood they had been set out ever since what they now called the Great Storm. Gray wisps of smoke immediately began to rise into the air, but everybody's attention was on a flickering pinpoint of light off to the east.

Stan turned to Jenny. "I guess it has to be a boat, doesn't it? What d'ya think, about a mile away?"

"Maybe further," she said. "It's hard to tell with the sun reflecting off of it like that. Do you think they see us?"

Stan turned around, shielding his eyes from the setting sun. "I doubt it. The sun's directly behind us. They probably can't see anything in our direction right now. The timing's about as bad as it can get."

Don traced the growing plumes of smoke down to their source. For reasons that now seemed inexplicable, they had built a signal fire to produce smoke, not flame. Once the sun set, it would be useless. "We need lots of dry wood, fast—not all this green stuff. C'mon, let's gather as much as we can while we still have some daylight to work with."

Everybody scrambled frantically, and within fifteen minutes, had collected a supply of dry wood. Kimo stood behind them, staring off toward the horizon with a dour expression.

As soon as the sun was down, they fed dry wood to the heap of leaves until a flame shot up a good five feet. They could no longer see it, but they knew the boat was out there. And though their vigil was useless, they knew sleep would be impossible. Like statues, they stood staring out into the distance.

"Depending on the type of boat," David speculated, "I figure it could be moving anywhere between three and thirty miles per hour. Either way, it'll pass the island by morning. That's if they don't see our fire before then and stop."

"If they were anchored, wouldn't we see lights?" Michelle asked.

"Maybe," Stan said, "but I think we'd have seen a light if they had sailed past, too. Maybe they just don't have their lights on. It's not like there's a risk of hitting another boat out here."

George piped in. "You think they wouldn't put their lights on if they saw our fire? More likely they just weren't coming this way at all, or they veered away and are halfway to Australia by now."

Marco argued, "No, I'm sure it was coming this way. I saw it first exactly east and it stayed to the east, so it must be coming toward us."

"Well," Stan said, "There's nothing to do but wait, I suppose."

"And pray," added Wayne.

As tinges of dawn flirted with moonlight, they stood as close to the cliff edge as they could, anxiously peering into the softening darkness. As soon as the first sliver of the sun appeared, they simultaneously spotted it no more than a quarter of a mile to the east. It was a white sailboat, with a single mast and its sails down, and it was pointed directly toward them—perhaps a round-the-world yachter making a rare visit to Henderson.

"It's anchored!" Stan called out. "They know we're here!"

Everybody began jumping, waving their arms, and shouting. It seemed that whoever was on board was still below deck, probably still asleep; or, if they did hear all the hollering, they were in no hurry to answer.

"It's not anchored," Kimo announced robotically from the back.

"How can you tell?" Don said. "It must be or it would have been past us by now."

"If it were anchored, the back of the boat would be facing us," Kimo said. "The current is coming straight towards us."

Jenny squinted against the rising sun. "I think he's right. It's still moving."

After fifteen minutes of nervous watching, Jenny quietly slipped away and walked back to the east beach. She knew that if she told the others what she was up to, they'd try to talk her out of it or even physically restrain her. But she'd already noted the water conditions—a light but chaotic surf indicated a current that was strong but by no means dangerous—typical early morning seas. It would be easy, and perfectly safe. If she needed to, she could just slip right back in through the north beach channel. It would be no different than the route she'd swum dozens of times before—but still, she knew they'd never let her go. Stan never liked her swimming through the reef, even after she'd done it so many times without any trouble. He seemed to think that just because she was pregnant, she was handicapped. In reality, though, swimming was about the only time she didn't feel pregnant.

She slipped out of her sandals and pareo and waded into the water. It was only once she made her way through the channel that Marco spotted her, pointing urgently and shouting her name. Stan pushed his way up to the front of the group, stood on the edge of the Point, and called out to her. He knew, however, that there was no way she would hear him, with the waves crashing against the Point and her head plowing through the water.

Once Jenny was safely through the channel, she stopped and treaded water, waving to the others to let them know she was okay. With her head out of the water, she could just hear their pleas to come back, but she pretended otherwise, putting her head back down and swimming northeast toward the boat. To get there, she would have to swim straight into the current, which was somewhat stronger than she'd expected, but that only meant the way back would be easy, like coasting downhill.

After a few minutes, it became clear that she wasn't making any progress into the current, but that the boat was still getting closer nevertheless. Apparently, it wasn't anchored. All she had to do was hold her own against the current and wait for the boat to drift to her. She laughed to herself about how strange it would be to those aboard to have a naked woman, especially a visibly pregnant one, board their boat from an island they likely assumed was deserted.

About thirty feet away, she starting shouting, but there was neither a reply nor sign of movement. Growing nervous and unsure of the wisdom of her actions, she nevertheless decided to attempt boarding, but the gunnels on the front and side were too high for her to grab. She swam along the port side toward the transom, hoping to find a ladder or swimming platform or something else to climb onto. Every few seconds, she stopped to tread water and call out, swallowing a fair bit of seawater in the process. That only added to her anxiety. Knowing that fear quickly drains energy from even the strongest swimmers only further increased her panic. She rolled onto her back and floated for a moment, taking deep breaths—she had to calm down.

She thought about abandoning her effort and heading back through the north beach channel, but quickly reasoned that the safest thing to do would be to board the boat. The way back to the channel would be with the current the whole way, but she needed to rest. She turned her head slightly and checked her distance from the Point. There was plenty of time: she could climb on the boat, rest until it floated to the Point, and then make the short, easy swim from there through the north beach channel.

After a few more deep breaths, she rolled back and swam the last few meters toward the transom. As she approached, she noticed the name of the boat, *Sea Salva*, painted in large, blue italics on the white hull, but with the final *a* blackened, as if partially burned away. Ironic but encouraging, she thought, that *salva* was the Spanish word for *savior*. Underneath the name, in smaller letters, was Newport Beach, likely the boat's homeport.

At the transom, she encountered a tall, forward-sloping stern. There was a ladder on the left side, but it was folded up, with the hinges three feet above the waterline—too high to reach. She noticed that the waves were lifting and dropping the stern a good foot, so she tried timing her lunges with the waves, hoping to grab the ladder when it was at its low point. After several discouraging misses, a larger wave brought the ladder down within her reach. She quickly lunged and grabbed the rung nearest the hinges. It took everything she had to hold on as the next wave lifted both her and the boat out of the water, then dropped her again, as if trying to rip her loose. But her adrenaline had now kicked in, and she had a death grip on the ladder. By synchronizing her movements with the rising and falling of the stern, she was finally able to claw her way up a couple of rungs until her feet found purchase on some kind of silver protrusion from the transom—perhaps an engine exhaust. She then stood and let go of the rung with one hand, and released a latch that held the ladder in its folded position. Both she and the ladder dropped back into the water. She quickly pulled herself up and stood on the bottom rung, calling out, louder and more insistently than before. Again, there was no response.

She looked again toward shore, and again assured herself she had plenty of time before the boat drifted past the Point, then climbed up the ladder and on to the deck. She immediately realized why there was no answer: there had been a fire. The cockpit was badly charred. A metal frame obviously designed to support a cloth roof was instead covered with melted, black plastic. The lack of a charred smell, however, indicated the fire likely was not recent. If anybody was still aboard, she reasoned, they probably needed her help more than she needed theirs. She waved toward the Point to signal she was onboard and okay, and then started to look around the cockpit.

The hatch leading down into the cabin was open. She stuck her head inside, again calling without a response. From the terrible mess below she could tell the fire had spread inside the cabin as well, though the damage was less extensive toward the front. The wooden steps leading down from the hatch were severely burned and looked too weak to support her. She carefully placed her weight on the outsides of the steps, where they looked stronger, and worked her way down. Inside, she quickly searched the forward and aft cabins, confirming the boat had been abandoned. The two aft staterooms were severely damaged, with almost nothing recognizable, but the forward stateroom was nearly untouched.

Her next thought was to somehow get the boat to shore. She went back up on deck to the steering wheel and gave it a spin to the left, before realizing how stupid that was: there could be no steerage as long as the boat was just drifting with the current; it was like turning the wheel of a parked car and expecting it to magically turn. She had to get the boat moving somehow if she was going to steer it.

Looking down, she saw the engine key still in place and turned it. Not surprisingly, there was no response, not even a click. She climbed back down to the main cabin to see if she could find the source of the problem, although she was unsure what she should look for. On the port side, she found a large electrical switchboard and turned on all the breakers, but nothing happened. A meter labeled "Battery" registered zero.

Climbing back on deck, she looked toward the island, trying to gauge the drift of the boat. On its present course, she figured it would float about a hundred yards off the reef. She guessed she had about fifteen minutes before passing the Point. If she didn't get off the boat before then, there'd be no way to swim back through the north beach channel—swimming into the current was impossible and trying to cross the reef in these waves would be suicidal. The Point was truly a point of no return.

"Anchor!" she shouted. She raced to the front of the boat and found a large anchor hanging off the bow. The anchor was attached to a heavy chain that wrapped around a capstan of some sort before disappearing into a locker below deck. Likely, the capstan was electrically driven, but there certainly wasn't any electricity to operate it. She was about to give up when she noticed a knob on the base of the barrel. She turned the knob counter-clockwise until the capstan began to rotate, allowing the anchor to drop, pulling chain out of the locker—the knob was some kind of brake, it seemed. "Well, that's some progress anyway," she mumbled.

She found a latch on the chain locker and opened it so she could watch the chain run out behind the anchor. She practiced releasing and tightening the brake to make sure she had control of the anchor, and then released the brake completely, letting the anchor fall freely. The chain seemed to rattle on forever, but she could eventually see it nearing its end. She assumed the end of the chain was fastened to something in the locker so that it wouldn't run all the way out, but not wanting to take a chance, she tightened the brake, making sure to lock it down hard. As the anchor rattled to a stop, she noticed that only a few feet of chain was left in the locker and that the end wasn't attached to anything. She silently congratulated herself for her foresight in stopping the anchor in time.

She watched the Point for a few seconds to check the progress of the boat, but its movement appeared unaffected by the lowered anchor. Then she looked again at the anchor chain. It still hung straight down. It took just a few seconds to understand what that meant: apparently the water was too deep, and the anchor hadn't found bottom. "Shit! Now what?" she said out loud.

A quick glance up told her there was no hope for the sails. Even if she knew how to set sail, the sails had been hopelessly damaged by the fire, leaving only charred lengths of rope hanging from the mast. She then focused on a small, deflated zodiac tied upside down onto the deck just behind the mast, but that too had been damaged beyond usefulness.

Out of ideas, she shouted toward the Point. "It's abandoned! Completely burned out. I can't do anything to stop it. It's just going to drift past. What should I do?" The boat was starting to gain speed as the current squeezed past the island. There were probably only ten minutes left before she'd have to give up and swim back.

On shore, Stan could only make out an occasional word from Jenny. It was obvious from her actions, though, what was going on. Well aware of the current and the risks she faced in getting back, he shouted, "Give up! Just get off the boat now before it's too late! Hurry up!"

Though she couldn't hear him, Jenny knew intuitively what Stan was saying. "In a minute!" she shouted back. Even if she couldn't save the boat, she could surely salvage some things on board. She scrambled around the cockpit, opening every storage locker she could find. Almost everything made of plastic or wood was ruined, and it would be too hard to swim back with anything metal. The stern locker on the port side presented a pleasant surprise, however: a large white cube marked 6-Person Lifeboat. It was a bit singed but didn't look terribly damaged. After wrestling it out of the locker, she studied the simple cartoon drawings instructing the user to throw it overboard while holding a rope tether. She did as instructed, quickly tying the rope to a cleat, only to watch the cube slowly sink beneath the surface.

She turned and climbed back below deck. In the kitchen she found some pots, pans, and metal utensils, which she threw up the steps to the cockpit. Near the navigation table, she found a few small knives and other tools, along with a compass. In the forward stateroom, under the bed, she discovered several lifejackets that appeared to be serviceable and a large coil of rope that looked as though it had never been used. Realizing she was running out of time, she threw the remainder of her things up through the hatch, then she climbed back on deck and surveyed her booty. It would surely improve things on the island—now, if she could just get the stuff ashore.

She sighed. "How the hell am I supposed to take this all this back?" She tied the two lifejackets together with the rope, passing it through some metal eyelets at the end of the pots and pans, and the soft cloth sacks that held the tools. Then she loaded the utensils, the compass, and smaller tools inside the pots and pans, and put the lids on. Not likely to stay, but she couldn't think of an alternative.

Just as she was about to jump overboard, she remembered seeing a nylon mesh bag in the forward hold where the fire hadn't caused much damage. She glanced at the Point and figured she had just enough time to grab it before she had to get off. She leapt through the hatchway, and as her feet landed on the charred top step, it broke clean through, sending her face-first down the four feet into the main cabin. The corner of the navigation desk caught her forehead and knocked her unconscious.

Stan raced back along the trail cresting the narrow ridge, frantically searching for some way down to the water—and to Jenny. Twice he leapt up onto a rock believing he had found a place from which to jump from the steep cliffs, but both times his hopes were dashed by the sight of violent surf smashing onto the rocks some fifty feet below. Ahead, he saw a yet another rock, flat and cantilevered out over the water—maybe far enough out to get him beyond the rocks that littered the water below. He bounded up, but stopped short when he saw the smooth, turquoise water of the reef-protected lagoon.

"Damn it!" he shouted. He had retreated past the protective reef— he'd almost certainly be killed if he jumped into the shallow lagoon. Besides, even if he survived the jump, he'd never be able to swim back out the channel in time to get to Jenny.

He turned back to the jutting Point itself, focusing beyond the Point, on the abandoned yacht drifting to the west, some hundred yards beyond the furthest rocks. *What the hell happened? Why didn't she come back up on deck?* Time was running out. He knew how strong the currents were as they swept past the island. He still had time to swim out to the boat if he could find some way off the ridge. Stan wasn't half the swimmer that Jenny was, but he'd be swimming with the same current that had the boat in its clutches. *What was she thinking, swimming out to the boat like that? For God's sake, she's more than six months pregnant!*

He retraced his path back out to the Point, now a little more slowly, looking once again for an entry point. He finally found a place that might just work: no overhang, but well outside the reef, with deep blue water below and no obvious rocks that might unpleasantly interrupt his drop. With no further thought, he backed up, and then burst toward the cliff's edge.

From the moment Stan's flailing limbs were airborne, it would be just two seconds before he would impact the water some fifty feet below—two seconds to second guess the decision he had just made. First, there was the immediate danger that he wouldn't clear the cliff and would be knocked unconscious even before hitting the water. Then even if he did safely enter the water without hitting anything, the surf might pound him right back onto the cliffs, the result being no better. But what if he was lucky and cleared the rocks, and caught a retreating wave? What next? There was, of course, no way to go back the way he came, so he'd have two choices, and precious little time to decide: he could swim a couple of hundred yards with the current to the channel and slip back through the reef and into the protected lagoon, or he could swim across the current and intercept Jenny and the drifting boat. By the time he got to Jenny, though, both he and the boat would be well past the channel, and with the current as it was, there would be no way back to the island.

As fast as his mind was spinning, that's as far as he got before his awkward entry crushed the wind out of him. After a few seconds of paralysis, he flailed his way back to the surface, desperate to refill his emptied lungs. When his head finally broke the surface, he realized he wasn't able to take the deep breath he yearned for. He slowly rolled onto his back and began weakly paddling away from the wall of rock.

It was a full minute before his lungs were able finally refill. He then realized that he had already made his decision. He had been paddling across the current toward the *Sea Salva*, and to Jenny. Whatever happened now, there would be no way back to Henderson Island.

Within minutes, he reached the transom and climbed the ladder. After a quick glance around the empty deck, he started down through the open hatch, noticing the broken step just in time to avoid falling on top of Jenny, still lying prone below. He carefully stepped over the broken step. Just as he reached her side, he heard Jenny groan. Well aware that there was nowhere to go and thus no hurry, Stan sat on the floor next to her, turned her gently onto her back and rested her head on his lap.

"You okay?" he asked.

"I … I'm not sure. I was going below to …" Suddenly recalling where she was, she tried to sit up suddenly. "We've got to go, quickly, before it's …" She swayed and collapsed.

"No, no. Relax. There's no hurry, everything's fine. Just lay down. Let me see if I can find you some water."

Stan grabbed a nearby seat cushion and slid it under Jenny's head, then rummaged through some overhead cabinets and found dozens of bottles of water, still intact. He opened one and brought it back to Jenny.

"Here, sip some of this." Stan lifted her head up to the bottle he was holding in his other hand. She took a sip and then lay back down. "How do you feel?"

"Okay, I guess. My head hurts, but I don't think it's so bad. How long … I mean, where are we? And how did you get here?"

"I swam out, and we're probably a little past the channel by now. Just relax, we're fine."

"No, let's go on deck. I want to see where we are. Help me up."

Stan helped her stand. "You sure you're okay?"

"So long as I move slowly, it's okay." She saw the fractured step. "Is that what happened?"

"Guess so. Can you get up?"

"Yeah, no problem." She slowly worked her way up the steps.

When they arrived on deck, they saw they were about a hundred yards off the reef, moving westward even faster now, and well past the Point and the north beach channel. At the most, they were maybe two hundred yards from the island itself, but with the reef in between, it might as well have been a thousand miles. Huddling on charred bench seats, they stared at the island that had been their home for the past three months. Stan thought it ironic that for so long they could only think about leaving, and now he wanted nothing more than to go back.

Back on shore, they could see all their friends walking along the beach as if in a funeral procession, mirroring the drift of the boat. Though they could keep up at a comfortable walking pace, Stan knew they were powerless to intervene as two of their best friends were slowly, inevitably swept away.

Stan soon noticed that Jenny was suffering from the heat of the direct sun and realized there was no point in staying on deck to watch the tragedy unfold. "Let's get you down below out of the sun. I'll see what I can find on board to eat, okay?"

"Yeah, I guess that's best." Jenny rose and climbed below slowly, still unsure on her feet. "I'm really, really sorry, Stan. I thought ..."

"Hey, you had no way to know. What's done is done. Let's not talk about it. We're safe, that's what counts."

Down below, Stan retrieved more bottled water and found some canned food with labels that were charred and unreadable, but appeared to be mostly intact.

"Well, I'm not sure where we're headed," Stan said, trying to sound upbeat, "but we've got all the food and water we need to get there. Whoever owned this boat was stocked to go around the world—and in style, too." He held up a bottle with the top half of a still recognizable Opus One label. "There's even some good wine here—or at least it was good once."

After finding a can opener in one of the drawers, he randomly opened two cans that turned out to be a can of corn and a can of sausages. Though she hadn't eaten since noon the previous day, Jenny was too nauseous to eat more than a spoonful of corn. She laid down in the forward cabin with her head on Stan's lap, and quickly fell asleep.

About an hour later, Jenny was awakened by a ray of sunlight from an overhead hatch slowly drifting across her eyes. Still a bit disoriented, she mumbled, "That's weird. Just clouds d'ya suppose?"

Stan had already noticed the moving ray of light, but hadn't placed any significance to it. Now that Jenny mentioned it, though, it did seem strange. He stood on the bunk, popping his head through the hatch. "That's weird, the island's on the wrong side. I mean, we're still next to the island, but we've turned around somehow. I don't get it, why would the boat suddenly turn like that?" He pulled himself the rest of the way through the overhead hatch out onto the deck.

Jenny weakly called up to him, "Check the anchor, Stan."

Confused, he walked to the front of the boat. The anchor chain was angled down into the water toward the east.

"Hey, I think it's caught on something! That must be what spun us around." He studied the shore.

"Are we still moving?" asked Jenny from below.

"Hold on, I can't tell yet … wait, I don't think so … No, we've stopped!"

"How far from land are we?"

"Not far at all. Just a few hundred yards, near the northwest point."

Stan went down below to help Jenny up on deck.

On the island, those following the progress of the boat saw it spin around. It didn't take long to figure out that it had drifted over an underwater ridge extending from the northwest tip of the reef. The ridge must have snagging the anchor. When they saw Stan helping Jenny on deck, they began to wave their arms, shouting.

Jenny pointed toward the excited group. "Can you make out what they're saying?"

Stan strained to hear over the sound of waves crashing on the reef, then shook his head. "Doesn't much matter, though. There are only two ways back, and neither's very easy. Either we go over the reef or we go directly into the current for a couple of miles to the north beach channel."

"I swim with the current pretty often, Stan, and I can tell you, there's no way we could swim back to the north beach channel. We'd need a boat of some kind."

"Maybe on a calm morning at high tide we could make it over the reef if we can build some kind of raft. It's not like it would have to cross the ocean or anything, it just needs to survive a few knocks against the reef."

"With the waves like they are now, I don't think anything would survive."

"Yeah, but time's on our side now. There's plenty of food and water on this thing, we can wait as long as we need to for more favorable conditions. Will build something."

Still not herself from the knock on the head, Jenny was uncharacteristically resigned. "We've both looked around the boat and didn't see anything."

"Come on, Jen. There's lots of stuff here. We just have to figure out how to make something with it."

They began scouring the boat, taking inventory of their findings. "This is incredible!" Stan said. "I had no idea how much storage space boats have. There's stuff under every floorboard and seat cushion."

Most of what they found had been rendered useless by the fire, but a lot was still in fair shape. Though escape was the primary objective of their search, they often found themselves thinking how much their existence on the island would change if they could get some things ashore with them. Snorkeling masks, stainless steel tools, flashlights and batteries, binoculars, jars, pots and pans, water bottles, day packs, real clothes, fishing tackle, a folding shovel of all things, and perhaps most importantly, a sideband radio. Though it was without power now, there was hope that the solar cells from the island's disabled radio could power this one.

But salvaging the boat, or some of the things on it, could come later, after they had figured out how to get themselves ashore. To that end, they had found no quick answers, but concluded that there were enough wooden doors and cabinets on board to piece together a rough but serviceable raft. It would take time, but time they had.

By evening, Jenny felt much better. She had a lump on her forehead, but no lingering pain or nausea. There was no way to cook on board, but Stan still pieced together a palatable dinner from the large variety of canned goods—even if it didn't live up to the standards they'd enjoyed on the island. They retired early, taking possession of the relatively undamaged forward stateroom. As they lay on the four-inch foam mattress, with real pillows and sheets, it felt like the Four Seasons, and the slow rolling of the waves rocked them into a deep sleep.

Chapter 12

"DID YOU HEAR THAT?" Jenny whispered, nudging Stan awake. Realizing it was silly to whisper, she looked up and called out, "Is somebody there?"

Hearing no answer, she turned back to Stan who was still trying to wake up, and then she lay back down. "I thought I heard voices. I don't know, must have been a dream or something."

"I didn't hear anything." He listened for a moment, then rolled over. "It's still early. See if you can get back to sleep."

A moment later, there was a sharp knock against the hull. Jenny and Stan leapt from their berth and raced up the hatch. Stan, arriving on deck first, was shocked to see Nani climbing onto deck from the swimming ladder in back.

"What ... where'd you come from?" Stan asked. Jenny climbed onto deck behind him.

"Surprise!" Nani said. "Happy to see us?"

"Us?" Jenny asked. Then glancing down behind Nani, they saw Kimo's head pop up just over the transom. Stan walked back and peered over the transom. Kimo was kneeling on a large, ragged, white fiberglass board in the water. It was too large to be a surfboard. Perhaps, it was a large windsurfer without the sail, or an old Sunfish.

"I don't—" Stan started.

"Not now," Kimo said. "The waves are going to build up again soon. We gotta go while it's still early." Kimo was obviously upset and hardly celebratory over the rescue. "I can only take one at a time. Who's first?"

Nani preempted Stan and Jenny, both still at a loss for words. "Jenny's first."

Jenny stepped to the back of the boat as if in a daze, hesitating before climbing down the swimming ladder. "I don't get it. So ... then you're coming back again to get Stan? Alone? Why did both of you come in the first place?"

Kimo glared at Nani. "Don't ask. Not now. I can swim the board back here alone, no problem. We just can't take three on this thing at once."

Jenny continued to stall, still trying to understand the plan, but Kimo was insistent. "Look, we can discuss it all later. For now, let's just go, all right? We need to do this while it's still high tide and before the afternoon winds kick in."

Jenny shrugged, and then climbed down the ladder and kneeled carefully on the front of the board, while Kimo braced it tightly against the hull of the *Sea Salva*.

"Lie flat, as far forward on the board as you can."

When she'd settled her bulging belly into place, Kimo lowered himself onto the back of the board, his legs dangling into the water, and paddled toward shore. A few minutes later, they arrived just outside the reef.

"Okay, we're going to catch a wave and ride it directly over the reef, so when I say, start paddling as hard as you can ... and keep your legs and head in close, just in case we hit something."

After studying the pattern of waves for a moment, Kimo shouted "Now!" and they began to paddle furiously. He'd timed it perfectly, sending them smoothly surfing over the reef.

Skimming just inches above the coral, Jenny realized there was no way somebody could swim through, and no way Kimo could go back out the way the came in. If they hadn't caught the very crest of the wave, and if it weren't high tide, they would have hit the reef and hit hard. She didn't even want to think about what it would be like being tumbled through the coral by the surf.

Once safely inside the lagoon, Jenny slid off the side of the board and began to swim the rest of the way in to shore. After a few strokes, she rolled over into a backstroke, intending to ask Kimo about the strange rescue plan, but he had already taken off, paddling eastward toward the north beach channel for the next trip. Jenny guessed it would be at least an hour before he got back to the stranded boat. He had a long, exhausting day in front of him. She rolled back to her front and swam the rest of the way to shore in a fluid crawl. As she stepped onto dry land, she was greeted by several of her friends, anxious to hear about the boat and the curious rescue.

Back on the *Sea Salva*, Stan had intently watched Kimo and Jenny navigate their way through the reef, somehow completely trusting that Kimo would succeed. As soon as he knew they were safely in the lagoon, he turned to Nani. "So, where'd that boat or surf board or whatever it is come from?"

Nani, who was also focusing on Jenny and Kimo, looked a bit more worried than Stan. She attempted to paste on a smile, however, hesitating slightly before replying. "It was in the bunker. I think it's a beginner's windsurfer, or at least that's what Kimo thinks. He found it on the east beach a few months ago, a week or so after the storm. He didn't want anybody using it, but I guess he didn't know how to get rid of it either, so he just put it in the bunker."

"But I don't get why you came out together. It doesn't make sense— now we have to make three trips back. And you must have left almost in the dark to have gotten here so early in the morning."

Again she hesitated, but now her façade of a smile began to melt away. "It's hard to explain. We had an argument yesterday." Apparently thinking about what to say, her expression saddened, perhaps for the first time Stan could remember. "Kimo didn't want to use the board," she began slowly, choosing her words carefully. "He said we should build a raft and try to reach you guys like that."

"A raft? You really mean like a Tom Sawyer raft? Yeah, fat chance. Even if you could get it out here through the channel, you'd never get back."

"That's what I told him. We argued about it for a long time. Sometimes ... sometimes, you just can't argue with him. He means well, really, but ... anyway, within a few days I'm sure he would have changed his mind and come out to get you. He would have either built something, or come out on the board."

"What changed his mind?"

"Nothing." She gave a half-heartedly smile. "Just before sunrise this morning, I went into the bunker and got it myself. By the time he saw me, I was already through the channel. He swam after me because he didn't think I would be able to rescue you myself, and he was probably right. But by then, all three of us had to be brought back, so he was rather pissed off, in case you didn't notice. I think he was also mad because I went in the bunker. I knew the combination because I'm the one that bought the lock back in Hawaii, but he didn't know that I knew it, so he didn't like that very much."

"He did seem to be in one of his moods ... he doesn't exactly hide his emotions well, does he? Anyway, I'm really happy to see you. I hope it doesn't cause too much trouble between you two."

"Don't worry, he gets over things quickly. He'll probably sulk a bit and yell about *the island rules*, then he'll be fine tomorrow."

"The rules? C'mon, this boat has some incredible stuff on board. It's going to really change everything, even if we can't get the boat itself fixed up."

Nani laughed nervously. "I doubt that. Kimo will probably release the anchor and set the boat free before he takes me back, and he'll certainly leave me for last." She could see Stan's incredulous look and continued with downcast eyes. "Well, in a way I agree with him. Think about it. When it comes down to it, have you ever really lived better or been healthier? I know, that's what Kimo is always saying, but it's really true. Even if you had everything on the boat back on shore, would it really help you get off the island? I understand everybody wants to get back, and if this boat had sails, or a motor, and people wanted to try sailing somewhere, okay, I can understand that. But just to take some food or tools off the boat? What's the point?" She hesitated, studying

Stan's stunned face, and then hung her head, adding faintly, "Well, that's the way he'll look at it anyway."

As Stan thought about how to reply, Nani turned to sit down, but abruptly straightened, staring off to the east, shielding her eyes from the morning sun. "Shit!"

Stan had never heard her swear. In fact, it was so completely out of character, it stirred a bit of panic within him. "What? What's wrong?"

"The sky. Look!" She pointed to a line of dark clouds off to the east. "We're going to have to wait it out. I just hope Kimo sees it before he comes back out through the channel—it's going to get rough out here."

The wind kicked up just as Kimo was starting though the channel, and the water immediately began getting choppy. He'd might make it out to the boat, but it was certainly too rough to return to shore over the reef.

"Shit!" he muttered. He waited just within the breakwater for a moment debating with himself, then resoundingly slapped the water in anger before turning the board around and paddling back to shore. Once on dry land, he carried the board back to the bunker and then briskly fled inland.

Jenny and her escorts slowly made their way back to camp, oblivious to the threatening weather and Kimo's abandoned rescue attempt. Jenny felt overwhelmed by the onslaught of questions about how she got trapped on the boat, what the boat was like, and what she knew of the ongoing rescue mission. Still in the dark about much of Kimo and Nani's plan, she felt ill-prepared to answer many of them.

After Stan gave Nani a brief tour of the boat, they treated themselves to some cold canned food and water, and then sat on deck to watch the rainsquall move in. Suddenly, a gust of wind slammed into the boat, violently rattling the loose ropes against the mast. Within seconds, the first drops of rain sent them scrambling down below. As the wind quieted, Stan took a seat, and Nani matter-of-factly removed her pareo.

She noticed Stan's widening eyes. "I hope you don't mind, but I really want to rinse the salt out of this thing. You really should do the same, you know—salt's not good for your skin. It can cause skin ulcers. Want me to hang your pareo up on deck too?"

Stan knew she was right, but hesitated, prompting Nani to unceremoniously snatch it off his waist. As she climbed up on deck to tie their pareos to the boom, Stan stared after her, unable to do anything but admire her perfect shape. The specter of being in the confines of the cabin, stark naked, with the soft drumming of rain on the roof was too much—it wasn't that he didn't trust himself, or her, but that he didn't want to feel so pressured and distracted; he felt guilty for even looking at her. He wandered into the forward cabin to look for some clothing.

When Nani came back a few minutes later, she found Stan dressed in shorts and a colorful collared shirt. He had even set out clothes on the salon table for her. Nani giggled at his modesty, but picked up the shorts, and stepped into them. "You're strange, you know that? It's cute." She pulled on the shorts and turned slightly to each side, gathering the loose waistband at her hips. "What do you think? Like them?"

Looking at her, Stan wasn't at all convinced that dressing had made his situation easier; she was overwhelmingly sexual no matter how she was dressed, and the baggy shorts just seemed to draw attention to the raindrops clinging to her pert breasts. She then looked playfully into Stan's eyes, smiled, and removed her hands from the waistband, letting the shorts slither down to the floor. Then laughing at him, she stepped out of the hopelessly oversized shorts and went forward to search for something that would fit. Stan's eyes couldn't help but follow her as she dug through the forward cabin, eventually finding an oversized white T-shirt with a colorful picture of Mickey Mouse on the front.

When she returned, she carefully studied Stan's face. After an awkward moment, she asked, "How'd you meet?"

"Meet? You mean Jenny?"

"Yeah."

"In college. We met at a frat party—or I guess to be more accurate, we met while trying to get away from a frat party. We literally ran right into each other trying to get out the door. She started griping about some asshole that was goading everybody into drinking beer until they got sick—he was the reason I was leaving too—some guy who reminds me of Bob in a way, just not as big. Anyway, we just started walking together. Sounds strange, but we didn't even know where we were going, just started walking. After an hour or so, we were talking so much we suddenly realized we were completely lost. I guess we were kind of following each other."

"So what attracted you to her?"

"I don't know. I suppose it wasn't as much what she was saying, but how she was saying it—her energy and enthusiasm maybe. She just has a great attitude about life and isn't afraid of anything, know what I mean?"

"Absolutely. Jenny is really an amazing person. I really admire her. I can't even imagine having the guts to swim out to this boat like she did. When did you know you were going to marry her?"

"It probably sounds silly, but the same night. Eventually we passed a late-night coffee shop, and I asked if she wanted to go inside to *get warm.*" He laughed a bit. "It was about a hundred degrees out and humid, so I felt completely ridiculous as soon as I said it. She didn't even hesitate though, just said, 'Yeah, I'm feeling a bit chilly too.' The funny thing is, we hadn't even seen each other in the light until we walked into that coffee shop—I wouldn't have even recognized her if I had seen her the next day—but I guess, I was already sold."

Nani thought for a moment. "That's a wonderful story. You two are very lucky."

"Well, I don't know about her, but, yeah, I feel very lucky to have found her."

After about an hour, the pattering of rain stopped as suddenly as it had begun. Stan climbed on deck to look around. "Damn it!" Stan shouted.

His urgent cry was enough to make Nani race up on deck, almost tripping on the step that had caused Jenny to fall. She immediately froze, then fell to her knees. "Oh my God!"

Stan raced to the front of the boat and checked the anchor. It took just a second to realize that the capstan brake had failed to hold up to the increased pull caused by the gusting wind. The last few feet of chain had paid out completely and both chain and anchor were now somewhere on the ocean floor, leaving the *Sea Salva,* once again, adrift. They had already been carried a good mile down-current of Henderson's western shore, well beyond any conceivable rescue, even with the surfboard. Stan just stared at the island, trying for the second time in two days to get used to the idea of being lost at sea.

"Unbelievable!" Stan said and viciously kicked the side of the cockpit. Nani began to weep softly.

They looked about, realizing that every minute they drifted made their escape that much more hopeless. But as the prevailing wind and current carried them westward, there was nothing to stop them. They hugged each other, unsure who was consoling whom, but both needing to know they weren't alone. After some time, they broke their embrace and watched the retreating island, hoping for a miracle they knew wouldn't happen.

Chapter 13

ONCE THE *SEA SALVA* had drifted past the island, the current weakened and their pace slowed. By midafternoon the island had vanished beneath the horizon, engulfing them in an infinity of ocean.

"I'm going down below to see if there are any maps," Stan dejectedly mumbled. "Maybe we can at least figure out where we're going. Keep your eyes on the compass so we know what direction we're headed, okay?"

Stan started to climb below, but then abruptly stopped and turned back to Nani, rolling his eyes. "Never mind. The compass doesn't mean squat."

"Why? What do you mean?"

"Just because we know where the front of the boat's pointed doesn't mean we know where we're going. We could be drifting any which way— frontwards, sideways, backwards. Christ, this is crazy! We don't know where we're headed or how fast we're going, and we don't know how far or what direction land is." Stan sat and cradled his head in his hands.

Nani rested her hand on his shoulder. "Kimo says Pitcairn is about a hundred miles to the west, and that's the direction of the current. Maybe we'll hit it."

Stan raised his head. "A little south of west is what he said, whatever that means. But it can't be all that far south; we saw it from the plane when we flew in from Mangareva. If we could just get this boat moving, even a little, we might be able to figure out what direction we're going and steer it somehow."

"Maybe we can make some kind of sail or something. Do you know anything about sailboats?"

"Obviously not, or I would have known to tie the anchor chain to something so it wouldn't slip away. How 'bout you?" Stan asked hopefully.

"No, I've been on sailboats, but that's about all."

"Well, I think you're right, we've got to find something that acts like a sail somehow." Stan began lifting cockpit seats, looking for anything that might be improvised into a sail. Inside the third compartment, he suddenly stopped rummaging and looked closer. "What the hell is a *storm sail*?"

"No idea. Why?" Nani replied.

"Because whatever it is, we've got one," Stan pulled out a light blue bag and peered inside. "It looks like it's actually in good shape. Jenny told me there was a lifeboat in here before. It must have been on top of the storm sail and protected it from the fire." He reached in the bag and took a small nylon triangle, not more than a meter on its longest side. "Well, whatever it is, it's tiny."

"Do you think something that small can really move the boat?"

Stan shrugged. "Let's just try. What do we have to lose?"

The storm sail had metal eyelets at each corner, so they found some salvageable rope to lace through, and then stretched two of the corners between two metal cables running from the deck to the top of the mast. They then tied the third corner to the deck, forming an upside-down triangle across the front of the boat.

Stan watched the sail fill with wind. "Now I guess we just wait and see if the boat moves."

After a couple of minutes they looked over the edge of the transom and noticed a slight ripple of water radiating from the back of the boat. Stan picked up a half-empty water bottle and threw it overboard, watching as it fell astern. After a minute, the bottle was about fifty feet behind them.

"It sure isn't a speedboat, but at least we're moving faster than the current. It's the best we're going to do, I suppose."

Stan went to the wheel and turned it slightly to the right, watching the compass for a few seconds. Finally the needle moved. The boat was turning. They spent the rest of the day learning how to steer, tossing debris overboard to see how they were moving relative to the water. They determined that to keep the boat moving forward, they could only steer about twenty degrees away from due west, otherwise the boat would slip sideways, and again, the compass would be meaningless.

Stan tried to be upbeat. "Okay, so Pitcairn it is. If it really is where Kimo said, we just might make it. It's going to take a lot of luck though—it's an awfully small island, and we're only going to get one chance at it."

"Hey, by the way, did you ever find any maps down below?"

Stan shook his head. "I did, but they're way too burnt to make sense of now. I'll look around some more, but I don't think any paper in the main cabin could have survived the fire."

"Is there any way we can keep track of where we are? I mean so we know how far we've gone at least? Does this thing have a speedometer or anything like that?"

"The speedometer wouldn't do any good even if it worked, I'm sure it would just tell us our speed with respect to the water, like throwing those empty bottles over. Without knowing what the current's doing, it's pretty useless."

"Isn't there a way to figure out where we are by the stars—or the sun?"

Stan opened his mouth to rebuke her for her naivety, but fell suddenly silent. He folded his fingers into a tent and looked up for a moment, then looked down again at Nani. "Yes, maybe. There might be a way. I think we could figure out our longitude if we had a good clock, and I think there was a watch down below. Let me think about it for a while. Can you take the wheel? Just keep the needle here on the *W.*"

Stan went below to find a pen or pencil and something that survived the fire that he could write on. Fifteen minutes later, he emerged carrying a watch and a scrap of paper.

"Okay, I think I've got it. The earth is about twenty-four thousand miles in circumference and it takes twenty-four hours to rotate once, so the sun should take an hour to move a thousand miles. That's six minutes to move a hundred miles. All we have to do is keep track of sunset or sunrise. Each minute earlier or later it gets, should be about fifteen miles of progress—actually a little more, like seventeen miles."

"Earlier or later? What does that mean?"

"The sun moves from east to west. So I think if we go west, sunrise and sunset should get later—six minutes later for every hundred miles we go. I don't know if that's exactly right because we're not really at the equator, and there must be seasonal changes too, but I'll bet it's not too far off."

"So you can figure out how far west we are, but what about north and south?"

Stan shook his head. "That's a lot harder. I thought about it, and I think we'd have to measure how high the stars or sun gets each day. I'm pretty sure that's what they use sextants for. But even if there was one on board, I wouldn't have a clue how to use it. Besides, we don't know what Kimo meant by 'a little south of west' anyway, so what difference does it make?"

"Well, then we just need to keep this compass needle a bit below the *W* and hope for the best, right?"

Stan stared into the distance. "Yeah, I suppose, but look at the bottle I threw in. It's not exactly in back of the boat. It's off to the left. I think that means the boat must still be going a little sideways, to the north. We'll have to compensate for that—kind of guess the angle and correct for it—then hope we see Pitcairn soon enough to correct our course so we don't sail past."

"What if we can't? What if we miss it?"

"Then we keep going until we find something, or somebody finds us."

"I don't think there's anything for thousands of miles, at least that's what Kimo says."

"Then we just have to find Pitcairn. Even that's probably three or four days away at this speed. The good news is that if we do get to Pitcairn we can send a boat or plane out to Henderson for the others."

Nani hesitated. "You know there's probably nobody on Pitcairn, don't you?"

"I know that's what Kimo said, but I thought there were fifty or so people living there. Are you sure he's right about that?"

"It's a complicated story, but I'm pretty sure. They left about a year ago. Didn't you read about it? It was a big story in the islands at least. It sure pissed off Kimo."

"Why, what happened?"

"They convicted a lot of the men on the island of statutory rape. It was some kind of cultural thing. I guess they always married very young there—it was a carry-over from the old Tahitian culture, but the New Zealand government decided to do something about it anyway, so they arrested a bunch of the men and put them on trial."

"Yeah, I do think I remember reading something about that now that you mention it, but I didn't know they'd evacuated the entire population."

"That's what I heard last. They all voted to leave because they didn't think they'd have enough people to keep the place going. The population had been getting smaller for a long time anyway, so it might just have been an excuse."

"Well, whatever we find there, it's where we're headed."

They decided to place their bet on a course of two hundred and forty-five degrees, and spent the next two days taking turns at the wheel. Although they had no idea whether they were on the right track, they both tweaked their heading whenever the compass needle fluttered even the tiniest amount. In fact, the light winds were so constant, they could have easily just fixed the wheel with a rope, but steering allowed them to feel they had at least some control over their destiny.

Stan's efforts to track their progress by timing sunset and sunrise were surprisingly successful. With completely clear skies, they were able to pinpoint sunset to within a few seconds or so, making their estimate of longitude accurate to well within five miles, if his calculations were correct.

At sunrise on the third day, Stan proclaimed that they had covered eighty miles, and all considered, they were still in good shape. They had eaten well and slept well, and the weather had stayed fair. And if their heading was correct, and if Kimo was right, they should see Pitcairn before the end of the day.

They often discussed their arrival at Pitcairn. From a National Geographic article he had read, Stan vaguely remembered there was only one bay that offered a safe approach to the island, the rest of the coast being nothing more than wild surf crashing onto unforgiving cliffs. According to the article, boats attempting to reach shore at any other point would instantly be dashed to pieces. He remembered its name, Bounty Bay, but unfortunately he had no idea where it was on the island. If it was on the island's west shore, they'd have to go around the island, which would mean turning and sailing into the wind—clearly impossible given their limited steerage. Even approaching the north or south shores would be almost impossible. So the truth, which neither was willing to articulate, was that their chances of finding the island, arriving there in daylight, and finding *Bounty Bay* on the east shore were, at best, very slim. Still, it was their only hope, so they clung to it dearly.

At about two o'clock in whatever time zone their watch was set to, Stan noticed Nani staring into the distance just off to the left, transfixed. He raised the binoculars he'd found below and followed her gaze, leaning forward. As he watched, a cloud moved slightly, revealing a sharp, dark outline behind.

"Unbelievable!" he said. "I think we've found it."

"Just behind the clouds, yeah?"

"Yeah, but let's not celebrate yet. There's a lot that can go wrong still." He made a slight counterclockwise correction of the wheel toward the emerging island.

Two hours later, Stan again raised the binoculars to his eyes. "It's definitely a bay. There's a building near the water, and I think I see a dock, but it's hard to be sure." He offered the binoculars to Nani. "Wanna look?"

"No, I've never been able to see through those things. So you think we're going to make it?"

"Actually, Nani, for the first time, I do, even if that means we just crash this damn thing onto shore where that building is. We're headed right at it. I don't see how we can miss."

They glided into Bounty Bay just before sunset. With no anchor, they had already made the decision to beach the boat, and worry about how to get off later. As it turns out, even that wasn't necessary. They were able to steer directly up to a sturdy concrete dock. The instant the side of the boat bumped, they jumped off the *Sea Salva* as if it were red hot, laughing at how silly they were being.

Nani immediately threw her arms around Stan. "I can't believe we really made it! You were great."

Stan wrapped his arms around her and held tightly. "Don't kid yourself. It wasn't me—we were just lucky. But we did make it, didn't we?" After several seconds, he realized their embrace was lingering more than a celebratory hug ought, and he reluctantly let go. "So what do you think? Want to head up the road?"

Nani looked around. Night was quickly approaching and it was already difficult to see. She could make out the outline of a long, low building near the end of the dock and a road heading off to the left, but nothing more. "Let's wait until morning when we can see a bit better."

"So what, then, spend another night on the boat?"

Nani sighed. "Yeah, I guess. There's really no choice. I'm tired anyway."

Turning back to the boat, they realized it had bounced off the dock and was now ten feet away. They laughed at themselves, as Stan dove off the dock, swam to the boat, and climbed aboard, where he found a rope. He tossed one end to Nani, and she pulled him in and tied up the boat. Then, grudgingly, they settled in for another night on board—Nani in the forward cabin and Stan out on deck so he'd hear if somebody came down the road.

Chapter 14

THE RAINSQUALL HAD STRUCK Jenny and her companions when they were about halfway back to the village. While they didn't know Kimo's whereabouts, common sense told them the rest of the rescue would have to wait until the next morning. They weren't concerned, since Jenny had told them the *Sea Salva* had plenty of food and water aboard.

Kimo failed to show up even after the rain had passed, but that too wasn't unusual—by now they had grown accustomed to his walkabouts or, as Russ had dubbed them, *pout-abouts*. Complain as they might about his erratic personality, nobody could accuse him of shirking the rescue attempt, and they knew he'd return as soon as the weather and sea allowed.

In the early afternoon, hours after the sky had cleared, Marco went to the Point to try some fishing and noticed the boat had vanished. He ran back to tell the others. For the second time in two days, everybody dropped what they were doing and followed Marco, this time along the beach to the northwest point, where the *Sea Salva* had been anchored.

Jenny was devastated. She ran ahead of the others at such a desperate pace that she soon collapsed, barely able to get up again. Don arrived at the island's northwest corner first, just in time to catch a glimpse of the retreating mast in the distance. By the time Jenny finally staggered her way to the others, she found them at standing like statues, staring off into the western horizon. It was an ironic mirror image of the scene two days earlier. Then the *Sea Salva* had brought them hope and excitement—now, without even touching land, it was leaving behind sadness and loss. Perhaps nobody was as excited as Jenny when it arrived, and certainly nobody felt her despair as it left.

Jenny strained to see the last vestiges of the mast, but was unable to focus through her tears. She normally was not one to cry, but the inescapable feeling that this was all her fault was too much to bear. When at last she was forced to concede that eastern horizon was empty, she collapsed to her knees. Physically and emotionally spent, she had no more tears to shed.

Don took a few steps toward her and rested a hand gently on her right shoulder. "Look, it's not your fault. It's just some unlucky timing, that's all. If Kimo had told us yesterday about the surfboard, we could have prevented the whole thing. It's his fault, not yours. You were the only one of us with the guts to do anything in the first place. We would have all just watched the boat float by if it weren't for you." As he was talking, he realized how angry he was at Kimo.

Don's acceptance that Stan was gone upset Jenny all the more, and she fell forward, burying her forehead in the sand.

Mary came over and kneeled next to her. "You said there was plenty of food and water on board, right? They'll be fine. For sure, somebody will find them. They'll be rescued, and I'll bet they'll get somebody out here to pick us up too, and you'll have your baby back in Pennsylvania after all. I'm sure they're going to be fine. We're all going to be fine."

The others began to crowd around, taking turns inventing happy, highly improbable scenarios, but Jenny ignored them. It was Mary's mention of her labor that was sitting foremost in Jenny's mind. If Stan were gone, she'd need to build an emotional fortress for herself and her baby. Wallowing in misery and self-blame was not an option.

"Christ, now what?" George asked, looking back toward the village.

They followed George's gaze to a column of black smoke blooming into the sky.

"One of the huts must have caught fire," said Don. "C'mon, we better go see if we can do something. Mary, stay with Jenny, okay?"

As the others jogged ahead, Jenny stood up, took a deep, resolute breath, then began walking with Mary behind the others.

Don made his way down the beach well ahead of the others. He quickly realized the smoke wasn't coming from the village itself, but from somewhere inland, closer to the airstrip. He slowed his pace, but still arrived at the source of the smoke just a few minutes before the others. Just in front of the bunker, Kimo was feeding what looked like trash into a fire. Don felt his anger and frustration with Kimo well up to unprecedented heights. He decided it was time to take action, but to do so, he needed the support of the others—he'd have to wait for them to catch up.

"Hey, what's that?" Don challenged in as matter-of-fact a voice as he could muster.

"Burning trash," Kimo said curtly, throwing a tangle of rope on the fire, and then walking back to the bunker. A few seconds later, he emerged with an armful of rubbish.

"Did you see the boat's gone?" asked Don.

"Yep."

Just then, David arrived. "Why're you burning all that stuff? Where'd it come from?"

Kimo remained silent, continuing to toss things onto the blaze.

"Hey, some of that stuff might be useful," David said. "We could really use those plastic bottles to carry water. We could even remelt the plastic and make it into lots of things."

Having finished tossing in his load, Kimo again headed back into the bunker. By the time he emerged carrying yet more junk, the others had all arrived.

Claire pointed to a smoldering suitcase on the outskirts of the blaze. "Hey, that's my suitcase!"

Kimo tossed an armful of trash into the middle of the inferno, and then turned to Claire. "You still don't get it, do you? This stuff—your suitcase and the rest of it—is the problem, not the solution. It's about time you guys faced reality, and this isn't reality. It's poison."

He scanned the group, intense beyond anything they had seen before, eyes ablaze with anger. "I'm tired of all your bitching and whining. You wanted to know what's in the bunker? This is what was in the bunker: a bunch of trash, that's all. That's all it's ever been. And as long as it's here, you guys are never going to accept reality."

"Where'd it all come from?" asked George.

"It's just shit that gets washed up on the island. You really think the beaches were always this clean?" He looked around. There were no replies. "When we arrived here, the beaches were a pigsty. Plastic, bottles, glass, everything you can imagine washed up over hundreds of years. We cleaned it all up, but it continues. Why do you think I get up so early every day? I walk the loop trail and look for trash that's been washed ashore. It goes into the bunker until the next flight out—which, as you know, hasn't been for a while. So the bunker was just a place to put stuff, like a huge trash bin."

Kimo shuttled more trash from the bunker to the fire, and then turned again to face them. "Look around you! The beauty of the sea, land, and air without contamination by man. Have you ever really ever been better off than this? Don't you get it?" Kimo began to make large sweeping gestures as he talked, and his voice grew more animated. "This is the best it gets, people; all this shit would just make your lives worse, not better. Look at it logically. Here you are, the luckiest people on earth—maybe even the only people left on earth—and all you guys can do is think about how to get back to civilization and throw it all away. That's what's crazy!"

Wayne raised his hand halfway. "What about the other stuff that was in there—the extra fuel, the first-aid kit, emergency food, stuff like that?"

A flicker of guilt crossed Kimo's face. "I never said all that stuff was there. I said the bunker was built as a shelter and was *intended* to hold stuff like that. This resort was new, and the bunker hadn't been stocked yet. If there had been stuff in there that would have helped during the storm, don't you think I would have opened it?"

He looked at Bob. "And yes, Bob, I looked for your matches after the storm, but they were already ruined by the water. There was nothing that would have helped in any of your bags. There was just the radio … and this." Kimo reached inside the waistband of his pareo and pulled out a hunting knife so long it could almost be a machete. He brandished it for a moment with eerie familiarity, as if it were a close friend from his past. Everyone recoiled. Kimo's erratic temper was intimidating enough, but this brought things to a new level. After a moment, he tucked the knife back in and resumed his work.

Any call to action Don may have been planning came crashing to a halt, but he braved one more question. "What about the surfboard?"

"Washed ashore after the Big Storm a few months back. A great example too: the one time we tried to use something from here— something that didn't belong on the island—look what happened. Now they're both gone... and so's the surfboard." He stopped again and glanced toward Jenny, just now joining the group.

"So why so secret?" asked Allison. "And why burn all this stuff now? I don't get it. And where's the stuff we brought with us?"

Kimo hesitated. "Look, it's time you guys understand something ... we're not going to be rescued."

"What do you mean we're not going to be rescued?" pleaded Michelle.

Kimo stared at Michelle, his eyes softening a bit, even growing somber. Then he stood to full height and addressed them in a deliberate, serious tone.

"I mean just that: we're not going to be rescued because there's nobody to rescue us. Look, guys, the radio wasn't broken ... at least not at first. I know the difference between a broken radio and ... I mean, there was nobody to answer. The radio was fine. David, you're a physicist, aren't you?"

"Yeah, so?"

"Can you really think of no explanation for what happened that night before the storm? Think about it: sudden, tremendous heat, strange lights in the sky, complete loss of radio contact, a burnt ship passing by. Really no ideas?"

"But we've all discussed it and there's nothing that can explain ... what do you mean by *strange lights*?" Even as he said it, he remembered the reddish glow the night before the storm.

"David, what causes lights in the north and south?" Kimo asked.

"You mean the *aurora borealis*?"

"It's called *aurora australis* in the southern hemisphere, but yeah, the northern and southern lights. What causes them?"

"Well, I'm not an astrophysicist, but I know they're caused by gamma radiation hitting the atmosphere. The radiation ionizes oxygen in the upper atmosphere and there's an interaction with the plasma in the earth's magnetosphere. When there are two plasmas with different vectors, you get a Hall Effect, and electricity is generated." He shrugged. "That's all I really know."

Kimo looked confused. "Well, I was always told it was the solar wind."

David shrugged again. "Same thing, really. Most gamma radiation is from the sun, so it's sometimes called solar wind."

Kimo quickly regained his confidence. "So what could cause the southern lights to appear so far from the poles?"

David thought for a several second. "An exceptionally large burst of radiation from the sun. A huge solar storm or a gigantic solar flare."

"Bingo. Look, I may not have a PhD in physics or understand all that stuff you just said about vectors and plasmas, but I do know the sun has storms that can interfere with military equipment. Imagine a huge explosion on the sun, a massive solar storm that causes enough radiation to bring the southern lights this close to the equator. Don't you think that might cause heating of the atmosphere?"

David thought for a bit and then nodded. "Well, theoretically, sure. I suppose it would be like turning up the power on a tanning light, but I don't know—"

"Exactly. It would broil the earth's surface. So this solar storm happened during our nighttime, which means by the time the sun rose here, it must have pretty much settled down. But imagine what it must have been like on the other side of the earth, the side that was directly exposed to the sun during this—whatever—solar storm. Look how hot the air got here, and the sun wasn't even hitting us. It probably would have just vaporized everything on the other side, but all we got is a light show. We're just really lucky it happened when the entire earth was shielding us."

He stopped to see if the others were following him.

"What I'm saying is that the only places that would survive would be places protected by the dark of night. That means a few Pacific islands in the southern hemisphere where it was still winter. In fact, since the heat started just after our sunset, and seemed to end just at sunrise, there's a good chance that we're *it*. We're all that's left."

Everybody stood in shocked silence, prompting Kimo to continue. "What I'm saying is that we're not just an island surrounded by an ocean, we're an island of life surrounded by a very dead world. We have to learn to survive here with what we have. And thinking about what's in the bunker that might make our lives more comfortable for a day or two, or doing reckless things to get off the island, just isn't going to help us survive. We're only going to make it if everybody come to grips with the facts and works together to survive."

"You mean you think that ... *everybody's gone?*" Jenny asked. "That's crazy!"

"Fine then," Kimo said. "The world's normal and they've just forgotten about us, and boats like the one yesterday appear all the time. Believe whatever the hell you want." Kimo turned and went into the bunker for the last load of rubbish.

Michelle turned to David. "Could it be? Does that make any sense, what he's saying?"

All attention turned to David. He ran his hand through his hair and looked at the ground, thinking before answering. "I don't know. Like I said, theoretically, I guess it could be. But I really have no idea how much the temperature could increase from a solar flare. I have to admit it makes more sense than a lot of the other things we've been discussing. I know that there are solar storms—big ones, sometimes. But to get hot enough to kill people? That's a whole 'nother story. I just can't say." He lifted his eyes and shook his head slowly. "Somehow, I never thought about the lights we saw that night."

As Kimo threw the last of the junk into the fire, he turned to the others. "All right, it's all gone. The bunker is no more. Now a new beginning. We are the world. I'm really sorry about Stan and ..." Kimo's voice caught noticeably. "I wish ..." He swallowed, then abruptly turned his back to them and ran off toward the farm. Only then did Jenny realize that hers was not the only loss that day.

The moment Kimo was out of sight, Don found a long stick and probed the edges of the fiery blaze, fishing for anything that might still be worth saving. The only thing he managed to push out of the debris was Wayne's carry-on, still smoldering but intact. Using the stick, Don lifted a charred flap of fabric and flipped it over onto the ground, revealing the remains of the bag's contents. "Anything in here worth saving, Wayne?"

Wayne stared at his bag in an almost catatonic state. "My Bible. Save my Bible."

Don picked through the black contents with the stick and pushed the Bible off to the side. It was already burnt almost beyond recognition. Then he pushed the bag back toward the fire. Wayne immediately attempted to smother the smoldering book with sand.

Somewhat dazed, the group wandered back to the village. On the way, David asked Jenny, "What'd he mean about the boat?"

"How would I know? It was just a burnt boat with nobody on board, that's all."

"That's probably what he meant: the fact that it was burnt. He's probably saying that was because of the solar storm or something."

Jenny bit back her tears. "I just can't believe what's happening. This whole thing can't be real. So that means there's nobody to rescue Stan after all?"

David shrugged helplessly. Michelle walked up next to Jenny and put her hand on Jenny's shoulder, but Jenny twisted away and walked briskly away toward her hut. Michelle hesitated a moment, then followed her.

David watched them go, unsure what to do. As soon as they were out of sight, he wandered to the north beach. He needed time to sort out the morning's events. He wondered if he could somehow calculate how much a solar activity of some kind might heat up the atmosphere, and how fast it might heat up and cool down. *I'd have to make too many assumptions*, he thought. *I'd just be guessing. It's theoretically possible though, and it explains the heat, the rain, why nobody's here ... and the lights! How could we have forgotten about the lights? We even said they looked like an aurora effect, but I told the others it couldn't be—we were too close to the equator.*

After strolling a few hundred yards down the north beach, he saw Claire standing ankle-deep in the lagoon, staring at the horizon. Perhaps, she also was trying to sift through the morning's revelations. He watched her for a while, thinking about the remarkable transformation Claire had undergone the past few months, how beautiful and strong she had become. Maybe there was something to what Kimo was saying—he, too, felt healthier and stronger than he ever had before. He hesitated for a moment, then walked up behind her. Realizing she hadn't noticed him, he softly called out. "Hey Claire, what's up?"

Without even turning to face him, she let out a sarcastic laugh. "Oh, you know, just the usual. Trying to figure out why the entire world has forgotten about us, or if there's even a world out there anymore. And then after I figure that out, I think I'll work on what it is that Kimo thinks he's trying to do here."

"Sorry. I know what you mean."

After a short, awkward silence, he continued, "I'm surprised Bob was so quiet. I had thought he would have been the most upset by Kimo's fire. He doesn't seem to be so anxious to get off the island anymore."

She turned to face David and again laughed sarcastically. "No, I'm sure he's not." She turned back toward the water and was quiet for a while.

Sensing that she wanted to say more, David walked up and stood next to her.

After a moment, she continued. "There's more to Bob's situation than you know. He didn't really come here voluntarily, and I'm not sure he can even go back anymore. Well, I mean I guess he could, at least as much as any of us can, but he'd probably be returning to an ugly jail

sentence—at least if there's a jail to return to—I mean, if some solar
storm didn't burn it up or something."

David waited to see if she would offer more.

"Anyway, my father is, or was, the district attorney of Los
Angeles."

"You mean he's *the* DA or *one of* the DA's?"

"No, no, he's it: the real *DA of LA*. Or, he was when we left." She
laughed a bit, but it was a sad laugh. "Anyway, Bob got into trouble a
few months ago. He accidentally rear-ended a police car, believe it or
not. Totaled it, in fact. Bob hadn't been drinking, but they thought
he had, so they searched his car and found some coke in the glove
compartment—not much, but, as you can imagine, the police were
looking for any excuse they could find to throw the book at him. I
begged my dad to help. He was reluctant, partly 'cause he really didn't
like Bob, but eventually he managed to get the case lost in the system
long enough for us to disappear for a few weeks. He figured after a few
weeks, things would calm down and then maybe he could make the
whole thing vanish without being too obvious.

"Anyway, one of my dad's friends had heard of this place, and my
dad insisted that Bob come here while things quieted down. He said a
few weeks of complete isolation would do him some good, with no way
back, no drugs, no booze, and no way to get into trouble. He didn't say
it, but I think he figured that if Bob and I were, I don't know, I guess
really by ourselves, maybe I'd see the real Bob and we'd break up. Well,
I suppose he was right on that score: it took less than a week here to
convince me that Bob and I were finished.

"So, my dad's certainly not going to help Bob when, or if, we get
back, and Bob knows it. In fact, my dad's likely to go out of his way
to make sure they throw away the key. I'm sure that's why he's not so
anxious to leave; he probably figures the longer he's away, the more
likely things will cool off back home. Of course, if Kimo's right, then I
suppose none of it matters anyway."

She hesitated a moment. "But this place has been a real eye-opener for me. It's as if I'd been the one on drugs all that time rather than Bob. I can't believe I followed that asshole around for so long."

"How'd you meet Bob anyway?"

"Just at a party. I guess I've always pretended to be somebody else, or maybe just tried to be what other people wanted or expected me to be. For instance, I really liked school and did well, but I always pretended to hate it because it seemed like the cool thing to do. I ended up at UCLA law school anyway, mostly to please my father, I think."

"You went to law school? I didn't know that."

"You never asked. Almost nobody does, and if they do, I just tell them I'm a student and nobody asks anything more. This was supposed to be my little vacation between law school and taking the bar exam, which, by the way, I missed a while ago. Anyway, everybody always expects me to be an empty-headed, blonde valley girl, so I guess that's who I try to be—people are more comfortable with that. But as far as Bob goes, I don't know what I was trying to be. Or do. I'm still not sure if he was a project or a way to get my father's attention … or whether I was just experimenting with something different. It all seems crazy now—another world. Anyway, now everything's fallen apart. Probably a good thing in the end."

She looked at David. "I'm sorry to gripe so much about my life. What about you? How'd you end up with Michelle?" Then realizing her question could have come off the wrong way, she added, "She seems like a really nice person."

"Yeah, Michelle's a wonderful person—the best. I know you don't see it here, but she is. She loves taking care of people: her kids, her parents … even Bob, in case you haven't noticed. She's a better person than I'll ever be. I suppose that's what attracted me to her. She took care of me at a time when, well, I guess my life wasn't going so well. Now … well, now it's all changed … I mean, between us. I guess when other people need her, she's more interested in them than in herself. And now she feels incredibly guilty for not being at home for her kids, and … I don't know … it just seems that we've both come to realize that we're very different people. I guess, too, when I stopped needing her so much, she began to lose interest in me. She needs to be needed, know what I mean?"

Claire nodded. "Funny that this place seems to have brought some couples closer together, and so quickly separated others. Maybe they should advertise it as a place to test relationships. Like the opposite of a honeymoon—you have to come here for two weeks before you get married."

They fell silent for a couple of minutes, absorbing the comforting repetition of the waves rolling onto the reef.

Claire nodded down the beach to the west. "I need to go for a walk. Want to come?"

"Sure."

A few minutes into their walk, David laid his arm across Claire's bare shoulder. Claire turned suddenly toward him and took him into her arms. They lingered in each other's embrace, both nervous with the realization that it was not a platonic, or even comforting embrace, but something they both desperately needed.

After a moment, David cradled Claire's face between his hands and brought her lips to his. Her kiss assured him that his advance was welcome, but not wanting to overstay his reception, David pulled away from her, intertwined his hand in hers, and continued their walk, neither of them saying a word.

David became immediately aware that his pareo made his physical response to Claire's kiss evident, but there was no way to shield his arousal without being obvious. Claire's downward glance told him she had also taken note. Embarrassed, he again turned to her, and they reengaged in their embrace, with even more abandon than before.

Then with no forethought, David pulled away Claire's pareo and let it fall to the sand. He looked at her to gauge her response, and she replied by reaching down and freeing him of his covering, letting it drop on top of hers. They lowered themselves onto the sand together, as if in slow motion. David gently rolled on top of her as she wrapped her legs around him. With their bodies now completely entwined, they hungered to be yet closer, and they quickly found the way, their lovemaking urgent and their pleasure quickly and simultaneously peaking.

They stayed where they were, unwilling to allow even the slightest gap to encroach between their bodies. Neither spoke for fear of losing the moment, both realizing how much they'd wanted and needed what had just happened. Their touch seemed the only thing separating them from the realities of Henderson Island—and of the world.

As reality gradually returned over the next minutes, they realized they weren't particularly well hidden. David risked the first words. "You okay?"

"Wonderful. How 'bout you?"

Reassured, he replied, "Even more wonderful."

"Really? Then promise we'll do it again?" she said.

"Okay, I promise, and maybe next time we can spread out the pareos first. I've got sand everywhere."

She kissed him again and held him as tightly as she could for a moment. "Let's get in the water before somebody sees us."

They waded out into the lagoon separately, until the water was up to their necks, then feeling sufficiently concealed, they floated into each other's arms.

After a few moments, Claire asked, "So, what wasn't going well?"

"What?"

"You said you met Michelle when your life wasn't going so well. What wasn't going so well?"

"Oh, I didn't really mean anything specific. My girlfriend had dumped me at a time when I was also having problems at work. I don't know, maybe she dumped me because I was being an ass about my problems at work. Anyway, I was pretty down when I met Michelle."

"How'd you meet?"

"In a park. She was out playing with her kids, and I was sitting on a bench. I was so self-absorbed, I didn't even notice them at first, but she somehow figured out I … well, anyway, she sat down next to me and just asked if something was wrong. If I was okay."

"Wow, that's pretty cool. So what did you say?"

David shook his head. "Claire, I don't feel comfortable talking about it right now."

"Sorry, I didn't mean to pry."

"No, no, that's okay, it's just that … I guess I feel a little guilty."

"I didn't mean to make you feel guilty either."

Claire tried to pull away, but David hugged her closer. "No, I don't mean guilty about us, I mean because I can't help her more, now that she needs me. You know, with her missing her kids so much. I've tried, really, but she doesn't want me—I think in a way she blames me."

"Blames you? For what?"

"For being here. In retrospect, I'm not sure either of us really wanted to come here. We saw an article and just started talking about it, and I think we both thought the other wanted to come, so we came. Does that make any sense?"

"Sort of."

After a few minutes of silence, Claire asked, "So now what?"

"I don't know." David's eyes suddenly turned serious. "We're certainly not going to be able to have a hidden affair here, so either we tell the others, including Bob and Michelle, or we just pretend this never happened. I don't like the second option. What do you think?"

"Yeah, I know we should tell Bob … and Michelle, and I guess the others, but I'm not so sure it's a good idea right now. Bob shouldn't care. For all I know, Michelle and Bob are already … well, I mean they certainly hang out a lot together. That might be another reason he's in no hurry to leave." She stepped backward. "But it might not be so easy. I don't know how Bob will react. He can lose his temper pretty easily, in case you haven't noticed."

"But how d'ya think he'll react if he discovers it by himself? Won't that be worse?"

"I don't know. He's not very predictable. His main problem won't be losing me, but the embarrassment of—I can't explain it exactly— he's always worried about his image. It would just be a lot better for everybody if he could pretend he was dumping me. Know what I mean?"

"I guess, but I don't like it. It means we're supposed to go back and sleep with our … in our huts? When we know we don't want to be there and they don't want us there?"

"Let's just think about it for a few days, that's all. Maybe there's some other way. This island's too small to have somebody like Bob mad at us."

David looked worried, as if he were unsure of Claire's intent. But seeing this, she kissed him deeply while dragging him playfully under water. Soon, they were making love again, this time like two giddy teenagers exploring each other's bodies for the first time. They finally collapsed, fully satiated, in the lagoon's warm embrace.

Chapter 15

STAN WOKE WITH THE rising sun, anxious to begin exploring. He rose from his makeshift bed on the deck of the *Sea Salva* and surveyed his surroundings, now illuminated by a brilliant, sunny sky. Bounty Bay was little more than a small ledge near the bottom of a tall cliff as it plunged into the ocean. His immediate thought was that though Henderson and Pitcairn were close neighbors, they were nothing alike. In contrast to Henderson's flawless sand beaches and protective reefs, Pitcairn's steep, rocky shores reached toward the sky, making the island appear like a small fortress in the middle of the ocean. It was easy to see why the *Bounty* fugitives were so attracted to it.

Just in front of the *Sea Salva,* a long wooden boathouse with a galvanized steel roof greeted him with the words "Welcome to Pitcairn Island" in faded, chipped blue paint across the front. The structure looked as if it might collapse at any moment. A wide concrete ramp led down from a concealed entrance into the water, and cliffs rose immediately behind the building. Just as Stan was about to go below to wake Nani, she appeared on deck.

"Good morning," he said. "I was just getting ready to go take a look around. Want to join me?"

"I guess. If there's anyone here, they're either not very sociable or they didn't see us come in last night."

They stepped off the boat and walked toward the boathouse, entering it like a pair of thieves. It was completely empty, short of some rotted ropes, various old poles, and similar junk. There certainly were no traces of recent activity.

"Not a good sign so far, is it?" Nani asked.

"C'mon, let's walk up that way." Stan pointed to a muddy road that took a hairpin turn to the right and slashed its way up the steep hillside behind the boathouse. The path took them up a couple of hundred feet before it finally leveled off at a small dirt clearing housing a cluster of metal-roofed, single-story buildings. A quick glance was enough to convince them that the structures were abandoned, but their curiosity prompted them to look through each one.

"Boy, they sure cleaned this place out, didn't they?" Stan said.

"Seems so. Let's not give up, though. It looks like there's more ahead. That must be the main village."

They took the muddy road up another few hundred yards to a group of buildings that appeared to have been the town center. A wooden flagpole, lacking both flag and halyard, stood in front of the largest structure, which seemed to be a town hall of sorts. And what was likely the church looked more like a house with a small cross above the front door. All the buildings seemed to be pretty much the same: simply shaped, shoddily constructed, single-story wooden structures with rusting metal roofs.

They walked from one building to the next, peering inside the windows and testing the doors. As they cautiously stepped across each threshold, calling out as they went, they looked for signs of recent activity, but found none. There was also nothing of any apparent value, just an occasional piece of old furniture that a previous owner probably wouldn't have deemed valuable enough to take with them.

Having explored all the smaller structures, they started toward the largest of the buildings—the one with the bare flagpole in front. As they approached, Stan said, "Hey, look at that." Next to the front door was a huge, badly corroded anchor with a plaque that pronounced it to be from the original *Bounty*. "And look at this!"

Stan was looking at a large wooden sign near the anchor that had a well-worn but still readable map of the island. They studied it for a few moments, trying to orient themselves.

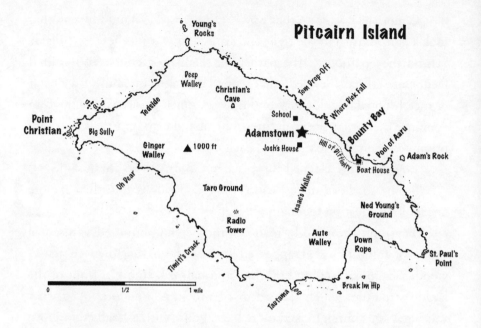

"Seems we're in the center of town right now," Stan said.

Nani pointed up the road. "Apparently there's a school up that way. Wow, this place is tiny, isn't it? Henderson seems gigantic in comparison."

"Look at the names of some of these places too: Point Christian must have been named after Fletcher Christian, Young's Rocks after that guy named Young—I forgot his first name, but I think he was an officer or midshipman or something like that. And here, look at this: Isaac's Walley—I think there was a seaman named Isaac Mills, if I remember right."

"I'm impressed! How do you know all that?"

"*Mutiny on the Bounty* was my favorite book when I was a kid. I knew the story by heart. I can't believe I actually ended up here. Do you know the story?"

"Of course. I grew up in the islands. The Tahitian women here finally took over and started a war with the men because they did nothing but get drunk and fight all the time. Actually, they didn't even have to do much of the killing themselves—they just let the men kill each other."

Nani giggled for the first time in days, as she pointed to another place on the map called Break im Hip. "I wonder how that got its name? And Where Dick Fall, and look, here's Oh Dear! There have to be some great stories behind these names. And why are they all called walleys instead of valleys? And why did this get named Adamstown and not Christian's Town?"

"That's after John Adams. He was the last male survivor of the original settlers, and I think he was the only mutineer still alive when the first visitor came to the island, twenty-five years after the mutiny. If you believe some of the accounts, he was kept as breeding stock after the women killed all the other men, but others think he was more of a dictator of sorts and the architect of the wars. Anyway, he taught all the kids to speak English and to read and write. When this whaling ship finally discovered them, he was already an old man. The islanders were all half or more Tahitian, but they spoke a strange sort of English."

Nani pointed to the door next to the anchor. "C'mon, let's go inside this one. The map says it's the town hall."

Like all the others, the door was unlocked and the inside looked like it had been uninhabited for years.

Stan suddenly called, "Hey, look at this! A radio!"

Nani wandered over to Stan who was playing with its dials and switches.

"Nothing. No power at all. If we can figure out how to get power to it though, we've got a shot at calling for help. Looks like it's in good shape too." Stan walked outside and looked up. There were still power lines connecting the buildings, so he went back in and tried the light switches. Nothing. The town hall appeared to be completely dead.

Nani and Stan left and continued from house to house, finding rags, rusted metal, ruined furniture, empty cans, and other useless junk, but absolutely no sign of another human being. Finally conceding they were alone on the island, they decided to take their time exploring. There was no hurry, and in fact, so long as there were still buildings to explore, they wouldn't have to face the inevitable question of what to do next. Heading farther up the main road toward the school, they spotted a blue house well off the main road that appeared to be in better condition than the rest. Curious, they both changed course and headed toward it. When they arrived, they found the door ajar. Against all probability, Stan knocked on the frame and waited for a response.

He leaned his head inside the door. "Hello?"

After a couple more attempts with no reply, Stan gently pushed open the door the rest of the way open and stepped through. The front door opened onto a kitchen-living room area that was still furnished and equipped, even if meagerly. Stan again announced their presence, this time with a little more force. "Anybody here?"

Receiving no reply, he walked in further, Nani stepping in behind him, and started looking around. Nani ran her hand across an old wood-burning stove, and then jerked her hand away. "It's still warm!"

Stan walked over to the stove and touched the top. "Well, it seems we're not alone after all. Maybe we should get out of here."

"Yeah, maybe you should," bellowed a voice from the front door. "Who are you and how'd you get here?"

They spun around in unison to face a man that could have been a prematurely aged fifty-year-old, or a fit, solidly-made eighty-year-old, with thick gray hair and a well-weathered face permanently darkened by years in the sun. His movements were slow and deliberate as he walked into the house toward them, but his dark eyes had the sparkle and intensity of a young man's. He wore a torn white T-shirt, tired jeans, and well-worn sandals. It had been so long since either Stan or Nani had seen a new face, they hesitated for what must have seemed to the man an unnaturally long time.

"So, what's your story?" he asked them again. "What are you doing here?"

"Sorry, we didn't mean to break in," Stan said. "We didn't think anybody was here." He hesitated, unsure what to say. "We got here last night. We need help. We ..." He looked at Nani for help. "I'm not even sure where to begin. How many people are here? We didn't see anybody else."

The old man stared at them for a few moments, looking confounded.

Nani stepped in front of Stan and restarted the conversation. "Hi, my name's Nani, and this is Stan. We came from Henderson Island. It's about a hundred miles east—"

The man laughed. "I know where Henderson is! But that's not what I asked. I asked what you are doing *here*—although while you're at it, you can tell me what the hell you were doing there."

Stan answered. "There're about twenty of us there. We've been stranded there for four months. We don't know what happened."

The man squinted his eyes at them. "Twenty people at Henderson? Bullshit. How'd they get there, and how'd you get here?"

Nani put on a disarming smile. "Can we sit down for a bit? It's a long story and hard to explain."

The man looked at her a moment before slipping into a reluctant, crooked smile that was almost a smirk. "Sure, why not? What else have I got to do? You're already in, so have a seat." He gestured to a ratty couch. "My name's Josh." He crossed to the other side of the room and sat in a wooden chair.

They began to explain the New Eden project to Josh, who seemed at first to find the story entertaining and funny. When they described the storm, however, his expression suddenly hardened and he leaned forward, growing more attentive, as they described the heat, rain, and loss of communication.

"So your radio just stopped working?" he asked. "Just like that? For no reason?"

"Well, we think it might have gotten wet in the storm," replied Stan.

"Got wet in the storm. Okay, maybe. Keep going. So how'd you get here?"

They went on to explain the strange events that led to their arrival at Pitcairn, with Josh seemingly testing them with questions now and then.

When they'd finished, he leaned back in his chair. "So … what're you going to do now?"

They looked at each other and shrugged.

"Try to get help, I guess," Stan said.

Josh laughed a little. "Well, you're not going to find much help here, that's for sure. Everybody left Pitcairn almost a year ago. Went to Norfolk Island. Everybody but my wife Marisa and me, that is. It was ridiculous for everybody to leave. Wait and see, they'll be back."

"So where's Marisa now?" asked Nani.

"Dead. She died during the … well, it must have been the same storm, a few months ago. Our radio stopped working too."

"Sorry about your wife," Nani said. "That must have been awful."

Josh shrugged as if he didn't care, but his eyes told otherwise.

"Wait," Stan said, "you mean your radio went out too?"

"Yep, still out. But everything's out now. The winds knocked out our windmill that powers our generator, and now our batteries are completely dead. Radio had power for a day or so after the storm, but nothing works on the island works anymore."

"But that doesn't make sense. Did something happen to the radio?"

"Look, I'm no damn electronics expert. I just know it didn't work. Go look at it yourself if you want. All I know is there was power 'cause it lit up when I turned it on, but there was only static when I tried it."

"So you haven't heard from anybody at all since then?"

"Not a soul, but didn't expect I would either. Not many people came to Pitcairn even when people lived here. Used to be different when people traveled by ship. Fifty years ago, we had ships stop by almost every week. Then ships got bigger and didn't want to take the detour no more. And people travel more by airplane now days anyway, so we sometimes went months between visits. Now, with nobody living here, I don't know why anyone would ever come this way. We aren't exactly on the way to anywhere, if you know what I mean."

"You have a boat here?"

"Nope, but you got a boat. What do you need another for?"

"We already told you, it's in bad shape—no sails and no motor."

"Well, like I said, I can't help. You'll have to figure it out yourself, but I guess you'll have plenty of time for that. Right now, I've got to go feed the chickens." With that, Josh stood up and walked out.

"Well, that was interesting," Stan said to Nani. "Somewhat abrupt, I'd say."

She nodded. "It's weird, too, that he didn't even know about New Eden, even though he's lived here his whole life. He didn't even believe there were people there."

Stan sat thinking.

"So now what do we do?" Nani asked.

"I guess if we're going to fix the boat or his radio, we're going to have to do it ourselves. So, I suppose we continue to explore the island. Doesn't seem like he's going to be any help to us."

After exploring the town a bit more and finding nothing but the same, they returned to the town center to check the map. They noticed a place labeled Radio Tower and decided to check that out next. The trail to the tower rose some thousand feet or so, and though the path was obvious enough to get them there, their progress was slowed by heavy overgrowth.

As the name on the map implied, they found a small, metal tower on top of the hill, still standing. There was no radio, however, nor even a hut. A few yards from the tower Stan found a pile of steel wreckage on the ground that he quickly identified as having been a windmill.

"So this must have been where they generated their power for the radio," he said. "The storm must have blown down the windmill. If there was a windmill, though, there must have a generator. If we find it, maybe we can still get power to the radio."

"Is that what this is maybe?" Nani had wandered more than a hundred feet away and was looking down at something.

Stan jogged over, then stopped short in disbelief. A large barrel-shaped object was cracked in two but connected with a tangle of broken wires. He walked toward the wreckage, afraid that getting closer would only confirm his suspicions.

When he got there, he knelt next to the two large casings, fondling the shredded wires and other bits. For a moment, Nani thought he was going to break into tears. Instead, he grabbed some nondescript bit of metal and threw it as far as he could.

"Damn it!" He suddenly grabbed his hand to stem a flow of blood. The piece of metal had sliced his finger as it flew from his grip.

Near the end of the afternoon, they went back to the *Sea Salva,* which now somehow seemed like home. After preparing another meal of canned goods, they opened a bottle of wine. Then sitting on opposite sides of the salon table like two negotiators, they sipped on their glasses of wine and took inventory of what they had learned so far.

"Well, no boats or planes," Stan started, "not even an airstrip. No radios or phones either, at least not any that work. In fact not much at all considering this was a real place just a year ago."

"Yeah, but it never was much of a town, was it? They never did have an airport, I don't think. What'd you say they had here before, like fifty people or so?"

"I guess. Something like that. I think there were more than that a long time ago. But let's not give up. There's plenty of food still, either growing or in those cans we found, and there are still some buildings we haven't gone in yet. Maybe we'll still find something useful."

"Do you think we can get the radio working?"

"Not without electricity."

"What about solar power or something like that?" Nani asked.

"You know how to do that? I sure don't. If that damn generator was working, we'd have a chance—maybe we could've built a windmill or turned it by hand or something."

"Maybe there's another generator on the island."

"I suppose. We'll keep looking, I guess."

"What if we can't find anything here and there's no way to get help?"

Stan sighed. "Then I guess we try to go back to Henderson

somehow—maybe on the *Sea Salva*. I don't see any way to get the engine fixed. Even if we knew something about engines, I don't think we'd have the right equipment. If we knew anything about sailboats, I suppose we could make some sails, couldn't we? I saw lots of old clothing and stuff like that around that might make some good sails. I'll bet that guy Josh could help us if he really wanted to."

"Maybe we should just wait until somebody ..." Nani stopped abruptly, afraid to continue her thought.

"Yeah, well, if some miracle rescue happens, it happens, but I don't know what the hell is going on anymore. It just seems so weird that both our radios, on two different islands, would suddenly stop working in the same way, acting like they were working but not connecting with anybody. Doesn't that seem weird to you?"

"Are you thinking about what Claire was saying? That maybe there was some catastrophe and there's no one out there to hear the radios?"

"Yeah, I guess. It seems to fit. But if it's true, that's all the more reason to get back to Henderson. Look, I think we should go see Josh again in the morning. Give him a bit of time to realize we're not a threat and see if he can help. Besides, like you said, there's lots more of the island to explore."

Nani took a sip of her wine and then got up from her seat and sat next to Stan, turning to him with a serious expression. "Stan, you know we might never get back, don't you?"

Stan raised an eyebrow.

"I didn't want to say this, but Kimo told me he was sure the radio *was* working. He's sure that Claire was right. He told me something about explosions on the sun or a big storm on the sun that might have ..." She stopped and leaned her head on Stan's shoulder, fighting back tears.

Stan was only half listening, intoxicated by Nani's presence. And having drunk more than half the bottle of wine by now, he was finding it difficult not to lean back on her; although he really only wanted her emotional support and companionship, he knew full well where that might lead. He shook himself back to reality. *How can I even be thinking like this with Jenny now—what is it—just ten weeks from delivering my son or daughter? God, what a mess!*

Nani, sensing Stan's self-reproach, stood and wandered to the forward cabin to curl up on the bunk she'd used the past few nights. Though her intent was to make it easier for Stan, her silent exit made him feel he was letting her down. She hadn't done anything wrong, after all. In fact, she had been almost heroic in her attempt to rescue them. He went to the main cabin and lay on his makeshift bunk, trying to rest and sort through things. Then, as his thoughts began to reflect back to Nani's comments about a solar storm, he drifted into a restless sleep.

Chapter 16

THE NEXT MORNING, NANI and Stan trudged up the road to find Josh. With no reply at his door, they walked back to town to consult the map, and decided to take the trail to *Point Christian*. Less than an hour later, they were on their way back to *Adamstown*, having found nothing but a trail leading through some overgrown areas that appeared to have been once under cultivation.

For Stan, the walk reinforced just how small the island was, and what it must have been like for the original settlers. "Twenty or so people living completely alone and isolated on this tiny rock for twenty-five years without even a glimpse of the outside world. Can you imagine?" As soon as he'd said it, he realized how analogous it seemed to their situation at Henderson. But before he could mention the irony to Nani, they spotted Josh standing outside his front door.

"What are you two up to today?" he asked.

"Nothing. We walked out to Point Christian this morning," Stan said.

"Why'd ya do that? There's nothing up there."

"Well, we didn't know that. Is there some place we *should* go?"

"Nope. Nothing left. Just pick a house, fix it up the best you can, and relax. Plenty of food and water on the island. Like I said, the others will be back some day."

Stan and Nani looked at each other. With a slight nod from Nani, Stan said, "We found out yesterday why your radio is dead. The windmill is down and the generator's smashed. You're batteries probably powered it for a day or so after the storm, but there's no way to recharge it. I don't suppose there's another generator on the island, is there?"

Josh laughed and shook his head. "They took everything worth anything. Used to be we had regular electricity in every house—the island had a real diesel generator. Cranked it up every night and ran it till morning. We had lights every night and kept our food cold. When the others left, I told them to take it with 'em—no way I was going to be able to bring barrels of diesel fuel up the Hill of Difficulty."

"Hill of Difficulty?" interrupted Stan.

"That's what we call the road up the hill from where your boat is. When the others were here, we'd use the windmill during the day just to run the radio but it didn't have enough power to keep the island going. When they took the diesel generator with them, the windmill was all me and Marisa had."

"Josh, we need to get our boat fixed up and get back to Henderson. My wife is due in ten weeks. I have to get back."

Josh scrunched up his face. "Due? Due where? What are you talking about?"

"I mean she's pregnant, and it's our first, and I'm not about to let her go through that alone on an island still living in the fifteenth century. I'm going back no matter what."

"In that thing in the harbor? No way. Impossible."

"How d'ya know that? You haven't even seen our boat."

"Yes, I have," he replied dourly. "I walked down this morning to take a look. It's a disaster. No sails, no motor... no chance. You're lucky that thing even floats."

"We can make sails. We saw plenty of cloth on the island. We can sew some sheets or something together."

Josh just stared at them, frozen, expecting them to say they were just joking. But after a respectful fifteen seconds or so, he said, "Are you serious?"

"Well, why not?" Stan asked.

"You don't know anything about sailing do you?" Josh was genuinely amused.

"We got here, didn't we?"

Josh stared intently at them for a few seconds before repeating his question. "You don't know anything do you?"

Stan locked eyes with Josh for a moment before finally shaking his head and smiling broadly. "No, not a thing. We got lucky."

"Yeah, I'd say so. All right, well, first lesson: a boat like yours weighs over ten tons and has a keel that is probably seven feet or so below the water surface. It needs a huge sail area to travel into the wind, which is where Henderson Island is—straight into the wind. Large sails aren't made of cotton or wool. They're made of heavy nylon, often carbon-fiber reinforced. If you made a sail out of sheets or cloth like you'd find here, and it was large enough to sail that monster of yours into the wind, the sails would be shredded by the first whisper of wind. You'd never even get the sails up. Forget it. That's why older boats, made before modern synthetic materials were around, used lots of small sails—because it was impossible to make big sails from canvass that were strong enough to survive. Your boat is called a sloop. Know what that is?"

"Isn't that just another name for a sailboat?"

"Nope. A sloop is a boat with one mast and two sails. Used to be that sloops were small, but now, with modern materials, they're making them a hundred feet long. You want to sail your boat into the wind, you're going to need large sails made of materials a whole lot stronger than you can find around here. Trust me. That boat's not going anywhere, at least nowhere upwind."

"Can we just wait until the wind changes and blows toward Henderson?"

Josh laughed. "Sure. That happens about one day a year. Then you could get about a third of the way there before the wind changes and blows you back—that is, if you're lucky and actually find Pitcairn again."

"So what do we do then, make a new boat?"

"It'd be easier, that's for sure. But you don't even know how to sail, so how's that going to help? This is the Pacific Ocean, not some lake! Go downwind to Australia or New Zealand if you want. It's probably just as realistic as getting back to Henderson."

Stan was quiet for a moment, prompting Nani to softly ask, "Could you help us? Do you know how to sail?"

"Yeah, I know how to sail, but no way in—what'd you say—two months? It would take ..." He drifted off for a moment, then continued with uncharacteristic sadness. "No, I can't help."

Stan jumped in. "What do you mean *no*? No you can't, or no you won't?"

Nani put her hand on Stan's forearm.

"No, I can't," Josh said, almost inaudibly.

Nani paused for a moment. "Why can't you help?" Her words were calm and cautious, but she kept her hand firmly on Stan's arm, urging him to give Josh space.

Josh looked at her. "Because I won't be around long enough."

Though she sensed what Josh meant, she continued. "Why won't you be around? What do you mean?"

"Just what I said. I won't be around. I have what they call an aneurysm. I'm not even supposed to be alive now."

After another moment of silence, Nani asked, "Can we help?"

"Nope. No one can help. That's why I didn't want to leave the island, and now it's why my wife is dead. I wanted to die here on Pitcairn, and my wife was staying with me just to keep me company until it was my time. And now she's dead instead."

"I'm so sorry," Nani said. "But of course you couldn't know that a storm was coming, and besides, you don't know what would have happened if she'd left."

"Don't patronize me! Just leave me be, okay? It's a big enough island for all of us, so you two go and do your thing and let me do mine." Josh turned his back on them and went inside.

Nani and Stan looked at each other, and then turned and walked down to their boat.

That evening, while they ate, Stan couldn't help thinking that Josh wasn't being entirely truthful.

"I know he could help if he wanted to," he told Nani. "We need to ask him again tomorrow. Somehow force him to help us."

"No, Stan, that's not the way. You can't force him to help. Think about it: he's dying and blaming himself for his wife's death, and you want him to work on a boat for you? How would you feel if you were him? Would sailing to Henderson be your top priority?"

Stan considered the wisdom in Nani's words. "I guess not," he admitted. "So, what do we do? He might be our only chance."

"We go back tomorrow and see if we can start the healing process. Do what we can to help him with his guilt. Make him feel good about himself. Then, maybe, he'll want to help us." Nani looked at him and wrinkled her forehead. "You know what an aneurysm is anyway?"

"Not exactly. I think it's like a blister on a blood vessel or something."

"So why's that fatal?"

"Well, I'm guessing he means it's in his brain, and if it bursts then it fills the brain with blood. I wonder how he knows he's dying of one? Maybe it's not even right. How would he even know?"

"We can ask more about it when the time's right. But for now, we should focus on his wife. That's what's really bothering him."

The next morning they climbed back up the *Hill of Difficulty* to find a homestead, eventually settling on a two-bedroom house in the center of town with a roof that was intact. They cleaned it up and brought in some of the more useable furniture from other nearby homes and from the boat. By midafternoon, they deemed it habitable. They saw Josh several times in passing, but always well off in the distance, and they resisted approaching him. Then just before sunset, they took him a bottle of wine from the boat. When he opened the door, he seemed somewhat suspicious, but pleased to see them.

Stan recited his rehearsed opening line. "I wanted to apologize for my attitude yesterday. I had no right to make demands, and I'm sorry about your situation and your wife."

"No worries, let's not talk about it." Josh said and opened the door wider, gesturing for them to come in.

Stan held up the bottle of wine. "Can we offer you some? We have plenty on board the *Sea Salva.*"

"Haven't had wine in many, many months. Sure, why not? You know alcohol wasn't really allowed on Pitcairn. I mean, we pretty much ignored the rules, but it was hard to get anyway during the last few years."

After finishing his first glass, Stan began the discussion that Nani had coached him through the night before. "You know, we've been discussing the storm for a long time—not just Nani and I, but back on Henderson too. We wanted to get your opinion on some of our ideas."

"Ah, so the wine comes with a price. Okay, shoot."

"We're just wondering about the storm, that's all. You've lived here a long time. Were there ever any other storms like it?"

Josh seemed relieved by the question. He leaned back in his chair and rested his head between clasped hands. "I've lived here for over sixty years—my whole life except the five years I spent in New Zealand—and I suppose it's the worst I can remember."

"What do you think it was?" Stan asked.

"What d'ya mean? It was a storm. What are you asking?"

"Well, I mean was there anything unusual about it? Was it hot, for example?"

Josh leaned forward and looked at Stan. "Very hot. That was the worst part. It just doesn't get that hot here."

Nani continued. "It was the same at Henderson. Really hot and humid, almost hard to breathe. We all spent the night in the water to stay cool."

"Can't exactly do that here, can we? No beaches on Pitcairn."

"It must have been terrible," Nani said.

Josh saw the discussion drifting back to Marisa's death. "Look, I don't need your pity, okay?"

The three fell silent. Stan had been curious about what killed Marisa—maybe the heat—but it was clear Josh wouldn't talk about it, so he continued leading into the key topic they had come to discuss. "Nani and I wonder what it was like in other places."

Josh thought for a long time, allowing Nani to intervene. "It happened at night. How could it get so hot during the night? Then it started to cool down around sunrise."

"Well, it happened," Josh said. "That's all that matters, I guess." Then he continued, his voice taking on an edge. "What are you trying to say?"

Nani studied Josh carefully. "There were some of us back on Henderson that thought it might have been some explosion on the sun or something that really heated up the part of the earth that was facing the sun—that we were somehow protected because it was nighttime. We think that may be why nobody answered the radio. Did you see how our boat was burned?"

"Hmmm." Josh rubbed his chin. "When did you find the boat?"

"About three months after the storm, it just drifted past the island," Stan said. "We think maybe it was burned by whatever caused the heat wave and the storm."

"Could be, I suppose, but then Christ, if it got that hot, everything must be … " Stan and Nani were silent, letting him think for a moment. "You really think that's why nobody answered the radio?"

Stan shrugged. "We don't know that's what's going on for sure, but it's possible. In fact, some of us think that's the only possible explanation." Although Stan wasn't convinced that was the case, he supposed it was true that *some* of them thought so.

Nani added, "And we don't know what would have happened if you and Marisa had left with the others. She might still have passed away."

"You're saying it might have even been worse on Norfolk Island?"

Nani and Stan nodded in unison.

Josh looked down and shifted in his seat. "So, you two have any more thoughts about what you're going to do?"

"We found a house down the path on the left. You probably saw us there. We thought we'd move up here for a while. Is that okay?"

"William and Glen's old house? Sure, do as you please. You don't need my permission and you're not going to get their permission. Go ahead."

The next morning, at their newly adopted house, Stan and Nani were awakened by shouting. Stan stirred in his bedroom trying to make out the voice. It was Josh, yelling outside their front door. "Get up! Time's a' wasting. Lots of work to do."

Stan went to open the door. "Hey, what's up?"

"You've got a boat to build, and I've got to teach you to sail."

Stan's heart leapt. "You're going to help us?"

"Don't get your hopes up. You aren't going to get back to Henderson any time soon. It might take a year or so, but you'll have a chance, at least if my head holds together long enough."

Disappointed by Josh's timeline, Stan nonetheless was ready to go. An hour later, they were sitting around a table at Josh's place.

"First things first. You guys need to know the timetable. I'm on borrowed time already. They said this thing in my brain should have blown by now. According to the doctors in Auckland, I'm already dead. Second, you can build when I'm not around, but you can't learn about sailing once I'm gone. So, first priority is learning. There's no boat to teach you with, so I'll tell you what you need to know, but if the doctors are right, you'll have to do most of your learning on your own *after* you've built the boat. Okay?"

"Sure. Where do we start?" asked Stan.

"Well, how much do you know? Do you at least understand how boats can sail into the wind?"

Nani and Stan looked at each other and shook their heads.

"Afraid of that. The key is that a sailboat is designed to only go forward or backward, but never sideways—kinda like a train on a track. Your boat down there has a keel that probably goes seven or eight feet below the waterline and prevents the boat from going sideways in the water. It would be like taking a sheet of plywood and pushing it sideways through water—no matter what you did, it would want to knife through the water instead, edge on, right? You can think of the keel and the rudder as kind of a track that your boat rides on. Think of a train: it can to forward or backward on its tracks, but never to the side."

Stan nodded. "Okay, but that doesn't explain how it can go into the wind."

"Hold on, you'll see." Josh went into the kitchen, took a large wooden spoon out of a drawer, and brought it back to the table. "So, let's say the handle of this spoon is the front of our boat and the round part is the back. Then let's say the wind is coming right at us from over there." He pointed across the room, toward the wall directly facing them. He then turned the spoon so that it was perpendicular to the imaginary wind. "Do you see how the boat could go in this direction? Directly across the wind?"

Stan blank expression prompted Josh to continue. "Okay, remember the boat can only go forwards or backwards. The wind is pushing the hull sideways, but it can't go that way, so where will it go?" He took a butter knife from the table and handed it to Stan. "So this is your sail. Now where do you want the sail to be? Put the sail on the boat so the boat goes forward instead of backward."

Stan played with angling the knife on the wooden spoon, finally setting it down at about forty-five degrees.

"Exactly," Josh said. "The wind is pressing on the sail, and the sail pushes the boat forward and sideways, but the boat can only go forward, so that's where it goes." He then pointed the spoon handle a bit toward their hypothetical wind. "Now where would you put the sail?"

Stan turned the knife to be more parallel to the spoon.

"Good. Now you're going into the wind, aren't you?"

Stan looked at the utensil arrangement. "Sort of, but just barely."

"What about now?" Josh asked, turning the spoon a bit more.

Stan turned the knife a little more.

"That's it. It's not as simple as that, but it's a beginning. Turns out that depending on the boat, you can go about forty-five degrees or so to the wind. If you get closer than that—that means more into the wind—the wind will just blow the boat backwards instead of pushing it forwards. It's called being *in irons* when that happens. Can you see that?"

"Yeah, so far."

"So, that's why you'll never get that boat of yours sailing upwind with homemade sails. You see, it's a battle. The wind is pushing the hull of the boat backwards, but the sails are pushing the boat forward. The closer you are to the wind, the weaker the force on the sail that's trying to move the boat forward and the stronger the force pushing it backwards. If the sails are too small for the boat, you'll lose the battle every time. Get it?"

They passed the next few hours listening to Josh, and though each point he made seemed to make sense, in the end it was hard to put it all together. If anything, they finished their session more pessimistic about their ability to remember or apply what they'd just heard.

"Is it really this complicated?" Stan asked. "I mean, do you really have to think about all of this while you're sailing?"

"No, don't worry about that. Look, in the end, what really matters is that you know where the wind is blowing from. The rest will become second nature after a while. You're only going to really get the idea by practicing. Unfortunately, Pitcairn isn't the best place to practice sailing. In fact, there's almost no place to sail here, so we're going to have to talk about that too."

Stan asked, "Then where did you get to know so much about sailing?"

"New Zealand. Marisa and I moved there a little over five years ago, and we stayed until they found my problem. I got a job teaching sailing to tourists there—didn't know how myself at first, but I learned enough to get around. We moved back here about a month before they evacuated this place, right after the doctors found my problem."

"I see. Well, so now what do we do about a boat?"

Josh looked concerned but then replied, "We have lunch, that's what. After lunch we'll talk about building a boat. I've been doing a lot of thinking about that."

After Nani served a little stew of zucchini, onions, and tomatoes, they again sat at the table to begin their lessons on boat-building. Once they were seated, Josh ceremoniously announced, "We're going to build what's called a proa, and we're going to make it the old-fashioned way."

Nani and Stan just looked at him, so he continued. "I've thought about it, and I think a proa is the best combination of being easy to sail and easy to build from materials we have on the island."

"Okay, but what is a proa?" Stan asked.

"Well, it's a Polynesian-type boat. You've probably seen a million of them in movies and magazines. Essentially, it's an outrigger canoe with a sail. So it'll be a canoe dug out from a tree that we'll pick out tomorrow, connected to a small missile-like hull off to one side called an ama. The ama is connected to the main hull by crossbeams called akas. Grab that red book over there and I'll show you a picture."

Stan fetched the book. Josh shuffled through a few pages until he found what he was looking for. "Look, see what I mean? That's the main hull where they're sitting. The missile-shaped log off to the side is the ama, and these two crossbeams are the akas. Here, see this board that goes down into the water on the side of the boat?"

"Yeah, kind of," replied Stan.

"That's called a leeboard. It's like the keel of your boat, but simpler; it prevents the boat from getting pushed sideways in the water—kind of like your railroad track. The boat in this picture also has a crab sail. See? It's like an upside-down triangle, with the wide part of the sail at the top rather than at the bottom. They're very efficient, but we're going to use a Bermudan sail instead. It'll be easier to make and will probably work better for sailing into the wind like you'll be doing."

When he realized he had lost them again, he explained, "A Bermudan sail is just a normal triangular sail. He looked at them hopefully, but they just shrugged. "Well, don't worry. I'll explain it all later. Anyway, the only tricky bit is that the ama has to always be on the windward side. Remember what that is?"

"Windward is the side of the boat that is upwind, right?" ventured Stan.

"Yeah, but I meant the ama. Remember what that is?"

Stan pointed to the picture in the book. "That's the outrigger part over here."

"Right. So the wind is always trying to tip the boat over toward the leeward side, and the weight of the ama on the windward side of the canoe balances the force the wind is applying against the sail. It prevents the boat from tipping over." Again, Stan looked confused. "Don't worry about that now. I'll explain it as we go."

"No, I think I get that." Stan tilted his head sideways to get a better look at the picture. "But if this outrigger thing acts like a counterweight and always has to be on the windward side, then how do you turn? I thought you said you have to tack to sail into the wind. If you tack, won't the outrigger be on the wrong side? The leeward side?"

"Exactly." Josh nodded. "There's hope for you yet. The answer is that you can't tack a proa. You have to do what's called shunting. Shunting means you change the direction of the boat when you want to turn. The bow becomes the stern, and the stern becomes the bow, and the sail reverses direction. That way the ama is always on the windward side. There is no front or back of a proa."

Stan felt discouraged. "Why can't we just make a regular boat, like the one we have now?"

"Because your boat down there needs ballast to keep it from tipping over. I'll bet your boat's got five tons or so of lead at the bottom of its keel. You'd never be able to build it by yourself. Even if you could, you'd need huge sails to move it, and if you tipped it over, it would sink. Okay? A proa is easy to build and light so it won't take huge sails to move."

"What about those boats with two hulls? Can we build one of those?"

"Catamarans, they're called. Yes, they'd be easier to make than something like your boat, but still harder than a proa. You'd need to make two identical hulls, and I'm not sure I'll be here long enough to even help you make the first. With a proa, you only need to make one hull. The ama is really just a log."

Stan looked unconvinced, but nodded.

"Anyway," continued Josh, "we're not going to start building just yet. For the next couple days, we talk—that's all. As I said, if you have to, you can build your boat without me, but you can't learn how to make it once I'm gone."

Chapter 17

DAVID AND CLAIRE WERE careful with their meetings the following week, making sure they weren't followed and that they had explanations for their absences. With time, however, they became emboldened and careless, bringing their escapades ever closer to the village. Most recently, they had found a small, sandy depression between two dunes that afforded them privacy only a couple hundred yards from the village itself.

"That was wonderful," whispered David, still entangled within Claire's legs. He turned his head to rest it on her shoulder, but then suddenly tensed and leapt to his knees. "Damn!"

Claire turned and immediately made eye contact with Michelle, who evidently had been watching from just a few yards away. Michelle met her look with empty eyes, showing neither shock nor anger. She said nothing, but just quietly turned and walked away.

"Damn it!" David grabbed his pareo and quickly wrapped himself. "I've got to go talk to her." He jogged after her.

Claire wrapped herself almost as quickly and followed a few yards behind David, unsure what to do.

"Michelle! Hey Michelle! Wait a sec," David called after her, but Michelle pretended not to hear. He caught up to her just as she got to the village, and then stopped short when he almost ran directly into Bob. Evidently, he had been waiting for Michelle, because she walked directly up to him and leaned into his huge chest.

Bob suspiciously eyed David and Claire, and then turned to Michelle. "What's up?"

Michelle shook her head. "Nothing."

Nervous, David approached Bob and Michelle. "Look, Michelle, I'm really sorry. We—"

"Sorry for what!" Bob glared at him.

Just then, Erik and Stefani, who'd been standing nearby, wandered over.

Claire stepped forward. "Bob, Michelle saw us making love in the sand dunes over there. We should have told you before, but I wasn't sure what you'd think. It's my fault."

Bob's face flushed red and his eyes opened wide. "You weren't sure what I'd think? Is that what you said? Then I'll tell you what I think. I think you're just the whore I always knew you were, and—"

"Bob, you can't blame them," said Michelle, glaring at David, but clinging tighter to Bob. "It's not like we're innocent, you know."

Bob bounded forward. Michelle put up a brief struggle to restrain him, but he pushed her away and stepped up toe-to-toe with David, towering over him. David didn't back away, but said nothing.

Bob looked down right into David's face. "So how long have you been fucking her?" He shoved David in the chest, knocking him back two steps, and then without giving him a chance to recover, jabbed him again. "Well? How long, David? You know I've been doing your girl too?"

David turned his back on Bob and was about to run when Bob struck him in the lower back with both hands, jackknifing him to the ground. David rolled to his side and curled in a fetal position, bracing for the onslaught that he knew would follow.

"Well, did you know that, shithead?" Bob kicked David in his kidneys, driving the wind out of him. "Say something, you little prick!"

Erik, realizing the situation could quickly become lethal, stepped between Bob and David, holding his palms out to Bob. "Please, Bob, leave him—"

"Get the fuck out of my way!" As Bob screamed, he grabbed Erik's right hand and flung him to the side like a rag doll. Erik was a large man, but Bob threw him backwards with such force that he had no chance of staying on his feet. Erik went down so quickly, he couldn't protect his fall. The back of his head struck a limestone outcropping with a sickening thud, stopping everyone cold—even Bob. They all turned to look at Erik, lying motionless on his back.

Michelle ran the few steps over to Erik and kneeled next to him, joined immediately by Stefani. Michelle quickly turned his head to the side, to see a large depression where it had struck the rock. Blood was freely flowing from the injury, not pulsing but rather steadily spilling out into a rapidly growing red puddle. Without skipping a beat, Michelle turned Erik's head back to its original position to prevent Stefani from seeing the injury.

"*Mein Gott!*" Stefani exclaimed seeing the expanding pool of blood forming below his head.

"Is he okay?" gasped David, still on the ground, unable to see what was happening.

Michelle pressed her hand against Erik's neck, feeling for his carotid artery, already knowing what she would find.

Stefani, meanwhile, ran her hands over Erik as if probing for some switch that might start him up again. She then turned to Michelle in a panic. "What do we do? Help him!"

Michelle shook her head and reached over to hold Stefani's hand.

Bob now appealed to the group. "It's not my fault—he tripped over that rock."

Stefani leaned over and hugged Erik, openly bawling. Claire went over and put her hand on Stefani's shoulder.

"Don't blame me," Bob reiterated. "He's the one that got in my face. I was just defending myself." With that, he walked off toward the Point.

Nobody knew what to do. They wanted to help but were powerless to do so. After a minute, Michelle stood and offered her hand to Stefani. "Come on, Stef, let's go back and sit down." After a moment's hesitation, Stefani took Michelle's hand and slowly stood up. As Michelle led her away, she walked in shock, staring back over her shoulder at Erik's body.

Recovering his wind, David sat up and turned to Claire. "Christ, I can't believe it. Look, maybe you should go on ahead with them. I'll head out to the farm and see if I can find somebody to help with Erik."

Shaken to her core, she could think of nothing else to do that made sense, even asking David if he was okay. "I guess. See you soon."

David made his way slowly to his feet and hobbled toward the farm. Minutes down the road, he ran into Russ and Jules, and, with difficulty, explained what had happened.

"Do you need any help?" Russ asked.

"I don't know. I'm not sure what to do. Do we bury the body, d'ya think?"

"Why don't I go and see if I can help Stef?" Jules said and then left briskly.

Russ noticed Don walking down the road from the farm. Soon the three men were standing over Erik, debating what to do.

"Maybe we should make a casket or something," Russ offered.

"With what?" David replied. "With the tools we have, there'd only be a skeleton left by the time we're done."

Don squatted next to Erik, looking down at him. "You mean he just killed him? Just like that?" He looked up at the others. "Isn't the real question, what do we do about Bob?"

"He wasn't trying to kill him," David said. "He was just mad and pushed him too hard."

"Either way, what do we do about Bob?"

"And about Erik," added Russ.

After several more minutes of discussion, they decided to head back to the village to get ideas from the women. As they approached, Michelle stumbled toward them, whispering, "What'd you do with Erik?"

"Nothing yet," David answered. "We weren't sure what to do."

"*Nothing*? Erik's still out on the sand alone? What if somebody wanders by and just finds him there, dead?"

"We just thought we should talk as a group about what to do first. Listen, I'm really sorry …"

Michelle waved him off. "Look, I'm not blaming you. You didn't do anything wrong. I'm just worried about Stef." She seemed about to say more, but was interrupted by Kimo's arrival. All eyes immediately focused on him.

He scanned their expressions for a moment. "What's going on?"

Claire stood up and walked away from the group, motioning for Kimo to follow her. When they were out of Stefani's hearing range, Claire explained. "Erik's dead. He tried to break up a fight between David and Bob, and Bob killed him—pushed him onto some rocks."

Kimo sighed deeply. "Where are they now?"

"Bob wandered off; I don't know where he is." She pointed to the west and said, "Erik, or his body, is over behind that sand dune. We didn't know what to do."

Kimo looked back to the village. "Where's everybody else?"

"Don't know. Maybe at the farm?"

Kimo focused on Stefani and, seeing she was well attended, sharply called, "David! Russ! Don! Come over here." He watched the three men hustle over. "We're going to have to bury Erik's body. That means digging a hole and making a casket. David and Don, you know that place a couple hundred yards down the north beach, where the sand mounds up really high?"

Don nodded.

"That's about the only place we're going to be able to dig a decent hole. Make a hole there at least four feet deep and at least a hundred feet from the waterline. Russ, head out to the farm and tell the others we need their help. Ask everybody to collect lots of palms so we can weave a basket big enough to put his body in. I want to have him buried as soon as possible. We'll worry about Bob later. For now, ignore him if you see him. By the way, who actually saw this happen?"

Claire and David tentatively raised their hands. Kimo looked at David. "Okay, tell me exactly what happened."

"Claire and I were coming back to camp, and Bob started to attack me. Erik tried to calm him down—"

"Just a second. Why did Bob attack you? Did he find out about you and Claire?"

David was distracted for a moment, wondering how Kimo knew. "Yeah. Well, actually Michelle found out and then Claire told—"

"Okay, it doesn't matter now. So Bob was pissed off and went after you—no shock there. Then what?"

"Well, Erik tried to calm him down. I didn't really see it. I was on the ground."

"I saw it," said Claire. "Erik stepped between Bob and David, so Bob grabbed him and whipped him around. Then he flung him backwards to the ground. Erik hit the back of his head on a rock, and, well, I guess that's all. He never moved after that."

Don looked at Kimo. "So what are you going to do with Bob?"

"Me? What am I going to do? What do you want me to do? Our island just lost another person—three down, nineteen to go. We're not doing very well, I'd say, but shit happens, so we deal with it—*all* of us." Kimo walked off in the direction of Erik's body.

By late afternoon, they had collected enough palm fronds for a casket of sorts. Everyone returned to camp and helped to slit the fronds into half-inch wide strips, which they wove into a large basket. Kimo then enlisted Don's help to lift Erik's body in. Stefani watched, nearly in a panic: a combination of grief and the fear of being alone. Jenny, having also just experienced a loss, put her arms around Stefani and spoke soothing words to her.

As the sun started slipping below the horizon, Bob arrived in the village. He walked in, ignoring everyone, acting as if nothing had happened. Stefani saw him and immediately went to Kimo. With a frightened calm, she asked, "What are you going to do? He murdered my husband."

Bob, who'd apparently overheard, made public his objection. "I didn't do a damned thing. He attacked me and fell backwards, that's all. It was an accident." He pointed to Claire and David. "Blame those two if you want to blame somebody."

Kimo locked eyes with Bob, whose face reflected a nervous combativeness. Then Kimo broke his stare and turned to the others, who were all looking back at him. "So what do you want me to do? We live on an island. You want to put Bob on trial, or you want me to play king and just decide whether he's guilty or not? And what then? You going to build a jail for him? Hang him? Flog him? Or maybe we should just set him adrift on a raft so he can starve to death." He suddenly looked at Jenny. "Sorry."

No one spoke for a long time, until Stefani broke the silence. "But you *must* do something. He murdered my—"

"I already told you, I didn't kill nobody," Bob screamed. "He tripped on a rock and fell—and that's all. So just drop it."

Kimo shook his head. "Bob, from what I understand, he didn't *just fall*, you threw him down. You may not have meant to kill him, but you lost your temper and caused his death. So just don't push it, okay? Just the tiniest bit of remorse might go a long way right now. Or do you even know what that is?"

Bob looked around the group and, realizing he had no support, stomped off to his hut.

Don turned to Kimo, who was standing next to him, and said, "You know this isn't over."

Chapter 18

IT WAS MORNING, AS they were bringing him breakfast, when Stan and Nani discovered Josh's body on the floor next to his bed. It was twelve days since they had arrived on Pitcairn—the very day they were to fell the tree that would become the hull of their proa. As expected as his death was, it was still a difficult blow to both of them. Once they had been able to get beneath his skin, they had really enjoyed his company and his remarkable stories of Pitcairn's history and culture.

Stan and Jenny had spent nearly all their time with Josh during those last twelve days, learning and relearning the principles of sailing and boat-building. He had sketched a detailed drawing of the proa and all of its parts, and quizzed them relentlessly on terminology and wind directions. He took them on walks and showed them the trees they would use for various parts of the boat; in particular, selecting the tree they'd use for the hull. He took them scavenging through the village to collect the tools they would need.

Nani insisted they stop work for the day to mourn his passing. Stan didn't complain—as the complexity of the project had unfolded the past two weeks, Stan had no choice but to concede there was no hope of being by Jenny's side when she went into labor.

They buried him next to Marisa's tomb directly behind their house, just where he had asked them to, and made a marker with a wooden plank. Stan found some black paint and neatly printed an epitaph on it.

Josh, the last of the Pitcairn Islanders,
spent his last days helping two strangers.
We knew him only a few days,
but will remember him forever.

Brush still in hand, Stan stood in front of the plank, feeling it woefully lacking. "I don't even know his last name or when he was born. We're not even sure we know the date he died." He turned to Nani. "You know, a few months ago I had an eight-to-five job writing software in Pittsburgh, and today I'm burying the last descendant of the *Bounty* mutineers and maybe one of the last people left on the planet—and I don't even know if I'll ever see Jenny again."

During the following two months, Stan and Nani shared the work of making the proa, but Stan had never experienced physical labor of nearly these proportions. Just hollowing out the hull took four weeks of intense work. After chopping down the tree that Josh had identified, it had to be cut to length (they had decided on twenty feet). Then came the most difficult step, hollowing it out using a tool called an adze. Using just the adze, the process would have taken months, but Stan found that he could carefully burn the wood he intended to remove, extinguish the fire, then easily dig out the charred wood. Josh had told them that the final steps of the process would need to be completed very slowly so that the hull's thickness would be as uniform as possible, but Stan went slower still, terrified that he would accidentally cut too deep and have to start over.

After trenching out the log, the next task was to open it—stretch it, like one might split a pea pod. Stan filled the hull with water and extremely hot rocks, then used a jack they'd found near the boathouse to slowly pry the log open. Then he placed wooden braces inside to hold the log open while the water was dumped out and the wood dried to set its new shape. He would then repeat the process, stretching it open yet further. Again, the fear of having to start all over slowed his work considerably, as Josh had warned him that if he stretched the wood too fast, it would split. He agonized over every stroke of the hydraulic jack, straining to hear the first sound of a crack forming. After five stretching cycles, he was able to open the hull to three feet, the minimum width that Josh had recommended.

While Stan built the hull, Nani focused on making a sail to the dimensions Josh had outlined. She searched the island, rummaging through all the old, rotten, canvas she could find for the best pieces. She then sewed them together using nylon string and some sailmaker's needles they'd found on the *Sea Salva*, reinforcing the corners, as Josh had instructed, with multiple stitching lines and patches of nylon sail they were able to salvage from the *Sea Salva*.

Once the main hull was finished, Stan began the far easier task of making the ama, as well as the akas that would connect the ama to the main hull. Then he and Nani found a fiberglass sheet that they shaped and smoothed into a perfect leeboard. For the rudder, Josh had told them to use a large oar they'd uncovered at the boathouse—that way, they could just pass it from one end of the boat to the other when they shunted.

Before adding the mast, boom, and sail, they took the unrigged hull down to the dock to ensure it floated. By itself, the hull was too heavy to carry, however, so they made a crude sled, on which they slid the hull down the Hill of Difficulty. At the bottom, they lashed the main hull and the ama to two akas using nylon rope from the *Sea Salva*.

"Ready to see if this thing floats?" asked Stan.

"Aren't we supposed to break a champagne bottle on its hull first, or something like that?"

"Hmm. We do have a bottle of champagne still, but frankly I'd rather drink it than waste it by breaking it. How about if we just bash it with an plastic water bottle instead?"

"Okay, but that means we need to name it. Any ideas?"

"I want to call it *Jenny*."

"I don't think you're supposed to name a boat after somebody that's still living. It's bad luck." But even as she said it, she realized that superstition wasn't the real reason for the pang of disappointment she felt.

"Well, I don't believe in luck, and this boat has no purpose but to get back to Jenny and … do you realize I'm probably a father by now?"

Nani smiled. "Okay, *The Jenny* it is then. I just hope it doesn't sink. I think I'm supposed to be the one that christens it though. It's supposed to be a woman."

They nudged the boat to the edge of the steep gravel beach. Nani then took an open bottle of water and smashed it onto the bow of the boat. "I christen thee ..." She hesitated, causing Stan's head to turn, then finally said, " ... *Jenny.*"

They half slid and half lifted the boat into the water, holding onto a rope tied to the bow. After watching it float for a minute, Nani said, "Well, I don't see any water inside."

"Yeah, so far, so good," Stan said, "but let's see how it does with some weight inside." He climbed into the *Jenny*, holding onto the sides, ensuring his first foot was secure before lifting in the other. Then realizing how stable it was, he stood slowly upright and rocked from side to side in a kind of dance. "This is really solid. I can't even get the ama to lift out of the water. Here, tie the rope to the dock and hop in."

After tethering the *Jenny*, Nani carefully stepped from the dock into the boat. Stan gestured to a paddle near the front. "Grab that paddle. Let's see how this thing moves."

After untying the boat, they paddled around in the quiet water protected by the concrete pier. At first, they tried to steer it like a canoe, by adjusting their paddling, but the boat didn't react. Stan then tried to use his paddle as a rudder, and the *Jenny* promptly responded. After steering in a few tight circles, they tied up their boat to the *Sea Salva*. "Nani, I can't believe we really built a boat. I've never felt like ... I mean I'm not sure I've ever done anything as satisfying as that."

"It *is* really impressive. But you know we have a long way to go."

"Yeah, I know. There's that little detail of learning to sail."

"And don't forget making the mast."

"Before we build the mast and stuff, why don't we see how the boat moves outside of the harbor?"

"You mean paddle it out into the ocean?"

"Yeah, let's try and see how it moves in the real ocean. We can always turn around if it gets rough, but we ought to see how it does in waves."

"Okay, tomorrow. Tonight, we celebrate." Nani leaned close to Stan, bumping her head onto his shoulder for a moment. Without thinking, Stan put his arm around Nani's shoulder and pulled her closer.

"Okay, but let's spend the night on the *Sea Salva*. If the weather turns bad, I want to keep my eye on our boat—on *Jenny*."

Over the last few weeks, Stan and Nani had overtly avoided letting their activities and discussions trespass into dangerous terrain, but now, huddled together over an after-dinner bottle of celebratory champagne, they found themselves drawn by the forces of nature.

With his hand draped over her shoulder, Stan idly traced his forefinger around the neckline of Nani's oversized T-shirt. As Nani's eye's flickered under his touch, they both realized they were balanced on a precipice, and with that realization, Stan's muscles suddenly tensed and he withdrew his arm.

"What's wrong?" Nani asked.

"Ah … I just hope the weather is all right tomorrow."

Nani stared at him. "Stan, we need to have a frank talk about this."

"About what?"

"About this—you and I. I know you're attracted to me, and I won't deny that I'm attracted to you too—and have been from the time I first saw you. But you don't have to be afraid of me. I know how you feel about Jenny and would never compromise that. And I know as well as you do that if something were to happen between us, we'd never forgive ourselves. So you don't have to worry."

She waited for Stan to nod slightly before continuing. "And you don't have to feel so guilty all the time either. Being attracted to someone else isn't something to feel bad about—it's just human nature, okay? It doesn't mean we can't support each other now and then, or that we have to run away every time we show emotional needs or feelings. For Christ's sake, we wouldn't be human if we didn't need emotional support now and then in a situation like this. We just have to understand it isn't going anywhere, that's all. We can be friends without being lovers."

Stan was both startled and relieved by her frankness. "Okay. Thanks for saying that. I'm not very good at that sort of stuff."

"It's not that. It's just that you're so nervous around me and I don't want you to be. You don't need to be. I promise, nothing's going to happen between us."

Her words comforted him, encouraging him to indulge in another glass of champagne. "Where are you from, Nani? I always wondered."

Nani laughed. "That's just what I was talking about! You know, I think that's the first personal question you've ever asked me."

"No, it's not."

"Then name another. Anything. How I'm feeling about being away from Kimo, my middle name, how old I am … name anything personal you've ever asked me."

"Come on, that's not fair. And besides, you still haven't answered the question. Where are you from?"

"I'm from everywhere, or that's how I feel sometimes. I've lived all over, but mostly on the islands. I was born in Tahiti. My parents separated when I was young, and I stayed with my father. He was in construction, and he moved wherever there was work for him, but always in the islands. People still say I have a bit of a French accent. Do I?"

"Not really. Just the tiniest bit maybe, but I like it."

The conversation continued, intertwined with sips of champagne; they were now well into their second bottle. Feeling more relaxed, Stan said, "You know, you were right."

"About what?"

"About being attracted to you. I still remember that night you first danced. I can't remember ever feeling so … I don't know … I guess, drawn in."

Nani enjoyed baiting Stan. "What do you mean *drawn in?*"

"You know what I mean." Stan looked at her only to get an impassive look. "I mean so sexually attracted to somebody. You were remarkable. I felt …"

Stan stopped, completely lost in the moment, nearly dizzy with

Nani's presence. He turned his head toward her, cupped the back of her head in his left hand, and drew her lips to his. For a few seconds, their kiss rid them of all ethical and moral boundaries, of all the chaos that had surrounded them over the past months, of all reality. For just a moment, there were no islands to go back to, no boats to build, no questions about the outside world, and no family to hold them back. But as Stan's hand dropped toward Nani's breast, Nani pushed away.

"Stan. We can't. We really can't. I want you too, but we just can't. I would hate myself, and you'd never, ever forgive yourself or me." She stood and walked around to the other side of the table.

"What do you mean, we can't? Why not? Nobody would ever know." He regretted it as soon as he said it, yet something kept him going. "I mean if we feel what we do, what's the harm? We don't even know …" He stopped, realizing it was the alcohol talking, and he was arguing with himself rather than with Nani—and he couldn't even convince himself. "Sorry. Of course you're right. It must be the champagne. Sorry." With that, he went up on deck to be by himself.

Early the next morning, they set out with the intent of paddling east from Bounty Bay to a stony mass called Adam's Rock. Though Adam's Rock was just five hundred yards away, it wasn't visible from shore, so Stan and Nani had consulted the map and devised a route for themselves. The first part of their trip would be in the protected bay through the Pool of Uaru. At the edge of the pool, they would round a point into the open ocean and sail about another hundred yards to Adam's Rock.

While they were in the protected waters, their going was slow but trouble-free. As soon as they neared the point, however, the height of the waves increased markedly.

"Should we keep going, you think?" asked Nani.

"If we can't make it through this, we don't have a chance in the open ocean. These waves are nothing compared to what we came in on."

"But they didn't seem so big then. I guess because the *Sea Salva* was so much bigger."

As intimidating as the waves were, their canoe knifed over them smoothly. The waves gave Stan the feeling they weren't making any progress, but at this point, that didn't matter much—the primary point of the this first trip was just to make sure no water got into the boat, and happily, none did. After a while, however, he realized they had made progress. Not far ahead, he saw Adam's Rock.

Stan stopped paddling. "For a first trip, that's enough. Let's head back. Keep paddling, on the right side—sorry, starboard—and I'll steer us around to the left."

"Didn't Josh say we should shunt? We could both just turn around in our seats and then you'll be in front and me in back."

"Yeah, I know, but I really want to see how the boat behaves as it turns, when the waves come in to the side of the boat. Let's just try."

Turning around was not exactly easy. It took much longer than Stan had expected just to get the boat to rotate, and when it finally did present its broadside to the waves, it began a disconcerting roll. "You swim well, don't you?" They both knew the question was rhetorical—there was no safe place to swim to anyway.

As they continued the slow leftward rotation, Stan felt himself begin to sweat, less from physical strain than from fear of maneuvering wrong and landing in the tumultuous water. Gradually, however, the waves approached them from astern, putting an end to the rolling motion.

"Woo-hoo!" Stan bellowed, shaking his paddle above his head. Though the maneuver was frightening, the outrigger had performed flawlessly: the ama had stayed glued to the water and the lashings had all held firm.

They pulled into the bay nearly two hours after they'd left, utterly exhausted from the paddling and tension, and more confident than ever—not only in their vessel, but in their ability to handle the open Pacific.

The next morning, they began rigging the boat. They placed the mast on a platform at the center of the boat that Stan had deliberately left thicker than the rest of the hull. The top of the mast was tied to the front, back, and two sides of the hull using four strong nylon ropes salvaged from the *Sea Salva*. To test its integrity, Stan climbed to the top of the mast, while Nani sat on the ama to make sure the *Jenny* didn't tip over.

Convinced that the mast was sound, they lashed the boom to the mast about a foot above the hull. They then lashed the leeboard to the middle of the port side, between the two *akas*. The next day, they attached the sail to the boom by threading a rope around the boom in a spiral and then through eyelets Nani had sewn into the foot of the sail. The sail was then attached to the mast by tying rope loops through another set of eyelets in the sail and around the mast. The sail could be then raised and lowered by a halyard looped through one of the *Sea Salva*'s pulleys that they had mounted on the top of the mast. The morning after they had finished the rigging, they walked out to the dock, and Stan tossed a leaf in the air. They watched the leaf drift away to the west.

Stan smiled. "Josh said we should wait until there was a gentle easterly wind before we try our first sail, and we've got it. I think we should take this as a good omen and go for it. What do you think?"

"Why not? Worst case, we lower the sails and paddle back. Conditions look perfect. So paddle out to Adam's Rock and start there?"

"That's what the man said: he said to start far enough out so that we wouldn't get blown back into the rocks right away. Plenty of room to allow for mistakes."

It took about an hour to paddle out to Adam's Rock. They turned the boat around so it was pointing toward the Bounty Bay, then pulled their paddles in. Stan took out the steering oar that would act as a rudder. One last time, he reviewed with Nani what they had gone over dozens of times already.

"Okay, the wind is coming at us from the right sides, so the sail will be on our left, and your end of the boat is in the front. Now we let out the mainsheet all the way, so there's no pressure on the sail, and we pull on the halyard to raise the sail. Can you reach it?"

Nani crawled over to the mast and pulled on the halyard, raising the sail smoothly up the mast. The sail whipped freely in the wind.

"Good. Now we pull in on the mainsheet until the sail stops flapping around—sorry, I mean luffing." He pulled in the mainsail until it was taut against the wind. "Now, we see what happens."

Sure enough, as soon as the luffing stopped, the boat began to glide forward, steering itself away from the wind to the left. Stan strained to hold the mainsheet and finally had to let go. The luffing resumed.

"It's really hard to hold the rope once the mainsheet fills up with wind. It got harder, too, when the boat turned. I can't hold it with one hand and steer with the other."

Nani replied, "So, let's try again, but remember to tie the rope off to that thing over there … the cleat."

"So I should tie it off while it's luffing and easy to hold, then steer a little away from the wind. Let's try that."

This time, using the steering oar, Stan was able to keep the boat on a course toward the dock. Over the next few hours or so, they sailed back and forth in front of Bounty Bay, making a few poorly executed turns, or shunts. They shunted by lowering the sail, turning the boat with the paddles, and then raising the sail again after reversing the front and back of the boat, passing the steering oar from one end of the boat to the other.

Once, as they were sailing with the wind, a breeze snuck over to the port side, violently swinging the boom and sail across to the starboard side. The sail put pressure on the ama, digging it down into the water, causing the boat to jerk and abruptly pivot.

"Well, I guess that's what Josh warned us about. Jibing, right?" Nani said.

"Yep, that's what we're *not* supposed to do. But it doesn't seem like it damaged anything."

They went on several more practice runs over the next few days, and made many more mistakes. But eventually, they learned to steer with reasonable skill and to identify and fix structural problems in the boat, such as weak lashings.

From the very beginning, when Josh had still been with them, they had said their final test would be a circumnavigation of Pitcairn. It would require them to sail to all points of the compass and give them a real open-sea experience without the risk of getting lost. So two weeks after their first sail, they set out in the early morning and finished their circumnavigation by midafternoon. It took a little longer than it should have because of their strict adherence to Josh's urgent warning to stay well clear of the island on the east, or windward, side. If a strong wind came along, he had cautioned, they'd be thrown onto the rocky shore and battered to pieces.

That night, they were tempted to celebrate with another bottle of wine, but after the last time, they were both afraid to let down their guards. Besides, it was now time for their real test: sail straight into the wind and find the little dot of an island some hundred miles away where their friends were. *That* would be the time for celebration.

Chapter 19

EVERYBODY HAD SHOWN UP at Erik's burial, except Bob, whom Kimo had told to stay far away. Jenny stood over Erik's grave, surveying the other islanders, while Kimo asked if anybody wanted to say something. Jenny soon realized that the fumbling silence and sideways glances were settling on her. She knew somebody had to say something, but her own thoughts were still on Stan, not Erik. She stared straight ahead, determined to outwait the others—surely somebody else would step forward. Just then, her baby gave her a sharp kick, as if prodding her forward. She rubbed her round belly, but the baby just wouldn't stay still, reminding her, yet again, that life would simply have to go on. She finally shuffled forward from the circle.

"Erik ... Erik was a good man. He died trying to help another person ... to break up a fight ... and to save a friend. I wonder how many of us would have done the same. I'll miss him, and I think the whole island will. He was ..."

She realized she had started to cry, and wondered whether her tears were for Erik or Stan. She couldn't even tell any more. Finally, she shook her head and retreated a few steps, hoping that with the ice now broken, somebody else would offer something. After a few more shifting looks, Stefani herself stepped forward, and spoke for a couple of minutes sorrowful German, before switching to English. There were no tears in her eyes, though, only determination.

"Our time together was short but wonderful. Nothing can give us back the time we now lose—we can only punish the person who took it from us." With that, she picked up a large clamshell full of sandy dirt and threw it on top of the reed coffin. Everybody turned toward her, shocked. The men then began covering the coffin with sand while the women walked back to the village, closely surrounding Stefani.

Claire walked right next to Stefani and put her hand on Stefani's shoulder. "Stef, listen. I know you're angry and hurt. I can't blame you. But it isn't going to do any good to get mad at Bob. He'll just hurt you too. Believe me, I know him. You have to let it go."

Stefani glared at Claire. "Don't worry about me. I can stand up for myself. Bob is a murderer and he must pay for what he did."

Claire shook her head. "Look, it wasn't like that. Bob didn't mean to kill … I mean, he didn't even mean to hurt Erik. It was an accident."

"Claire, that is your problem. It has been always your problem. We saw the way he treated you. He was mean to everybody, but he treated you terribly and you let him. You made excuses for him—it is even what you do now—but I will not. Kimo is the only person with the courage to stand up to him. In fact he's the only guy here with any guts at all."

For the next few days, Bob managed to stay away from Stefani, but the island was small, and their paths crossed occasionally at a distance. Three days later, however, as people were gathering for dinner, he ran directly into her.

Stefani walked up to him, looked him in the face, and said in a calm, steady voice, "Bob, I want you to leave the island."

Bob laughed, but then noticed her flat expression. "You're serious? How do you expect me to do that?"

"Build a boat or a raft. Or just swim—I do not care. Just leave. I give you one week."

The others all stopped what they were doing and turned toward the scene. Bob glanced around at the different faces, realizing he had to say something, but he still couldn't bring himself to apologize. "You've got to be kidding. Erik fell, that's all. I'm not going anywhere, and you better watch your damn mouth."

"One week," she said again, and then walked calmly away.

"What the hell was that about?" Bob boomed. "You guys all with that bitch on this?" In unison, the onlookers looked away, as if they hadn't heard the altercation.

"Well, are you? Don, are you with her?"

Don hesitated, then turned back to Bob. "Bob, you've got to understand. She just lost her husband. She needs time, that's all."

Bob turned to Wayne. "How 'bout you?"

"It … it's not that simple," Wayne replied.

"Yes, it is. Are you with her or with me?" Bob was quickly losing what he had left of his temper when Kimo walked up.

Kimo stopped in his tracks, sensing the tension. "All right, what now?"

There was complete quiet. "Don, what's going on here?"

"Stef told Bob he had to leave the island within a week, that he had to build a boat and leave."

Bob nodded his head. "Yeah. Can you believe that?"

Everybody was silent for a good minute or so, just waiting for Kimo to say something.

Finally, he said, "Christ, what next? All right, I guess we can't go on like this, but I'm not willing to pass judgment on what Bob did when I wasn't even there. We're going to have to be fair about this. Have a trial or something."

"A trial?" Bob threw his arms up. "For what? Because Erik fell? How the hell are you going to have a trial?"

"I'm not going to," Kimo replied. "Neither are you and neither is Stefani." He turned to the others. "Tomorrow, the rest of you are going to sit together and discuss this for as long as it takes. You decide what's to be done. You want to send him floating off to his death in a raft, go for it. You want to send Stefani off on a raft instead, that's fine, too. You can decide he's innocent, you can tie him to a tree for a month, cut off an ear … for all I care, you can give him an award for being such a nice guy. I don't give a shit, but whatever you decide, it's final and it's over. Done. Understood?"

"Hey, you're talking like I'm not even here!" Bob interjected.

Kimo raised his voice yet one level above Bob's. "Then leave!"

Noticing that Kimo's hand was resting on the hilt of his knife, Bob grumbled, then walked off.

As soon as he was out of earshot, Russ said, "I don't know anything about this. What am I supposed to say at a trial? I don't want to get involved—it'll only upset people."

Kimo turned to him. "Russ, all I can say is tough shit. I don't want to either. You really want me to play God here? You want a dictator deciding what's right and wrong, without even asking what others think?"

Russ just shrugged his shoulders.

The next morning, Kimo told Bob to spend the day at the Point, and Stefani at the farm with Michelle, whom he decided should also be excluded from the discussion because of her recent ties to Bob. Then, with no preamble, he abruptly left the others at the main table under the lean-to.

"That's it? So what are we supposed to do?" Russ said when Kimo was out of earshot.

"Claire, you're the lawyer," David said. "What do you think we should do?"

Claire glared at David. "I'm *not* a lawyer—just a law *student*. And, anyway, I don't think that means very much here."

Jenny looked at her. "I didn't know you were studying law. I know you said you were a student, but I thought ..." She stopped, realizing she was on the verge of saying something rude and foolish. Before she had time to extricate herself, however, Claire saved her.

"No, that's okay. I know I don't exactly fit the lawyer profile."

Lynda said, "But you and David were the only ones to really see what happened weren't you? Maybe you two should just decide what to do."

"Don't lay that on us!" she growled. "You think that's the way justice works? The witnesses decide if the accused is guilty? There's a reason we have judges and juries, you know."

George offered a compromise. "Well, maybe it would help if you at least tell us again what happened."

David and Claire recounted the events, answering questions as they went. When they were through, Don asked, "So what if this were back in the States? Would Bob be guilty of murder?"

"That depends on what a judge and jury says," Claire repeated.

"I know," David said. "What I mean is, what if a jury decided it was an accident that killed him, but Bob did something violent to cause the accident? Would it be murder?"

"It's still not clear. It could still be considered murder if he meant to cause grievous harm to David. It might be called voluntary manslaughter if it were considered *in the heat of passion*, or involuntary manslaughter if completely incidental. It's complicated."

George asked, "So what would the punishment be?"

"First of all, I don't know. I was going into contract law not criminal law. But second of all, what difference does it make? We're not there; we're here. It's completely different. We don't exactly have a jail, you know. What can we do, fine him?" Claire was obviously becoming frustrated at being the target of so many questions.

Marco took the moment of quiet as an opportunity to comment. "It is true that it is different here. I think the island would be better if Bob is not here. It is not the first time he attacked somebody, and it will not be the last. He is big, strong, and mean."

Jenny said, "I may not like him either, but does that give us the right to get rid of him? If we decide to get rid of him, then who's next? Besides, I don't think anybody has claimed that he even really *intended* to hurt Erik."

"Well, I don't completely agree with that," Don said. "It sounds to me like he did mean to hurt Erik—just not to kill him—and according to what Claire said, that's still murder."

"All right then, what are our options?" David asked. "I hope we all agree that some kind of execution isn't appropriate, so what does that leave other than just closing our eyes to the problem?"

They all looked at each other.

George spoke up. "So, what did they do on ships, for example, to punish people? They flogged them, or put them in irons, right?"

Jenny answered, "They put them in irons until they could get back to stand trial, but there is no place to get back to in this case. And you want to flog him? You gotta be kidding! It would be completely senseless. I don't know about the rest of you, but I won't have anything to do with that! We're not a bunch of animals."

"Jenny's right," Claire said. "We need to think about the intention of punishing a crime. Punishment can be used as a deterrent to others, as revenge, to rehabilitate, or just to try to prevent or deter Bob from committing another crime. There's no way that corporal punishment rehabilitates, and I would really question whether it sets an example for others. He obviously didn't mean to kill Erik, so a deterrent makes no sense either. So what's the point? Just revenge? I don't see what that accomplishes either."

Wayne said, "So then if corporal punishment is out, and you say it makes no sense to execute him, and if there's no way to put him in jail, then we just forget about it—is that what you're saying?"

"No, that's not what I'm saying," Jenny retorted. "But we have to be sensible."

Allison now entered the fray. "Sensible like Bob was? Stefani lost her husband because of an unnecessary, violent act. We can't just look the other way, or it'll be one of us next."

"Okay, then what about making him do extra work for a few weeks, or something like that?" suggested David.

Wayne exploded. "Extra work? Who's going to enforce that? So what's the message in that? Bob killed somebody so he has to do some extra work? How 'bout a time out? The fact is, almost anything we do with Bob is more of a punishment of us than it is of him … unless it's to get rid of him."

"Get rid of him?" David asked. "I thought you were big on the Bible and your Christianity. Doesn't the Bible say to forgive?"

"I think it also says an eye for an eye, a tooth for a tooth, so I don't know what you want to do with that," Don said.

Again, there was a pregnant pause.

Wayne took a deep breath. "Actually, I'm glad you brought up the Bible. I think that's where we should look for answers—and not just about this. We should think about Noah." Seeing confused faces, he continued, "You know, Noah, from Noah's Ark? Don't you guys get it?"

"No." David sighed in resignation. "Can't say that I do."

"Don't you ever think about why God spared us? Why he put us all here on this island and timed everything so that we survived the solar storm?" Again, he words met inquisitive looks. "Don't you see? This is the ark. Instead of a flood and a boat, he chose to scorch the earth and keep us protected on this island."

Jenny asked, "Are you serious?"

"I'm not saying I have it all worked out, but you've got to figure that whatever God does, he has a purpose, right? So you tell me, what else did God have in mind by gathering us together on an island so far from—"

"Okay, okay, I get the idea." David was exasperated. "But what does all that have to do with Bob?"

All eyes went to Wayne. "What I'm asking is, do we want Bob on our ark?"

"But according to you, Wayne, God put Bob here," David argued. "Doesn't that mean God wants him here?"

"Maybe God's giving us a choice—a test. Maybe he wants to find out if we know who should be on the ark and who shouldn't. Maybe he wants to see if we have the wisdom to tell right from wrong, and the strength to do something about it."

David turned his head away in disgust, so Claire took over the argument. "So how would you intend to get rid of him, then?"

"I suggest that we put him on a raft with food and water, float him out beyond the reef, and let God decide what to do with him."

"Let God decide? Now that's some rationalization!" David said. "I suppose if you had a gun and shot him, it wouldn't be you that killed him because God would decide whether the bullet hit him. You just pulled the trigger—God sent the bullet to its mark. Is that it?"

"Wait a minute, David," Don calmly stated, "I don't think his suggestion is so silly. I might not agree with the ark business, but we do need to decide who we want on the island. Like Marco said in the beginning, Bob is trouble, and the island is better off without him. Can you honestly argue with that?"

"And are you willing to be the one to carry out the sentence?" David said. "Are you willing to kill?" Receiving no answer, he turned to Wayne. "What about you, Wayne, are you willing to take a life?"

"We can ask Kimo to do it," Wayne said. "Besides, like I said, it's God's choice what happens to him. Our decision will only be that he can't stay on the ark. God is asking us to choose right from wrong."

After a moment of silence, Claire said, "There are a lot of people here we haven't heard from. Personally, I think that's the worst idea I've heard since I've been on this island, but I'd like to see how the others feel about Wayne's suggestion."

Jules said, "I'd rather we vote in secret somehow."

George hopped up from his seat. "How 'bout a Yes jar and a No jar, and each of us has one shell to put in whichever one we want?"

Welcoming the chance to switch gears, the group decided to break so they could collect shells from the beach and find two suitable clay jars. When they returned in about half an hour, they engaged in another lengthy argument about the exact wording of the proposition upon which they would be voting.

That night, as the sun began to set, Kimo and Stefani returned to the village and started dinner. A little while later, Bob ambled in carrying some fish. Kimo looked up at Bob, and then motioned for he and Stefani to follow him to the main table where the others were still meeting. "Okay, everybody, let's call it a day. What'd you decide?"

Noticing their dodging glances, he prompted them more sternly. "Come on, what'd you decide? Somebody say something!"

Nothing, just more silence, shifting eyes and downturned faces. "Don, you tell me. What did you guys decide?"

"We really didn't, I guess. We had a lot of really good discussion, but it's not easy."

"You got to be kidding! All day, and you decided nothing at all? Did you even decide if we should do anything? Or whether Bob was even to blame?"

Emboldened by the lack of verdict, Bob intervened. "I'm not—"

"Shut up!" Kimo cut him off. "Don, did you guys even decide if we should do anything at all with Bob?"

"We took a lot of votes, but we couldn't really agree."

"And I don't suppose it will do any good to continue the discussions tomorrow, will it?" Seeing their obfuscating expressions, Kimo continued. "Never mind, I should have known. All right, go eat dinner." He glanced at Stefani, who returned his look with shrug and raised eyebrow that clearly said, "I told you so."

Francesca, Stefani's closest friend on the island, walked over to her. "I'm sorry," she said almost in a whisper. "I know it must be disappointing, but it wasn't easy. There was just not a good answer."

Ignoring Francesca's apparent attempt to be discrete, Stefani finally broke her silence, addressing the entire group with frightening coolness. "There is only one answer, and everybody knows it. You are only too weak to say it. Yes, I am disappointed in all of you, but I expected it."

Then turning her icy expression toward her nemesis, she restated her demand. "Bob, you have one week to get off the island." With that, she walked back to Kimo, who rested a hand on her shoulder and steered her toward the north beach.

Chapter 20

STAN SURVEYED *JENNY*, TIED snug against the *Sea Salva*. He and Nani had built a small, raised deck around the mast, below which they'd stocked enough food and water for a week. They had fastened a cushion to one side of the deck, toward the ama, upon which they planned to sleep in shifts. In the bottom of the proa they had also stashed away several key items that they'd stripped from the *Sea Salva*—knives, pots and pans, the compass and the radio, hand tools, some extra rope, and two life preservers—as well as some things they had found on Pitcairn—an ax and a few other tools, a few books, and some maps. If they did make it back, Henderson would be a changed place.

"Well, we're as ready as we can be," Stan concluded.

"And you still think we might make it in three days?"

"Dunno for sure, but, yeah, I think so. Maybe even two days. Depends on the wind. We just have to make damn sure we don't miss Henderson."

"You don't really think we could miss it, do you? We found Pitcairn, and that's a lot smaller than Henderson Island."

"Yeah, but Pitcairn is higher, and easier to see from a distance. Besides, we were going downwind before, so we could steer a straight course all the way here. You know what it's going to be like going back: we're going to have to make huge zigzags. Josh figured ten miles southeast, then ten northeast, back and forth all the way, and hope that we end up in sight of Henderson. We could end up a long way off. I mean, if we keep careful track of our turns, we should end up within five or ten miles—close enough to see the island—but what if there's a storm when we arrive and we can't see it? Or what if we arrive at night?

And remember he also told us reefs are hard to see from the ocean side, especially in the late afternoon."

"At least we have Josh's maps now. That's more than we had when we came here."

"A map doesn't help, if you don't know where you are."

"But you said you had that worked out, that you were going to plot out every turn like we did when we sailed around the island. Besides, we can still keep track of when sunrise and sunset is each day. It's still a six-minute time change on the way back, isn't it?"

"Sure, I know, with the compass and watch we should be fine, but what if … oh, never mind, I'm sure it's fine, really. I just don't want to take it lightly, like it's going to be easy. We've practiced enough, haven't we? Let's just make sure we wait until the weather's perfect before we start."

"And until we have a full moon."

Five days later, four full months after arriving at Pitcairn, the sky was clear as far as they could see to the east, and the winds were blowing at about fifteen knots from due east. Stan and Nani figured conditions were about as favorable as they could get.

The two started out just after sunrise, heading southeast, with Stan at the steering oar. Within four hours, they had lost sight of Pitcairn. Every hour, Stan dropped a log into the water, attached to the back of the boat by a rope. As the boat glided forward, the rope would fall back behind the boat. By using the watch to time how long the rope took to run out, he estimated their speed at about four miles per hour—although, assuming the current ran at about one mile per hour, it was more likely just under three. Seemingly on track, with an overcast sky, but moderate winds and light seas, their confidence grew, and by early afternoon they were in high spirits, gliding effortlessly over the gentle, long swells. By nightfall, they had shunted northeast and back again to the southeast, and were getting ready for their second northeast leg of the journey.

Stan showed his marked-up map to Nani. "Too cloudy to get a

reading on the sun, but as near as I can tell from our log measurements, we're about a third of the way there. We should be about here." He pointed to a cross well to the south of a straight line between the islands. "So during the night, we only need to keep the course we're on."

"Shouldn't we shunt again during the night?"

"I don't think we need to, and I rather do it in daylight in case something goes wrong. If we stay on our course, we'll be right about here in the morning." He penciled in a light X to the northeast of their current position. "All we have to do is stay as close to the wind as we can and check the compass to make sure the wind doesn't shift. Then in the morning, we shunt back to the southeast, and we should be on our final course. Easy. We might even make it by tomorrow afternoon if the winds hold up."

"So you want to take the first shift or shall I?"

"Why don't you—it looks calm and you already have the steering oar. I'll try to get a few hours rest then take over. If anything strange happens, wake me up right away, okay?"

Stan worked his way across the hull to their makeshift bed and lay down.

He couldn't really sleep, but was lulled in and out of consciousness by the waves as he lay comfortably in the makeshift bed. After what he supposed was a few hours, he gave up trying to sleep and took over for Nani while she rested.

The rest of the night passed uneventfully, and Nani slept soundly through the early hours of the next morning. Wanting to take a log measurement of their speed, then shunt back to the southeast, Stan finally tried to wake her about an hour after sunrise.

"Nani! Time to get up. We need to turn this thing back to the southeast or we're going to miss Henderson."

Nani lay there for a moment and then stretched. "That was the best sleep I think I've ever had. I want my own bed that moves like that." She sat up. "Want something to drink?"

"Some water would be great."

As she looked crawled to the center of the boat where they had stashed their water bottles, she noticed something was off. "What happened during the night? The boat seems to be moving differently than it did yesterday—the waves are more gentle or something."

Stan shrugged. "I don't know. We also slowed down a bit. I took a log reading last night—seems we're moving about half the speed we were during the day."

Nani looked up at the sky. "Were you able to get a time for sunrise this morning?"

Stan shook his head. "Too cloudy. Here, take the steering oar so I can make another measurement with the log."

As she took the oar, Stan threw the log overboard, watching the second hand of the watch while the rope paid out. After writing down the number of seconds it took to become taut, he froze, staring back at the log.

"What the hell is this all about?" he asked himself out loud.

"What's what about?" Nani followed Stan's gaze.

"Look at the log. It's floating off to the side." The rope was out a full fifty feet, but was angled at least thirty degrees off to the starboard side.

"That's weird, it's always gone almost exactly behind the boat before. You think there's a current or something?"

Stan thought for a moment. "A current should pull the boat the same way as the log. So even if there were a current, the log would still be behind us."

"Did it do that last night when you took a reading?"

"I don't know. I just timed how long it took. I couldn't actually see where the rope was. Let's just try again."

He pulled the log in and then carefully placed it directly behind the boat. The result was exactly the same. They both stared thoughtfully at the log until finally Stan concluded, "I think the only thing it can mean is that we're not going forward anymore, but somehow sideways."

He crawled to the middle of the boat to look at the leeboard. Sure enough, the lashing had come undone, and the board had floated out of the water. As he lashed it back down, he said, "At least it's easy to fix. We're lucky it didn't actually come all the way loose."

With the leeboard back in place, they again threw the log overboard and this time watched it drift directly backwards.

"That's better. That must have been the change in the boat's motion that you noticed. I guess the waves were hitting the boat at a different angle. I didn't even notice it until you mentioned it." Stan took his speed measurement and compass heading again, and then started to record their position on his map. "Damn it!"

"What's wrong?" Nani asked.

"What's wrong is that we don't have any idea where we are, that's what. We're now officially lost at sea."

"You mean we don't know how far to the north we went last night?"

"What I mean is I have no idea where we were going all night, because we were going sideways—and that could have started an hour ago or just after dark."

They sat silent. Then Nani asked, "Do you think we should try to go back to Pitcairn?"

"Who the hell knows? Pitcairn might be closer and higher, but Henderson is bigger. It's a crapshoot either way."

"Then we go on and do the best we can, that's all. And if we can't find Henderson, we can always turn around and try to find Pitcairn again. Hopefully we can get a good time measurement tonight and at least see how far east we are. We should be able to do that, right?"

"Yeah, if we have a clear sky, but you know that won't tell us anything about our north-south position, so we'll still be lost. But it's all we can do, I suppose. I wish I had taken a time reading this morning. Anyway, we'd better shunt back to the southeast now, or we're sure to shoot past to the north of Henderson."

For the rest of the day, the winds remained steady. The cloud cover broke periodically, but unfortunately covered the western sky when the sun set, making it impossible to pinpoint the time of sunset and get a fix on their position. After dark, they were much more diligent than they'd been the night before, checking the direction of the tethered log by moonlight and paying close attention to the feel of the boat in the waves.

As morning approached, stars littered the eastern horizon; there would be no problem getting an accurate time reading. Watch in hand, Stan anxiously awaited sunrise. Nani watched the horizon with him. Then almost simultaneously, at the first sliver of sun, they shouted, "Now!"

Stan checked the watch. "Six thirty-three and, let's call it twenty seconds." He checked the numbers he had written on the chart, "Almost seven minutes later! That means we've passed it."

"By how much?"

"About ... about fifteen miles or so. We must have made better time than I thought."

They turned to scan the western sky, but saw nothing but a dark bank of clouds that had rolled in from the north.

"So, we have to turn around," Stan said. "At least we know how far we're off, though, and we'll be going downwind, so we can go any direction we want. Which way do you want to try—to the northwest or the southwest?"

Nani shrugged and looked at the map. "Why don't we go just straight west? Looks like that's your best guess."

"Yeah, but it's just a wild guess."

"So we try. What else is there to do?"

They turned downwind to the west, toward the cloudbank. With the wind and current at their back, they were making good time, and Stan estimated they'd be at Henderson's longitude in two or three hours. They glued their eyes to the western horizon, hoping to make out some solid shape.

After about two hours of watching, Nani said, "We really should have seen it by now. What do we do?"

"We pick a direction, north or south, and try that. If there's nothing there, then we try the other way, but we should be at about the right longitude. We'll just go north and south until we find it. We've got enough food and water for at least another few days.

"Let's try north first, okay?"

"Sure. Then we have to shunt. The sail's on the wrong side." As soon as they worked the sail around and maneuvered the boat to a northerly course, they both saw it: land, perhaps two miles to the northwest.

"I can't believe it," Stan said. "It's probably been there for the past ten minutes, and we were just looking in the wrong place. It was behind those stupid clouds—and behind our sail."

"It is Henderson, isn't it?" asked Nani.

"What else could it be?"

After about an hour, they were just a few hundred yards off the southeast corner of the island. Stan veered north, paralleling the coast, heading toward the two channels that would carry them safely into the lagoon. However, as they neared the point where the rocky coast dissolved into the reef protecting the lagoon and the east beach, the winds picked up and shifted a little to the north.

"Well, it's definitely Henderson," noted Nani. "We should be able to see the Point soon. We're getting pretty close to shore, aren't we?"

"Yeah. The boat's pointing north, but the wind must be pushing us sideways a bit. I can't steer any further east 'cause the wind's shifted. If we lose the wind, we'll get pushed right into shore. I think we'll make it, though."

Five minutes later, the wind changed yet again, shifting their course yet closer toward the island.

"We have to shunt away from the island," called Stan urgently, "and quickly."

They spilled the wind out of the sail in order to move it to the other side of the boat, but as soon as the sail lost its wind, the boat was blown downwind toward the island. They both looked at each other in a panic, realizing there was no way to complete their turn in time; they were just thirty yards from the rocky surf and bearing down quickly.

Stan shouted, "Leave the sail down and grab a paddle! We have to get this thing away from the rocks."

Just as they veered it away from the coast, they felt a gentle but ominous bump underneath them. It wasn't big enough to cause damage, but nudged them yet further into shore.

"We're not going to make it!" Even as Stan said it, the boat hit another hidden rock, this time jarring them to a halt, tossing both Nani and Stan hard against the side of the boat. Before they could figure out what to do, another wave lifted them up a few feet, then slammed the *Jenny* down onto the same rock, splitting the hull right down the middle.

PART II

†

The Boy that Didn't Belong

Chapter 21

I'M TOLD THAT ONE's first clear memory is often associated with trauma: an event significant enough to cause a child to think back on it the next day, and the day after, and the day after that, year after year, forging the memory deeply into the recesses of the child's mind. That's exactly what happened to me when I was six years old.

I have no recollection of what led up to the events of that day, and I suppose it doesn't matter. But the gist of it is that Kimo claimed I pushed his son, Teiki. Of course that's possible. Teiki and I were just kids, after all, and I imagine we often blurred that fine line between playing and fighting. What I do remember so vividly, though, was being whipped with a bamboo cane. Kimo was holding me down, urging Teiki to hit me. Even more than the physical pain, I remember the panic of being held down and Kimo encouraging Teiki to swing harder and harder. Then, of course, I remember Dad running up to us, shouting at Kimo, "Hey, what the hell are you doing! Cut it out!"

"Just a little training session, Stan, that's all. Keep going, Teiki. Ignore him."

Then Kimo gripped my arms tighter, digging his fingers deep into my tiny muscles, causing excruciating and unnecessary pain; at six years old, after all, I was hardly a threat for escape. Where would I go anyway?

Teiki glanced briefly at both Dad and Kimo, unsure what to do at first, then gleefully continued to bear down on my bare bottom. Teiki was only five and a good three inches shorter than I, but bamboo makes an effective whip; between that and Kimo's fingers pressing into my arms, my pain was very real, even if overshadowed by sheer emotional terror.

As Teiki laid into me again, Dad reached out and ripped the rod from his hands, raised it high above his own head, and held it there, glaring at Teiki. Teiki backed away and raised his hands in defense, crying in fear that the bamboo would be turned on him. Kimo flung me violently to the side and stood. He stared at Dad and then, in a flash, grabbed the bamboo rod from Dad's hands.

Dad must have been petrified to confront a furious Kimo, armed with his ever-present knife, but he calmly turned to me and said, "Adam! Go to Mom, now!"

Kimo, however, turned his fiery eyes on me "No! You stay right there. You leave here and I'll whip the life out of you. I want you to watch this. It's time to straighten out a few things."

It's not that I chose to obey Kimo over my own dad, but rather that I was too frightened to move, so I stayed to watch what was to haunt my dreams for months and control my life for years. My father was a strong, fit man, but no match for Kimo, and they both knew it. Kimo had pinned him facedown on the ground before I could see what happened, and was pressing his shin across the back of Dad's neck. My father was completely quiet, obviously in pain and unable to move. Kimo turned to me. "Now watch this. This is what happens when you don't do as you're told."

With that, he tore aside Dad's pareo and brought the bamboo rod down on Dad's buttocks and back, making a cracking sound I'll never forget. With the first stroke, a line of bright red slashed across my father's back. The pressure on his neck prevented him from screaming I guess, but the pain must have been unbearable. Kimo proceeded to whip him relentlessly, leaving long, red streaks. And after some time, Dad was screaming despite the pressure on his neck.

The other thing I remember is what stopped the beating. As you might guess, it was Nani. I remember her running up as fast as she could and laying right on Dad's bloodied back, defying Kimo to hit her instead. He almost did too. He raised the bamboo rod as if to strike, when she turned and looked directly into his eyes, daring him. He froze for a few seconds, and then threw the stick into the brush. He stood, scooped up Teiki, who was almost as terrified as I, and headed off, calling back to me, "You don't belong here!"

I admit my memories may be distorted by my fear and colored by the stories told to me since, but those words stick out with perfect clarity. "You don't belong here." Something in the way he said them scared me more than anything else that happened that day.

As soon as Kimo was out of sight, Nani lifted herself off of Dad, sat on the ground next to us, and began to cry with me. Finally, she stopped and looked up. "Go home as fast as you can and stay there." Only too happy to leave, I ran to our hut as fast as I could, blinded by my tears. Then, as the story goes, my father couldn't move, so Nani had to wait there until others came to help carry him home. They brought him to our hut where he spent several days in agonizing recovery.

Many of us were scarred by the events of that day.

My scars were purely emotional. From then on, everybody says, I stopped playing and took life too seriously. It was also the beginning of what would become a complicated and oppressive relationship with Kimo: I hated him and was terrified of him, but also emulated him and was somehow possessed by him. I loved Dad, but Kimo was all I thought about, and as much as I hate to say it, it was he who I secretly aspired to become.

Dad suffered physical scars from that day, but even deeper emotional scars. I believe he never got over his failure to protect me. From then on, he was quieter and more passive, possibly realizing that the best way to protect me was to avoid and even submit to Kimo rather than challenge him.

And though I didn't know it then, I suppose Kimo was changed by what happened: I think, after a while, he realized he'd crossed a line that day from which he could not retreat. From then on, he isolated himself from the rest of us, destined to bear the role of dictatorial king of the island.

Teiki bore similar scars to his father's. An insult to Teiki became an insult to Kimo. He withdrew from normal children's play, forced to become, in essence, the prince, with whom nobody would dare argue. As you might expect of a young, isolated child, Teiki quickly became aware of his status and did everything he could to play the role. Perhaps because I was the only older child on the island, Teiki and Kimo seemed to make me a target. I did my best to avoid them and to blend into the background as much as possible when they were around.

That day, too, marked the beginning of a childhood rivalry between Teiki and me, one that was to bloom into something dark, complex and consuming.

Chapter 22

In a way I suppose it's appropriate that I was born just as the sun began to rise on January first, or so we believe from David's calendar. Of course, I was too young to remember my father's return from Pitcairn, just over a month later, but it must have been spectacular. Nani and my father walked into the village from the east beach while everybody was having lunch. Perhaps everybody would have been less shocked had the two of them sailed into the lagoon and had been spotted while still out at sea. But they just walked in from the east beach trail, my dad in sandals and something called shorts, and Nani, barefoot and naked. Apparently their boat had sunk so fast, she didn't even have a chance to get her shoes, and then lost her pareo while struggling to shore through the violent water off the east shore.

I can only imagine how happy Nani and my dad must have been to finally get back after everything they'd been through—and not just on Pitcairn, but upon arriving at Henderson. They were almost killed when their boat was blown onto the rocks just south of the east beach. We call that spot Shipwreck Rock now. I've often climbed down the cliff there and, once, on a calm day, even swam out to the exact rock that crushed their boat—but that'll come later in my story. Anyway, there aren't many places down on the southeast part of the island where it's possible to get safely in and out of the water, so all in all, I'd say they were very, very lucky.

My dad still tells me how thrilled he was to meet me—his new son. I can't believe that of course; I'm sure he just says it for my benefit. How could he possibly have set aside the shock of learning that my mother had died just an hour after I was born? How could anybody? What I do believe, though, is that he always loved me and never blamed me—or anybody else—for her death.

Even now, everybody tells me how much they miss my mother, especially when there's a crisis of some kind. I wish I had known her. They say she had real guts and often talk about her like she was a hero. As I was growing up, I was unimaginably proud when somebody told me I looked like her or did something that reminded them of her.

As I already mentioned, I was just over a month old when my dad returned. Michelle and Claire had labored to keep me alive those first weeks, nursing me on goat's milk. Nobody expected me to live without a mother. I figure that's why they didn't name me for so long—somehow if I had no name, it wouldn't matter as much if I died. Or maybe they thought I had to survive a couple of months to earn a name.

They tell me Nani had little to say when she and Dad arrived to see Stefani prominently perched by Kimo's side. Kimo must have been just as surprised to see Nani, but made no apologies for Stefani, who apparently made a point of nudging closer to Kimo. Nani, in turn, seemed preoccupied with my father's reaction to the news of Mother's death, fully sharing in his initial shock and subsequent grief—and I'm sure that's true.

I don't really know when Stan and Nani became a couple—they've never shared that with me. I suppose it happened quickly: after all, they're both open about the attraction they felt for each other from the onset—from the moment they awkwardly bumped heads on the airstrip. At the same time, they're just as open about my dad's feelings for my natural mother. Nani says Dad loved my mother as deeply as any man can love another woman, and Nani never pretended to replace my mother in either my heart or my dad's. But still, even though neither she nor anyone else ever tried to hide the fact that she wasn't my real mother, I grew up thinking of Nani as Mom. I suppose it could seem strange that I refer to Jenny as Mother, but call Nani Mom, but I've never had any problem with the apparent conflict. And lest there's any doubt, Nani has always treated me as her own—I could have had no better mom. But regardless of their relationship, the story goes that about a week after their return, Mom and Dad, together, finally gave me a name: Adam.

And as for the relationship between Kimo and Stefani, I'm told that began the very week Erik died. I suppose all the raw materials were there: Kimo had lost Nani, and Stefani had lost Erik. On top of that, Kimo was the only person who took control of the situation the day Erik was killed. Stefani likely realized that her only path to retribution lay with Kimo, since he was the only person with the power, both in will and physicality, to punish Bob. I also think Stefani told Kimo exactly what he wanted, and needed, to hear: not only was it okay for him to take control of the island, it was necessary, for everybody's benefit. So, the combination of mutual loneliness, loss, and need for control quickly bonded them.

By the time my father returned to Henderson, Stefani had already had a significant influence on Kimo and, through him, life on the island. She must have become pregnant with Teiki almost immediately after they got together, since he was born just less than a year after I was. He was the first person to be conceived *and* born on Henderson, a distinction with respect to me that Kimo was quick to point out.

There's still no shortage of speculation about how Stefani solved the Bob problem. About two weeks after Erik died, Bob simply disappeared, without trace or explanation. David tells me that they searched for him for all of an afternoon before declaring him gone, and I imagine it was a half-hearted search at that, probably done with the hope of not finding him. There was certainly no mourning that night. Even Michelle, who was the closest to Bob, recognized that the island was better off without him. From what I understand, no one ever asked either Stefani or Kimo about Bob's disappearance, and if anybody knows anything about it, they certainly haven't offered to share it with me.

Chapter 23

IT'S PROBABLY DIFFICULT TO imagine what life was like on Henderson by the time I reached my seventeenth birthday—the day everything was to change. We were two very different generations, separated by at least twenty-five years: the Elders and the Youngers, as we came to be called. We Youngers thought of the island as our entire universe, while the Elders thought of everything in terms of their "Old World." We had never worn shoes and scrambled freely over the rockiest parts of the island, while it seemed that the Elders always struggled to make or repair shoes just to walk over the well-worn paths. We Youngers knew every variety of fish in the lagoon, every coral head, and every nook and cranny in the rock cliffs, while the Elders talked about animals we couldn't even imagine: huge animals called elephants with long noses like eels, so strong they could lift a person; tigers, that could kill humans with one swipe of their arms; unicorns, that looked like goats but were large enough to sit on, and with a single long horn sticking straight up; giraffes, with necks longer than a person is tall, so high they could eat from our tallest trees.

There is also no end to the stories the Elders told us as we were growing up. They talked of islands beyond the horizon called continents that were so big you could put thousands of islands like ours inside. About mountains taller than our island is long, and villages called cities, where thousands and thousands of people lived in buildings that looked kind of like the bunker but were so tall they reached the clouds. They said these buildings had stairs that magically appeared to carry people up, and then disappeared when they reached the floor above. They talked about things called "machines" that showed pictures that moved just like the real world moves, and with sounds, too. Other machines that could think, and do arithmetic even faster than David, and still others that could fly and carry hundreds of people from place to place at speeds it's embarrassing even to mention. They said that some of the stars we saw at night were machines too—not the stars that shoot across the sky, and not the ones that rotate slowly during the night, but the ones that move in a straight line from one horizon to the other; they somehow stayed up in the air hundreds of miles above the earth without falling.

It was all inconceivable to us, but why would they make it up? Yet they did. They even admitted that some of their stories weren't true, like the one about the fat man with silver hair that dressed in red and brought us gifts once a year in a flying boat. They had told us that story for years, insisting it was true. Only after Kimo told us otherwise did they finally admit it was a lie.

Then there were the stories that even the Elders couldn't agree on. Dad said that in the Old World, they had groups of people called "religions." I didn't understand it exactly, but I gathered that religions were elaborate histories of how the world came to be, and that people believed in these religious stories without any real evidence. Dad told me that people just had faith that these stories were accurate stories of the universe and its history. There were many different religions in the Old World, each with its own heroes, explanations, and traditions, and that often they didn't agree with each other. He said that great wars were fought because of these different versions of history, even though both sides stood without a shred of evidence. Somehow people felt that winning a war would be proof that their religion was the right one.

Wayne, when he was still with us, told these religious stories the most, like about how the world was created, and about the first man on earth, also named Adam. He insisted it was true, but Dad told me it wasn't. Dad told me to always ask Wayne for proof—to challenge his stories—yet Dad expected me to believe his own impossible tales, like the mountains that spit fire, and the cold, white, fluffy rain that fell in the Old World. Where was his proof for that? As we got older, we simply decided not to believe anything we couldn't see. We listened and pretended to believe what the Elders said, but really we didn't. Secretly, we laughed at them.

Our parents tried so hard to teach us mathematics, writing, reading, geography, history, and so on, but we were all terrible students. Even when we did believe what they were saying, we didn't see any value in most of it. At seventeen years of age, I was probably the best of all the Youngers at reading and writing, but I was still not very good. In fact, it wasn't until many, many years later, and with a lot of help, that I learned to write well enough to even attempt this chronicle. The lessons that really meant something to us were how to make tools, build shelters, twist rope, fish–practical things. And though I was deathly afraid of him, Kimo was our real teacher.

One of the most important changes that took place during the seventeen years after Mom and Dad's return from Pitcairn is that we gradually separated into three distinct groups called Kitchens. I'm not sure, but maybe the Kitchens started as a more convenient way to prepare meals for a growing population that began to have different eating habits. Regardless, Kitchens soon became more than eating groups; there was a special allegiance to members of one's own Kitchen, as if we were family. Each Kitchen even had a different, I guess one could say, *philosophy* about the island, and about how to live.

Don's Kitchen settled in the middle of the village. Even after seventeen years on the island and nearly seventy years old, Don and Mary were still healthy, though neither moved quickly anymore. When I was young, Wayne was the leader of the Kitchen, but he simply disappeared one day when I was ten. Some believe he slipped off one of the trails that trace the top of the cliffs and was washed into the ocean—probably at the south end of the west beach trail, where the water breaks directly onto the cliffs. Dad, however, suspects that Kimo might have had something to do with it. Wayne's wife, Allison, and their children—Jill, who's thirteen, and Pete, age nine—have stayed pretty much to themselves since it happened.

Russ and Jules and their fifteen-year-old, Sarah, were also part of Don's Kitchen and were also always keen to avoid conflict. Russ began walking with a cane after his broken leg healed several years ago—I think I was about six years old when it happened. But Jules was still very vibrant and active.

Marco, also in Don's Kitchen, spent most of his time fishing alone. He was showing his age, but was still active and healthy. My father tells me he was never the same after Francesca died eleven years ago, and that they were a very close couple. The Elders think she succumbed to something they call cancer; she just got weaker and weaker until, one night, she passed away in her sleep.

Michelle was the final member of Don's Kitchen. She acted as our doctor. I wrote "acted," because she really didn't have the tools to heal or treat her patients effectively. She tried so hard and cared so much, but there was so little she could do. When Linda died of appendicitis, for example, she was completely crushed. She said it would have been an easy thing to deal with if only she'd had the right equipment. She told me that in the Old World, they used to cut people open and fix problems like that—they called them operations. They'd put the person to sleep first, and when the patient woke up, the problem would be fixed. Although they couldn't fix everything that went wrong, Michelle said an operation could have easily saved Linda. Regardless, Michelle always seemed unhappy to me. She was so nice to everybody, it just didn't seem fair for her to be so sad all the time. We often tried to cheer her up, but when I was young, Mom explained to me that some people are only happy when they are unhappy. I'm not sure that really makes sense, but somehow it did to me then.

Our Kitchen was called Stan's Kitchen, and included my mom, my dad, and my little sister Tia who was ten. Tia was really only my half-sister, but we were as close as any brother and sister could be. I had another brother just two years younger than I, but only for a few days, and of course I don't remember him. I don't think Mom and Dad know exactly why he passed away, except that he was born too soon. I guess in the Old World, babies could survive when they were born early, but here, it's something everybody worries about.

David and Claire were in our Kitchen too, along with their fifteen-year-old daughter Jenny (named after my mother), Daveetoo, who was thirteen, and little Tommy, who, at five, was the youngest person on the island. Daveetoo's real name is just Dave, like his father, but somehow we started to call him Daveetoo. Nobody really knew if the *too* meant the number two, or *also*, but that's all anybody ever calls him.

Kimo's Kitchen was clustered on the east side of the village, nearest the Point. It included Stefani, their son Teiki, who was sixteen, and Teiki's younger sister Matahina, who was just short of fifteen. Teiki and Matahina were very close. In fact, I often thought Matahina was the only person that Teiki really liked—he virtually doted on her at times, perhaps because he had no other friends upon which to spend his affections. It was still strange, though, because they had completely opposite personalities: he was introverted, moody, and sullen while she was outgoing, fearless, and loved by everybody. Dad and Mom often said that Matahina was a lot like my mother Jenny.

George and Sue were also part of Kimo's Kitchen, along with their fifteen-year-old son Nick and their eleven-year-old daughter Lisa. But then Sue died while giving birth to their third child, who also died just days after being born, before even earning a name. Dad told me that in the Old World it was common for women to give birth in their late thirties, but that here it was very dangerous.

Lynda was also in Kimo's Kitchen, along with her two children Lois and Clark, both thirteen. Linda and Lynda became pregnant at the same time, never explaining who the father was. We know they shared a father, though, since Linda and Lynda made it clear Lois and Clark were half siblings. Most of us assume they recruited Kimo for that role since they were so quick to join his Kitchen shortly afterward. And as I said before, Linda died of what the Elders believed was appendicitis when Lois and Clark were only four.

Kimo himself was probably fifty or so, but none of us knew for sure, not even Mom. He stood out among the Elders because he was so much more active and fit. Mom and Dad said he looked the same as he did nearly twenty years earlier, but, of course, that must be an exaggeration. His dramatic mood swings, which never had any apparent cause, seemed to grow increasingly severe over the years. Within an hour, he could go from being a caring teacher, to an angry, almost psychotically cruel dictator, and then back again. Mom could sometimes anticipate his mood changes and even help what we called "the good Kimo" return, although she harbored no residual love for him—concern, sometimes, but not love.

Every Thursday and Sunday night, the Kitchens all got together in the Center for gatherings. Together, we'd eat huge, wonderful meals that sometimes took all day to prepare. And occasionally, if Kimo had been in a particularly good mood that day, he would provide pork for the feast. (Only Kimo, and just recently Teiki, were allowed to hunt the pigs that ran wild on the island—a rule they said was intended to maintain control of the pig population.) Then, after dinner, and after some coconut wine or beer, we would sing, tell stories, or perform skits.

During recent years, however, our gatherings became more quarrelsome, with each Kitchen pressing different opinions on the others.

Don's Kitchen believed that this person they called God was planning the things that were happening, and that our island was just part of his plan. They felt we should stay on the island until God told us what to do; when God was ready for us to leave the island, he would provide a way. They used to have a burned Bible that they said had answers to a lot of our questions and problems, but it disappeared the same day as Wayne. Since then, they spent a lot of time just trying to remember what it said and were always talking about it. They also believed that they could make things happen by thinking hard—they called it praying. But praying was strictly banned by Kimo—he said it was dangerous to believe that just hoping for something would make it happen. He said that people had to work for things, not wish them.

Our Kitchen tried to convince the others that we should all build a boat to get off the island. Our Kitchen's Elders—really just Dad and David—insisted that if we stayed on Henderson, we would meet the same fate as the ancient Polynesians, because we didn't have what David called a critical mass; what he meant was that our population had to grow if we were to survive, but Henderson Island would never be able to support more than a hundred people. So at the very least, they thought we should find a way back and forth to Pitcairn, which we knew had many things we needed. If we could just get there, they argued, we'd be able to use Pitcairn's resources to build a real boat and maybe then sail to a larger island. David and Dad believed there might still be land out there that was livable and that we ought to try to get there.

But even if our Kitchen could have convinced the others, it would have been almost impossible to get to Pitcairn. When I was fourteen, Dad helped us build three tiny outrigger canoes based on what he'd learned from Josh. They were fine for one person paddling in the protected lagoon or even venturing beyond the reef when it was particularly calm, but in the open ocean they would have been a joke. They were toys, nothing more. Henderson just didn't have any trees big enough to dig out a real boat, and we didn't have tools to cut logs into boards from which you could make a boat.

Even with a boat, there would be the navigation problem. The compass and watch on *Jenny* had been lost along with everything else when Mom and Dad were washed onto Shipwreck Rock. David spent a lot of time studying the stars, sun, and moon, determined to create something we could use to keep track of the time and date, as well as our exact location on the earth. He built a large sundial on a platform of concrete, with all sorts of carefully placed sticks and stones that cast complex shadows that only he understood. None of us dared touch it. Even Kimo left it alone out of respect. David tried many times to explain how it worked and what all the markers meant, but I just pretended to be interested.

Dad always said that it was easy to figure out where you are when you're in the same place for seventeen years, but quite another to navigate at sea without a map or compass in search of a speck of land the size of Pitcairn. He insisted it was a reckless proposition at best. Although it'd be possible in clear weather to see Pitcairn once you got within twenty miles or so, on a cloudy day, you'd likely sail on past without a glimpse. Mom and Dad were not disillusioned by their luck in finding Pitcairn, even with a compass; without a compass, they knew such an attempt would be akin to suicide.

In the end, though, all that really mattered was what Kimo's Kitchen thought, and that meant what Kimo himself thought. He vehemently argued that the odds of safely getting to another island and back were very low, and said we simply couldn't take the risk. Our population was small, he argued, and to needlessly lose people in reckless endeavors would make our long-term survival impossible—the only hope for humankind was for us to stay on Henderson and work together. So while he agreed that getting to Pitcairn was important, he said it would require us to take risks we simply couldn't yet afford. His solution, then, was to wait until we had safely grown our population to a point where we could afford the loss. Although his logic felt kind of cold, it seemed to make sense.

When times were good, our gatherings were great. When times were hard, we fought. If, for example, we were going through a dry spell, David or Dad might argue that our water supply would never hold up as our population grew, so we had to figure out how to get off the island. Kimo argued that we would have to ration water so we could support more people with what we had. Wayne, and after he disappeared, Don, would argue that as our population grew, somehow there would be more water—God will provide, they always said, and they were right: the water did always come back.

What divided the Kitchens the most by the time I was seventeen, though, was our dwindling raw material for making tools. Our supply of tool rock was all but exhausted. A few years earlier, Kimo had moved all the remaining pieces into his hut so he could ration it out. After that, it was a rare occasion when he'd offer a new chunk, and each ration seemed to become smaller and smaller.

David, trying to take the matter into his own hands, became obsessed with trying to find metal on the island. He told us about all the things we could do with metal, aside from making tools. But he never found any, so we remained a "Stone Age society," as the Elders always put it. Over the years he did manage to make a reasonably transparent glass, it was sharp, but it broke much too easily to be used for tools. We really had no solutions. And when we expressed our concern to Kimo, he simply said, "For now there's enough, and that's all that matters. We just need to conserve."

I never understood just what Kimo held against me, but he seemed to look for opportunities to torment me as I was growing up. By the time I was seventeen, though, I pretty much knew his limits and was able to avoid confrontation. I also knew enough to stay well away when he was in one of his bad moods. But even then, he continued to find excuses to put bamboo to my backside or put me in isolation.

Isolation was Kimo's practice of punishing someone by locking them up in the bunker for a day or so. In isolation, you were in complete and utter darkness, with no food, water, clothes, shoes, or any civilized way to relieve yourself. And because there was virtually no air exchange with the outside, it soon became hard to even breathe. By the time I was introduced to isolation, Kimo had modified the bunker for the sole purpose of making it more uncomfortable: he'd covered the floor with a mixture of our island-made cement and pieces of David's glass, making it impossible to sit or lie down. There were only a few places you could stand without cutting your feet. Kimo argued that this "improvement" allowed him to dole out short sentences and still make people want to obey. I can certainly agree with that. Even a half-day in the bunker was an unbearable experience.

I went to isolation more often by far than anybody: six times in all. I also received the record sentence of two days, which I earned by arriving for work at the farm at a time that Kimo perceived as late. Obviously, I had been sentenced by "the bad Kimo." I wonder if I would have even made it had Mom not snuck me some oranges and bread in the middle of the night. We both knew what she was risking—we didn't know exactly what Kimo would do, but it certainly wouldn't be pleasant. I think he'd actually forgotten that Mom knew the numbers that opened the lock, and of course, Mom wanted to keep it that way.

To be fair to Kimo, I was the only one who ever received such arbitrary justice. Most of us had never even been inside the bunker. It was more of a threat than a punishment. So just maybe, at least in part, the problem was with me. My relationship with Kimo had never recovered from the whipping just over ten years earlier. I feared him, hated him, and in a very strange way, worshipped him.

Chapter 24

TEIKI STARTED IT. HE was always looking for opportunities to taunt me, because he knew I would back off rather than risk Kimo's wrath. It was my seventeenth birthday, and I had gone fishing at the Point in the early morning, and had managed to wrestle a huge tuna unto the rocks by myself. It was the best catch of my life, and I was convinced it was a good omen. Determined to get the monster back to our Kitchen myself, I'd pierced its gills with a stick and slung the fish onto my back, resting the stick on my right shoulder so that its weight was shared by my back and shoulders. It was on the way back when I ran into Teiki. He was coming from the opposite direction, and we met right where the trail from the village splits, one path leading to the east beach, the other back to the Point.

"What's that?" Teiki asked, trying to hide his admiration.

"Tuna. Beautiful, isn't it?" I tried my best to sound friendly, but I had a bad feeling trouble was on its way.

"What're you going to do with it?"

"Take it back to our Kitchen. Maybe dry some for later in the week."

"No, it's too big for just your Kitchen. I'll take it for Thursday's gathering."

I glared at him. It was Monday—it would be rotten by the time the next gathering came around. My answer should have prompted no argument, and I suppose it didn't. Instead, he reached out and grabbed the stick. I didn't let go, but somehow he knocked the fish onto the ground. I looked down and saw it covered in sand. I was infuriated. I'd been so proud of having brought in the huge fish alone and was looking forward to showing it off to Mom, Dad and the rest of our Kitchen.

I refused to yield to Teiki as I should have, and as he certainly expected I would—it was simply accepted that Teiki was second in command on the island, his orders enforced by Kimo himself. "Leave it alone," I said. "It's mine. Catch your own fish. There are plenty more out there." I kneeled and started to wrestle the fish onto my back again.

"I order you to give it up for the gathering *now*! If you don't, you'll go in the bunker." Teiki had just recently started to ask for things by saying "I order you." He was probably just trying to test whether he really could give orders, but even Kimo didn't give commands so directly.

"No way!" I told him. "You know the fish will rot before Thursday. You want it? Just try to take it! You and Kimo don't own the ocean, and I'm sick of your orders."

Just as I started back on the path, I saw Kimo walking toward us from the east beach trail, well within earshot. He jogged up to us, squarely blocking the path back to the village.

Teiki was quick to his side. "Dad! Adam stole my fish. I was bringing it back for Thursday's gathering, and he's trying to take it away for his own Kitchen."

Kimo studied Teiki suspiciously. As unlikely as it was that either of us had caught such a magnificent fish, I'm sure Kimo realized how much more unlikely it was that Teiki had; Teiki virtually never went fishing. And what's more, Kimo knew that saving the fish until Thursday was ludicrous. But a quick look at him told me that none of this mattered. Perhaps, if Kimo had been in one of his more rational moods, he could have found a way to salvage Teiki's lie, but this time, it was clear that "the bad Kimo" was blocking my way. I knew this just wasn't going to end well. So knowing I wouldn't get far by rationalizing, I stupidly decided to ignore him. I veered off the path in an attempt to get around him and get back to the village.

"Don't turn your back on us, kid!" Kimo shouted. As I walked away, he grabbed the stick from behind me and tore it off my shoulder, inadvertently spinning me around. I backed away a few steps. "How dare you steal from Teiki! I promise you one thing: you'll never steal or talk to him like that again."

I stared at them with the most sullen, rebellious expression I could contrive, but Teiki was relentless. "I told him he'd go to the bunker for this, and he just laughed at me." Kimo's eyes burned into mine. Somehow I knew this time was different. This time, there would be no isolation. His words from so many years ago, "You don't belong here," suddenly came back to me in full force.

As if reading my mind, he said, "No, not this time. This time, we end it. Both of you come with me." He gestured south down the east beach trail, indicating we should walk in front of him. I knew that was a bad sign. I didn't know what he had in mind for me, but the path he was signaling us toward was the least traveled one on the island, leading away from both the village and the bunker. Imagining the worst, I again defied him, backing up toward the Point instead of following his direction. At that, Kimo pulled out his knife and pointed it down the east beach path. "Last chance. That way. Let's go."

Kimo rarely pulled out his knife, let alone waved it in such a threatening way. Just resting his hand on its hilt was always enough to silence any activity he didn't approve of. I turned my back on him and ran, not even thinking about where I was going. Since he was blocking the path back to the village and had insisted I go down the east beach trail, I instinctively darted down the only remaining path: the one leading back to the Point. I often wonder now if he had planned that all along; if he had reasoned that by ordering me down the east beach trail, he'd get me to run to the Point, where he really wanted me.

Regardless, I knew that if he got hold of me, I'd learn more about his knife than I ever wanted to. So my only hope was to stay out of his reach. I knew the island as well as Kimo, maybe better, since mine was a child's knowledge of every nook, rock, and cranny. I was faster on my feet than he was too. But if he caught me, I'd be no match for him in a fight, with or without his infamous knife.

As I ran, I heard Kimo behind me. "Teiki, leave the damn fish. Follow me."

I turned my head and saw them both following me, Kimo keeping pace, but Teiki staying well back, as if he knew something terrible was about to happen that he did not want to be part of. I was nearly halfway down the ridge when I realized my error: I was running down a funnel, trapped on both sides by cliffs and violent surf. I glanced behind me to see if there was a way to turn around and get past Kimo back to the main island, but there wasn't: the Point is narrow and has only one trail. Kimo also knew I had no escape, so he slowed his pace to a casual, deliberate walk. With no where to go, I slowed as well, keeping just a few yards in front of Kimo's knife, thus delaying my inevitable arrival at the end of the Point.

There was only one place to enter the water safely from the ridge that stretched out to the Point, and even then, you had to take great care, jumping as far out as you could from the cliff edge into exactly the right spot. It's where my dad dove off to swim out to Mother on the boat—he was the first to actually brave the jump, earning it the name Stan's Leap. Stan's Leap was a slightly overhanging ledge, about twenty-five yards short of the very tip of the Point, and the entry was off to the northwest side of the ridge. Though it was an overhang, the rocks littering the water below extended far enough away from shore to required one to jump quite some distance out. As children, leaping off that spot was like a right of passage. We weren't allowed to do it, but we did anyway. So, fortunately, I knew the spot well. Although I also knew a slight error would lead to certain death.

I had just jogged past Stan's Leap when I realized it was my only chance of escape. All that lay ahead was a dead end, and Kimo and his knife would soon have me pinned against the unforgiving tip of the Point. I immediately spun around and darted back, directly toward Kimo, and the Leap, hoping to get there before him. Quickly realizing my intent, Kimo sped up and lunged forward to intercept me.

He arrived at the Leap just before me. Without even looking, I dove, head first, as far out as I could, knowing I wasn't yet at the right spot.

Right away, I was able to see that I had been lucky—I would enter the water well clear of the rocks. The adrenaline of entering the water, face first, from such a height blinded my senses, but as soon as I surfaced, I felt a sharp pain in my left hip. Apparently Kimo's knife had managed to reach me just as I had dove.

I didn't know how deep the cut was, but I could still swim. Eventually, the blood would attract sharks, but I had more immediate problems. I considered my options: I was a strong swimmer and could easily get back though the north channel, but Kimo would expect that—where else could I go? I looked the other direction, towards the Point. The surf was so high and the cliffs so steep that there was no conceivable way to get out of the water there. So my choices were to stay put and drown, or perhaps become shark food, or swim toward the north beach channel where Kimo would be waiting for me, probably just inside the reef, knife at the ready. And with Kimo having already drawn blood, there was no doubt about his intentions. I treaded water, looking up at Kimo and Teiki, slowly drifting with the current toward the north channel.

Finally deciding on a course of action, I started to slowly swim to the north beach channel, intentionally dragging my left leg. Kimo and Teiki could probably see the blood in the water but had no way to know the cut wasn't disabling. As I'd hoped, Kimo turned and walked back from the Point, heading, I'm sure, to the north beach to meet me. He knew exactly where I was going. There was no need to hurry, the outcome was inevitable.

As soon as his back was turned to me, I changed course and began swimming as hard as I could, directly into the current toward the Point. Though the waves were high, the current was weaker than usual. I didn't know how long I could maintain the pace, but I was making progress into the current. If I could make it back to the Point, then perhaps I could swim around to the east beach side. I didn't dare slow down even to look and see whether Kimo had been fooled. Regardless of whether he'd seen me, I had no other options.

Once past the tip of the Point, I turned toward the east beach channel, hugging the reef as closely as I dared. The current weakened considerably on the other side of the Point, giving me hope for the first time that I'd get through the channel before utter exhaustion took over. Just as I entered the channel, I heard Teiki shouting. I stopped and treaded water, listening. Teiki was warning Kimo that I had changed direction. Now, I'd have to beat him there. So, as hard as I had been swimming before, I somehow managed to go yet faster.

Finally, I made it through the east beach channel into the quiet waters of the lagoon. In water up to my hips, I put my feet down and staggered toward the beach, completely spent. I could only hope that I'd have enough time to find a place to hide and rest for a few minutes before Kimo got there. By the time the water was down to my knees, however, I saw Kimo running along the east beach trail toward me, with Teiki far behind. There was no escape now. I could hardly stand up, let alone run, so I slowly continued to shore. As I finally stepped onto dry sand, Kimo was waiting, knife in hand. Somehow I had to stall him and gain a few minutes to rest. So, doubled over, hands on my knees, I tried to speak between gasps. "So ... is this ... how Bob ... disappeared?"

He stopped. "You never knew Bob. You don't know anything about him or what happened."

"I know what I hear... and I hear he disappeared not long after Erik died. ... Everybody thinks you killed him."

"If you really want to know, then yes, it was my job to take care of the problem. He killed Erik and would certainly have killed again. There was no way to tolerate somebody like that on the island, so someone had to solve the problem. What, you think it's easy to do my job? You think I wanted to kill him?"

"I didn't say it's easy ... I just asked—"

"Everybody wants me to make decisions for them, solve their problems, and maintain order, except when it interferes with what they want. Everybody wanted Bob gone, but nobody had the balls to do anything about it. They wanted it to happen by magic somehow, so they could just pretend it had nothing to do with them. So it was my job, and I did it. Well, they got what they wanted in the end. Poof! Gone! Nice and clean, like he never existed. Christ, they never even asked about it. They didn't want to know."

"But you had no right to make that decision by yourself. And what about Wayne? You make him disappear too?"

"Wayne was of no value to the island. He didn't work—thought God would do his work. He and Allison were too old to have more children, and he was disruptive, too. He was leading people against me with all his Jesus talk. It was bad enough when he kept his shit-talk in his own Kitchen, but when he started to talk to Teiki about … Why am I telling you these things? I don't have to defend myself to you, or anybody else for that matter. I did what I had to do." He took a step towards me.

"But you always say how important it is that our population grows and we all stay together."

He stopped again. "We need a growing *productive* population, not useless people that just consume our food and water or kill off other people."

"So why me? You afraid I'll kill somebody?"

"As a matter of fact, yes, I think you will. Teiki. Eventually. The two of you won't be able to survive on this island together. Ultimately, it will have to be one or the other. I've tried to get you to understand that there needs to be a leader—one leader—but you just never get it. And Teiki should have been the first, the oldest. Jenny had no right to come here when she was pregnant. Eventually, I won't be able to …" He seemed uncertain how to finish, but his thinking was interrupted by a noise behind him, somebody slipping on a rock. We both looked to find Teiki approaching us, somewhat hesitant. Then Kimo turned back around and lunged at me.

I was ready—the short conversation had given me enough rest to be able to jump back from his thrust. I turned and ran south along the beach, Kimo following at a slow jog. At first, I easily increased the distance between us, but I was tiring quickly. After a couple of minutes, I realized that, again, Kimo's experience was getting the best of me. Running in the sand was laborious, and he'd been smart enough to move slowly and conserve his energy. He knew I wouldn't be able to keep up the pace I had set. I, too, slowed to a jog, staying just out of his reach, about twenty yards in front.

As we continued our half-paced chase, Kimo called out to me. "Okay, here's my deal. This is between you and me. If you stay on the beach, we keep it that way. We'll have a fair fight, without the knife. But if you head back to the farm or the village, it'll be more than just you and me. I'll make it between me and your family."

I didn't answer. I needed to save what little precious energy I had left. Besides, it wasn't exactly a fair deal—maybe if he really did throw the knife aside, gave me time to rest, and tied both his hands behind his back, it would be an even fight—but even then, I'd probably still lose. The steadiness in his voice told me he had far more energy left than I did; in addition to being exhausted from the swim and the run, the cut on my hip was still bleeding. It hadn't cut into my muscle, but I had left a lot of blood back in the ocean and on the beach. My one advantage should have been my youth and endurance, but right now even that seemed to be on his side.

After about a mile, I began to feel dizzy and knew I couldn't keep pace any longer. So I suddenly darted away from the ocean toward the cliffs, and ran to a spot I recognized from years of exploring the island as a child. Of course, there was no place I hadn't explored, but this particular spot was a favorite. I loved to climb up the cliff right in this spot because, while it seemed impossibly steep, there was a series of solid, well-placed handholds that made the climb easy. If Kimo didn't know the holds, which was likely, it would buy me time. He'd either have to study the rock as he climbed, or find a different way up. As we approached the cliff, Kimo accelerated to a sprint. I used my last burst of energy to stay ahead of him until I could leap onto the cliff.

Just as I bounded up to the first handhold, Kimo reached for my heels, missing by inches. He didn't try to follow. I suppose he assumed I'd reach a dead end or that I'd just dangle a few moments before tumbling back into his clutches. But after watching me climb nearly a third of the way to the top, he must have realized his error. He began scanning the cliff for another way up to the east beach trail that skirted the cliff. Of course there were none, so he started up the same route I had taken. I had no doubt that he could make it to the top, but he'd have to spend a few precious minutes to find the holds that I knew by memory.

I arrived at the top of the cliff and stumbled south along the east beach trail. After just a dozen steps, however, I realized how futile it was, even with the lead I'd built. There was nowhere to go. I was injured, exhausted, and alone, and Kimo had my family as hostages. Only two things were certain now: soon, Kimo and I were going to face off, and right now, I had the advantage over him—and in all likelihood, I never would again.

I walked back to where Kimo would soon arrive at the top, all the while, my anger growing at the words that had haunted me for so long. How could I "not belong" on my own island? It was like telling me I shouldn't be alive. I knew what I needed to do. I bent down, as if in a trance, and picked up a large, jagged rock, and perched myself on an overhanging shelf where I could watch him finish his climb.

He was a couple of yards from the top and feeling for the last handhold he would need to haul himself to the top. As he extended his arm and probed for the hold, I watched, utterly devoid of thought and feeling. Then as his hand found it, he looked up at me, and I dropped the rock onto his head. He twisted, managing to avert the blow, but lost his balance, somersaulting down the thirty-foot cliff. Although I knew there'd be no way to survive the fall, it wasn't until I saw Kimo's head rebound off a protrusion near the bottom that it dawned on me: it was over.

It's terrible to admit, but I actually raised my fist in triumph. A wave of accomplishment and pride passed over me. It was more than just relief from escaping death, too: I was celebrating victory over my archenemy, a victory punctuated by gruesome death.

But after basking in my triumph for a few seconds, it occurred to me this might be too good to be true. He might not be dead. This was, after all, Kimo. I stared down at him, watching for movement, thinking how impossible it seemed that Kimo could be actually be dead but imagining, if he were, how much our lives would change. I headed down the east shore trail to another, easier path down to the beach. Once on the sand again, I cautiously walked to Kimo's body, having, by now, convinced myself that it would be gone when I got there. Relief flooded over me as I mounted a small sand dune and saw his mangled figure among the rocks.

Next to his body lay his knife, still in its sheath but torn away from his side during the fall. I had so often thought of all the things I could do with it. So many times, I eyed that blade in envy, knowing I would never be allowed to touch it. Now, it would be mine. Hungry for its feel, I reached down and pulled the knife from its sheath.

My heart raced as I held the shiny blade in my hand, surprised at how heavy it was compared to our stone knives. I ran my finger down the blade. It was the first time I had touched metal, and I was astonished by its cold, smooth surface. Finally, I picked up the belt and sheath. As I tied it around my waist, I couldn't wait to get back and tell everybody. I was a hero.

Chapter 25

HAVING CLIMBED BACK UP to the east beach trail and now heading toward the village, my leg began to throb. After limping along about a quarter mile, I noticed Teiki down below, walking south along the beach, unaware of the shocking scene he'd soon discover. I opened my mouth to shout, but caught myself—I had no idea what to say. Sometimes emotions are like waves: those that lift you to greatest heights, drop you into the deepest troughs. My wave had crested, and I was starting to feel a slow, steady decent as I watched Teiki. His walk was unsteady and his pace faltering. I sensed that he regretted our confrontation and wished Kimo hadn't involved himself. He undoubtedly expected to encounter a gruesome scene ahead, but surely not to learn that his father and protector was dead.

More somber now, I turned away and continued to the village. When I got there, it was nearly lunchtime, each Kitchen crowded with people. I walked along the beach, around Kimo's and Don's Kitchens, so I could tell my own Kitchen the news first. As I arrived, Mom and Dad were both preparing food. When they looked at me, their faces flushed with shock and panic.

Mom ran toward me. "What happened?"

"What? It's nothing. Just a cut." I was confused. I had often come home with cuts and injuries. Why, just now, would a little blood cause such a panic?

"Not the cut—the knife!" Dad said. "Where'd you get that? Where's Kimo?"

I had forgotten that I was wearing Kimo's knife. But now that they'd noticed it, it was time to claim my moment. I stood up straight, puffed out my chest, and told them. "Dead," I said. "He's dead."

"Where? How?" asked Mom.

"He's on the east beach, about halfway down the beach. He fell down the cliff." Then realizing how unconvincing that must have sounded, I added, with a burst of pride, "I killed him."

Mom grabbed me by the arms. "Oh my God! How did it happen?" Then she turned to look at my sister Tia, who was walking over to see what had happened. "Tia, not now!" Mom yelled. Tia looked confused but obediently wandered away.

We sat down and I explained the day's events as accurately as I could. When I finished, Mom and Dad were completely silent—hardly the reaction I expected.

"We've got to tell the other Kitchens," Dad said. "Give me the knife. We'll hide it under that for now." He looked worried and somber as he pointed to a large rock nearby.

"Take off the knife?" I said. "Why? It's mine now."

"Adam! Take it off now!" he said.

Not used to such urgency in his voice, I reluctantly did what he asked.

Dad looked at Mom. "We have to talk to the others."

Mom stood frozen for a moment, as if she hadn't heard us. Then she looked up and said she'd come along right behind us—she needed to check on Tia first.

As Dad and I approached the Center, blood still running down my leg, everyone was quick to gather around. But before either of us could say a word, Teiki ran in, pointing at me. "He murdered my father!"

Suddenly, I could feel all eyes on me. "He was trying to kill me!" I retorted. "He attacked me with his knife. See?" But as I gestured toward my wounded leg, I realized how crazy it must have sounded—Kimo attacked me with a knife, and *I* killed *him*? Not likely. I needed to tell the story from the beginning, but Teiki hadn't given me the chance. Instead, I'd been forced into the defensive.

"Bullshit! Dad and I caught a tuna at the Point this morning. Just as we were bringing it in, Adam hit him with a rock from behind. Dad fell onto the rocks and then Adam took our tuna. I climbed down to see if I could save him, but by the time I got down, the waves had swept his body away." He pointed at me again. "You just plain murdered him!"

"What a liar! Kimo fell down a cliff onto the east beach, not off the Point. Why don't you tell the truth? He was trying to kill me, and you were egging him on." Amazed at the boldness of his lie, I had unwittingly changed my story from having killed him in self-defense to him falling down a cliff.

"Then how do you explain the fish back there? Are you telling us you caught it fishing from the east beach? A tuna inside the lagoon?"

"No, I caught it at the Point. But Kimo chased me down the east beach." As I spoke, I realized it must have sounded as though I was making my story up as I went.

Stefani began to wail. For the second time, she had lost her mate to violence in a series of events that was murky at best.

Michelle immediately started walking toward Stefani, but stopped when she was passing in front of me, her forehead in a frown. "Adam, try to show a little sensitivity. His father and her husband is dead. This isn't the time to argue about who's to blame."

Of course she was right, but I couldn't stop pressing. "Well, anybody who wants to know the truth, come with me. I'll show you his body."

Everybody just glared at me. I turned away in anger and ran to our Kitchen, with Mom and Dad close at my heels.

Back at the Kitchen, Dad tried to explain, even though I wasn't listening. "Don't you see? It doesn't matter what happened. Kimo's gone. That's all that matters. Like him or not, he was their leader—our leader. Life will be different now and people are afraid. Right now it's not a matter of what the truth is, or exactly what happened, but coping with…" He hesitated, fumbling for how to continue. He shifted his look toward Mom and shook his head gravely. "Can you even imagine how things are going to have to change?"

Dad's argument only infuriated me. Was I supposed to just let Kimo kill me? I wanted to go to the beach, where I could be by myself for a while, but wanted to take my knife with me. I went over to the rock where Dad had hidden it and lifted it up. The knife was gone. I looked at Dad, but his expression indicated he was just as surprised by its absence as I was. Now, I was convinced the whole world was against me—even my own Kitchen. I just had to get away. I ran down the north beach and hid in Lone Frigate Cave for the rest of the day, staring off at the horizon, yearning to know whether there really was another world somewhere out there.

Chapter 26

Dad was already outside the next morning when I exited the hut I shared with Tia. He looked serious.

"Good morning, Adam."

"Is it? Have they come to their senses yet?" I was still in a very sour mood.

He gave a deep sigh. "Look, Adam, it's not so simple. Don, Russ, and I walked the entire way down the east beach yesterday afternoon. There's nothing there."

"What do you mean nothing there? You didn't find Kimo?"

"Trust me, he's not there. Are you sure he was dead?"

"He was dead. Teiki must have moved him. You must have at least found his blood on the rocks. It was pretty messy."

"Come on, Adam, be serious. How could we have found his blood? We didn't know where to look. Besides, what difference would it make? Teiki would just claim it was your blood—that you set it up to look like Kimo fell. You were bleeding pretty badly, remember."

"What about my fish?"

"Teiki brought each of the Kitchens large tuna steaks yesterday afternoon. He said we might as well enjoy the fish he and Kimo caught. It was a tuna, wasn't it?"

"It was a *huge* tuna, Dad, you should've seen it." My pride dissolved quickly into incredulity. "You mean they really believe Teiki's story?"

"Look, what I've been trying to explain is that right now nobody cares who's right. There is no *right*. They know you killed their leader; it doesn't matter *why*. Maybe it will later, but right now, they're just frightened. They've been led—we've all been led—by Kimo for more than fifteen years. Our world's about to change, and in case you haven't noticed, it's a pretty small world we live in—and a world that doesn't see much change. Can you understand that?"

I tried my best to understand, but just couldn't. Change was a good thing, not something to fear. I wanted to confront everybody and force them to understand. At the same time, though, I guess I could understand them a little; to some extent, I was afraid too. A world without Kimo was a world I had never known.

"I sort of understand being afraid about that," I said, "but it's still not right. What do you expect me to have done, just let him kill me?"

"No, of course not. Just try to understand, that's all. We're with you. The entire Kitchen is. I hope you know that." He looked at me, but I didn't reply. "C'mon then, let's go to the Center and try to make peace. If people ask, please, just stay calm. *Slowly* explain what happened, but don't lash out at Teiki. It won't help. Show remorse and even pity for Teiki. And for Stefani too, okay?"

Mom, Dad, and I wandered over to the Center with David and Claire, trying to show unity. Both Kimo's and Don's Kitchens were there, huddled in separate groups, as if they were expecting us. Any hope we'd had of a quiet entry was lost when Teiki emerged from the crowd.

"So my dad's murderer is back. Got some more stories for us this morning?" He turned and faced the others. "So. What are you going to do about him?"

They looked around at one another. Then finally, Stefani stepped forward. "Come on, you can't pretend this didn't happen. He didn't murder just my husband, but the chief of the island—your leader. Kimo was part of all of you, and his murderer is standing right in front of you. If you let him get away with this, then who's next?"

Her appeal met a pregnant silence. I imagine it was a virtual replay of the aftermath of Erik's death some seventeen years ago. Resolution, however, required a leader—someone to come forward and take control—the lack of which confirmed Kimo's absence more than ever.

Finally, Teiki responded. "If nobody else wants to settle this, I will."

I wasn't afraid of Teiki. Perhaps I should have been, I don't know. I was a year older, but we were about the same size. I was probably faster and fitter, but Kimo had been diligently training Teiki how to fight, both by hand and with a spear. I had often watched their lessons from a distance, trying to learn what I could, but there's no question Teiki was better trained. Training doesn't tip the scales of a flat-out brawl, however, and that's what the next few seconds were. As he started toward me, I likewise ran forward, and we grappled each other to the ground. I was so blinded by fury, I don't even remember who yanked me out of the fray, but we were both pulled away so quickly that no damage was done. Now restrained, we stared at each other, eyes locked in rage, until Dad grabbed me and steered me back to our Kitchen.

"This isn't over!" I heard Teiki shout after me. "Don't think for a second it's over."

Chapter 27

THINGS WERE HORRIBLE AFTER that. We all shared the food from the farm and the fresh water spring, but the Kitchens wouldn't even speak to one another—it was as if we lived on different islands, unable to see one another, let alone interact. Dad called it a "cold war."

Convinced that Kimo's Kitchen would seek retribution, we kept a guard throughout the nights. I suppose they, in turn, expected us to come after Teiki. And Don's Kitchen just wanted to stay out of the way, as though speaking to either of the other Kitchens would be seen as taking sides.

The worst, though, was that things simply stopped getting done. The garden began to fill with weeds after just a week of neglect. Everybody took what he or she wanted without regard to maintaining the farm's productivity. People were uncomfortable working together, whether on the farm or on other projects. Our gatherings were cancelled through an unspoken agreement. The younger children, no longer allowed to play freely around the island, were constantly herded back into the protection of their own Kitchens.

I began to feel a frustration that was probably akin to what Kimo must have felt so often. Didn't they know what was going on? How could they just sit around and watch the island go to hell like this? Couldn't they see for themselves what needed to be done? We needed to work together! I actually began to wonder whether a world without Kimo might be worse than one with him.

A few times, somebody would step forward and try to make peace. Dad tried twice, once to get everybody to come to a Thursday gathering and once to get people to spend time weeding and reseeding the garden.

Nobody raised an objection; they just ignored his proposals. There seemed a pervading fear that if they did what Dad asked, somehow, it would acknowledge him as the new leader or us as the lead Kitchen. Mom tried to encourage others in more subtle ways, but that too was hopeless. There was no malicious intent behind the chaos, and I'm sure we all hoped it would stop, yet it persevered in the face of reason.

This was the mood leading up to lunchtime two weeks later, when we noticed Tia was missing.

"Food's ready, where's Tia?" asked Mom.

"I don't know. I haven't seen her since early morning," replied Dad.

"I specifically told her not to leave the Kitchen alone. Adam, could you go find her?"

"Sure, Mom."

I headed out to the farm, figuring she probably went to get something for our lunch. I shouted her name as I went, waiting a few seconds between calls to listen for a response. As I walked past the bunker, I heard a rustling sound. I thought it might have been a pig or a rat in the bushes, so I ignored it and kept walking. But then I heard the noise again. Now curious, I crept closer to take a look.

It was then that I noticed that the lock on the bunker door was missing. In its place was a stick pushed through the hasp, keeping the door closed. I stopped and studied it for a good minute or so. I had never seen the bunker without Kimo's lock. Why on earth would it be unlocked now? Only Mom and maybe Teiki knew how to open it. I looked around, and then crept toward the heavy concrete door. I was suspicious that it was some kind of trick, but was too fascinated to stay away. When I got to the door, I called as loudly as I could. "Anybody there? Tia?"

There was no answer, but of course I didn't expect one. It made no sense that she would be in there, and even if she were, the bunker was virtually soundproof. I reached out for the hasp, my pulse racing, and ran my fingers over its cold, smooth surface. Then I pulled the stick out and slowly opened the door. I half expected Kimo to appear and scream an objection. What I was doing would have been unthinkable just a few days ago. It may seem strange that this simple act of opening the door could have been such an emotional threshold, but the bunker was the ultimate taboo. Aside from Kimo's knife, it was the only proof that there really was a world beyond ours.

With the door fully open, I called into the darkness. "Tia?"

I heard a weak voice. "Adam?" I couldn't see her from where I was standing, and I knew from experience she couldn't walk out. She would be blinded by the light and in pain from standing on the sharp floor for so long. I stepped inside, and as my eyes adjusted to the shadows, I saw her standing naked in a back corner. Furious, I stepped in to pick her up and carry her home.

Just as I reached her, the door slammed shut, and we were immersed in darkness. Suddenly the whole set-up became clear. Tia had been the bait, and I the fish—and I had a pretty good idea who it was doing the fishing. Instantly, my anger transformed into guilt. Poor Tia had spent most of the morning in the stifling, uncomfortable bunker, forced to suffer because of my personal war with Teiki.

I set my pareo down on the sharp floor, which allowed Tia to sit down.

"What happened, Tia?"

Through her sobs, she replied, "I was walking along the beach. I didn't go far from our Kitchen, really."

"Don't worry about that, just tell me what happened."

"I was on the beach, and he just grabbed me. He picked me up and ran off with his hand over my mouth so I couldn't yell. I tried—"

"Who grabbed you, Tia? Who was it?" Of course I knew, but I needed to hear it anyway.

"Teiki. I tried to get away, but he was really rough with me. I could hardly breathe, he was squeezing me so tight. He carried me here and pushed me in. It really hurt."

"What hurt?"

"My shoulder mostly, from where I fell. I think it's bleeding. Can you get us out of here? I hate this place. I can't breathe in here."

I took a while to answer, not wanting to admit my helplessness. It was heartbreaking to know she was suffering. "I'll try. Just rest for now, Tia. Stay quiet and rest." That, I knew, was the secret to surviving in the bunker, and there was no way to know how long we'd be there.

I tried to puzzle through what had happened. Obviously Teiki had planned things carefully. He must have known the numbers to Kimo's lock, which wasn't really surprising. He forced Tia into the bunker and closed it with a stick, figuring the stick would attract my attention. Teiki was probably waiting nearby, knowing that eventually I'd head to the farm looking for her. When I walked by, not noticing the missing lock, he tossed a stone into the bushes near the bunker door just to get me to look—that was the noise I'd heard. Once I noticed the stick, he needed only to wait until my curiosity got the best of me, as he knew it would. The real question was what he intended to do from here. Did he really mean to let us suffocate in here? Was he really that cruel? Perhaps, if it was just me, but both of us? He was arrogant and mean, and certainly hurt, but not cruel.

I had no idea how bad the air would get with two people inside, but I knew it was going to get difficult quickly. We could shout for help, but nobody would hear us and we would just use the air more quickly. All we could do was hope that somebody would figure out where we were. Maybe if they knew we were here, they could force Teiki into opening it. Then I remembered that Mom knew how to open the lock. That gave me hope, but still, it would be a long time before they'd think to look for us in the bunker. I suppose I should have asked Mom to take the lock off the bunker as soon as Kimo was dead, but I didn't think of it.

I settled in for a long wait, adjusting to the silence. One of the most disconcerting things about being in the bunker was the absolute quiet. You couldn't even hear the ocean when you were inside. There was no other place on Henderson Island where you could go and not hear the sounds of the ocean. The first time Kimo sentenced me to isolation, the silence drove me to near panic. I had never experienced quiet before. When I tried to explain it to the other Youngers, they couldn't even grasp what I was talking about.

About an hour later, while Tia slept on my folded pareo, I felt my way over to the door. I really don't know what made me do it, but I leaned into it with all my weight, more out of frustration than anything. It swung open, offering no resistance. I stood in the bright light, wondering why Teiki had left it unlocked. Or maybe it hadn't been unlocked the whole time; maybe Teiki had silently unlocked it later for some unknown reason; maybe he felt guilty. But there'd be time for solving puzzles later. I picked up Tia and carried her home.

Nobody was at our Kitchen when I arrived. They were probably all out looking for Tia, and now, maybe for me too. I laid Tia on her bed, and headed straight for Kimo's Kitchen, determined to have it out with Teiki once and for all.

As it turns out, I didn't have to go to Kimo's Kitchen to find Teiki, he was waiting for me in the Center. Of course, I should have been more suspicious—he was just standing there with a wide, mischievous grin—but I was too consumed by rage to stop and think. Several of the others were there too, including Mom and Dad. They surely saw us, and must have suspected that some kind of game was afoot, but they were all preoccupied forming a search party for Tia.

As I approached Teiki, he turned his back to me and started to run off to the east beach. I took chase. Within a minute he got to the trail branching left toward the Point and without hesitation headed that way. He was making exactly the same mistake I had with Kimo a couple of weeks ago—running into a trap. I chased him down the ridge of the Point, right past Stan's Leap without any thought about what I'd do when I had him. As he reached the well-worn ground at the tip of the Point, he reached down, grabbed a fishing spear, and spun around to face me. I stopped short, just managing to avoid impaling myself, then jumped back just in time to avoid Teiki's jab. I was lucky. He would have speared me with the first strike had I moved a split second later.

Again, I had been manipulated. That's why the bunker wasn't locked! All he'd really wanted to do was to goad me into coming after him on his own terms—at a time and place of his choosing and, of course, in plain site of witnesses. The spear, of course, had been carefully planted there, waiting for our arrival. Now, while defending himself from what everybody would see as an irrational and unprovoked attack by me, he'd kill me. He'd claim it was self-defense—just as I had claimed when I killed Kimo.

Did he really think he could get away with this? It seemed crazy, but maybe it wasn't: if he were the only one to return from the Point alive, his would be the only story told. Besides, by now I knew the island had much less interest in truth than in avoiding conflict. Okay, I suppose there'd be Tia's story, but that would just sound like the crazy story of a ten-year-old; it would never hold up against Teiki's word and what they had witnessed themselves. In the few seconds I had to think things through, I marveled at his ingenuity.

Teiki advanced on me steadily and with surprising care, driving me backward with jabs of his spear. I could outrun him, but the time it would take me to turn around would be all he needed to ram the spear home—I'd never make the first step. My only hope was to keep my eyes focused on the point of the spear and rely on my reflexes to jump back in front of his jabs. I backed down the narrow ridge, away from the Point. Teiki kept pace but seemed afraid to close the gap between us.

We were replaying the scene from two weeks ago with Teiki taking his dad's place, and like before, there was just one way out: Stan's Leap. My plan took shape. All I'd have to do is back up until I was at the Leap, dart to the side, and dive out as far as I could. I would then swim my way back to safety, this time taking the easy way, right through the north beach channel. I wasn't afraid of Teiki intercepting me in the lagoon. I could take him in the water, with or without a spear. I only had to dodge his jabs another twenty feet, and then I'd be there. I could only hope he wouldn't guess my plan.

But then suddenly the entire scenario made no sense. Why was Teiki being so passive with the spear? If he were really trying to kill me, why didn't he just do it? I might be able to dodge one or two jabs, but really I had no chance against his spear. All he needed to do was charge. Besides, he must have known perfectly well I was about to take my escape dive; he had planned the entire scenario, so he couldn't have forgotten about Stan's Leap. In a moment of clarity, I realized that once again he was manipulating me. For some reason, he wanted me to take that dive.

That was it! He must have rigged the Leap so that it would somehow make the dive fatal—there were dozens of ways to do that. It was brilliant! The story would be that I came after Teiki, and he ran down to the Point to get away. I chased him until he had no choice but to fight. He grabbed a fishing spear that somebody must have accidentally left there. He tried to fend me off but not to kill me, even though, he would argue, he easily could have. Then I dove off Stan's Leap but somehow didn't make it ... I was killed falling onto the rocks or something. He had the perfect revenge for his father's death in plain sight of everybody. He would be completely without blame. I wouldn't know it until later, but Teiki had strung a couple of ropes across the safe diving spot, so that I would certainly have tripped as I dove, stopping my forward momentum and sending me straight down, head first, onto the rocks. After I fell, he'd simply untie the ropes and toss the evidence into the ocean behind me.

I had one advantage now: if I was right, he had no intention of actually hurting me with the spear. I waited until he feigned the final charge that would force me to dive. As he lunged, I quickly turned left and took a step toward the water as if I were going to dive. Teiki fell for my ruse and relaxed his grip on the spear so that he could run to the edge to watch my fall. In that split second of opportunity, I whipped around and, using both hands, grabbed the spear about a foot from its tip. He had the advantage of controlling the safe end of the spear, but I had the leverage.

We wrestled for mere seconds before I changed the direction of my tugging, throwing him off balance. He lost his grip on the spear and was flung closer to the edge. Though he fought to stay upright, it was a hopeless battle with physics. As he fell, he desperately reached out for one of the ropes he'd rigged earlier. And then, I don't know how he found the strength, but he managed to arrest his fall by grabbing onto the ropes. At that point he was stuck, dangling thirty feet over rocks and a surf that was even more ferocious than usual. He was safe, but only as long as he could hold onto the rope, and as long as the rope held—neither was going to last long. I could already see his grip loosening.

I watched him dangle on the rope for half a minute, trying to muscle his way back up. Failing that, he began to swing his legs, to and from the cliff edge, I believe hoping that he could somehow get far enough away from the cliff to drop safely into the water. But, as I said, the surf was unusually violent that day, and even if by some miracle he managed to swing far enough out to avoid a directly impact with the rocks, he certainly knew he would be smashed into the cliffs by the waves. Perhaps if it had been a calm day, and he were very lucky, but I suspect he had chosen this day because of the high surf.

By now we had quite an audience—curiosity had driven several people from the Center out to the north beach, which offered an unobstructed view of Stan's Leap. I'm sure they all saw Teiki hanging. Some of them were probably already running out to us, but that would take a couple of minutes, and by then it would all be over. I had only to walk away, and Teiki would tumble to his death, leaving no blame on my shoulders. Now, it would be my story to tell. I'd explain the trap he laid out, even show everybody the ropes he'd rigged to send me to my death.

I hovered above Teiki for yet another fifteen seconds, watching his strength sap away and his fingers slowly open, now too weak to even swing his legs for fear he'd lose his grip. I can't begin to describe everything that raced through my mind while I watched his struggle. It was as if time had frozen. My first thought was that Kimo was right: the island just wasn't big enough for the both of us, so either he or I had to go. Teiki's and my harmless childhood rivalry had grown into a blood feud that could never be quelled. And who was there to settle things between us? None of the islanders could even make a decision about the farm, much less something like this. Besides, the Elders were slowing down—it was our island now, and it was time for leadership to move on to the Youngers. I suppose Kimo always knew it would pass on either to Teiki or me, but now I knew it had to be me. There was no other way.

But then I realized how easy it would be for me to become another Kimo, and that scared me. My greed for his knife, my quickness to assert my physical superiority, and most important, my thoughts at that very moment: that killing Teiki served some greater good. Wasn't that the way Kimo had rationalized killing Bob and Wayne? The island was better without them, so it was okay for him to "make them disappear?" In fact, wasn't that exactly what I had told Dad after I killed Kimo? Now here I was, passing the same life-and-death judgment over Teiki. Besides, was Teiki really evil? Perhaps he didn't know that I'd killed his father in self-defense. Was it possible that he hadn't heard our conversation on the east beach? Come to think of it, he probably hadn't—he arrived afterwards. How would I have reacted if he had killed my father?

And where would it all end if we kept killing each other—even if we had reasons? The three Kitchens might have different opinions regarding what to do, but we all agreed that the key to survival was to work together, not to kill one another.

I suddenly knew that I had to be better than Kimo. I lay on my stomach and reached down, grabbing Teiki's wrists just as his fingers lost their grip. I tried to pull him straight up, but couldn't. With my own strength quickly waning, I began to swing him from side to side, until he gained a small foothold on the rock face. With his legs now supporting some of his weight, I was finally able to wrestle him back up to the top. By the time he was safely on the ridge, we were both far too tired to even think about the spear that was still within easy reach. Instead, we stared at each other, gasping. His expression was impassive, indicating neither gratitude nor blame.

My respect for Teiki increased enormously that day. I had always looked down on him—he was merely Kimo's minion, someone younger and weaker than I. But this was a well-considered, intelligent plan, even if a vengeful one. I hated him for what he had done to Tia, but for the first time, I respected him, even if as an enemy. I suspect, or at least hope, that he harbored similar feelings toward me.

Dad was the first to arrive at Stan's Leap. The rest of our Kitchen followed close behind. Ignoring Teiki, Dad helped me up, put his arm around my shoulder, and shepherded me back from the leap that was his namesake.

By the time we arrived at our Kitchen, my story had been told. Tai emerged from her hut to corroborate what she could. Mom disappeared for a moment, then returned holding Kimo's knife, presenting it almost ceremoniously.

"Adam, I'm the one that took your knife. I'm sorry, but do you understand why?"

"Because you were afraid of what I'd do with it?"

"No, Adam. I did it because you just can't get things by killing, even if in self-defense. That's what Dad was trying to tell you. It couldn't be yours just because you killed Kimo. You had to earn it, Adam, and you did that today by not killing. Today, I'm proud of you—and so is everyone else. It's yours now."

Reflecting on Mom's words, I hefted the knife in my hands. Somehow, it now felt even heavier than it had just days earlier.

Chapter 28

THE NEXT MORNING, I waited a while before heading to the village center. I knew that by then, everyone would have arrived to get water from the spring and would be gossiping about the previous day's events. Sure enough, everybody was there. No one spoke to me but they certainly took note of Kimo's—or, now, my—knife on my hip.

I walked directly up to Teiki. "Teiki, I'm going to the farm. Want to come and help plant some corn?"

Teiki stared at me intensely, and I stared back, knowing everybody was watching. I was uncertain how he would respond, but Dad had talked me into trying. Because I had saved his life, Dad felt Teiki might welcome an opportunity to even the score. And if Teiki joined me, he was certain everybody would follow—where Teiki went, his Kitchen went, and if our two Kitchens were aligned, then Don's Kitchen would be just a step behind.

Without breaking eye contact, he finally flashed a thin smile. Without responding directly, he turned to his Kitchen-mate, Nick, and ordered, "You come, too."

I surveyed the others, and tried to address them the way the Good Kimo would have. "The farm's been a mess lately. We could use everybody's help getting it back in shape." With that, Nick, Teiki, and I headed off toward the farm. I leaned over so that only Teiki could hear me and said, "Thanks." He didn't say anything, but I thought I noticed a slight nod of acknowledgement.

Within ten minutes of our arrival at the farm, all three Kitchens had shown up in full force. Most of the Elders and all of the Youngers were there, even little Tommy. We worked quickly, our spirits buoyed by the camaraderie that only physical labor can nurture. By lunch we were all hungry, thirsty, tired … and happy.

Within a week, the island had returned to what it was before Kimo's death, with Stefani surprisingly resigned to the situation, and Teiki at least appearing to be cooperative. Nevertheless, I often found myself looking over my shoulder, not altogether certain they were as accepting as it seemed. The other Youngers, though, and even many of the Elders, began to treat me as their leader, asking me questions like: "Should we plant more yams?" "Are we going to have a gathering tomorrow night?" and "I found some Old World rope down by the east beach that's been washed ashore; can I take it? Still, I felt uncomfortable giving orders and tried to avoid it. Instead, I made suggestions that some people interpreted as orders.

All of it made me curious about how people were led in the Old World, so I discussed it with Dad one evening.

"Dad, where you used to live, what was it called again?"

"Pittsburgh, you mean?"

"No, I mean the big group, the 'country,' I think you called it."

"The United States?"

"Yeah, that was it. In the United States, how were the people led?"

"We called it *governed*, and it's not an easy question, Adam. It got really complicated by the end. There was a group of people called congress that made the rules and laws, another called the supreme court that interpreted the laws and decided when the laws were actually being broken, and then a single person called the president, who made sure the laws were followed. At least that's how it was supposed to work, but it was complicated, because each group had power over the other."

"But you said everybody voted to figure out who would govern, right?"

"Well, yeah, but it really wasn't that simple. Groups of people called states voted to figure out who would represent them in congress, and all the people voted together to decide who would be the president—States were almost like our Kitchens, but much bigger of course. Then congress could vote to get rid of the president if they felt he was breaking the laws they made. But the president chose the judges of the supreme court, and they could decide that the laws congress made were illegal. That's why it was so complicated."

I can't really say I understood, but thought if so many people lived that way, then maybe it made sense. "Now that Kimo's gone, do you think we should do something like that here?"

Dad laughed. "Not a chance, Adam, it was way, way too convoluted, and we're much too small."

"What should we do then? Everybody is asking me things as if I was Kimo, and I don't feel comfortable just taking over like I'm him. I know we need a leader, but why should they want me?"

"I don't see what the problem is, but if you want, just ask them who they want to be in charge. We're way too small for anything more than that."

At the gathering that Thursday, I stood up and waited for everybody to pay attention. "With Kimo gone now, I'd like to talk about who should be in charge of the island. I think somebody has to decide simple things, like what to plant, when and where to build more huts, when to kill a pig, and things like that, and it just seems we ought to decide as a group who it will be. I think we ought to have a vote."

Mary asked, "Why don't you just keep doing it like you've been doing the past week? It seems to be working out pretty well."

"Because some people might not agree, or maybe in a month I won't be doing such a good job. It just seems we should all decide that together rather than just have somebody just take over. You know what I mean?"

Teiki asked, "So, does the winner get the knife?"

His question both surprised and upset me; the knife was mine. "I don't understand why the knife should be ..." I stopped, realizing the question was a test. The knife was the island's, I realized, not mine, so the island should vote on who made decisions regarding its use. Teiki left me no choice. Reluctantly, I replied, "Yes, I think the leader we vote for should have the knife and decide what to do with it. That makes sense."

Tia said, "I vote for you, Adam."

Don broke in. "No it doesn't work like that, Tia. You have to vote secretly, so nobody knows whom you're voting for. Usually what you do is nominate a few people, then everybody votes for one of the people that's nominated."

Happy to have somebody else involved, I asked, "Don, since you know how it's done, can you lead the vote?"

"Sure, I guess."

"How do we mominate people?" asked Tia.

Don chuckled. "It's *nominate*, and all you have to do is say, 'I nominate Adam.' It means that you would like him to be on the list of people we can vote for."

"Okay, then I nominate Adam," Tia said.

"Alright, I don't think we really need to second the nominations or anything. Anybody want to nominate someone else?" Don asked.

There was a pause, then Stefani said, "I nominate Teiki."

"Anybody else?" Don looked around at everyone.

"I think our leader should be an Elder," I said. "I nominate Stan."

"Thanks, Adam, but I don't want to be nominated," Dad replied. "We're all getting too old to run this place anyway. You Youngers know the island better, and it's time you took over. Can I decline the nomination?"

"I guess so," replied Don. "Any other nominations? Any other Elders? Does everybody agree with Stan on that?"

David piped in. "I do. It's their future, not ours. Besides, we may know more about the Old World, but that's not what matters here. Teiki, Adam, and the others know more about the world we live in than any of us ever will."

Don didn't seem convinced, but after waiting another moment, he continued. "Then I guess we only have two nominees, Adam and Teiki. So, everybody get one shell from the beach. We can use those to vote." Then directing his voice to Tia, added, "But just one!"

We each got a shell from the beach and returned to the village center where Don had set out two clay jars. Don then told us to sit in front of the jars, with our back to them. He told us to put our own shells in our own jars, then cover our eyes with our hands. One by one, everybody walked past and dropped a shell into one of our jars. The jars were so close to each other that there was no way for us to tell just by listening which jar had received the shell each time. I'm told that some voters gave an exaggerated show of their preference, but most shielded their drop from the others.

When the last vote was cast, we turned around and faced our jars. Don told us to each count the shells we had collected. We both eagerly reach into the jars and pulled out our booty. Even as I was trying to count mine, I glanced to the side and saw that there were only two shells in Teiki's hand, obviously Stefani's and Teiki's. Teiki showed no reaction—he knew he had no chance to win—but as his eyes scanned the group of faces, his face suddenly contorted with anger, and then just as quickly, melted into dejection. It was then that we realized that our efforts to make the vote secret had failed: Teiki's own sister, Matahina, had voted for me, and everybody knew it.

I felt obligated to say something to both the Elders and Youngers. I wasn't sure what I should say, but I was anxious to share a couple of ideas from my talk with Dad the night before. "Thanks for your shells everybody, but I'd really like to come up with a different way than just having one person in charge. I'm not sure one person being totally in charge is a good idea. I don't mind making small decisions, about what to plant or what to do on a day-by-day basis, but I think big decisions, about how we're going to live, or if we should try to leave the island, and things like that, should be made by all of us, not by one person—at least I don't want to make them. I'm thinking we should make a council, with one person from each Kitchen, and the council can make the important decisions and rules for the island. They can also decide to have a new vote anytime they want, so if I start making bad decisions, they can replace me. I'm just thinking, in the long run, that'd be better than having a single leader."

After further discussion, we agreed that each Kitchen would choose one representative however they wanted to, and that the next night we'd hold our first council meeting. To make sure our Kitchen didn't have two votes, I would attend the meetings but not be able to vote. Then I announced that the upcoming Saturday, we'd have a special gathering and roast a pig. Teiki acted surprised when I asked him whether he'd be willing to hunt down one of the pigs, and prepare it for cooking. He readily accepted, trying unsuccessfully to hide his enthusiasm.

The next evening, we had our first council meeting. The chosen group consisted of Teiki, Don, and David. After waiting at least fifteen minutes to see if anybody would start the meeting, I finally decided to start it myself.

"I guess the main thing I thought we should talk about tonight is what we're going to do about the rules about using the stuff that washes onto shore. I mean, do we want to keep living the way we always have, or do we want to change?"

Don replied, "Adam, I think we know you well enough to know what you mean. What you're trying to ask is, 'Should we try harder to build a boat?' Right?"

I hesitated, not wanting to admit to being so transparent. He had me pegged, though. "Yeah, I guess that's the main question."

Don replied, "Personally, I don't have a problem trying to build a boat, but I think it's pretty crazy to try to go to another island. It would be really dangerous, and besides, where is there to go? I don't really see the point. I know you guys don't want to hear it, but I think Wayne was right: we'll know when it's time."

Prepared for his objection, I replied, "But how do you know it's not time now? Our supply of stones for making tools is almost gone, and the stones we have left are really lousy. I remember working with stones the size of a coconut when I was a kid, and now we just have these tiny things. Dad says there are really good stones on Pitcairn, and even metal tools. Maybe this is the time."

"Now that *is* a good thing to discuss," David added. "We don't have a knife or axe worth a damn. We keep trying to reflake the same tools, and they just get smaller and smaller. Teiki, what's left of the rocks that Kimo was keeping?"

We all turned to Teiki, who grudgingly replied. "Nothing, unless he buried them somewhere. He used to keep them under his bed, but there's nothing there now."

"We've got the glass," David said. "We can make pretty sharp tools with that."

"Yeah," I said, "but you know it breaks almost right away. It's okay for some things, but it's not strong enough to replace stone. David, what do you think about trying to get to Pitcairn to get some good rock?"

He thought for a moment. "I agree that we ought to try, but don't think it's going to be easy, even if we can build a boat. The hardest part is going to be knowing what direction to go without a compass." David was always talking about a compass. But as far as I was concerned, it was another one of the magical things that might or might not have existed in the Old World—after all, how could a simple needle always point north? The Elders told us about "magnets" and "magnetic fields" and things, but really, how could two rocks attract each other without even touching? How would one rock even know the other was there?

"You study the stars and the sun all the time," I said. "Can't you figure out which direction to go? You always say you know where Pitcairn is. You even have a stick in the observatory that points to it. Couldn't you figure it out on a boat too?"

"Sure, if the weather was clear, and if I could see the sky, and if I had a watch." Again he was talking in old-speak. Watches and clocks were another thing the Elders always talked about—things that kept track of exactly how much time had passed, and could predict when the sun would rise and set.

"My mom and dad made it. They said they knew where they were."

"They had a clock *and* a compass on board, and even then, they were lucky."

"Yeah, but they couldn't even really steer their boat. Besides can't we make a watch or a clock?"

David and Don just laughed. Teiki and I locked eyes with each other, both feeling the fools. I felt stupid arguing the point further.

"How close do we have to get to Pitcairn before we see it?" I asked.

"Stan said the highest point was a thousand feet or so above sea level," David said. "So I calculated that you could theoretically see it from forty miles away, but that's if the sky is perfectly clear and the ocean is perfectly calm. There's no way to know how close you'd really have to be. Maybe, if you're lucky, fifteen miles before you'd know for sure that you were seeing land. The other problem is that it's almost due east. I've got some ideas on how you could figure out how far north or south you are, but not east or west, not without a clock."

"So then you could make sure we're not too far north or south, but you couldn't tell us how far we had gone?"

"Exactly ..." His enthusiasm dissolved into uncertainty. "Well, at least theoretically. I'm not sure how accurate even north and south would be on a boat. So you could take a chance, but you could easily miss the island too."

"But I want to take the chance. We need to. Our tools are getting worse and worse."

That was true, but for me it wasn't the tools at all. The fact is, I was just dying to go somewhere. Anywhere. It seemed I had stepped on every inch of our island, and I desperately felt like I needed to see some of what the Elders kept telling us about, and find out what was real and what wasn't.

David looked at me. "Well, if you're asking whether I have a problem with you trying to build a boat, the answer's no—go for it. In fact, I'd love to help. It'll be fun. I just don't think it's going to be as easy as you think—and remember, miss Pitcairn and there's nothing for thousands of miles. Kimo was probably right in not trying."

Teiki had been quiet the entire time, but now opined. "I think it's a great idea. We should try to find Pitcairn."

I looked at Teiki, in shock. I was sure he'd disagree. All along, I had assumed that David would side with me, Teiki would vote against me, and Don would be the deciding vote. And for this particular issue, I was pretty sure Don would say yes in the end, but I had never expected to sway Teiki to our side. I was grateful for his support, but naively so, as I would later discover.

Chapter 29

WHEN I TOLD DAD of the council's decision, he looked disheartened. "Look, Adam, I know you're keen on building a boat, but I keep telling you, it isn't that easy. There aren't any trees even close to the size we need to make a real boat. It's one thing making little canoes for paddling around the lagoon, but you're talking about a whole different thing to make a boat that can survive in the open ocean."

"So, how did you make boats back in the Old World? You told me that you used to cut the trees into flat pieces then build boats piece by piece. Why can't we do that?"

"We called them *boards*. So how're you going to cut trees along their length into boards without any metal? Then how will you hold it all together without nails or screws? There's just so much you don't know. You've never even seen a real tree, just these overgrown weeds we have here on Henderson."

"How 'bout if I could get you some metal? How much do you need?"

Dad laughed. "I don't have any idea. To start with, enough to make a saw. That's a thin piece of metal—"

"I know what a saw is, Dad. You've told me before. What if I can get you some metal?"

"More than just that knife you have. It would take some *real* metal. Enough to make a hammer and nails too. Talk to David," he added dismissively, "he's the guy that's always trying to make stuff."

A few days later, during an unusually calm high tide, I went down to where my mom and dad's boat had sunk seventeen years earlier. I swam out to the very rock they'd hit and began diving, looking for debris from their boat. The water was only ten or fifteen feet deep around Shipwreck Rock, and the bottom consisted of small rocks, almost like coarse sand. Of course, any wood would have been long since carried away by the currents, but since metal was heavier, my hope was that there'd still be bits nearby. Sure enough, during the next hour or so I was able to find two dark red objects that appeared to be some kind of tools I couldn't identify. They were so unlike the bunker's lock and my knife that I could only recognize them as metal by their weight.

I was disappointed, but brought the bits back to my father and David anyway. They confirmed that had once been metal tools, but were quick to agree they were useless both as tools and scrap metal.

Dad rubbed his forehead and then looked at me. "But actually, this makes me think of something. There may be another place to get metal, and I mean a lot of it."

"Yeah?" I asked, doubtful.

"Yeah. And we should have thought of it before." Dad looked at David, who just shrugged in response. "You know how I told you that the anchor of the *Sea Salva* got stuck on an underwater ridge off the northwest point?"

"Yeah! You think we could find it? How big was the anchor?"

"It's not just the anchor, it's the chain too. There's plenty of metal there, believe me. Much more than a person can lift. But don't get your hopes up. First of all, it isn't going to be easy to find. I know about where it is, but only within a hundred yards or so. And it might be too deep to even get to. And on top of that, it's beyond the reef, so we'd have to go there in the little boats on very calm days. Then, even if we do find it, it's probably impossible to bring back through the reef—too heavy."

"But we can try!"

"Yes, we can try," he agreed, his voice sober. I think he made the suggestion just to keep me busy and distract me from my ambition to leave the island. "First thing, though, we're going to have to see much better underwater. We can't exactly feel our way along the bottom out there."

"So, how do we do that?"

"David, how good a piece of glass can you really make? Think you could make a lens for a diving mask?"

"Diving mask? Even if we can make the glass, how the hell are you going to make the rest?"

"Wood. We can carve something that fits Adam's face exactly, then seal it to the glass with some gum that we boil down from tree sap."

"Well, you work on that part, and I'll see if I can make a decently clear piece of glass. I've been playing around lately adding some of that lye we use for soap. Seems to make the glass clearer. Give me a few days, and let me see what I can do."

"So what's this *mask* for?" I asked. "I can see fine under water without a mask."

"With a good mask, you can see as clearly as in air. If you're going to spend any real time underwater, you'll need it."

The whole next week, I used my knife to carve a bowl that fit almost perfectly over my face, covering my eyes and nose, and resting just above my mouth. Then Dad and I cut out the bottom of the bowl in a shape that perfectly matched a small bit of clear glass that David had managed to produce. He was very proud of the little piece—a rough circle probably not more than a couple of inches in diameter. We then sealed the wood to the glass with hot gum, and made a pigskin strip that pulled the entire contraption tightly against my head.

I felt ridiculous as they marched me down to the beach.

"Just try it," Dad said. "I know you think you could already see underwater, but just try it."

I waded into waist deep water and submerged my head. It's hard to explain the world it opened up for me. It was thrilling—I thought I could see underwater before, but all of a sudden I could really see. After paddling around a bit, I stood and laughed. "Okay, you win! This is really amazing!"

"In the Old World," Dad said, "we had tubes called snorkels that bent around our heads, so we could breathe without turning our heads out of the water—we can try to make something like that, too, maybe using bamboo. We also had tanks that we wore that held enough air for us to breathe under water for more than a half an hour. In Hawaii, your Mother and I did it once and …"

"Yeah, Dad, I know. You told me a hundred times: scuba diving. You used to dive down a hundred feet and breathe under water. Hey, can we go out tomorrow and look for the anchor?"

Dad looked at David and then back at me. "I suppose so. If it's calm. If we do find it, we'll need some way to mark it, then figure out how to bring it up to the surface. It's not going to be easy, you know."

"Let's worry about that later, Dad. First, let's just try to find it."

Chapter 30

SIX DAYS PASSED BEFORE conditions allowed us to safely paddle outside the reef in our three canoes, but that sixth day was worth waiting for, with a very quiet surf, light current and perhaps most importantly, a high tide peaking in the late morning. We decided that Dad, Mom, and I would go on the first trip, Mom and Dad because they would best know where to search, and I to swim down in case we wanted a better look at something. Mom and Dad generally agreed where the *Sea Salva* broke free of its anchor, but couldn't confine the search area to less than a hundred yards in any direction.

Shortly after sunrise, we went out through the north beach channel, and quickly made our way down current to the search area. When we arrived, Dad tied my canoe to his while I slipped into the water with my mask. I swam for a good thirty minutes before grabbing onto Dad's canoe, exhausted—the canoes could easily hold their own in the light current, but swimming against it was still exhausting.

"I didn't find anything yet. I can see the bottom, but not clearly."

"How deep is it?" Dad asked.

"Right here? Maybe thirty or forty feet. If I swim down even a few feet, it's a lot clearer. It's like there's a cloudy layer or something right near the surface."

"How wide is the ridge?"

"I wouldn't call it a ridge exactly. It's about the same depth a long way out and off to the west too. The bottom drops off steeply over there to the east, almost like a cliff. I can't tell how deep it gets, but it's a really long wall. I didn't see the end of it. It's going to be hard to find anything here without knowing better where to search, but I'll keep trying."

"And I guess the anchor is probably stuck somewhere on the wall in really deep water. All you'd see up on this shallow area is the chain, and that'll probably be buried in the sand by now."

"Well, we're here, so I'm going to keep looking for a while."

I swam back and forth across the plateau for another half hour before climbing back into my canoe. All of us were pretty exhausted by then, so we decided to go back. We had timed high tide well, so we were able to paddle the canoes right across the reef rather than fight our way all the way back to the channel.

Back at our Kitchen, we recounted our findings to David and Claire. David listened quietly, then finally asked, "So what if you had a way to see the bottom clearly, right from the boat as you were paddling around. Interested?"

Dad must have known what David meant because he smiled right away, but I sure didn't.

"Like one of those submarine things you told us about once?" I asked. "That'd be cool, but how can we do that? We can't even build a real boat."

"No, not a submarine, a glass-bottomed boat. If I can make a piece of glass big enough, we can make a window in the bottom of the boat. We might even be able to lower it a couple of feet below the surface to get a better look at the bottom. What d'ya think? Want to give it a shot?"

David was always excited about trying new things, but most of his ideas didn't work, so, generally, I tried not to get too excited until he actually succeeded. Still, it seemed worth a try. The job of making the new boat itself fell to Dad and me. Hollowing out another little canoe would take a long time, so we decided to just make a small raft, where one person could lie on his stomach and look down into a little wooden tube while being towed by a canoe. The wooden viewing tube was really just a hollow piece of driftwood we found, less than two feet long and maybe six inches in diameter. David's piece of glass would be mounted onto the bottom of that.

Over the next several days, the others began to show a lot of interest in our progress. Before long, almost everybody made a point to stop by at least once a day to check on things and even offer help. The entire project was the most exciting thing our island had ever seen—at least in my memory. My underwater viewing mask got the most attention, especially with the Youngers. I let them all try it, and even though it leaked on everybody else's face, David was suddenly overwhelmed with demands for glass. He agreed to supply it on the condition they help him at the furnace.

From the beginning, Matahina, Teiki's sister, showed the most interest in our project. She was with us almost every day, virtually from sunup to sundown, offering to help in any way she could. We called her Mati for short. I remember the day Mati and I were swimming together, adjusting the fit of her new mask. We were standing in the waist-deep water, and she was showing me where her mask leaked. I used my knife to shave the high spots for a better fit. She was just a little girl—that's all she'd ever been to me—but at that moment, as she stood next to me, her head just inches from mine, I got this odd feeling. Even now I can't describe it—an emptiness, maybe, or like I had a stone in my stomach. I lost track of what she was saying.

"Hey, Adam! Are you listening to me?"

"Sorry, I was thinking about something. What'd you say?"

"I said, 'Can you take a little away right here, around my left eye?'" I reached out to take her mask.

"What were you thinking about anyway?" she asked.

"Nothing." That wasn't entirely true. I just couldn't answer—partly because I was embarrassed and partly because I didn't quite know.

"Nothing? So you were just ignoring me then? That's naughty. I'm not going to vote for you next time." She laughed, pushed me backward into the water, and swam away.

She had a wonderful laugh and always teased with it, ever since she was five years old. But now, as she was growing up, it took on different character. I watched her swim off, wanting to swim after her, but somehow afraid to. Instead, I waded back to shore, where Mom was sitting in the sand. As I wrapped on my pareo and tied my knife around my waist, Mom said, "Mati's growing up. She likes you, you know."

"*Likes me?* What do you mean?" I was both annoyed and intrigued.

"I mean she wants you to pay attention to her. She's becoming a very beautiful girl, isn't she?"

I looked away as if I didn't care, or didn't hear. But Mom was right, she was beautiful. Her full, blonde hair and smooth, flawless, tanned skin that was just starting to reshape itself to accommodate her changing womanhood.

"Adam. You be careful, okay? Don't forget, you killed her father. There's still a lot of tension there."

"Come on, Mom, don't be silly. What do you think she would do? It's just Mati."

That evening, back at our Kitchen, David handed his masterpiece to Dad, cradling it with both hands. "So the problem was that the glass kept cracking when it cooled. I cooled this one very slowly, over three days. The clarity isn't perfect, but it's the best I've ever made."

Dad held the window up so we could all look through it. It was so clear, I couldn't imagine anything more transparent. Dad was less enthusiastic. "Well, not exactly Waterford, but it's not bad. It'll do, I think."

"So is Waterford the type of glass you used in the Old World to look into water?" I asked.

They laughed, but didn't bother to answer. I was too embarrassed, or maybe too proud, to ask again. There were so many times I just didn't understand what made them laugh. Sometimes I hated their inside jokes.

The next morning, we fit the glass to the hollow driftwood tube and sealed it using hot gum. We carried the tube into the lagoon and tested it. It was wonderful. I was sure that if there were an anchor or chain out there, we'd find it.

Just a few days later, the weather and tides cooperated and we were ready to search again. Dad and I paddled our canoes out through the north beach channel, I with the glass-bottom boat in tow. Once we reached the underwater plateau, Dad held my canoe while I dove down to find a rock we could tie up Dad's boat to. After securing his canoe, I climbed back into my canoe and Dad boarded the glass-bottom boat, lying down with his face over the viewing port. I'd wanted to search first, but he knew best what we were looking for and I was the stronger paddler, so this way made more sense. I towed Dad while he searched the bottom, occasionally pointing right or left to tell me which way to go. Before long, Mati appeared in the third canoe, paddling close beside us.

The glass was just a couple of feet under the water's surface, but it made a big difference. Not only could we see better, but we were able to cover a much larger area since the boats were so much easier to move against the current. Still, Dad saw nothing promising. To tell you the truth, we weren't even sure what we were looking for, and we knew that after so many years there might be nothing to see.

By early afternoon, the weather began to look uncertain, so Dad transferred back to his canoe, and we tied the glass-bottom boat to our makeshift mooring. There was really no choice but to leave the glass-bottom boat out, since there was no way it would make it across the reef, and it would be very difficult to paddle it all the way back into the current.

Dad, Mati and I arrived at our Kitchen to find everyone waiting, curious what we'd found.

"The area's really large," Dad said, "and I know for sure we went back over the same spot a few times. What we really need is a systematic way to search."

"So why don't you put markers on the bottom so you have kind of a grid, then spend like a day or so in each area?" David suggested.

Dad nodded his head. "Like underwater signs. We could tie different numbers of sticks to rocks with short ropes, then drop the rocks into the water to mark the corners of different search areas."

And that's exactly what we did. Over the next two weeks we went out searching four more days, still only during calm high tides. As we went, we carefully marked off the areas we had finished searching, so while we didn't find anything, at least we could see progress. Dad and I went out every time but there was always an argument over who would be in the third boat. Mati edged her way in three times.

It wasn't until the following week that we found something. It was a bit embarrassing, too, because it wasn't Dad and I with our glass-bottom boat who found it, but rather Mati, who'd been swimming off by herself, towing her canoe with a rope tied to her ankle. She often did that when she went searching with us: paddle up-current a bit, then jump off and let the current carry her and her canoe over the search area. The area she found it in was one Dad and I had searched just the day before without seeing anything. I suppose we'd been looking for something more striking.

"Check over here," Mati had called to us. "There's some kind of strange pattern on the bottom."

We paddled over to see what she was looking at. Dad dismissed it even after she showed it to him. It wasn't anything more than a wandering line of coral growing out of what was otherwise a sand-and-rock bottom. I looked, but couldn't tell what she was seeing; by now, though, I had come to realize that my vision wasn't as sharp as everybody else's. I don't mean to say it was bad, but Mati could see things I couldn't.

"Let's at least check it out," Mati urged. Then, allowing no argument, she abandoned her canoe and disappeared underwater, forcing us to grab its rope to prevent it from drifting away. She surfaced about thirty seconds later.

"There's something there. I can touch it, but I can't pick it up."

"Is it metal?"

"How am I supposed to know? I'm just saying there's something down there that's long and skinny, and has coral growing on it—but it's not just coral. There's something underneath."

I put on my mask and swam down. It was deep there, maybe

forty-five feet. I was impressed that Mati had made it so far down, and frankly, if I hadn't known that she'd just done it, I probably would have given up before I got to the bottom. After barely touching it, I returned to the surface gasping for air.

I took a few deep breaths before reporting to Dad. "There's definitely something there, but I can't tell what it is either. Let's try to follow the line in the sand and see where it goes."

We tracked the line to the east until it plunged over the wall and we couldn't see it anymore. To the west, we could follow the line for about a hundred feet or so, but it never really got any shallower. If this was it, it wasn't going to be easy to get it back to land.

The next day, we returned with a long rope tied to a heavy rock—David's idea, of course. We tied the free end of the rope to my canoe, and I hugged the rock against my chest as I slipped off the back of my canoe. The rock pulled me down quickly, without wasting any energy. When I arrived at the mysterious line in the sand, I let go of the rock, and with plenty of breath left, was able to dig around the line and confirm there really was something there. I even lifted it just a little.

I returned to the surface with still plenty of air left. "I think that's it!"

"Can you get a rope through one of the links?" Dad asked, pulling up the diving rock.

I really had no idea what he meant by links—in fact, I still wasn't sure what a chain was, even after my dad had described it to me many times. "I'm not sure," I replied, "but I think I can get a rope underneath. Want me to try?"

"I suppose. I'm sure we can't lift it now with the ropes we have, but we can at least tie our glass bottom boat to it so it's easy to find the next time we come out."

I took another dive down with the diving rock, but this time untied the rope from the rock and tied looped it around the chain. When I surfaced, we tied the glass-bottom boat to the rope. I swam back to my canoe, still tied to our original mooring. One more dive down to salvage that rope, and we were on our way home.

That night at our Sunday gathering, we told everybody what we had found.

George was the first to comment. "Look, I may not be a real sailor but I've been on sailboats like the *Sea Salva* and watched people pull up anchors. A boat that size probably used an electric winch. If the chain and anchor are as heavy as I think, we're going to have to lift it with an incredible force. Even if we had a way to pull up that hard, it would sink all of our little canoes combined—and that's if the anchor's not stuck in the rocks and sand, which it probably is by now."

As always, George's opinion wasn't exactly encouraging, but I liked that he had said *we* rather than *you*.

"Then we'll have to lift it a little at a time," I said, "with lots of ropes and lots of canoes. We don't even need canoes, just things that float: logs, reeds, some of that really light, white stuff that sometimes floats onto the beach—what do you call it, Styrofoam or something? If we make enough floats, we can lift it."

Dad tossed across a bit of broken rope. "Here's another problem we're going to have to deal with."

I picked it up and studied it. The inside was rotted and the outside badly frayed. "So, what's this?"

"That's part of the rope you brought up this morning—the rope we were using to tie up the glass-bottom boat. We're lucky, another day or two and it would have broken."

"Then we're going to have to figure out how to make the rope last longer in the water."

Of course, Teiki couldn't resist joining the naysayers. "What I want to see is how you're going to get this chain and anchor through the reef. Or are you planning to drag it all the way back to the north beach channel? That'd even be more fun to watch."

The group went silent. Despite his sarcasm, we realized that Teiki had hit on the real problem. Getting it up to the surface was going to be tough enough, but how would we get it back to the island?

I stood up and faced him. "So then we have to make a new passage through the reef, out near where the anchor is now."

"A passage through the reef? You mean like a new channel?" Teiki laughed. "This gets better and better."

"We can do it!" I insisted. "We'll find the deepest and shortest way through the reef, probably the place where we bring our canoes back in now, and then we'll dig the rock and coral out until it's deep enough for the anchor. It doesn't have to be that deep, probably just five feet or so. If we all work together, we can do it."

"Well, good luck," Teiki said. He stood to leave.

"Okay, you don't have to help," I said. "And if we get the anchor back to the island, you don't have to have any of the metal either. Any metal we get should be divided between everybody that helps with the project."

We locked eyes. He broke his stare just for instant to glance down at my knife, then turned away and began walking toward his Kitchen.

The next day, we broke into three groups. Many of the better swimmers, including myself, and eventually even Teiki, were in the group charged with clearing a passage through the reef. By looking carefully, we found an easier place to clear than the one we'd been crossing in the canoes. Clearing it wasn't easy, but it wasn't as bad as we'd expected either. We were able to tie ropes to the coral heads and rocks, then back up toward shore where we could get better footing. One rather large coral head was exceptionally hard to move, but also provided the biggest payoff once we finally loosened it using a long pole to pry it out of the sand.

By the end of the week, we had a safe passage for swimmers, our small canoes, and, hopefully, the anchor. To his credit, Teiki ended up being one of the most helpful workers in the group. Each day, he was reluctant to start, but then after watching us struggle for a while, he inevitably thought of a better way to do things. So long as we followed through with his idea, he worked as hard as anybody. In the end, we christened our new passage the Anchor Channel. It dramatically shortened our journey out to the chain and allowed us to go in and out during any tide.

A second group, led by my dad, twisted hemp ropes that were thicker and stronger than anything we had made before. They also tried waterproofing the ropes by covering them in hot tree sap. That part was horrible, dirty work, to put it mildly, but it did seem to protect the rope.

David led the third party, making floats that we would use to lift the anchor chain to the surface. The idea was to sink the float—by securing heavy rocks to it—down to the chain. Once the float reached the bottom, someone would dive down, tie it to the chain, and then cut away the rocks, causing the float to pull up on the chain. By stringing enough floats along the length of the chain, we hoped to lift it to within a few feet of the surface. We had a few Styrofoam blocks that floated very well, but most of the floats would be bundles of dried wood.

Each project seemed difficult, even impossible at times, but within three weeks, every team had made enough progress to allow us to test our concept. So when we awoke a few mornings later to unusually calm seas, we set out. We loaded rocks into our canoes and dragged the Styrofoam floats behind our canoes

Once Dad, David, and I were through our new Anchor Channel, with our canoes tied to the rope extending down to the chain, we immediately went to work. We tied enough rocks to the first float to make it sink, then released it, watching it slowly shrink as it sank toward the chain. Once it reached bottom, I took hold of a diving rock and rode it down. As fast as I could, I tied the float to the chain with a short piece of rope that Dad had waterproofed. I then surfaced for a short rest, before taking a second dive. I then cut through the rope binding the rocks to the float, and drifted back to the surface as I watched the float, freed of its counterweight, shoot up a couple of feet, tensioning its tether to the chain.

"It worked!" I said, almost before I had surfaced. "It's off the bottom. Let's do the other one."

"Okay, okay," Dad said. "Rest a minute. There's no reason to rush things, this is going to take a while. How far did the float pick it up?"

"About a foot."

"All right, which way do you want to go—toward the anchor or toward the end?"

I shrugged and looked at David.

David said, "I'd rather get the free end first, then work our way to the anchor."

I attached the next float about ten feet from the first, further away from the underwater wall. Like the first, as soon as I cut away the rock, the chain lifted a few feet further off the bottom. The seas were still calm, so we paddled our canoes back through the Anchor Channel and brought out two more floats, made from wood rather than Styrofoam. Their size made them a bit clumsier to handle, but they worked almost as well in the end.

Even with the Anchor Channel, we had to stop work in the late morning because of the strengthening current and wind. But by the end of that first day, we had attached six floats, the chain now forming an underwater arch of sorts, with the top of the arch some twenty feet below the surface. It still didn't look like the metal my knife was made from, but there was no longer any doubt that's what it was.

That night, after dinner, Dad and David and I met to plan our next steps. "Making the floats is easy," David said, "but we have to work fast. I don't know how long those ropes will last, and eventually, the wooden floats will get waterlogged and lose their buoyancy."

We all nodded, but knew it all depended on the weather.

The sea was a bit rougher the next day, but we went out anyway. We reached the free end of the chain with our second float, which once released, sent the entire string of floats up to the surface, dangling the chain just a few feet below. We then started working our way towards the anchor itself, and by afternoon, found the point where the chain plunged off the edge of the underwater plateau. We were now pulling on the anchor itself, stuck somewhere on the underwater wall. As thrilling as it was to see the chain suspended just below the surface, it was discouraging to see it disappear almost vertically into the dark waters beyond the ridge. There was simply no way to know how far down it was.

That night, we again worked on our strategy. George seemed to know more about anchors than anybody else, but it still wasn't much. "All I know is that they have big, flat blades that dig into the bottom. If you drag the anchor along the bottom, like the floats are doing now, the blades just dig in deeper. If you want to pull the anchor out of the bottom, you have to somehow pull perpendicular up from the bottom—and if it's in that underwater wall, that means directly away from the wall. Then the blades should pop right out."

"So then we have to pull from the east, somehow, from the deep side of the wall?" I asked. "How are we supposed to do that? There's no place to pull from."

"I understand the problem, I'm just telling you that's what you need to do, not how to do it. With most of the chain already up and floating, the anchor itself probably isn't that heavy, but I still don't know how you're going to do it: you'll never be able to keep a large boat or raft up-current from the anchor long enough to pull it up, and obviously the water is way too deep there to tie ropes to the bottom like you did on the plateau."

George had dropped the *we* and returned to using *you*. I had to somehow bring him back into the fold. "How 'bout tying a big raft to the reef, with a long rope?"

"There's no way we can possibly make a rope that strong," Dad said. "And think about how long it would have to be."

"Then why not use the anchor chain itself?" David suggested. "We can take the chain of floats along the outside of the reef and pull it up along the reef. Once we get the chain up-current from the anchor, we should be able to pull it up."

Dad argued, "You'd never be able to pull all those floats into the current like that. You have any idea how much force there must be now on the anchor chain?"

At a loss for better ideas and despite George's advice, we decided that, conditions permitting, we'd go out in the morning with a half dozen floats, attach them as far down the anchor line as we could, and release them, hoping we could pull it out by brute force. And if we couldn't, at least we'd get a better idea of how deep and how fast it was stuck.

Early the next morning, I walked ahead of Dad down the north beach to begin our attack on the anchor. As I neared the Anchor Channel, I could see a few of the floats bobbing in unusually calm waters just beyond the reef. Something wasn't right, though. The floats were all in a jumble, rather than strung out in a line.

I ran down the beach in a panic. All the work we'd done was lost. I dragged one of the canoes toward the water, intending to paddle out to the floats, without even considering what I'd do once I got there. Then I heard Dad shouting behind me. "Adam, the floats are floating free!"

"I know. I'm going out and to see if we can save them!"

"No, no… they're still tied to the chain, but the current isn't pulling them!"

I looked at the floats again. He was right. If they had broken free, they would be in a line stretching to the west, not jumbled all together like this. My heart leapt as I realized the significance of what was happening: the current had disappeared or even reversed itself.

We had to act quickly. We paddled two of the canoes out through Anchor Channel, dragging behind the three weighted floats. When we got to the float closest to the anchor, our hopes were sky high. The anchor line plunged straight down rather than angling off toward the east. I wasted no time. I grabbed my diving rock and the nearest float. We were in deep water now, so I couldn't just drop the float to the bottom this time. Instead I held both the float and my diving rock as I descended along the chain. When I got to about forty feet, I let go of my diving rock and quickly tied the float to the chain. Then, stretching my breath to the limit, I cut the tether holding the float to its counterweight. The rocks fell away and the float jerked up, but it was held fast by the anchor chain.

I swam back to the surface, took a couple minutes to catch my breath, pulled up the diving rock and repeated the process with the next float. The result was the same.

I saw David and Mati on the beach watching us, probably wondering why we'd gone out without them. I called back to them. "Make some more floats, as fast as you can. We're right over the anchor now. There's no current."

As they scrambled off, I descended with the last float and attached it, with the same result. Frustrated, I resurfaced, climbed back into my canoe, and started paddling toward shore.

Before I had made it even twenty feet, I heard Dad shout, "It's coming up!"

I turned to see the three new floats nearing the surface. That meant the anchor must be free. I quickly donned my mask and dove off the canoe. I immediately saw a dark shadow about thirty feet below. The anchor must have been closer than we thought.

Back at the surface, I reported my findings to Dad. His response sounded more cautious than excited. "Okay, it's up, so let's not lose this thing now. We've got to get the free end back through the channel as quickly as we can. Otherwise, when the current kicks in, it's going to sweep the whole thing away to Pitcairn."

Things went quickly from there. Mati came out in the third canoe, and she, Dad and I paddled the string of floats attached to the free end of the chain toward Anchor Channel. As soon as we reached the lagoon, Teiki, David, and the others were there, ready to pull it to shore. All we in canoes had to do was herd the floats away from the reef and through the opening.

Behind us, as the anchor neared the channel, it caught on the bottom, but we gave it no chance to dig in. As soon as we felt resistance, Mati and I went down with another two floats and attached them directly to the anchor. We were surprised to see it was no more than three feet long.

By afternoon, we had more metal than I had ever imagined in front of us. We stretched the chain out as far as it would go along the beach and measured it: about two hundred feet. I figured that was about six feet for each of us, with the rest of the chain and the anchor set aside as community property, to be controlled by the council.

"So, how're you going to divide it up?" Dad asked.

"We just count the links, then everybody gets the same number."

"No, I mean how are you going to separate the links?"

"Can't we just break them?"

"With what?"

Teiki, apparently eager to have his own share, said, "By bashing them with rocks."

I could tell from the twinkle in Dad's eye that once again, we Youngers were about to become the butt of yet another Elder joke. But he didn't say anything, so Teiki grabbed a rock from the shore and began pounding. The other Youngers followed suit, so I couldn't help but pitch in too. I mean, really, how difficult could it be?

After half an hour, we hadn't succeeded in doing more than knock some of the red layer off the chain—what David called rust; the chain was still that strong after all those years. I realized then, just how much metal would impact our lives. I also realized I didn't have to baby my knife as if it had been made of David's glass. My dad had always told me not to worry about it so much, but Kimo had so seldom used it that I just assumed it was because it might break, like our stone knifes.

The other revelation of the day was that, there in front of us, was proof that at least some of what the Elders had been telling us was real. There was another world, and they really had made metal in large quantities, and it really was as strong as they claimed. Could that mean they were also telling the truth about the buildings that touched the clouds? About ovens that boiled water in seconds without any flames? About boxes that carried people up and down buildings and even to the moon? Regardless, though, it meant that the story of the *Sea Salva* was true, and that there were lands beyond our horizon.

David may have been even more pleased with our treasure than I was. After we gave up our pounding, he finally intervened. "Okay, enough watching you guys suffer. Now, you kids are going to learn to be blacksmiths."

"What's a blacksmith?"

"Somebody that works with iron or steel. We're going to heat it up until it's bright red or orange. That makes it soft so we can bend it or smash it with a hammer on an anvil to make it thinner, like for a knife blade. We'll be able to break the chain with no problem when we get it to the furnace." It was then that we all realized how difficult this was going to be. What hammer? And what was an anvil anyway? And how would we hold the pieces of hot metal?

"What about all the rust?" Dad asked.

"Well, I'm not completely sure," David admitted. "I know that, theoretically, if the temperature is high enough, just plain carbon will reduce it—the carbon from the charcoal will draw oxygen from the iron oxide and form carbon monoxide, leaving the iron behind. I only know that in theory, though, so we'll just have to play around with it. Worst case, we melt it again. Look, if the Romans and Greeks figured it out, so can we. It's going to be fun."

Chapter 31

AFTER WEEKS OF TRIAL and error, we learned to melt the anchor and chain, cast it into simple shapes, then hammer the castings into tools that far outperformed our deteriorating stone tools. By Elders' standards, I suppose they weren't much, but they revolutionized our lives. We made better axes to cut down trees, saws that could cut boards from the trees, nails to hold the boards together, and hammers to drive them in. We also made cooking pots and frying pans. And Teiki finally got his own knife, though not as shiny and perfectly formed as mine.

Six months after we salvaged the anchor and chain, we finished building our first boat. It was small—just twelve feet long—but it was enough to show how little we knew about boats. All the seams leaked until we learned to cram sap-soaked hemp into the gaps between the boards. We made sails by weaving hemp fibers into fabric, but within days, they rotted, and were torn to ribbons in the lightest winds. But in time, we learned to waterproof the sails by soaking them in grease. Once we had a leak-tight boat with sails, we tried to sail in the lagoon, with Dad as our teacher—but it wasn't long before I realized that trial and error would be a better teacher. Once we were able to sail downwind, we began to turn into the wind—we could get the boat pointed to the wind, but couldn't make forward progress. It took another two months to get the hull and sails adjusted so that we could go up and down the north lagoon.

Then, with everything we learned building the small boat, we set out to make our first real ocean-going vessel. We decided to name it the *Enterprise*. The name came from the Elders—they said it was the name of some famous ship that flew to the stars—but I just liked the name. The *Enterprise* was twenty-five-feet long and had three sails and two masts: a large one close to the front and a smaller one nearer the back. Running along the length of the boat was a narrow keel. When we put enough rocks in the bottom of the *Enterprise*, the bottom of the keel was about four feet below the waterline, and the *Enterprise* could sail close to the wind—without the rocks, it was unstable, and the wind would push the *Enterprise* sideways.

Perfecting the *Enterprise* and learning to sail were my obsessions the next year. I worked on little else during the day and dreamed of nothing else at night. Every time we had to rebuild something to make the boat more seaworthy, I felt crushed. I just wanted to sail somewhere—anywhere, as long it was beyond our horizon.

Once we felt the Enterprise was ready, we built a small, flat deck in the middle of the hull, and covered it with a wooden roof. Many nights, I slept in that cabin while the *Enterprise* was tethered to a coral head in the lagoon. I loved the gentle rocking, and sound of the small waves lapping against the hull.

Except for Mati, the others helped out more as a way to pass the time, which is not to say they didn't contribute, rather that I couldn't count on them. The issue was that they were far less interested in getting to Pitcairn now that we had sound tools again. We had moved into the Iron Age, which meant the rocks that were so precious to us just months before were now all but worthless. And since they figured the burned-out world beyond Henderson was of no use to us, they weren't about to risk their lives in "useless explorations." The Elders had settled into a routine and had no interest in excitement or change, and the Youngers were either afraid or suspicious of what might lie beyond—if the Elders' stories were true, what was out there was incomprehensible; if fabrications, then what was the point? Only Mati and I felt the need to know and were compelled to take the risk to find out. And it was thus that Mati, by far, was the most enthusiastic participant in the project. In fact, if it was possible, she seemed to love sailing as much as I did.

Teiki also showed a keen interest in the boat—he understood every detail of its construction and made suggestions that were vital to its final design—but he never set foot in the boat nor lent a hand building it.

David's role centered on navigation, and he seemed to love the fact that we'd begun paying attention to his observatory and his teachings. I studied for long hours with him, trying to understand how to use the stars to figure out where we were, and I sort of got it, even if he thought I was a slow learner. Of course, David was also enthusiastic about making new tools to help us build our boat. Once he showed us all the work that was required to fire up the furnace, I began to really appreciate how hard he must have worked over the past seventeen years.

Finally, we got to where we felt comfortable sailing the *Enterprise* along the north coast outside the reef, and we set out on our first real adventure: to sail around Henderson. We figured it was a trip of about thirty miles if we kept well away from Henderson's east coast—and I can tell you, Mom and Dad warned me more than a few times about getting too close to a windward shore! It was early spring when Dad and I completed that first circumnavigation and the next day, Mati and I set out to do it again, this time going the opposite way around. She was so disappointed at not having been included in the first trip, I felt I owed it to her. Besides, I never tired of sailing.

Though I didn't tell Dad, Mati was by far the better sailor—I always felt nervous with Dad at the rudder, but never with Mati. What I most appreciated was her eyes. She could see things that I couldn't make out if I were half the distance away. The evening Mati and I returned from our sail around the island, Dad and I immediately began to plan our first real trip—an easy downwind sail to Pitcairn. There was never any doubt that it would be Dad and I that went. I can't say he was enthusiastic, but he was willing and capable, even if increasingly nervous as the voyage became more real. I think that Mati always knew Dad would go with me on our first trip, but she was still disappointed when I told her. She pled her case enthusiastically, but to no avail. Though I would have preferred to take Mati, Dad would recognize Bounty Bay, know his way around the island, and even know what we should take back with us. Besides, Mom didn't like the idea that Mati and I go together.

She wouldn't even let Mati stay with me overnight on the boat in the lagoon.

With his knowledge of navigation and the stars, David was the only other reasonable candidate to be my co-explorer, but he just wasn't comfortable sailing. Plus, he still had no ideas about how to gauge our east-west progress. But he did make a little device to help us figure out how far north or south we were: it was made out of two sticks, hinged on one end. If we leveled one stick on the horizon and pointed the other at the sun right at its highest point during the day, a little gauge at the hinge would show the angle between the sticks, and that would tell us how far south we were. He called it a sextant. We practiced several times and it seemed easy to use, but that was on solid ground, which didn't move as we tried to line the sticks up. I wasn't sure it'd be so easy on a boat bobbing wildly on an endless ocean.

David had tried to make a compass, too. He placed a sliver of iron, which he called a needle, on a piece of wood floating in the water. He said he'd hoped the needle would point toward the North Pole, but it didn't. He tried and tried, but each time, the sliver would move around aimlessly, just as common sense suggested it should—after all, how could a piece of metal know which way to point?

In the end, he told us, "I guess you really need a magnet for it to work, not just iron. I wish Kimo hadn't gotten rid of that radio; it would have had a magnet in its transformer."

More gobbledygook. As diplomatically as I could, I replied, "Well, it was worth a try." Behind his back, though, we Youngers enjoyed a good laugh at his expense—just another of his crazy ideas.

Regardless of what we thought, however, David said one of the objectives of our first trip to Pitcairn was to find one of those mysterious compasses or, at least, a magnet so that he could make one. Our second objective would be to find a watch or a clock that still worked—that, he said, was our only hope for figuring out our longitude, even with a compass. Dad said most watches and clocks worked on batteries that would be dead by now, but he hoped to find an older kind that you could wind up. I, too, preferred to find one that worked without electricity—as often as it had been explained to me, electricity just didn't make sense. Anyway, I didn't care much about David's two objectives; for me, the trip was a chance to see a new world.

Dad and I figured it might take two days to get to Pitcairn, then we might stay there for a week, depending on the weather. Sailing back again would be upwind and take a bit longer, so, all in all, the entire trip should take no more than two weeks. We'd stock the *Enterprise* for three-weeks, though, partly in case we missed Pitcairn, and partly because we wanted to see how the boat and supplies held up in case we'd wanted to take a longer trip some day—to Mangareva, for example.

Mom wasn't thrilled about Dad and I both going, but she accepted it without argument—I guess because she knew there was no way I'd be dissuaded and that I'd be safer with Dad along. I also like to think she trusted my sailing skills and decision-making ability—but if so, she was sorely mistaken.

Chapter 32

THE NIGHT BEFORE WE were to set off, I was too excited to sleep. I got up before dawn and was on board the *Enterprise* by sun-up. Within an hour, Mati swam out to join me. She must have been awake all night as well.

"I wish I could go with you," she said. She seemed sad, an emotion I hadn't often seen in Mati.

"There'll be other times. It's just that for this first trip we need one of the Elders who knows what we're looking for, and Dad's actually been to Pitcairn."

"I know, but there will only be one first trip. Where is he, by the way? I thought you wanted to be off right after sunrise."

"Probably saying good-bye to Tia and Mom. I'm sure he'll be here in a moment. So why doesn't Teiki have any interest in sailing? He seemed interested enough in building the boat."

"I don't know. And you know that he doesn't even like it that I sail. Neither does Mom." She brightened suddenly, and gave me a broad smile. "Teiki did have some good ideas on building the boat, though, didn't he?"

"For sure! Great ideas, like how to attach the rudder to the hull. I just don't understand why he doesn't want to go on the boat, even in the lagoon."

Just then, Mom walked out to the beach and called to us. "Adam, Dad's not feeling well. I think you're going to have to wait for another day."

"What? No way, we're all ready to go! What's wrong?"

"Just a stomach flu or something, I think. Nothing serious, but he certainly can't go on a boat. He was throwing up all night."

I turned to Mati. Her eyes were already pleading with me. Mom followed my gaze and realized what we were considering.

"Mati, your mom and brother would never let you go. Besides, neither one of you has even been off the island."

"Sure we have. We sailed around the island together, remember?"

"You know what I mean. You've never been any place other than here. Besides, you've never been away together … overnight."

"What difference does that make? Besides, you and Dad have told us so much about Pitcairn, it feels like I've been there a hundred times. She's a really good sailor too."

Mom hesitated, obviously struggling to answer. "Mati, why don't you go and ask your mom. It's up to her, not me." I may have been voted the leader of the island, but parents were a still higher office.

Mati dove off and swam ashore. I followed just behind, anxious to plead my case with Mom. But as soon as I was out of the water, Mom started in on me. "Adam, there are some things you just don't understand yet. Why do you think Mati spends so much time on the boat? And why she's so interested in sailing?"

"Because she's the only person on the island who wants to know what's really out there, that's why."

Mom stared at me for a moment. "Look, Adam, I can't explain it all now. But being on this island, while it's forced all of you to grow up so quickly in many ways, in other ways you're all just still children. I have to check on your father now, but we really need to have a long talk sometime—about growing up." She walked back to our hut, and I swam back to the *Enterprise*. I knew Mati's mother would say no, but I was still hoping that somehow this would be the day. I was so anxious to go, I even considered going on my own. Just minutes later, though, Mati came running back, her wide grin telling all.

In retrospect, I guess I felt more than a bit odd leaving without proper good-byes. But Mati said she didn't want to give anyone time to change their minds—and I didn't either. So not fifteen minutes later, we'd made an abrupt departure, paddling the *Enterprise* out through the north beach channel. Beyond the reef, we promptly set sail and starting downwind to the west, parallel to the north shore. The winds were light, as they usually were at this time in the morning, but we knew they would increase as the sun climbed. Before long, we saw both Youngers and Elders walking along the beach, waving to us, easily able to keep pace with the *Enterprise*.

"Scared?" I asked Mati as we waved back to them. She giggled. "No way. Excited. You know that."

"You look a little nervous."

She looked away from me. "Not really ... not about the trip, at least."

"Then what?"

"Nothing. I'm fine." She still wasn't looking directly at me—Mati always locked eyes with me when we were talking.

"Mati, I know you're not fine. What's wrong?"

"Nothing, really. It's just I'm not sure Teiki will be too happy about my leaving, that's all."

"So, what'd he say?"

"Nothing."

"What do you mean *nothing*? What'd he say?"

Mati was silent, prompting me to belatedly figure out the obvious. "You didn't tell him, did you?"

She finally lifted her head. "Not exactly."

"What's 'not exactly' mean?"

"It means I didn't tell him. He wasn't around."

It was my turn to be silent a moment. "He's going to be furious."

"So what? He hates that I sail with you anyway. He even slapped me when I got back from our sail around the island."

"You never told me that. What an asshole! Maybe we should turn—"

"No!" She turned her back to me.

I thought for a bit, then said, "No, I suppose not. Teiki doesn't own you. Besides, it's really up to your Mom, not him."

Mati hung her head, looking down at the water, then abruptly walked toward the front mast. "C'mon, let's let out the sail some more. The wind's right at our backs."

We adjusted our sails and picked up speed. The spectators now had to walk briskly to keep up with us. As we got to the westernmost part of the island, about to head into the open ocean, we noticed Teiki for the first time, standing at the northwest point. I'd have been more comfortable had he been cursing at us or waving us back or something, but he just stood there like he was made of wood, staring at us, his arms folded.

Mati stared at him, too, and then quietly scolded me. "He's not an asshole. Sometimes I think you are. He's just hurt … and jealous." In a rare moment of wisdom, I remained silent.

By midmorning, the winds had picked up and Henderson had completely disappeared, even from Mati's sight. And with the sun now too high in the sky to really gauge its direction, we had to steer by the wind and the feel of the waves, hoping the sea would remain constant until we could get a better idea of where west was. I tried to use David's sextant to see if the maximum height of the sun had changed, but as I had suspected, with the motion of the boat, it was hopeless.

Conditions were magnificent that afternoon, and the *Enterprise* flew downwind riding flickering whitecaps. Hours later, when the sun touched the horizon, we finally got an accurate check on our westward heading, and were reassured to find we were only a few degrees south of our intended course. We had a brief celebration, though we both realized that just because we'd finished the day on a westward heading wasn't proof we hadn't gone off course. We had a cold meal of dried fish, bread, and fruit as we watched sunset fade into darkness. It was eerie and more than a little disconcerting to be so alone and so far away from land. We didn't talk about it, but I sensed Mati shared my uneasiness.

It was a cloudless night, so it was easy to stay on course. David had forced us to practice using the stars to find south so many times, we could do it in our sleep: imagine a line starting at the head of the Southern Cross, extending through the bottom. Eventually, the line hits another bright star that we call the Compass Star (I think that's a name we made up and that it had another name in the Old World, but none of us know what it was.) Point to the middle of the line that connects the cross to the Compass Star, and that's south. David and Dad told us that in the northern hemisphere, there was a star that was exactly north, called the North Star, and that at night, it wouldn't move at all—the other stars would just rotate around it. That would have been more convenient, but we made do with the stars we had.

All night, we took turns steering and sleeping. If our speed estimates were good, and if we didn't drift too far off course, we figured we'd spot at Pitcairn as sunrise. Of course, if we didn't, the one huge advantage we had over Dad and Mother's trip more than seventeen years earlier was that if we had to, we could turn and sail into the wind, searching both north and south until we found it.

The next morning, as the sun rose, we saw Pitcairn, straight ahead, no more than five miles away. The cliffs and mountains rising out of the sea were breathtaking. Dad had often told me that Pitcairn was over a thousand feet high, but I couldn't appreciate what that was until this moment. Pitcairn's mountains were ten times as high as Henderson. It also had real mountains and hills--Henderson, of course, was flat. From the many maps of Pitcairn that Dad had drawn for our trip, I could tell we were heading a little north of Bounty Bay. We changed course to the southwest for fifteen minutes until we saw the bay opening, then easily glided the *Enterprise* in.

The concrete dock was exactly as my father had described: a huge monolith of concrete protecting a pool of calm water. Building that must have been a great project! It was more than fifty feet long and five feet wide. Beyond the dock was the most incredible building I'd ever seen, many times the size of any of our huts and with an all-metal roof. Of all the times Dad and Mother described Pitcairn, they had never mentioned the fantastic metal roofs!

We lowered the sails and paddled to the lee side of the dock, tying the *Enterprise* up to a metal ring that looked like it'd been designed for that purpose. We gawked at the building. This must be what my father had called the boathouse. It was then that I realized what was missing: the *Sea Salva*. I suppose after almost twenty years, there was no reason to think it should still be there, but it was still a disappointment. We had heard so much about it, and I'd been keen to see what the Elders called a real boat.

As if oblivious to the significance of the moment, Mati immediately leapt onto the dock and ran off to the boathouse. I ran after her, and we ended up in an undeclared race of sorts.

"Hah, I won!" she said, touching the side of the boathouse.

"Okay, okay, but only because you got a head start. But did you see the roof? It's made of metal."

Mati wasn't listening. She was already exploring the immense building that now engulfed us. It must have been twenty feet wide by forty feet long, with a ceiling too high to touch, even if we jumped. I wondered why anybody would make a building with a ceiling higher than a person's head. Besides some rotten wood and rope, the only thing we found was a metal pole, perhaps two inches across and twenty feet long, still shiny and free of rust. I reached down with both hands to pick it up, expecting it to be very heavy, but was shocked at how easily I could lift it. It was hollow, but it still seemed way too light to be made of metal. Then I remembered that David had told us there were metals other than iron; maybe this was one of them. We'd have to take that back with us for sure.

Mati soon ran out of patience and insisted we go up to the town. We left through the front of the structure and turned right, expecting to see the trail up to Adamstown, what my dad called the Hill of Difficulty. What we saw, though, wasn't like any trail we had seen before. It was more than five feet wide and carved right out of the steep hillside. The trail was overgrown with grass and weeds, but there was a narrow path down the middle that was still clear for walking. We weren't sure if that meant people had been there, or whether it was an animal trail, like the ones our pigs made on Henderson.

The spectacle at the top of the cliff was even more remarkable than the boathouse. There were dozens of huge houses, all made of wood that had been sawn into boards, and all at least partially covered with metal roofs. They were in pretty bad shape, but we could only imagine how impressive the city must have been at one time.

And just as we'd been told, there were forests with trees much larger than we'd ever seen, some almost two feet around. And the ground changed as we climbed. The sand and gravel that we'd seen around the boathouse disappeared, and by the time we got to the top, the earth had become soft dirt with a reddish hue, and the rocks round, smooth, and heavy—nearly the opposite of those on Henderson.

We spent the day exploring every building we could find, virtually running from one to another. There were so many things we just didn't understand. We found what we recognized as the radio only because of Dad's detailed description. We twisted knobs and flipped switches but nothing happened. That wasn't the point, though; the point was that it existed!

David had told us that anything that looked electrical, no matter how beat up it was, should be brought back. And, if it was too large, we should look inside it and salvage anything magnetic. We were supposed to find magnetic things by touching them with my knife to see what stuck. And I had to admit that after all the things I'd seen that day, I was actually beginning to believe that magnets do exist, and that if we could find one for David, he could build his compass.

We failed utterly with respect our second goal, to find a watch or clock. Dad had drawn pictures, so we had a pretty good idea what we were looking for, but there was just nothing close. Yet, our search was just beginning as the day drew to a close.

I managed to catch one of the chickens running around the island, while Mati labored to light a small fire in front of what we guessed, based on Dad's descriptions and map, must have been Josh's house. We dug up some yams to go with our chicken and cooked dinner. Afterwards, we sat by the fire and planned where we'd search next and what, among our discoveries so far, we should take back with us. As we talked, the sun began to set, and Mati's enthusiasm seemed to turn to nervousness.

"Well, I guess the radio comes back with us for sure," Mati said. "Think we should bring some more metal back?"

"I don't think so, at least not just because it's metal. But remember those things we saw that look like tools?"

"You mean in the big flat building in the main city?"

"Yeah. We should probably bring those. I'm sure David knows what they are. Anyway, we should really search the buildings more carefully tomorrow and maybe even walk to the radio tower that Dad was telling us about. David said there would probably be some of those magnet stones up there in the wreckage."

The wind shifted suddenly, blowing smoke into my eyes. I rose to toss more wood on the fire, so we wouldn't have to relight it in the morning, and then sat back down upwind of the smoke—next to Mati.

There it was again, that strange need to get closer to her—to put my arm around her and pull her to me. And the closer I leaned toward her, the stronger the feeling. There was no satisfying it. It made me nervous—even afraid—but even fear couldn't quell its power.

As I resisted the urge to obey these strange feelings, Mati moved closer, as if reading my mind. She rested her head on my shoulder and burrowed her nose into my neck. From there, the mysterious avalanche gathered momentum. The more we touched each other, the closer I had to get. Almost dizzy, I kissed her forehead, not knowing why. She kissed my lips and that, too, had to become more. Our kisses had to become deeper, my hands had to find new skin to touch, and our bodies had to get closer. If she pushed me away, I'm not sure I'd have even been able to stop. We were in a place that was so completely foreign to us, yet we were only lost in one other.

I won't go into the rest of the details of that first night on Pitcairn, but to help understand how strange it all was, it's important to consider just who we were. I was the oldest Younger on the island, the next older person being more than twenty years my senior. And Mati was just a few years younger than I. Simply put, there had been nobody to show us how to grow up. We had no role models to show us passion or romance. So there was no way to understand what was happening to us as we matured or what we were supposed to do about it. It wasn't until much later that I realized Mom had seen this storm coming and had tried her best to warn me of it on the day we left. I hadn't understood—and even if I had, I wouldn't have believed it.

That night, we responded to each other by nervous and awkward instinct... and, I might add, with enthusiasm. In our passion, we went beyond the verbal, communicating on a much deeper level, and in our brief interludes of reason, we were too confused and embarrassed to talk about what was happening. We slept in short intervals, taking turns cradling our heads on each other's lap, in wonder of what had happened. As we watched the fire slowly burn down to embers, we formed a silent pact to just accept our new status. There was no need to discuss it: we had become a corporation of two, inseparable and invincible. From that night on, it was going to be us against the world, and the world didn't stand a chance.

Chapter 33

THE NEXT DAY WAS short. We spent almost all morning with each other, then gathered a leisurely lunch before beginning to look around the island. Once we were underway, though, we saw nothing different than we had the day before. It didn't matter to us, really. We weren't due back for another ten days or so, and we were together.

We decided to spend the night in Josh's house. We cooked outside and then carried our food in and ate at a table we'd cleaned up earlier. After dinner we lit some candlenuts and discussed what we should do next. Mati was leafing through some half-rotted papers she'd found in a corner when I brought up the thought had been bothering me all day. "We've got more than a week before we have to go back, but I'm not sure there's anything left for us to do here. Do you think we should just go back tomorrow?"

"I don't know." She stopped shuffling through the papers she'd found and looked at me. "Do you want to?"

"No. It just feels ... I mean, they're probably worried about us, and there's nothing to do here. I don't want to go back yet, but I guess I feel guilty somehow."

"Well, I don't want to go back either. What's going to happen when we get back? What are they going to say? Do we even tell them about ... what happened? I mean about us?"

"I don't know. What's Teiki going to say? What *can* he say?"

She gave a short laugh and shook her head. "I'm not worried about what he'll say, but about what he'll do."

"What he'll do?"

"Adam, Teiki never forgave you, and I don't think he ever will. He and my mom are very bitter about what you … about what happened."

"What about you? Do you blame me for what I did?" It had, until that moment, been a subject we'd deliberately avoided, but now we could discuss anything.

"What a silly question!" she said with awkward laugh. "What do you think?"

"No, seriously, how did you feel? Weren't you pissed off like Teiki and your mom?"

"I … I don't know. Sort of, I guess, but … I always knew Dad wasn't fair to you, and I knew your story was true. I think everybody knew; it's just that nobody wanted to say it. You know, Dad didn't always treat me fairly, either. It was like sometimes he loved me and sometimes he hated me, and I never knew which it was going to be. It seems mean to say, but in a way, I was happy about what happened … though I couldn't ever admit it." She looked me in the eye. "Teiki idolized Dad, though. And Teiki was Dad's life."

"So Teiki and your mom are still upset?"

Her expression turned grave. "*Really*, upset. I mean like they'd-like-you-dead upset." Seeing my surprise, Mati continued. "I didn't really mean that the way it probably sounds. They're not bad people … they're actually really good, but … well, I don't know if you can understand how much Kimo's death affected them."

I was quiet, thinking about her words.

"Adam, in the beginning, I convinced them that I was spending time with you to find ways to hurt you … or, not really *you*, but your reputation. I didn't really *say* that's what I was doing, but I had to make them believe it or they wouldn't have let me spend time with you. Teiki wanted people to turn against you, or even better, for you to be off the island. To sail off and never come back. That's what he really wanted. That's probably why he supported your boat project. He was hoping you'd never come back."

"I'm surprised your mom let you come with me."

She looked at the floor. "She didn't," she said, almost in a whisper.

"I didn't ask her 'cause I knew what she'd say, and I really wanted to come with you."

I thought for a moment, reflecting on how difficult this must have been for Mati. "Well, it's not going to help if we come back empty-handed after being away for two weeks."

She walked over to me with a ragged sheet of paper in her hand. "Hey, I'm not so good at reading. Can you look at this?"

I leaned over her shoulder and looked at the page under the flickering light of the burning candlenuts.

"It's a map. That's Pitcairn there." I pointed to a small island.

"Yeah, I know that, but what's this island up here?" She pointed to a spot to the northwest.

"It says it's Mangareva. That's the island the Elders all flew in from. It was supposed to be a huge city with almost a thousand people."

"That's what I thought it said, but the spelling was a bit funny. How far do you think it is?"

"I can't tell exactly. Was there more to the map than this?"

"There was, but it fell apart when I picked it up. Besides, it was all moldy, so you couldn't read the rest. Can you tell from what's here?"

"Well, we can guess, I suppose, just by looking at the size of Pitcairn, but I remember Dad saying Mangareva was about four hundred miles away or something like that."

"A four-day sail."

I wasn't sure whether she was proposing something or just making a comment, but decided if she wasn't proposing it, I would. "Maybe even a little less with good winds. Want to go?"

Her growing smile told me that was the response she wanted to hear. "Why not? We've got lots of food and water on board, and if we get there, can you even imagine what they'd all say when we got back? Do you think we can find it?"

"Sure. Look how big it is compared to Pitcairn—it's huge—and we found Pitcairn, didn't we? We even have a map now and know what direction to go, even if we don't know exactly how far it is. It's north and west. That's cool, too, because the more north we go, the easier it will be to get back to Henderson. We won't have to sail directly into the wind to get home."

I looked at her, but couldn't gage her expression. "So, you wanna go?"

Suddenly, Mati jumped into my arms. "First thing in the morning. But now there are other things I want to do."

Chapter 34

We had intended to depart first thing in the morning, but the sun had almost reached its zenith by the time we pried ourselves from each other's arms.

"What are we going to bring with us?" Mati asked. "We'll be going directly back home from Mangareva, so we need to load up whatever we're going to take now."

"Well, the radio for sure, and some of the metal rope that connects the houses here—David said they use that for electricity, so that should make him happy—and the old tools we found."

"Okay, but we can't bring everything on our first trip, or we won't have an excuse to come back."

"Oh, and there was that long metal pole we found down in the boathouse."

We loaded up the boat, replenishing what little food and water we'd used on the way to Pitcairn. Full of excitement, we pushed away from the concrete dock and started on a northerly course, riding an already brisk easterly wind. We joked freely as we left Pitcairn in the distance, bristling with confidence in the future and in ourselves.

We easily stayed on course through both the day and that night. The next morning, we awoke, thrilled, to find we were being escorted by a pod of dolphins. The wind was unusually strong for morning, but the skies were clear and it was wonderful to see the *Enterprise*'s bow cutting through the sea just behind the dolphins. I did a quick check of all the rigging, and everything was perfect. I threw the log overboard and carefully counted out the seconds until the rope was taut, concluding that we were moving at about six miles per hour. A few hours after sunrise, I tied down the tiller and announced, "I'm going to catch us a fish for lunch."

"We can marinate it in some of the lemons we brought," Mati said.

I got up to fetch my fishing line and tackle, and Mati noticed that I had tied down the tiller.

"Here, let me steer for a while. I don't like leaving it tied down like that. I know it looks like we're going straight, but we might drift off course without noticing."

"You didn't seem to mind tying it down yesterday when we took a break."

Her eyes twinkled. "Well, sometimes I guess it's okay, but I like steering anyway."

She crawled back to the tiller while I went the other direction to dig out my fishing gear. As we passed each other, I heard a sharp cracking sound and looked up just in time to see the front mast topple over to the port side, almost hitting Mati. The next thirty seconds passed in complete confusion. First, the boat leaned over frighteningly far to the port side as the fallen sail filled with water and sent the boat into an abrupt left turn. We both grabbed the starboard gunnels to hold on the best we could. As the boat whipped around to the left, the wind was suddenly at our backs. Fortunately, we realized what was going to happen a split second before it did: the rear sail suddenly jibed, crashing sharply to the other side. Had we not intuitively ducked at that very moment, we would have been knocked overboard and left in the ocean, probably unconscious. Then in no time, the turn finished and the boat was pointed into the wind, the rear sail flapping freely and the front two sails well under water. Our situation had changed so quickly from second to second, there had been no way to settle on a strategy. And by the time we could figure out what to do, there was nothing left to do. It was over before we even had a chance to be frightened.

"Come on," I said, "we better get the other sail down fast, before it luffs itself to bits."

Raising and lowering the sails had become so second nature to us, we had the other sail down in no time, without even discussing what we needed to do. Then we stood and looked around the boat, surveying the situation.

I said, "I guess the wind was just too strong for the starboard stays."

Even if you know how to sail, you might not understand some of the terms I'm using, since Dad admitted there was an awful lot he didn't remember—I think some of our words are made up. The *Enterprise* had two masts that we just called the front and back masts. The masts were about two inches in diameter at their bases. Each had a horizontal "boom"—strange name, but that's what we called them—that was attached to the mast with a bit of metal that David made.

Five ropes that Dad called "stays" held the front mast up: three connected the top of the mast to the front and two sides of the boat (forming a triangle of sorts, with the mast in the middle) and then two more tied about halfway up the mast were connected just to the two sides. The back mast was supported the same way, except the stay at the top went to the back of the boat rather than to the front. The stays were waterproofed hemp rope, about a half an inch in diameter, and were connected to the masts by lashings. It all seemed like overkill to me, but Dad was always saying that breaking a stay or losing a mast could sink the boat—at least that's what Josh had told him.

There were three sails on the *Enterprise*: a "jib" that was in front of the forward mast, a larger sail we called the front sail that filled the triangle made by the front mast and its boom, and then the rear sail, which was fastened to the back mast and boom. The sails were connected to the masts, booms, and front stays by lots of little rope loops, each about a foot apart. At least that's the way the Enterprise was just a few minutes earlier—now, there was only a rear mast and sail.

As we looked overboard at the mess of sails and ropes, along with the boom and mast, we saw the mast hadn't just toppled overboard, but had also broken right in the middle.

"I don't get it," Mati said. "If the stays broke, then why is the mast broken? Wouldn't it have just toppled over into the ocean? It should have just fallen down, not broken, don't you think?"

"Yeah, it seems that way." I was confused. "Maybe one of the top stays broke, then the mast broke because the lower stays didn't break. Then when the sail fell into the water, that broke the lower stays."

"I guess."

"Well, one thing for sure is that we better figure out what to do with all that crap. It's really pulling the front of the boat down. We're lucky it's so calm right now. If a big wave comes along, it'll probably break right over the top of the boat and sink us." I looked at the pile, not sure where to start. "Do you think we can even pull that mess back in?"

"Not with the sails full of water, no way. We have to somehow bring the sails in first, or just cut them away. That's probably the safest."

"I'm not cutting anything away! Who knows what we're going to need to fix this." I grabbed my knife and started to climb overboard.

"Wait! At least tie a rope around yourself in case the current pulls you away."

There was no current, or if there was, we were moving with it, but I decided not to make an issue of it and did as she asked. In fact, I was curiously pleased that she was thinking about me.

Once in the water, I cut the rope loops that attached the sails to the front mast. I suppose I could have just untied the loops, but they would be easy enough to replace; the sails were what we needed to save. I climbed out of the water, and with the sails now free of the mast and boom, we were easily able to pull them on board. The mast and boom were heavier, but still not difficult to pull back in once the sails were gone.

I inspected the broken rope stay. "That's weird. Look right here where it broke. There's no sap on the rope. No wonder. It's completely rotten. Here, feel it."

I handed her the rope. She scraped her fingernail across the rotten area and it flaked away. She then scratched at the rope that was still waterproofed, and it held firm.

"It can't be. That's … it's impossible." Mati turned away, buried her head into her hands, and started to weep.

"What? What can't be?"

She violently shook her head.

"Mati? What is it?"

She ignored me. I knew she had to think through things by herself first, and that once she did, she would tell me what was bothering her.

My attention drifted to the mast. What was bothering Mati became immediately obvious. "Mati, look at this!"

She lifted her head to look. The mast had been cut more than halfway through with a saw, right where lower stays were attached, just under their lashings.

For the first time I could remember, Mati began to openly sob, "I'm so, so sorry. I never thought … how could he do something like this?"

I knew exactly what she meant, but it was impossible to be angry in the face of her tears. "It's not your fault," I told her.

"Maybe it is. I was always telling Teiki what we were working on. I should have guessed that was why he always asked so many questions about sailing, when he … I even saw him playing around a few weeks ago, putting boiling water on some pieces of waterproofed rope. I asked him what he was doing, but he just said he was playing around. He must have been trying to remove the waterproofing. It seems so obvious now, and I feel like such a fool."

I jumped up and checked the other stays on the broken mast. "Look at this, Mati. The others are fine."

"So he only messed with this one?"

"Yeah, it seems so. Why would he do that?"

"Because he knew we'd be sailing downwind to Pitcairn," she replied, still sobbing.

It took me a second to understand. "Of course! He didn't want it to break on the way to Pitcairn; he wanted it to break on the way back. He just weakened the top starboard stay, so it would break when we were on a starboard tack. There's less tension on that rope when we sail downwind, the rope wouldn't rot for a few days anyway. He wanted me to get far downwind from Henderson, then make it impossible to get back."

Only then, did I realize the most terrible thing of all. I put my arms around Mati's shoulders. "Mati, he had no way to know you'd be coming with me."

We spent the next couple of hours bobbing around in the middle of nowhere, consoling each other, without a thought about what we should do next to escape our predicament. For me, it was infuriating, but for Mati, it was much, much more. Even though she liked me (or, I'd like to think, even loved me), she'd always looked up to her brother, believing that underneath it all, he was a good person who simply liked to compete with me. Never was she forced to take sides in our quarrels, pronouncing one of us right and the other wrong. Now that there was a clear right and wrong, she'd have to make some serious adjustments in her thinking. If we were successful in fixing the damage, she'd also have to face going back to Henderson and dealing with her brother directly.

As strange as it may sound, after a while, I found myself feeling sorry for Teiki, though I confess not too much so. Mati was the one person he seemed to really like—I suppose he even loved her in his own way—and he had unwittingly sent her to possible death. It was almost painful to imagine what he must have felt as he stood at the northwest corner of the island, with his crossed arms, helplessly watching his sister sail off to the disaster he knew would befall us.

Mati's voice shook me out of my thoughts. "We'd better check the rest of the boat. He probably did the other mast too."

"You're right. Maybe other stuff too, especially things that would only break when we sail into the wind. Knowing Teiki, he wouldn't have relied on just one weakened point."

We examined every part of the boat we could, even those under water. I was most worried about the keel itself, but fortunately it looked fine. The extra rope we had stored below the floorboards, however, had apparently been swapped out for untreated rope, and had already completely rotted away. In addition, the rear mast had been rigged the same as the front, and the rudder had been cut halfway through, right under the tiller so it could only be seen from the water. It was a miracle it hadn't broken already, but again, the stress on the rudder was almost nothing while sailing downwind to Pitcairn.

We weren't in any immediate trouble, so we decided not to rush things. The one thing we couldn't afford now was to do something stupid. Better to think things through during the night. There'd be plenty of time to make repairs in the morning.

Unlike the exciting churn of a boat knifing its way through the sea, bobbing adrift can be very unsettling. Sleep, that night, was uneasy, allowing plenty of time for reflecting on unanswerable questions. What would Teiki have done if Mati *had* told him she was going with me rather than Dad? Forbid her to go, I'm sure, but on what grounds? Or what if we had been in shouting range when he found out Mati was on the boat? Would he have revealed his plan in order to save her? Was his intent to kill Dad and me, or just to leave us stranded on Pitcairn? Or did it even matter to him?

We both awoke early the next morning and began making repairs. As luck would have it, they were pretty easy. We used the metal rope from Pitcairn to make new stays, much stronger than the old ones. Then, rather than try to repair the broken front mast, we used the strange metal pole we'd found in the boathouse. With the new metal stays, there was probably no need to strengthen the rear mast, where Teiki had cut part of the way through, but just to be sure, we lashed part of the broken mast across the weakened area. The rudder was the most difficult to repair, but since it hadn't broken yet, we were able to reinforce it with bits of spare wood we had on board.

Our biggest problem now was figuring out where we were. By the time we were ready to set sail, we had been aimlessly adrift for almost a full day. We no longer had a clear heading for Mangareva, Pitcairn, or Henderson. After much discussion, we decided to press on to Mangareva. Although it was the farthest of the three, it was also by far the largest, and therefore, we supposed, easier to find. Besides, we weren't willing to concede defeat. Perhaps if our problems had been accidents, we'd have turned around and let discretion be the better part of valor. But there was no way I was going to let Teiki stop us. His thwarted sabotage simply proved to me that Mati and I were invincible. So with our boat stronger than it had been when we left Henderson, we took our best guess and got underway.

Chapter 35

I HAVE NO IDEA when we sailed past Mangareva or how close we came. The realization that we were lost was a gradual one. We'd expected to get there two or three days after the repairs, but as we waited for dawn a full five days after our setback, we had no choice but to finally accept that we had missed our mark. We were lost at sea.

As the sky began to lighten, I anxiously watched Mati, standing at the very front of the boat, leaning into the front stay and peering at the horizon. Having long since accepted that she had, by far, the sharper vision, I hardly ever relied on my own eyes anymore. "See anything?" I asked.

"I don't think so. Clouds off to the northwest—almost due north. Maybe there's something there, but I don't think so. There's certainly nothing anywhere else." We both fell quiet, not wanting to verbalize our fears.

"You think we should turn around?" Mati finally asked.

"I don't see how that'll help. It's not like we've dropped bread crumbs behind us."

"Bread crumbs? I don't understand."

"Oh, it's just a story Dad used to tell me as a kid. Something about a boy dropping bread crumbs behind him in the woods so he wouldn't get lost, but then something or other ate the crumbs and he got lost anyway. It doesn't matter. What I mean is that if we don't know what direction we're going, or how far we are from Mangareva, then it's not going to help to turn around and try to find it. Which way would we go? I don't have a clue whether it's in front, behind, to the right, or to the left of us."

"So then what do we do, just keep going?"

"I was thinking about that last night. It wasn't on the map you found, but David always drew maps for us that showed Mangareva at the southeast tip of a long chain of islands. I think they were called the Society Islands or something, and the rest of the islands were all over to the northwest. There were lots of other islands to the north of Mangareva too, but he said there was nothing to the south except Pitcairn and Henderson. So, I think our odds of finding land are much better if we head north."

"That's where the clouds are too, so that's probably a good idea. We can see for sure there's nothing in the other directions. At least there's a chance there's something behind the clouds."

"Maybe there's some rain too. It would be good to top off our water supply. We still have plenty now, but I guess we don't know how long we'll be ..." I couldn't bring myself to say "lost."

Mati suddenly grinned. "So, we have plenty of food, too, especially with that mahi-mahi you caught yesterday, and we have each other. Not too bad, huh?"

She was right. And her optimism was contagious. I sure wasn't anxious to get back to Teiki and Henderson anyway. And there was bound to be something out there for us, somewhere. Maybe sailing into the unknown wasn't so bad after all.

For the next two weeks, the *Enterprise* sailed briskly on gentle seas without a glimpse of land. But we kept going forward, as straight as possible. We reasoned that if we went in a straight line, eventually, we'd have to hit something, but if we started to go in circles, we might never get anywhere. There were enough light rain showers to replenish our water supply, and the fish were abundant, so we were never at risk of starving or dying of thirst, but by the end of the second week, we were on a fish-only diet and getting pretty sick of it. The other thing that began to run out was our enthusiasm. Every day, our boat leaked a little more. We pushed hemp caulking into the separating boards, but from the inside of the boat, we just couldn't stop the water completely. We found ourselves bailing more and more every day, and it was becoming tiring. We still enjoyed sailing, and we weren't tired of each other's company, but we wanted desperately to know where we were. And the *Enterprise* seemed to be getting smaller and smaller—we longed to walk more than fifteen feet in a straight line.

Of course it was Mati who first spotted land. Early one afternoon, she pointed tentatively off to the east, as if she were afraid of scaring away whatever it was she saw. It looked like clouds to me, but I dared hope she saw something more.

"What is it?" I asked.

"There's something there." I think she was afraid to say "land," but I knew from her expression that's what she meant.

I immediately changed course toward the cloudbank. After an hour of sailing and squinting off to the east, I could finally see some substance behind the clouds, but it looked to be thirty or forty miles away. But even from that far away, I could tell that whatever we were looking at was high—much higher even than Pitcairn—and very large.

Over the next hour, the clouds thickened and moved toward us, and then it finally began to drizzle. We lost sight of land, but by then, we were so close there was no way we'd miss it.

By the time we could see the island's shadow again, the sun was setting. We estimated we had just a couple more miles to shore. Fortunately, it was nearing a full moon, so we had enough light to keep us from accidentally running aground. The rain stopped just as we approached land. The dark coastline was difficult to see, but almost right in front of us, there was a snug little bay, well protected from the waves. It was almost like a circle, about two hundred feet across, with an opening just fifty feet wide. We could tell by the waves that the water inside was sufficiently deep for the *Enterprise*.

As we entered the bay, the wind died down and the water settled to almost dead calm. We veered into the slight remaining wind, dropped our sails, and lowered a small anchor we'd found on Pitcairn, which fell nearly twenty feet before finding bottom.

The diffuse moonlight cast dark shadows on a sharp, craggy

shoreline, resulting in an eerie and forbidding scene. As much as we desperately wanted to go ashore, we decided it would be smarter to wait until morning.

For the first time in two weeks, we both slept without one of us keeping watch—or rather we tried to sleep. Our leaks had worsened to the point where we still had to get up several times to bail, but even without that, we were just too excited to sleep; we were surrounded by a world we had never seen, and a world that, in just a few hours, would answer so many of our questions.

At the first hints of light, we crawled out of our little cabin. The cloud cover had lifted during the night so we got our first real look at our discovered land. It was unbelievably big. Perhaps this was no island at all, but instead what the Elders called a continent. Off to the west, two huge mountains sloped gently upward all the way from the ocean until they disappeared into the clouds. I guessed we were at least thirty miles away from them and that they were maybe thirty miles away from each other, but these were just guesses—I had never seen land stretch such enormous distances.

"It's so big!" Mati said.

"But look at the land." I pointed to a little outcropping no more than thirty feet from the boat. It was dark black, with no vegetation—no soil, no dirt, not even a blade of grass—just horrible, twisted black rock that was even more sharp and irregular than Henderson.

Mati shifted her focus from the horizon to the nearby shore. "Oh my God, no wonder nobody survived! I can't even imagine the heat it would take to have done all this!"

I couldn't respond. I think I was as devastated as the land around us. All my dreams to see the world, and it looked like this! Kimo and the other Kitchens had been right: there was nothing for us here, nothing but tortured, barren, black rock, stretching as far as we could see along the shore and up the sloping mountains. We stared in silence, absorbing the site of the dead land and the implications it carried. Mati shuddered. I draped my arm around her shoulders and pulled her closer.

"I can't imagine either," I finally replied. "It looks like the slag that

David gets in his furnace when he melts glass and something goes wrong. The sun must have melted everything."

Mati began to weep, and I wasn't far behind.

"Look, it goes down into the water, too." I pointed into the crystal clear water, which revealed the same black rock all the way from shore to where we were anchored. "It must have melted the land and then poured into the water."

As the sun rose from behind the mountains, the ambient light increased steadily, and leaden shadows began to reveal a bit of color.

Mati finally broke her silence. "Look way up there on the mountain. I can see green and yellow areas. Maybe it isn't all like this."

I couldn't see it yet, but was happy to hear her optimism, and tried to build on it. "Want to swim ashore for a look around?"

"I guess, but just a quick look. I think before we do too much exploring, we should sail along the coast and see what else there is. Maybe even find a beach where we can pull up and fix some of the leaks."

"I suppose, but I really want to see what that rock's like."

"Adam? What if …"

"What?"

"What if everything is like this and there's no way to find our way back home?"

"Hey, don't think about things like that. Let's just see what's here and not worry, okay? C'mon, let's go ashore."

"Okay. Looks like there's a little place over there where it would be easy to get in and out." She pointed to a dark beach about a hundred feet away that was nestled between two rocks. We cast off our pareos, dove in, and swam over. The tiny beach was steep and more gravel than sand, made up of the same black rock, but broken up by the waves over the years. Despite our situation, after having been at sea for three weeks, I felt a tremendous burst of pride in taking those first steps onto our new world.

I went to an outcropping and lifted up a loose bit of the strange rock. It was light, as if half air. And walking on the stuff was tricky because there were so many holes to step into if you weren't careful. "Well, you were right about one thing," I told Mati. "The way to explore this place is by water, not by walking around on this stuff. It'd probably take us an hour to walk just a mile."

We set out for a short walk along the coast to the north, with no intention of going more than a hundred yards. We just wanted to get to a high point where we could look around. While I was focusing on the tricky footing, Mati called to me. "Look! There's some green ahead."

I looked up and saw it: a patch of grass. It was shorter and thicker than any grass on Henderson or Pitcairn, but it was bright green. It was as if whatever melted the ground had completely missed that section of land. "Maybe the melted rock flowed down from the mountain like water, pouring into the sea, and it just flowed around this area. Maybe there are other areas like this that weren't destroyed, too—all those green areas you saw up in the mountains."

Mati didn't answer. She had stopped short and was staring, transfixed. I followed her gaze to a magnificent building just beyond the grassy patch. In fact, it was completely surrounded by green. We walked closer to get a better look. It was amazing. It was in perfect condition and even larger than the boathouse we'd seen on Pitcairn. It was made of little rectangular reddish-brown stones and large sheets of glass. It had what looked like little curved, reddish boards for a roof rather than the metal sheets of Pitcairn, but it still looked extravagant. What was most impressive, though, was that at least half the building must have been glass! Facing the ocean was a window covered by a piece of glass that was bigger than an entire wall of our hut on Henderson. In front of the huge window was a big, flat cement surface.

We carefully approached, walking across the soft green grass onto the smooth cement surface. We peered in the largest of the windows. It was as amazing on the inside as it was on the outside, and again in perfect condition.

Mati asked, "You think this area was once one of those big cities that the Elders talked about, with hundreds or thousands of buildings like this?"

"Probably. I guess so." I ran my hand along the glass. It was as smooth as the sides of my knife blade and so clear you couldn't even tell it was there. It was so overwhelming that it frightened me, and it was clear that Mati was a bit scared, too. I put my left arm over her shoulder to try to comfort her (and perhaps to take comfort from her), and she put her right arm around my waist to pull me closer.

"Think we should go in?" she whispered.

"I guess so. That's what we're here for, isn't it? I'll bet it has everything David wants."

We walked a few steps to a door, and I pushed on it, but it wouldn't budge. "It's stuck on something."

"Try pulling on that round thing," suggested Mati.

There was a shiny, round, metal ball on the door. I tried to pull it and turn it, but it wouldn't budge. "Maybe you have to put something in this little slot here to open it," I said. "Should we try to break one of the glass pieces?"

"No, please don't. They're so beautiful. There must be another way."

I tried to ram the door with my shoulder. It didn't give way but there was a slight cracking sound. We looked at each other.

"Try again," Mati said.

I rammed the door harder and was rewarded with a louder cracking sound, like that of breaking wood. Without prompting, I hit it a third time, and the door flew open. We stood there, staring, but afraid to step inside. The floor was made of smooth, polished stone that was glistening as if it were wet, even though it was completely dry. Everything was perfectly shaped and clean.

I scanned the room, trying to find something, anything, that looked familiar. I spotted a round disk on one of the walls with numbers around the outside, but it took me a moment to realize why it looked familiar: it was just like David's descriptions and Dad's drawings.

"Look, a clock!" We cast aside our fears and ran across the shiny floor to the opposite wall. I gently lifted it from the wall and set it on the floor near the door. If we did get back to Henderson, we had just accomplished one of our two primary objectives. Now if we could only find a compass.

We wandered into an area that we guessed was for cooking. Everything was made of perfectly shiny metal. My eye wandered to several knives that had been pushed into a wooden block. I withdrew the largest: a knife almost as large as my own back on the *Enterprise*. "Here's something we can take back as a present for Dad."

"What about me?" Mati asked with an exaggerated pout. "I want a knife, too."

"Then it's yours." I ceremoniously handed her the knife. "A treasure from the Old World."

Mati giggled and took the knife. "What do you suppose this place was?"

"Maybe a hut where lots of people lived, maybe for a whole Kitchen. That's all I can figure."

Mati's attention turned to a large piece of glass shaped like a bowl. It sat on a stand about waist high and was covered with sharp facets that made it shimmer in the morning light. "Adam, look at this! Isn't it incredible? See how beautiful it is? Can we take it with us?"

"What would you do with it?"

"Nothing, I just want it to remember this place and to show to others. I didn't really want this knife; we can give it to your Dad if I can take this instead."

I walked over to the bowl and picked it up. A small piece of paper on the bottom read Waterford Crystal. I was dizzy.

"Are you okay?"

It took me a moment to answer. "Yeah, I suppose. It's just that Dad and David were teasing me once about Waterford glass and, well, it just hit me all of a sudden: this is their world ... the Elders. It means it's *all* true. Everything they told us and we laughed at. Their world really did exist, just as they said it did."

She kissed me on the lips. "And it means it's all possible, too."

I looked at her quizzically.

"I mean it can all exist again," she explained. "We can do all those things they always talked about. We can make them again."

As I set the glass object down by the door, I realized she was right: all of it was possible. There was so much to learn, explore, and rebuild, but we could make it all happen again.

I was starting back toward Mati, when I was distracted by a large black rectangle of glass across the room. I wandered over and ran my hands over the smooth dark surface, wondering what its purpose might be. There were a few protrusions on the bottom with words written next to them. I touched one of them and the dark glass immediately lit up. Then the perfect image of a person appeared underneath the glass. The person was looking right at us and talking! He spoke English, but I admit I was so confused I had no idea what he was saying. It took me a moment to realize this must be what Dad called a television.

Suddenly a new voice screamed from behind us. "Police! Freeze!"

We spun around. Just outside the door, there were two men dressed in identical blue clothing, both extending one arm and pointing some sort of metal object at us. Survivors! This changed everything. Were they explorers from another island like us, or were they from here and somehow managed to survive the devastation—maybe in the green areas we had seen up in the mountains?

Clutching my arm, Mati whispered, "What does he mean, *freeze*?"

"I don't know," I whispered back. "Let's just be friendly." I started to walk over to greet them.

Before we could even think of what to say, the taller one commanded in the same demanding voice, "Put your hands up!"

I couldn't understand why we should raise our hands, so I looked at Mati, but she seemed just as confused. They repeated their command a third time. Although we didn't really understand, Mati extended her arms toward them, like theirs were to us. I imitated her, thinking that was probably what they were asking us to do. Maybe extending their arms to us was a confirmation of their friendly intentions, even though their voices didn't sound too friendly.

As we began to walk slowly toward them with our hands extended, they backed out of the doorway and onto the concrete surface. They seemed to be afraid of us. So as calmly as I could, I said, "It's okay, we're friends."

The taller one shouted, "I said, drop the weapon and freeze!"

Mati started toward them again, but just then there was a deafening sound, louder than a crash of thunder, and one of the blue men's metal objects jerked backwards.

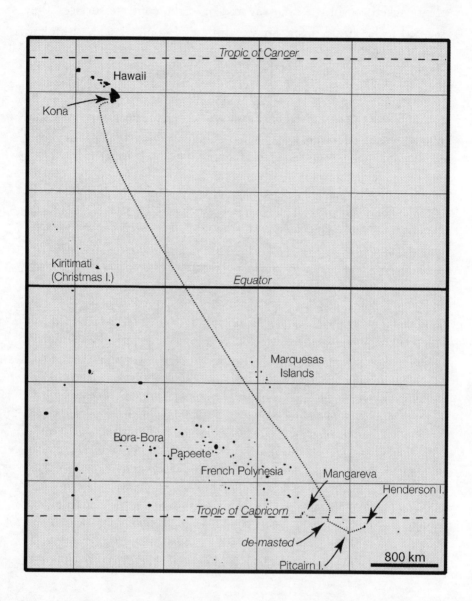

Tropic of Cancer

Hawaii

Kona

Kiritimati
(Christmas I.)

Equator

Marquesas
Islands

Bora-Bora

Papeete

French Polynesia

Mangareva

Henderson I.

Tropic of Capricorn

de-masted

Pitcairn I.

800 km

Part III

✝

Odd Clients

Chapter 36

AT APPROXIMATELY 9:11 A.M., Officer Tate and I responded to a silent alarm at a vacation home on Kiholo Bay owned by Jim and Jay Sanders. We arrived at the rear of the house at approximately 9:28 a.m. and immediately noticed that a rear patio door had been forced open. We heard noise from within, so it was evident that the perpetrator was still inside and making no effort to conceal him or herself. Because of that, we suspected it may have been the owners who forgot their key, forced open the door, and then neglected to shut off the alarm, but we called for back-up just in case. We stationed ourselves on opposite sides of the broken door and looked inside.

We observed a man and a woman in the living room, both roughly twenty years of age, picking up and examining various objects. Neither wore any clothing or shoes. The woman was carrying a large kitchen knife in her right hand.

As they were unaware of our presence, I signaled Officer Tate to observe them from the doorway before announcing our presence. They spoke freely to each other with no concern of being overheard and appeared to be role-playing, making fun of the items they were examining. The man began to run his hands along the surface a television, then jumped back in surprise when he pushed the power pad, turning the TV on. At first I thought he was startled by the noise, afraid it might alert somebody, but he made no effort to turn it off or lower the volume; rather, he seemed entranced by the local news broadcast.

I signaled to Officer Tate, and we entered the doorway with our guns drawn. We clearly identified ourselves as police officers and ordered the pair to freeze. They immediately turned to face us. They made no effort to escape, but ignored our command to freeze. They exchanged a few words with each other that we were unable to make out above the sound of the television.

I then ordered the intruders to raise their hands. They ignored that command as well. Again, they looked at each other, pretending not to understand, even though we had already heard them speaking English with one another. I repeated the order a second time. This time, the two slowly extended their arms straight out, as if mocking us. With her hands extended and holding the knife, the female began to advance on us in no apparent fear of our drawn weapons. It appeared to us that she and her companion were on drugs of some sort.

The man then claimed they were "friends." I thought they might be claiming to be friends of the owner, though that seemed very unlikely. We backed away, stepping outside the door, keeping a safe distance from the intruders while giving them time to respond to our orders, but we were soon on the patio, backed up against the lava field that surrounds the bay, and could retreat no further.

I ordered them to freeze a final time, but the female continued to advance on our position. I then fired a warning shot over the female's head. The warning shot seemed to shock both of them, as they stopped their advance, froze, and became completely focused on our guns; however they continued to refuse to raise their hands as instructed.

Despite their erratic behavior, the pair did not appear to be hostile. I then commanded the female to put down her knife and she promptly complied. We feared they would resist arrest if we tried to restrain them, and because back-up had not yet arrived, we were concerned about putting ourselves in a position in which we'd have to shoot them unnecessarily. We therefore waited for help to arrive.

At this time, the male suspect began talking to us. He said, "We sailed from Henderson. How many of you are there?" We refused to respond and ordered them to remain silent. They complied.

A second squad car arrived five minutes later, and we proceeded to handcuff the two suspects. They did not physically resist arrest, but seemed surprised that they were being restrained. We proceeded to wrap a blanket around each of them and asked them where they had left their clothes and shoes. They claimed that they left their pareos on their boat and had no shoes. We didn't believe this, considering the sharp lava surrounding the point of entry to the house, but as we escorted them to our squad car, I noted that they walked across the lava, seemingly without discomfort, strengthening our suspicions that drugs were involved.

They were reluctant to get into the squad car. They did not physically resist, but had to be prodded a bit into the back seat. They appeared extremely agitated as our car drove away. They whispered to each other the entire way to the station, but we were unable to make out what they were saying. Their reaction to entering Kailua and the police station was again consistent with the use of hallucinatory drugs: staring at signs and into streetlights, almost hypnotically.

After escorting them into the station, we read them their Miranda rights. When I asked if they understood what I had said, the male suspect took this as permission to speak openly. He repeated that they had sailed here from Henderson Island and said there were another thirty of them "still back there." He also said, "We thought you were all dead," but didn't specify whom he meant by "we" and "you." He then asked the same question he had earlier, regarding how many of us there were and where we were.

Given the state of undress in which we found them, they were unable to produce any identification. They gave their names as Adam and Matahina, but refused to provide either last names or addresses. We proceeded to book them, cut a few hairs for a DNA search, and issued them jumpsuits. When they figured out what the bright orange jumpsuits were for, they removed their blankets right in the middle of the crowded police station, oblivious to the stares they were drawing, and unhurriedly donned the jumpsuits before we could show them the restrooms. Again, the awkwardness with which they put on the jumpsuits was consistent with the influence of drugs.

The couple had still not acknowledged that they understood their Miranda rights, and given their behavior, it seemed possible that they really didn't understand what was going on. They seemed anxious to talk to us, but until they acknowledged understanding their rights or were represented by council, we did not want them talking. Accordingly, we instructed them to remain silent, escorted them to separate detention rooms, and contacted the DA's office to get further instructions.

Officer James W. Meade

Chapter 37

THAT WAS THE POLICE report prepared by Officer Meade. I was assigned to the case the same day and admit I had read it through the first time with disinterest. My initial interview was just after lunch, with the male suspect named Adam. I was struck by Adam's appearance the moment I opened the door to the detention room. He was of average height, young, fit, and darkly tanned, and sported long, unkempt, sun-bleached blond hair with a matching scraggily beard. There was an intensity about him that one seldom finds, and it quickly dominated my attention.

After sizing him up for a moment, I stepped forward and introduced myself. "Hi, I'm Bill Riley from the public defender's office. I've been assigned to represent you." I extended my hand; he looked at it, but refused to take it—he didn't seem angry, but rather lost.

After a moment, he replied, but even then, very cautiously. "I'm Adam. What does it mean to *represent* me?"

I was relieved that his English was good. I couldn't even understand half the people I represented. This guy might be on drugs, but at least we weren't going to waste hours trying to communicate through interpreters. "It means I've been asked to defend you against the charges that are being brought against you."

"What charges, and where's Mati?"

I glanced at the police report. "Mati is Matahina?"

"Yeah, Matahina. We call her Mati."

"Mati's down the hall in another detention room. I've been asked to represent both of you, so I'll see her in a moment. Now, the charges against you, as I understand it, are likely to be breaking and entering,

314

burglary, illegal drug use, assault with a deadly weapon, and public indecency. Do you understand what all that means?"

He looked genuinely confused. "No, not really. Is it because I pushed open the door to that hut?"

I couldn't help chuckling. "*Hut*? Look, I know that area, and that's not exactly a hut—more like a mansion. But yeah, that's part of it. The police report also says that you were, well, completely naked."

"We had to swim ashore and didn't want to get our pareos wet. We thought we'd only be on shore for a few minutes."

"All right, let's start from the beginning. What's your full name and where are you from?"

"I already told the man in blue: I'm Adam and I'm from Henderson Island."

"I know, it says that here. But what's your family name?"

He looked at me blankly.

"Who are your parents?"

"Stan is my dad, and my mom is Nani... and Jenny was my mother."

I thought, *Oh, boy. Here we go again.* Somehow, we got all the crackpots here in Kona, and they all seemed to find me at some point in their illustrious careers. Well, that was okay, actually; to tell you the truth, I enjoyed the weirdoes. In the beginning, I was deluded, as are most law students, into believing I'd be saving innocent people from unfair prosecution. It didn't take me long to realize that they were almost all guilty, and that my job was nothing more than to assure fair treatment and, usually, barter for lighter sentences. The rare innocent clients I had defended never even got to court; the cases were always dropped well before then. Of the cases that did get to court, I lost almost all of them, and the few victories I did chalk up were cases I won on some technicality, despite the fact that everybody, including me, knew the defendant was guilty, so I typically didn't feel very proud of winning.

So mine wasn't exactly a rewarding occupation, and by any measure, my twenty-year pursuit of that occupation had been remarkably unremarkable. Somewhere along the line, as I lost my idealistic zeal, I came to realize I wasn't the great defender I once thought I'd be—and, I suppose, that all lawyers imagine they'll be. I had even come to dread the possibility that I might have to actually defend a truly innocent person someday—what if I lost, and because of my mediocrity, an innocent person wound up in jail?

Don't get me wrong, it's not that I was lazy. I worked hard at my job—very hard—with hours long enough to eliminate any possible social life or long-term romantic relationship. It's just that I still didn't seem to get anywhere. And of course, as I was busy calibrating my own legal abilities, all the local private law firms were doing the same. It wasn't long before they, too, realized I was nothing special. That's how I gradually became chained to this unrewarding and boring existence as a public defender, enlivened only by the weirdoes and their far-out tales—and I could already tell this one was going to be a whopper.

"Okay," I said, "we'll come back to your parents later. But what were their full names?"

All of a sudden he seemed to get it. "Oh, you mean their *other* names?"

"Sure, I guess that's what I mean, their other names."

"I don't know. They told me once—I know they had other names—but I forgot."

I sighed in resignation. "All right, so where's this Henderson Island?"

"It's about a hundred miles east of Pitcairn."

"And where's Pitcairn?"

"About three hundred miles south and east of Mangareva."

"Uh-huh. Well, I hate to ask, but where's that?"

He looked completely bewildered, as if I were an idiot. "You don't know where Mangareva is? It's a big island. There were once almost a thousand people living there."

"I see. And how would you get there from here?"

"I don't really know because nobody's told me where we are now.

About three or four weeks to the southeast, I think, but I'm not exactly sure. So where are we anyway?"

"You don't know where you are?"

"No."

I decided to play along. "This is the town of Kailua, on the Kona shore of the big island of Hawaii."

"I've heard of Hawaii. My dad went there with my mother once. Are there many people alive here?"

"Here on the big island? Not that many. Oahu has more people." If you ignored the words he was saying, he seemed perfectly sane, even likeable. I looked forward to hearing more of his delusion, but there was no time for that right now. "Look, we need to worry about you, not … well, let's just focus on you for now. In just an hour, you'll go into court for your arraignment. You know what that is?"

"No."

"A judge is going to ask you how you plead to the charges I told you about earlier. We really need to focus on that, so tell me what happened. Start at the beginning."

"The beginning? You mean of the trip or just today?"

"Let's keep it simple. How 'bout starting when you arrived at the house they claim you broke into."

"Well, we were surprised to see the house. It seemed in perfect condition, too. We thought at first it must have somehow survived the Great Storm, but now I guess it was built afterwards, right?"

"I don't really know, just keep going. What happened when you saw the house?"

"We didn't mean to stay on land long, but we had to get some things to take back to Henderson, and it looked like we might find them inside."

"What sort of things?"

"A clock and a compass mostly."

A goddamn scavenger hunt? I thought. We'd have to come back to that when there was more time. "Okay, so then what?"

"So, then I pushed through the door and we looked around. We found a clock and, I think, a television, but then the two guys in blue came."

"Okay, look, you've got to stop calling them that. They're policemen, and you should address them as sir, or officer."

"Okay." He silently mouthed the two words as if practicing.

"The report says they told you put your hands up, but you kept walking toward them. Why didn't you do what they told you?"

"They just shouted 'freeze,' but we didn't know what they meant."

I stared right in his eyes, but he didn't even flinch. Wow, this guy was good. He could tell a tale as convincingly as anybody I had ever met, and I was pretty good at reading people. I played along. "It means you should stop moving and stay absolutely still."

"Oh. Well, we didn't know. My dad said it was something that can happen to water when it turns hard and transparent, like glass. Why didn't they just ask us to stay still?"

"Good idea. I'll recommend that to them." *Yeah, right. I'll just use that argument in court: But Judge, they told my defendants to turn hard and transparent. They really tried, but just couldn't* … "So what happened next?"

"We tried to talk to them, but one of them made their gun …"

He seemed stuck, so I offered, "Fire?"

"I guess. Anyway, it scared us. We'd never seen a gun before. The Elders had told us about them, but we didn't know that's what they were holding until the one guy made it fire. Luckily, it didn't hurt us."

"That's because he missed, and I'm quite sure he meant to. I understand one of you was carrying a knife and wouldn't drop it."

"Mati had a knife we found in the other room, but she never would have …" His expression turned to disbelief. "Did they think she was going to attack them?"

"I don't know what they thought, but she's lucky it was Officer Meade—most officers wouldn't have fired just a warning shot. In fact, he may even be reprimanded for not doing more. Are you on any drugs or anything?"

"I don't know what that means."

"Drugs. Like smack, acid, coke, meth … anything?"

"Sorry, I don't know what those are."

Absolutely straight-faced! He was good. "All right. Look, we don't have much time before we go into court, and I still need to talk to your friend. Mati, was it? Is she your girlfriend or something?"

He frowned for a moment, then smiled and said, "Yeah, I guess she is."

"How old is she?"

"Sixteen."

"And you?"

"Eighteen."

"And your parents are back on this Henderson place?"

"Yes."

"Okay, I need to go talk to Mati. I'll see you in about an hour for the arraignment. Somebody will come and get you and walk you into court."

I laughed to myself as I walked out. For twenty years, I had listened to bullshit, from real artists, too, but this guy was the craziest. Did he really think anybody would believe that shit?

Mati was seated with her back to me as I opened the door. When she heard me enter, she stood, as if frightened, and turned toward me, leaving me momentarily speechless. She was an absolutely stunning young woman with long, full blonde hair surrounding dark brown eyes that seemed out of place, but somehow reached out toward me. Her cheekbones were high, and her flawless complexion obviously darkened by a lifetime in the sun. I remembered the police report that so mechanically described her as being found stark naked in the Sanders house. I was sure there were more elaborate stories going around the police station right about then. Even through her orange jumpsuit, it was clear she had the body of a full-grown woman. Without any ID or proof of age, though … well, it was going to be a mess. If she really was sixteen, she'd go to the juvenile system, but what would the courts do with somebody that claimed to be underage, but didn't look underage and had no proof? Probably try her as an adult.

The girl's story was consistent with Adam's, down to the names of the places, times, what they had misunderstood, and so on. It was one thing to hear a crazy story from one person, but quite another to hear the same story from two different people. It meant they had worked out the story in advance—every little detail. It also meant these kids were a lot smarter than I had given them credit for. Mati's demeanor was much like Adam's: confident, energetic, likeable, and both frightened and defiant at the same time. If she was sixteen, she was incredibly mature for her age. She, too, denied having a last name, so I asked her about her parents.

"What were your parents' last names?"

"I don't know. I think they had them, but I'm not sure 'cause we never used them. My mother's name is just Stefani and my Dad's … was just Kimo."

The split second of hesitation before "was" caused me to suspect there was more information to be mined. "Was? Did he die?"

"Yes, about a year ago." Again, I detected was just a hint of nervousness in her response.

"I'm sorry. How did he die?"

She looked down at the floor. "He was killed."

"Killed, like murdered? How?"

"He was pushed, and fell onto some rocks."

"Who pushed him?"

She hesitated. "Adam. But he had to."

Though it obviously disturbed her, she seemed to give no consideration to lying. I waited, but she offered no further explanation, and I didn't want to open another can of worms just then. Still, I wondered, if it were a lie, then what was her motive? And if it were the truth, then why was she making up so many other things? After the interview, I explained the upcoming arraignment process to her and started for the door. Then, as an afterthought, I turned and said, "Mati, name some of the others that were on this island with you."

"Well, in our Kitchen, there's myself, my mom, and my brother Teiki. Then there's George, Nick, and Lisa, and—"

"That's good. How old is Lisa and what color hair does she have?"

"She's eleven and has brown hair. Why?"

"No reason, just curious. Short hair, long hair?"

"It's really long, but why?"

I left without answering.

It was lunchtime by the time I finished with Mati, so I went across the street to my favorite deli and ordered my usual turkey and swiss on white. I sat at a table in back, and between bites, mulled over my odd new clients.

Adam and Mati hadn't actually taken anything from the Sanders house, but they obviously intended to. I knew the DA wouldn't pursue an indecency charge since the couple was on private property and had not intended to be seen. The police hadn't found any drugs or paraphernalia, so it was unlikely that any drug-related charges would be levied. The charge that would certainly be pressed—and would likely stick—was breaking and entering, which they both freely admitted having done. I still wasn't sure they recognizing it as a crime. They'd be on shaky ground, but the DA office would probably go for a burglary charge, if nothing else, so they could offer to drop it later as part of a plea bargain. The charge I was most concerned about, however, was assault with a deadly weapon. Based on the police report, the DA would have a straightforward case—they'd merely have to show that any reasonable person would feel threatened by a naked woman approaching with a large knife—didn't sound like a stretch to me.

So the charges seemed clear. The real puzzle now was how to deal with their lack of identification—I knew that wasn't going to go over well with the court. I checked my watch and realized I'd better think that through in the courtroom. Judge Dean was notorious for his machine-gun approach to justice and wasn't particularly keen on lawyers that held up his pace.

I entered the courtroom just as the bailiff was calling the court to order. I took my seat in front of the bar and nodded across at Frank Dickerson, sitting at the prosecutor's table. I wished we weren't first on the docket; I was accustomed to having very little time with clients before an arraignment, but this was the first time I didn't even know their names going into the courtroom. The only sensible and responsible course was to ask for a continuance, although I was a bit wary of doing that. I had asked for continuances before, of course, but this would be the first time I'd try to delay a simple arraignment. In fact, I couldn't remember anybody ever asking to continue an arraignment. I thought back to law school, trying to remember what grounds could be used for such a request.

Before I could come up with anything, the bailiff called our case and escorted in Mati and Adam. They looked like two three-year-olds on their first trip to Disneyworld, eyes darting in every direction, absorbing images but not able to process them. I stood and gestured where they were to sit. As soon as they were settled, I turned to the judge. "Your Honor, I'm Bill Riley, representing the codefendants." (Judge Dean and I knew each other well, but he was big on formality.) "I've only had a few minutes with my clients and don't feel I can represent them adequately during these proceedings without more time. I'd like to request a continuance."

"Would you mind if we at least hear what the charges are first?"

"Sorry, Your Honor." Oops, I had gotten ahead of myself. Not a good start.

The bailiff read the charges. It was exactly as I predicted: breaking and entering, burglary, and assault with a deadly weapon.

"Good. Now, Bill, what's the problem? This is only an arraignment. It's a bit unusual to ask for a continuance, wouldn't you say? All you've got to do is plead guilty or not guilty."

"Your Honor, there's some confusion regarding the names and identity of the defendants, as well as their ages. I need additional time to discuss this with them in order to ask for a fitting bail."

Frank remained silent. His turn would come, and he knew my gyrations would work in his favor in the long run. Judge Dean stared hard and long at the defendants; I'm sure he'd already figured out the issue. But then he took the unusual step of addressing them directly. That made me nervous, since I hadn't prepared them for such a discussion—in fact, I had specifically told them not to say a word—but I could hardly tell the judge not to speak to them. There was nothing for me to do but hope they didn't launch into another of their crazy stories.

"So, Adam and Matahina, I see you haven't given the court your last names. Why is that?"

I reluctantly nodded to them to respond. Adam was obviously frightened by the proceedings, but still answered first. "I don't have a last name—at least I don't know what it is."

Mati quickly added, "I don't either."

"And do I understand correctly that you've given the court no address or form of identification?"

I took the risk of answering for them, hoping to make it clear that I wanted communications to go through me. "Your Honor, that's why I need a little more time with them."

The judge looked at all of us sternly for a good ten seconds. "You do understand, don't you, that by asking for a continuance, you are giving up your right to a speedy trial?"

"Yes we do, Your Honor."

"Okay, the court will schedule arraignment for two weeks from today. Bailiff, take the defendants back into custody."

I didn't want a two-week continuance; I only wanted a day or two at the most. Not asking me how long I needed was probably the judge's way of telling me that while he couldn't deny my request, he wasn't happy with it, and that he was in control of his court.

But a continuance was really my only choice—or at least that's what I like to think. Without family, an address, identification, or last names, there was simply no way Mati and Adam would be given the opportunity to post bail. So without a continuance, I risked getting into the arraignment process, being denied bail, then having to come back later and beg for bail, at which point I'd be forced to explain why they'd refused to provide their names in the first place—and that would sit even more uncomfortably with the judge than a continuance. Besides, if I got the information I needed the next day, perhaps I'd be able to talk the judge into moving the arraignment forward. But all I could do at this point was hope—and get to the bottom of the story.

Chapter 38

THE FOLLOWING AFTERNOON, I again stopped in to see Adam and Mati, but this time together, as I was curious to see how they'd continue their charade in front of each other. Before heading to the interview room, I checked in with the police chief to see if he had gotten word on their DNA profiles. He told me they found no matches at all—as if neither of them had ever existed. That should have been surprising to me—shocking, in fact—but for some reason, it wasn't.

Shortly after I arrived at the interview room, they were escorted in from their cells, Adam just slightly before Mati. Of course they'd been housed separately, so they immediately jumped into each other's arms. I gave them a minute before asking them to sit so we could get started. As soon as he was seated, Adam asked, "Can we go now?"

I almost laughed, until I realized he wasn't joking. "No, not exactly. Do you understand that you've committed a crime—a felony?"

Mati replied, "We just pushed open a door, that's all. We can fix it, if it's broken. Besides, we already spent a whole day in this place."

"And I broke the door, not Mati. At least let her go."

"First of all, I can't let either of you go. It's not up to me. Second, the problem isn't just that you broke the door, but that you went into the house intending to steal things. And third, Mati is at least an accomplice to the crime. You admitted to me yesterday that you would have stolen things if the police hadn't showed up. Oh, and fourth, it was Mati, as I understand it, that was actually holding the knife."

"But we didn't hurt anybody or take anything. What's the big deal? It was just a mistake anyway—we didn't know anybody lived there.

We really need to get back home. We need to let them know there are others alive."

Again, their mannerisms appeared rational and sane, but their words indicated otherwise. "I'll do what I can, but don't expect miracles. Right now I need to know more about you—everything about you. Start by telling me how you got to the Sanders house."

"You mean from the boat?"

"No, go back further. Tell me about the boat. Where did it come from? Where is it now?"

Adam smiled and looked at Mati. "We built it on the island and sailed it here. It's about a hundred yards or so south of the house, anchored in a little bay."

"Why were you on this island—what was it, Henderson Island? What were you doing there?"

"I don't understand," Adam said. "That's where we were born."

"Okay, then what did your parents do there? Are they still there? Can you call them?"

"Of course they're still there, but I don't get what you mean by *call them.*"

"I mean call them—like on a phone?" I held up my phone for emphasis.

They looked at each other blankly before Adam appeared to get the idea. "Oh, I know what you mean. No, there aren't any radios on the island. There used to be one, but I never even saw it."

"Look, you've got to help me out just a little here. I'm just not getting this. Who are your parents, and what are they doing on this Henderson Island?"

Adam replied, "I told you who they are yesterday. My dad used to live with my mother in some place called Pittsburgh, in the United States. They went to Henderson on vacation a long time ago, like eighteen years ago, before the Great Storm."

"And they just stayed there?"

"Of course they stayed. There was no way to get back after the Great Storm."

"You brought up this Great Storm yesterday too. What's that about?"

"The Great Storm. You probably have a different name for it here, but that's what we called it."

"Called what?"

"I don't know, I wasn't born yet, but it's when the heat and rain came and, you know, destroyed everything."

I shook my head. "So let me get this straight. You say your parents went there on vacation and a storm came that, what, destroyed their boat so they couldn't get back?"

"No, there was never a boat on the island. So when nobody came to get them, there was no way to get back."

"I thought you said you built the boat that took you here. That took you almost twenty years? Must be quite a boat."

By now Adam seemed as frustrated as I was. "No, it only took a few months, but we had to make metal tools from the anchor—it's complicated to explain."

While I was trying to find a new vector for my questions, Adam took the opportunity to throw in a question of his own. "So what happened here during the Great Storm, and what about the rest of the world? Are other people alive?"

I couldn't begin to know how to respond to such a ridiculous question. And how in the world could I defend these two when they lived in some absurd fantasy world and spoke such gibberish? In the end I decided to completely ignore the question and catch him off-guard. I locked eyes with Adam, and asked, "Adam, who's Lisa?"

Adam looked suspicious. "Lisa? How do you know Lisa?"

"Never mind, just tell me who she is."

"She's George's daughter and part of Kimo's Kitchen, with Mati."

"How old is she?"

"Lisa? Eleven, I think, almost twelve. Why?"

"Describe her hair."

"Long, straight … and brown. I don't get it, why are you asking?"

"Where's Kimo?"

He swallowed and softly replied, "He's dead."

"How did he die?"

He finally broke my stare and looked at the floor. "He fell." He wasn't a very good liar after all. I waited, silently.

Eventually Adam looked back up at me. "I killed him."

Remarkable—there was no way they could have prepared their story to such a depth, which meant there must have been a seed of confused truth somewhere in all of it. Separating that from the bullshit—that was going to be the challenge. I had to check a few things before continuing.

"Hold on for a few moments, I'll be right back."

I knocked on the door and waited for the guard to let me out. "Sal, you got somewhere I can be in private for a minute or two?"

He pointed to an empty desk. "You want me to take them back?"

"No, I just want to check on a few things. I'll come back in a moment."

I quickly unrolled my computer and googled *Henderson Island*. There were millions of hits that included the two words in separate contexts, but didn't see any that pertained to an Island named Henderson. So I added quotes to restrict my search, but *"Henderson Island"* produced nothing. I tried *"Pitcairn Island"* next. There were thousands of hits, the first of which was a Wiki entry that reminded me why the name was so familiar: it was from a book I had read as a teenager called *Mutiny on the Bounty*. The Wiki said that Pitcairn had been uninhabited for nearly twenty years now. Scanning the rest, I learned that the closest island to Pitcairn was San Juan Bautista, which was about a hundred miles to the east.

I googled *"San Juan Bautista Island"* and found just a few very old hits, which led to short descriptions of an uninhabitable island covered with worthless sandstone and bird dung, lacking any fresh water sources. Its only claim to fame was the multitude of scattered rocks around the island, which were hidden just below the water's surface, making it "an extreme hazard to navigation." I did one more search on *Mangereva*, and after i-Search politely corrected my spelling, I found that it did exist and was called home by a few hundred inhabitants. It was also roughly where Adam said it was. Still, this Henderson Island they claimed to have come from didn't even exist. Mangareva also didn't have anywhere near the thousand people that Adam said it did. Not a lot of help, but I needed to heed Sal's signals to hurry and get back—he didn't like leaving suspects alone.

Sal let me back into the detention room and I continued my interview. This time I went slower and just let them talk while I took notes. They told me the original twenty-two inhabitants—Elders, they called them—had arrived on the island almost twenty years ago. Of those twenty-two, fourteen were still alive. There were also fourteen offspring of the twenty-two that they called *Youngers*. Cute. The only contact anyone had with the outside world was with some guy on Pitcairn Island named Josh. Adam's mom and dad had met Josh eighteen years before, when they somehow managed to sail there on an adrift boat named the *Sea Salva*. I asked Adam how his mom and dad had found the boat, but his explanation didn't make much sense.

I had to wrap things up anyway. I had several other cases going that day and, besides, I needed time to sort out their story. I explained that they would have to stay in jail for a while and that without an address, family, friends, or identification, the court wasn't about to just let them go. Their disappointment was palpable.

As I stood to leave, I gave them each a pencil and some paper, and asked them to write down the names of everybody on the island, including as much as they could remember about each of the Elders and their previous lives—even the Elders that had died. I figured if there was any truth to their story, I might find something useful in their notes. And if they were making it all up, then I'd find a discrepancy somewhere, no matter how well rehearsed.

A full agenda the next day prevented me from seeing the pair, but I took advantage of a last-minute plea bargain in another case to leave the office early and look around the Kiholo Bay neighborhood where the alleged break-in took place. Kiholo Bay, about fifteen miles north of the airport, is a state park popular for snorkeling because of its crystal clear waters and jagged rock bottom. And as much as the water is spectacular, the land is desolate. There's no fresh water or vegetation, just black lava as far as you can see—in fact, the coastline there is less than two hundred years old, formed by a massive lava flow from Mauna Loa. To my knowledge, the Sanders home is the only house in the area. Frankly, they never should have been allowed to build the place—I've often wondered whom they bribed to get the building permit, but I guess you can do whatever you want if you have enough money.

I went specifically to look for the boat that Adam and Mati claimed was anchored just to the south of the Sanders house. Since it was a gated home, I asked a police officer to meet me there—I didn't want to be accused of trespassing myself. When we arrived, I feigned interest in the crime scene, and then told the officer I wanted to survey the surrounding area a bit. I gingerly made my way south across the lava flow and walked along the water's edge. I soon came upon a narrow, well-protected cove that fit their description perfectly. I wasn't exactly surprised to find no boat there. I snapped a few pictures of the empty cove before heading home.

Although I'd planned to spend my evening relaxing in front of the TV with a couple of beers, I found my interest wandering back to the inconsistencies between what I'd found on the Internet and Adam and Mati's strange story. I pulled my notes from my briefcase and hopped back on my computer to see what else I could piece together. Googling *"Sea Salva"* produced a lot of hits, but nothing I could see that was relevant to a boat lost at sea: I tried combining the name with *"boat fire,"* *"shipwreck,"* *"lost at sea,"* and about every other related term I could think of, but nothing showed promise.

So I decided to search for their island again. I typed in *"Hendreson Island."* And, surprisingly, this time there was a hit—just one. Just as I clicked on the link, I realized I'd misspelled Henderson, but by that time, the page was already loading and it was too late to correct my error. The link took me to a line in a British history site that was really about Pitcairn Island: "Pitcairn Islanders would often take the hundred-mile trip east to Hendreson Island to collect the miro wood that they used to make carvings, which they traded for food and other staples when ships passed nearby."

That was peculiar. Obviously somebody else had had problems inverting the adjacent keyboard letters. Even stranger, every reference I had previously looked at said the only island even near Pitcairn was this San Juan Bautista, so now what was this about Hendreson Island? Confused, I again searched *"San Juan Bautista Island."* This time I read through the hits for a good half hour. Still, there wasn't much; the only new thing I found was that San Juan Bautista had been bought by the airline mogul Chris Stetson, just before he'd vanished eighteen years before, and was then protected as a UNESCO World Heritage Site.

I vaguely remembered the story of Stetson's disappearance, but not the details. So I quickly googled *"Chris Stetson" disappearance* and got the full story: He had been sailing in the South Pacific near Tahiti when the massive Typhoon Gita passed through. After weeks of intensive, high publicity searching, he was pronounced lost at sea along with his crew of five and an unclear number of guests that may have been on board. Interesting—didn't tell me much, but there did seem to be a few odd intersections with Adam and Mati's story.

The next morning, when I awoke, I realized I had been dreaming about Adam and Mati. I couldn't remember exactly what I had dreamed, but as I lay thinking about it, I somehow came to the realization that I believed them. That's not to say I believed their story, but that I believed that they believed their story. I suppose it was watching Adam struggle with his lie about killing Kimo that convinced me. I began to sweat. I had the frightening feeling that I might finally be representing true innocents. I just hoped I wouldn't fail them.

Unfortunately, due to a barrage of critical court appointments in Hilo, it was another two days before I could get to the jail again to talk to them. Even then I had only a few moments. I again asked that they be brought to the interview room together, thinking it would be good for each of them to see that the other was doing well. The problem was that neither of them *was* doing well: they looked depressed, confused, and scared, as they asked again, with even more urgency, whether I had come to finally let them go. Rather than answering, I pulled out my phone and showed them the picture I'd taken the day before of the little bay.

"This look familiar?"

They both jumped out of their seats and Adam grabbed my phone. "That's where the *Enterprise* is!" But then, he became more interested in my phone than in the photo. "How'd you make this? It looks just like the real place."

"I took this picture just a couple of days ago. There was no boat."

They looked confused and worried. Rhetorically, Adam asked, "You mean it's not there any more?"

Mati turned to Adam. "It probably sank. Remember how much water was coming in?"

Adam melted back into his seat, dropping my phone on the floor.

"Sank?" I said as I picked up my phone. "So you think it's still there? Underwater?"

"Mati's probably right. We were leaking about an inch of water every hour. It would have sunk by now." He looked utterly dejected, his forehead sinking into his hands.

Mati put her hand on his shoulder. "We'll still get back. We can build another one."

Seeing no reason to argue, I moved on, reiterating many of the questions I'd posed before, but to which I hadn't gotten satisfactory responses. Did they know anybody here on Hawaii? Could they remember their last names? Relatives' names? Their answers were the same. I finally asked if they had made their lists for me. They both gave me several pages of what looked like first grade handwriting, and then again begged me to let them free. They still didn't seem to understand why they were being locked up and fed what Adam called "food that tastes like mud." Even with as callous as I had become over the years, it actually hurt me to tell them they were going to have to go back to their cells.

Chapter 39

THAT NIGHT I AGAIN lay restless in bed, thinking about my two strange clients. I shouldn't have believed them, but I did. Even worse, though, was that I was getting emotionally involved. The next morning I got up right at sunrise, grabbed my mask and snorkel, and drove to Kiholo Bay. This time I snuck around the Sanders house directly to the bay. Logically, I was confident I wouldn't find anything, but part of me wasn't so sure. I needed to be sure. From a nearby gravel beach, I slipped into the water and started swimming out to the middle, but the moment my mask was in the water, I saw a boat. The craft had obviously just recently sunk and was lying on its side in about twenty feet of water. If the sun had been higher the last time I was here, I would have seen it from shore.

This changed everything. I decided to do something I hadn't done in all my twenty years of work: to blow off my morning court appearance. I knew it would be at the expense of what little was left of my already waning career. I went home, sat in front of my computer, and pondered all my notes together with Mati's and Adam's lists, determined to find some connection between them and the real world.

I read through Mati's list first, but there was nothing of any help. Her spelling and grammar were that of a nine-year-old and her penmanship wasn't even up to those standards. There were no last names or backgrounds that looked searchable, just misspelled first names that could have easily been made up. I moved on to Adam's list, which was notably more legible and understandable, but still contained spelling quirks. Again, I was amazed at how well his descriptions aligned with Mati's, down to the most minute detail. Then about halfway through his list, I hit pay dirt. One of the islanders, a woman Adam named "Claire"—"Klar" according to Mati's list—was listed as forty-four years old. Adam had remembered that she came from a place he wrote down as "Lost Angels Ease" and that her father was the DA there. *I should be able to check that,* I thought. *How many DA's of Los Angeles could have lost a daughter eighteen years ago?*

Just a couple seconds on i-Search gave me what I needed: eighteen years ago, District Attorney William Johnson lost his daughter when Typhoon Gita virtually wiped out the entire system of islands named Mangareva. The islands were home of a small resort named New Eden, where his twenty-two year old daughter, Claire Johnson, was staying with her fiancée, Bob Simpson. My first thought was to contact this William Johnson, so I googled his name, hoping to find contact information. Unfortunately, he had died of a heart attack more than ten years before. I made a note to find his next of kin, but that would take time—right now, I had some new leads to follow.

Googling *"New Eden" Mangareva*, I found out that New Eden was once a resort emphasizing a native Polynesian lifestyle, with a few grass huts and not much else. It was established some eighteen years ago, and was open only a few weeks before Typhoon Gita closed it permanently. The specific island the resort was on wasn't identified but was described as "near Mangareva's capital, Rikitea." The resort was founded and owned by Chris Stetson—the same guy that had established San Juan Bautista Island as a World Heritage Site! For a split second, I wondered whether they could be the same island, but then realized it couldn't be—San Juan Bautista was more than three hundred miles from Mangareva.

The most recent reference to New Eden discussed its demise. The day before Typhoon Gita hit, Stetson had gone to Mangareva in his yacht and picked up two New Eden employees, an Alan Filsner and a Janice Pedit, for a two-day cruise, reportedly in the direction of Tahiti. All were presumed dead when his yacht disappeared the day Gita tore through.

Searching for more information about Typhoon Gita, I found that the storm had been categorized as a massive Category 5 storm. It had initially been expected to miss populated islands entirely but had taken an unexpected southeastern turn during the night and hit Mangareva dead-on. Unprepared, the Mangareva airport was utterly devastated, as was its capital, Rikitea. There were extensive fatalities—over half the island's population! It took a full week before boats from nearby islands were able to bring food and water, provide medical help, and re-established radio communications. The damage was so severe that nothing was found of the New Eden vacationers or their huts—with no concrete or stone houses, every structure on all the secondary islands in the Mangareva chain had been utterly erased. Cross-searching *"New Eden" typhoon victims* pulled up the names of the lost vacationers. They matched Adam's and Mati's lists perfectly! Was it possible that they had survived and somehow gone unfound for almost twenty years? It seemed impossible, but …

I went back to reading about Typhoon Gita, following a satellite image of its path. After it leveled Mangareva, it continued southeast, passing thirty miles to the east of Pitcairn Island, now as a Category 3 storm. If I understood the maps correctly, it missed San Juan Bautista, but would have likely been close enough to make quite an impression. Could that have been their Great Storm?

Taking a different approach, I again googled *Sea Salva shipwreck*, this time without the quotes, and limited my search to entries between seventeen and eighteen years old. The first few hits were irrelevant, but the fourth was a short report in a maritime log about a boat named the *Sea Salvation* from Newport Beach. It was part of a pleasure flotilla sailing from Los Angeles to Sidney, but due to a propane leak, it caught fire just south of Easter Island. Unable to extinguish the fire, those on board were able to safely off-load to other boats in the flotilla. The *Sea Salvation* itself was abandoned while still ablaze, and presumed to have sunk. I supposed it was possible that the fire had eradicated the "t-i-o-n" from the name. In fact, it was too close of a coincidence not to be the same boat.

I spent the next half hour trying to put the puzzle together, but one big piece still didn't make any sense. Why did the one old reference call the island Henderson, (or actually Hendreson) while all the new ones called it *San Juan Bautista*? Moreover, if the two islands were one and the same, then why would the people of Pitcairn have routinely gone there for additional natural resources, when all the references made it clear it was "an uninhabitable sandstone island covered with bird dung," not to mention "extremely hazardous," and "surrounded by a multitude of rocks just below the surface?" The descriptions of San Juan Batista were also incompatible with Mati's and Adam's, even though the island was located in the exact spot on the map that they said it would be.

I decided to dig deeper into the history of this San Juan Bautista. It took about thirty minutes, but I finally found the clincher: the island was discovered by a Captain James Henderson in 1819! They just had to be one and the same. I picked up the phone and called Derek, a friend of mine who consulted with companies to help set up their websites.

"Hello?"

"Hey, Derek. This is Bill."

"Yeah, I can see that! Do you realize it's only ten o'clock in the morning?"

"Yeah, yeah, but I need some help with a case. Got a minute?"

"I guess. I'll do you a favor and keep my video off, though. You probably don't want to see what's on the other side of this call."

"So, this may sound like a ridiculous question, but if money was no issue, would it be possible to change the Internet?"

"Change the Internet? I don't get what you mean."

"Let's say there was some place, say an island, that you wanted to hide—change its name, description and location everywhere on the Internet so that nobody would ever go there. Could you?"

"I guess anything can be done with enough money, but it would be virtually impossible. Don't you remember the story of the company called Google?"

I made the mistake of hesitating, allowing him to continue what I feared would become a technical tirade. "You don't remember Google? You know the verb *google*, right?"

"Sure, google means to search for something."

"Well, that's not its original meaning. Originally, google was a name for the largest number that could sensibly exist: ten multiplied by ten, one hundred times. It was spelled differently, like g-o-o-g-o-l, but it was pronounced the same way." My video was on, so he must have seen my body language urging him back to the point. "Anyway, about thirty years ago, two guys formed a company named Google—it was named after the number, but they spelled it wrong for some reason—and the company became a big success. You don't remember it?"

"Not really, Derek, but I'm not a computer guy, remember?"

"Obviously. Well, anyway, Google was so successful, it took over the entire Internet search industry—they had a complete stranglehold on information access for several years. And that's where our current meaning of the word google came from: for such a long time, everybody typed their key words into Google's engine, so to *google* something was the same as searching for information on it. Then fifteen years ago or so, the company completely crashed—almost overnight—along with this other company named *Yahoo*. You must remember that."

"Go on." I did remember it now, but only generally.

"There were actually two things that used to happen way back then that led to the crashes. The first was that people began to bomb searches. Bombing is where searches are deliberately redirected to the wrong webpages. Do you remember that incident back when we were in college, where if anybody searched for *miserable failure* they were routed to the home page for George W. Bush's White House? That's bombing. So in your case, if somebody searched for one island, they would get results for another island instead. Back in the day, bombing was easy if you had enough money, because it didn't actually change any underlying data—it just corrupted the indexing—and that didn't take a lot of work. But, like I said, that was only one of the things that people used to do. The other thing—what really crashed Google and Yahoo—were worms. Know what those are?"

My silence told him what he expected. "Well, I won't get into it, but the point is that some contractor who worked on occasion for both

Google and Yahoo was able introduce worms that went into all the big data centers. The worms selectively corrupted the actual data—not just the indexing."

"How could he do that?"

"Actually, it was a *she*. The worm just worked in the background of these data centers, searching webpages for certain text strings or image patterns. When it found a target word or string of text, it would substitute a new text string. She even fixed it so the worm would search image files, like maps, for text strings and paste the new text images on top, even matching fonts. What was so amazing was that worms this lady developed were so invisible that nobody noticed them for years."

"So that really happened?"

"Yep. Various people and companies had bribed her to modify the Internet to favor their interests over their competitors'. In the beginning, the changes were subtle—that's why nobody figured out what was happening—but eventually she got too bold and changed things that were obvious. Once they knew something was screwing with the data, they were able to find her worms. The worms were easily eliminated, but the damage they caused couldn't be reversed so easily since the worms left no record of what they'd changed, and even back-up's had been corrupted. With time, people reported incorrect data and things got back on track, but there was no universal fix. Anyway, since Google's and Yahoo's businesses were completely based on data integrity, well, they both quickly went out of business. That's what allowed Apple to launch i-Search, which of course is what everybody uses today. A single employee destroyed two multibillion dollar companies virtually overnight."

"So, then it is possible to hide an island?"

"No, the point is that it's *not* possible. Not anymore. When all this happened is when the Bureau of Data Integrity was formed to audit search engines and data storage centers. So with BDI's constant comparative verification routines, it's impossible. Anything like that would be found almost immediately."

"Derek, let me get this straight. Twenty or so years ago, it wasn't just possible; it was being done. People with enough money could and were make massive changes to databases worldwide. Is that right?"

"Well, that long ago, sure."

"So let me try this again. If I had a infinite amount of money eighteen years ago, could I have changed the name of an isolated, unpopulated island somewhere in the Pacific Ocean, then modify its description to discourage further visitors, say, by adding navigational hazards and making the island less appealing than it really was?"

"Back then, sure. Piece of cake if you had the money. That wasn't what you asked."

"It's what I meant to ask. So what if I wanted to prove it. What would I have to do?"

"Hmm … well, I guess you'd have to go to a physical library somewhere and find real books that predate that time. I think there's still a library in Honolulu. Remember, any books written since then probably got their information from the Internet, though, so they would be wrong as well. In fact, come to think of it, even if a book were written before then, but was printed in the last fifteen years—like one of those print-on-demand books—would probably still be wrong. The worms would have affected electronic book images, as well."

"Okay thanks, I owe you one. Later?"

"Yeah, bye."

Was it really possible that, at one time, a worm (whatever that was) could have altered every piece of electronic data about Henderson Island, renaming the island to San Juan Batista, and changing its description? If that had really happened, though, wouldn't people who had been to Henderson notice the mistakes and try to correct it? It seemed farfetched, but as I thought about it, I realized it wasn't. From what I gathered, few people had ever been there—maybe a dozen, max—and even if, by some small chance, those few people saw that somebody had referred to the island by a different name, would they care enough to actually complain about it? And so what if there were errors in the description? To whom would such a person complain anyway, and then, who would care enough to investigate? Besides, if they were electronic, people's personal notes and records would have been doctored too, thwarting any possible investigation.

I remembered an example from law school, in which an article in an important law journal referenced a prior case that never existed. After a few years, there were hundreds of references to the same bogus citation. The case had soon become accepted as law because it had been referenced so often and had gone unchallenged. The more I thought about it, the more I realized that if something were changed on the Internet for just a couple of years, it too could simply become the truth.

I made a mental note to visit the old library in Honolulu next time I was there.

I drove to the city jail to see my clients. If possible, they looked even more dejected than before, not to mention downright emaciated. After three days of incarceration, the vitality that had radiated from them when we first met had vanished. They greeted me mechanically, without their usual eagerness. I suppose they'd given up on me—they weren't the first, believe me.

"Okay, I found your boat," I told them. "What was it called?"

"The *Enterprise*," replied Adam listlessly.

"Yeah, *Enterprise*. Well, I found it. It's on the bottom, just where you said. I also checked a few more things. Tell me more about this Great Storm."

They looked at each other and shrugged in unison, then Adam began. "We weren't even born then. I, or we, just know what the Elders told us."

"Well, what did they tell you about it?"

"That it was really hot at first—so hot that they had to go in the lagoon to keep cool—then there was really hard rain and wind for a couple of days. They thought the rest of the world was all destroyed." Stan shrugged and looked around. "I guess not all of it was, though."

"They thought the rest of the world was destroyed? Why?"

"Kimo said, or they all thought, that it wasn't just a storm—we, or they, thought it was something else. When nobody came to pick my parents up, they just thought—well, that everybody was gone. Why else would nobody show up?"

"Let's back up. How did they all end up on this Henderson Island in the first place? I thought they were supposed to be on Mangareva?"

"I don't know what you mean. I know they said they all came from Mangareva on what they called an airplane—like a boat that flies—and I know Henderson had another name back then, too."

"Was it San Juan Bautista?"

"No," Mati interjected, "I remember. They called it New Eden."

Adam nodded. "That's right. I remember now. They didn't want everybody to know where it really was, so they called it New Eden."

I leaned back in my chair. The pieces were starting to fall into place. Stetson must have bought Henderson Island with the intent of turning it into this resort island, but in order for it to be successful, he'd have to ensure the island remained unpopulated and unvisited—except for, of course, his employees and visitors. To achieve that end, he probably paid this data manipulator at Google a lot of money to redirect all Internet queries about Henderson to San Juan Bautista Island, essentially wiping out Henderson's identity and history. Further, then, he likely had her infect data-storage centers and alter records to make the island sound desolate and unlivable—I had to admit, the rocky navigational hazard was a nice touch. And these worms, or whatever Derek called them, must have simply missed the one reference I found because the key word was misspelled as Hendreson. And even then, the only reason I found it was because I used quotation marks in my search, disabling i-Search's spell checker. So for all practical purposes, Stetson had succeeded in electronically wiping Henderson Island off the face of the earth.

As far as the resort guests, they'd get information about this place called New Eden, which they'd be told lay on one of the many small Mangareva Islands. But then upon arriving in Mangareva, they'd take a three-hour plane ride to Henderson, which, from what I could see, was likely the most remote place on the planet.

Then Typhoon Gita whisked through, wiping out New Eden's

Mangareva base as well as Stetson's yacht, erasing all physical pointers to New Eden's actual location on Henderson. And since the rest of the world was told that Mangareva had been flattened and that New Eden was on one of Mangareva's islands, the evidence would have been conclusive and consistent: the resort had been lost along with all its guests. There wouldn't have been the slightest reason to launch a search or even an enquiry. Meanwhile, the vacationers were hundreds of miles away on Henderson Island, and perfectly safe.

To compound matters, Pitcairn Island, the only other piece of land that was even remotely close to Henderson, had been abandoned, dramatically reducing the already near non-existent maritime traffic in that part of the Pacific. No wonder no boats came by: not only was there no reason to go to Henderson; there were some good reasons to avoid the entire area—officially, it offered nothing but navigational hazards, and as a World Heritage Site, off-limits by international law.

The irony of it suddenly struck me: conventional wisdom was that the Internet had made it almost impossible to hide anything, but in this case, it was used to successfully hide an entire island for almost twenty years!

I came out of my trance and looked back at the couple. "So nobody came to pick up your parents when they were supposed to. Weren't there radios or boats on the island? I mean, what made them think that this Great Storm had wiped everything out—other than the fact that nobody came for them?"

They looked at each other as if realizing for the first time what I was suggesting: that there might have never been a Great Storm, or at least in the sense they'd always thought.

Mati replied, her tone somewhat defensive. "There was a radio, but nobody answered."

"And there weren't any boats on the island," Adam said. "We couldn't build any boats either, because the trees are too small on Henderson, and we didn't have any metal to make a saw... or nails."

Maybe their radio didn't work, but on the other hand, maybe it did and they just couldn't get a signal through. I wondered what kind of radio it was, but knew it would be senseless to ask. A VHF radio would have been completely hopeless. And even a sideband radio, which was more likely, would have never been heard farther away than Mangareva, which from what I saw on the map, was the only populated land within hundreds of miles. So with Mangareva destroyed by Gita, their only hope would have been a satellite radio or phone. I continued to press. "And the storm?"

"Well, the Elders said it was really hot and that, if it was that hot there, it would be even hotter in the rest of the world. They said the sun would have destroyed everything."

"But why? It's often hot and humid before a big storm. What's so unusual about that?"

"Storms aren't common at Henderson. In my lifetime, I've never seen anything like what they described. David and Kimo said it was something called a solar storm, like a big explosion on the surface of the sun. The only reason we survived is because it happened at night."

"So let me get this straight. Just because it was really hot, then rained really hard for a couple of days, you—sorry, they—thought some kind of huge solar storm killed all the people in the whole world except the people on your island? I have to say, Adam, that doesn't make a whole lot of sense."

They again looked at each other, as if communicating telepathically. At that moment, I realized that everything they had believed their entire lives was collapsing very, very quickly. Eventually, Mati broke the spell.

"There were the lights in the sky! There were strange lights in the sky caused by the ... from the explosion on the sun, and ..."

She seemed to be searching for words, so I tried to help. "Lights in the sky? What kind of lights?"

"I don't know. Just lights." She looked into the air above me, as if she could see them. "Dad said they were bright red. He called them Southern Lights ... or, another name. I forget."

Adam took over. "David said that when there are explosions on the sun, it's like a storm. He said the sun shines really little things, too small to see, and they cause some kind of change in the earth's atmosphere that causes the colorful lights in the sky."

"Could it have just been a full moon, maybe shining through storm clouds that were building? Or maybe just an unusual sunrise?" I didn't realize until after I asked, that these were rhetorical questions. There was no way either of them would know—it was evident that Adam was just echoing words from this guy, David. Yet, this was the part of the story that didn't make sense. It was possible the story of the lights had been distorted over years of telling, but then again, it must have made enough of an impression to convince them there'd been a solar disruption large enough to destroy civilization.

"There was also Josh, on Pitcairn," Adam said. "The storm killed his wife too."

"Tell me about him."

Adam told me about how his parents sailed to Pitcairn and met an old man that had also been isolated by the storm. The storm had knocked out the island's power, so Josh had had no way to contact anybody either. Mati interrupted his story, her eyes pleading with me to believe them. "But there's also the land here, where we anchored. It's all burned and melted. How did that happen, and how did anybody survive that?"

I couldn't help but laugh. "It's lava, from a volcano—from Mauna Loa, to be precise. The land around where you're anchored was formed about two hundred years ago, when molten rock flowed down the side of the mountain and into the sea, and then froze there. I can see how you might think … well … anyway, I assure you it wasn't because of a solar flare."

All of us were quiet for a while.

Finally, I broke the silence. "Okay, listen. You say the rest of the people are still on the island, right?" They nodded. "Let's take a look for them."

"Look for them?" Adam asked. "You mean by boat?"

"Nope. You'll see." I reached in my briefcase and pulled out my computer.

Mati and Adam wrinkled their foreheads as they watched me unroll my computer to face them on the table, go onto Satview, and search for *San Juan Batista Island*. But as soon as the satellite image appeared, they simultaneously shouted, "That's Pitcairn Island!"

"No, that's San Juan Batista Island, your Henderson Island." I brought up the labels, and the word *San Juan Batista Island* popped up right across the satellite image. "See?"

Adam was insistent. "No, it's Pitcairn. Henderson is over here." He pointed to an unlabeled shape on the far right of the screen.

I scrolled to the left. If this was really San Juan Batista, as the map claimed, then Pitcairn should be a hundred miles west. Nothing—just open ocean. So I scrolled back to the right, past the island labeled as San Juan Batista, to the blob that Adam said was really their Henderson Island. There was obviously something there, but there was no label. Satview claimed there was nothing there.

I decided to double check the coordinates that night back at home, but based on what I was looking at right then, I was sure he was right. It seemed Satview, for some reason, labeled Pitcairn as San Juan Batista Island, and gave no name to the real San Juan Batista, or Henderson Island. I tried to blow up the image of the unlabeled island, but the highest resolution offered by Satview was only five-kilometers-per-inch. Adam and Mati were able to show me some of the island's gross features, such as the Point and the farm, but there was no way to confirm anything with these images.

For the next few minutes, Adam shot out an annoying string of questions: "Where did those pictures come from?" "Can you get pictures of any place like that?" "Why was there a mistake in labeling the island?" I fended them off the best I could, but he was dissatisfied with all my answers—as was I.

Finally I rolled up my computer and leaned back in my chair. "Look, I believe you. It's the most amazing story I've ever heard, but I believe you. The question is what do we do now?"

Adam looked relieved. "So we can go now? We don't have to stay here?"

I took a deep breath and slowly exhaled. "I'm afraid it's not that simple. No matter what the reason, you did commit a crime, and you can't expect the DA to just accept this crazy story. If I told him all this, he'd just laugh at me. We need to find some absolute, simple proof that explains why you don't have a name, an ID, or a place to live, and why it was okay for you to break into that house. Right now I don't know how to do that." They pleaded with me, almost hysterical about going back to their cells, so although I knew better, I said I'd try to talk to the prosecutor.

I knew Frank Dickerson well. He'd been an assistant DA for almost as long as I had been in the public defender's office, and we had crossed paths many times. He wasn't the smartest or most interesting person in the world. Come to think of it, he was downright pedestrian. Nevertheless, we had become friends outside of our professional lives—perhaps a commentary on my own existence. I made a quick call and was surprised to find he had a few minutes for me if I could come right away.

Reluctantly, Sal agreed to leave Mati and Adam in the interview room for a half hour while I stepped next door. I told Frank the story as simply as I could, leaving out the more complicated and tortuous parts.

He was shuffling papers the entire time I was speaking, but when I stopped, he finally looked up at me. "So what do you want then? You looking to plead this thing out?"

"Frank, were you listening to anything I was saying? These two need help, not a jail sentence."

"Look, they're guilty. We all know it, and it sounds like they freely admit it. How they got to Hawaii is none of my concern. All you've told me so far is that there are some glitches on the Internet—that somebody may have tampered with some data, what, twenty years ago or so? Why does that make it okay for these two to break into a house and threaten a police officer with a knife? Isn't that a bit of a stretch?" He must have seen my look of disappointment, because his voice suddenly softened.

"Come on, Bill, be realistic. What do you expect me to do? What would you do if you were me?"

"How 'bout at least recommending a reasonable bail? Or releasing them on their own recognizance while we figure this thing out?"

"Sure. No problem. As soon as they tell us who they are, and provide some identification and a little evidence that they're not a flight risk. It sounds like an interesting story, Bill, but awfully hard to believe, don't you think? Even if it's true, if I released them based on that, I'd be laughed out of the office, and you know it."

"Yeah, I know, but I believe them. It all fits together. Look, help me out a little at least. What would it take for you to recommend releasing them until their trial? I'll research this thing carefully and lay the whole thing out for you."

He drummed his fingers on his desk. "With no identification or even a last name?"

"What if I personally vouch for them and let them live with me?"

"Bill! You can't be serious! You've been at this game as long as I have. You should know better."

"Yeah, I should, but let's say I do it anyway. I'll put up the bail money if you ask for something reasonable."

Frank stood and let out a long sigh. "Sorry, Bill, I just can't, and you know it. Listen, I've got a hearing in five. Maybe we can talk more tomorrow, okay? And bring me some proof, not just a story."

Well, I tried, and I can't say I was surprised. "Sure. Good luck in court."

Even as I walked out I was planning my next steps. The easiest course would be to leave them in jail a couple more weeks, finish the investigation, and then present it all in court. On the other hand, there were other riskier, but faster, avenues: I could go directly to the judge with my story. Or perhaps, better, to the press.

Chapter 40

As SOON AS I returned to the jail, I knew something was wrong. Normally the jail was quiet and lethargic, but now everybody was running around in confusion.

"What's going on?" I asked the desk sergeant.

"Your clients just bolted," he growled, as if it were my fault.

"Bolted? You mean ran away? How?"

"They attacked Sal, that's how." Sal, who'd been the guard of the detention room for as long as I can remember, should have retired years ago—he'd be a pushover in any kind of physical confrontation.

"So where are they now?"

"You tell me, they're your damn clients. Out there somewhere." He pointed his thumb over his head toward the door. "You know perfectly well there's no place for them to run, and the sooner and quieter they return, the better it'll be for them."

"When did it happen?"

"Just a couple minutes ago. Sal went in to bring them some water, and they pushed him back against the wall, closed the door on him, and ran."

"That's it? Ran? So how did they get past everybody? Isn't that why you have guns and tasers and shit?"

He shrugged and turned up his hands. "They were fast. We yelled at 'em, but they were gone before we could do anything. It's not like we keep our guns out and armed, ready to shoot everybody that walks through the door." That explained his comment about them returning quietly. Explaining to the police chief or the press how two unarmed kids in orange jumpsuits just ran out of a police station full of armed cops wasn't going to be fun.

"Is anybody out looking for them?" I asked.

He gave me a frozen stare. "No, we thought we'd give them a fair chance. You know, count to a hundred first before we send anybody out. What a stupid question! Of course we're looking for them. Don't worry, they won't get far."

I could only imagine how lost they must be. In their bright orange jumpsuits, they'd be about as subtle as a marching band sneaking through a library. And even though Kailua wasn't exactly New York City, it would probably seem like it to them, given what they were used to. They wouldn't have any idea what to do or where to go; and not only didn't they have any money, they probably didn't even know what money was. They hadn't even known what a gun was. There was no doubt they'd be captured almost immediately. I just hoped it would be peaceful. I wished I had taken more time to explore the story about Adam killing that Kimo guy. He didn't seem like the violent sort, but it worried me just the same.

It seemed fruitless, but I decided the only way I might be able to help was if I found them before the police did—or I suppose more likely, be there when the police found them. It was a long shot, but why not try? I quickly walked out the door of the station and stopped just outside the threshold, trying to imagine what I'd do in their situation, running as fast as I could, afraid, unfamiliar with everything I saw, and grossly conspicuous in bright orange.

I looked around, hoping to spot something that might be familiar to them. The answer was obvious: the ocean. If I were they, I'd work my way to the ocean as quickly as I could. The court and jailhouse sat together on a corner in a busy part of town. A right turn from where I stood would provide a straight shot to the wharf: three long blocks, with no place to hide. It was impossible to imagine that Adam and Mati could have made it to the wharf without being spotted. There'd be one hell of a commotion, and surely the police would have them by now. Instead, the street looked normal.

So maybe I needed to rethink this. Adam and Mati must have realized they'd never make it in a direct dash to the ocean, in which case they'd have had to buy some time, either by hiding near the courthouse or going down one of the narrow alleys that parallels the ocean, perhaps ducking into doorways as they went, and then making a dash for the ocean down a quieter street.

Just then, I heard shouting from somewhere behind the police station. I took off jogging down the side alley to the north, following the noise. Three short blocks later, I saw an officer sitting on the curb, holding his head with one hand, and yelling to a second officer. With his other hand, he was pointing east, directly away from the ocean. I couldn't hear what he was saying, but it was clear that he'd been hit on the head, and perhaps momentarily knocked out. I looked in the direction he was pointing and saw two orange jumpsuits in the middle of the road. For a moment, I thought it was Mati and Adam, lying dead in the street, but it seems instead that our young fugitives had realized that wearing bright orange wasn't the way to blend in with the city's surroundings and had simply discarded the suits right then and there. I wasn't so sure their current state of undress would help them blend in any better.

Using the jumpsuits as their cue, the police ran inland, fanning out to cover the side streets. I remained convinced, though, that those kids were headed to the water. Tossing their jumpsuits inland was likely a decoy, to give them enough time to head the other way—if so, it was quick thinking on their part. I discreetly backed away from the corner, and then slowly jogged the opposite way, toward the ocean.

An unusually impressive surf crashed against the concrete wharf that day—not at all an appealing place to go swimming. Still, from their perspective, it was probably safer than roads filled with cars, people, and lights. I stood on the wharf and scanned the horizon, unsure just what I was looking for.

Out of the corner of my eye, I caught a brief movement. I looked harder and thought I saw two heads briefly pop above the surface a couple hundred yards away. Before I could refocus, however, they were gone again. It had to be them. And if it was, again, I had to give them credit: it would take a lot of guts to jump in the water and somehow expect to escape by swimming. These weren't exactly friendly waters.

I stood watching, waiting for them to pop back up. It was like trying to track a pod of dolphins: they swam under water, surfacing every half-minute or so, and then disappearing again before I could really focus on them. Once I determined that they were going north, I extrapolated their path and realized where they were headed. A dozen sailboats were moored about five hundred yards offshore and nearly a mile to the north.

I watched them for a long time before deciding what to do. For right or for wrong, I decided not to report them. I'd try to get to them first, and talk them into turning themselves in. But not now—it was too late in the day, and I knew they'd spend the night on one of those boats, so I'd surprise them the next morning. I stayed another few minutes, until they were too far out to see, and then turned back toward the police station and my car.

As I was driving away from Kailua, I laughed out loud to see the police moving farther inland. I laughed even harder when I turned north onto Queen Kaahumanu Highway and saw a helicopter swooping in to join the search. But as I continued home, the situation lost its humor. I realized they'd be caught despite the idiocy I had just witnessed. It was imperative that I find Adam and Mati first, and convince them to turn themselves in.

Chapter 41

I HAD A SHORT hearing in the morning that I couldn't miss, but nothing after about ten o'clock that I couldn't move to the next day. As soon as I finished at the courthouse, I drove up to Honokohau Harbor, where I rented a small Boston Jet Whaler and headed south along the coast.

I wasn't particularly handy with boats, but fortunately the sea had settled down during the night. I buzzed south about three miles to the cluster of sailboats moored in front of Kailua. I'd guessed it wouldn't be too hard to figure out which boat they'd climbed onto, but when I got there, I saw that it was even easier than I'd expected: there was one empty mooring ball and there had been none the day before. These particular moorings were long-term leases, and the boats had pretty much become a part of the Kailua panorama—I suppose once a month or so, one of them might come or go, but that was about it.

So now they were more than just thieves; technically, they were pirates. It wouldn't be long before someone reported the boat missing, and then the Keystone Kops were bound to figure out where their fugitives had fled. The question now was where they were headed.

I turned around and raced the Whaler back to Honokohau, jumped in my car, and drove north to Kiholo Bay. Where else would they go but back to their *Enterprise*? It was all they knew, and contained everything they owned; besides, it was a well hidden little cove. And they sure couldn't go back to Henderson on an unprovisioned sailboat, so they'd need some time near land to prepare for their trip. I guessed that with the light morning winds, they'd make it to Kiholo Bay in four or five hours. Even with my late start, by car, I could get there before them.

By one o'clock, I was parking next to the gravel road about a hundred yards before the gate to the Sanders property. I awkwardly worked my way along the lava around their house to the cove. I sat down on the small black gravel beach, half hiding behind a rock outcropping, and waited.

A half hour later, I saw a sailboat drift into the harbor, Adam visible at the wheel and Mati working the sails. I was impressed by how quickly they turned the boat into the wind and brought down the sails. The boat was about thirty feet from the rocks on either side, and maybe fifty feet from the little beach I was on. Without even dropping anchor, they both dived overboard and swam down toward their sunken boat. I stripped to my boxers, slipped into the water, and quietly breaststroked my way to the opposite side of the boat they had so recently acquired. I quietly paddled to the back and climbed up the swimming ladder with as much stealth as I could muster, as they continued surface diving near the front.

I'm far from an expert on sailboats, but I could see that the boat they had taken was a forty foot or so sloop, obviously well past its prime but evidently serviceable. I sat in the cockpit facing the swimming ladder, anxious to see their surprised expressions when they climbed aboard. Maybe once they realized how easily I had found them, they'd be more inclined to turn themselves in. As odd as it may seem, it was only then that I began to wonder if I had reason to be afraid of them. Just as I was considering swimming back to shore, I heard somebody climbing up the swimming ladder in back. A few seconds later, I saw Mati's face peek over the transom. Rather than surprised, she looked defiant—even angry.

"What are you doing here? How'd you find us?"

"It was pretty obvious. Where else would you be? Why'd you take off like that? It was a stupid thing to do."

She almost bounded up on deck in total disregard of her nudity. "We don't belong in a place like that. We didn't do anything wrong and we just want to go home."

"But there's a process you have to go through. You can't just run away. Where's Adam?"

"Right here." I whirled around to see where the voice had come from. He had used Mati's entrance as a diversion while he had somehow climbed onto the deck behind me. He looked relaxed and in full control, possessing a quality quite unlike anything I had seen in him before. He wore a huge sheathed knife on a belt, which seemed even more ominous because it was the only thing he was wearing. My guess is that if I had been carrying a weapon of some kind, the knife wouldn't have been sheathed, but rather pressed against my throat by now. I felt pretty foolish to have thought I was going to surprise them.

"Adam! I'm glad to see you—both of you."

Adam climbed down to Mati and wrapped his right arm around her shoulders. "Why, so you can take us back to that … jail?"

"Look, you've got to understand. You need to go back, and you need to do it on your own. If you wait until they catch you, they're not going to be very friendly, and you'll end up spending a lot more time in jail."

Adam vigorously shook his head. "We're not going back there. Even Kimo never put anybody in isolation for more than two days. We're going back to our own island."

"You can't go back in this boat. You stole it. It's not right. Besides, they'll catch you and then they'll really come down hard on you. Stealing a boat is a very serious crime."

"So what are we supposed to do? If our boat was still floating, we'd take that, but you already saw where it is. We talked about it last night: we'll borrow this boat till we get to Pitcairn, then build our own and leave this one there for somebody to pick up. Eventually, somebody will find it and return it to whoever owns it. What else can we do?"

"You can let me take you back and go to trial. We can explain what happened, and you'll be really free. We can probably get the coast guard or the navy or something to take you back and rescue the others."

"I don't know who they are," he continued. "And besides, you've already told us we're guilty, right? So we'll go to jail again, for even longer. That's what you said. Besides, I'm not so sure the others need to be rescued. I think Kimo may have been right all along: there's nothing here for us. Henderson is our home."

I was arguing, but only half-heartedly. It was so compelling to see them like this: free and full of vitality—they really did need to go home. Jail would just turn them into the rest of us, and what a waste that would be. Besides, after requesting the continuation, how long would it be before Judge Dean would even bring this to trial? I could hardly make promises.

"But you can't possibly make it to Henderson," I said. "What'd you say, it would take three or four weeks? Do you have food and water on board? Do you even know how to sail this thing?"

"We just brought up the fishing gear and water from the *Enterprise*, and there's already lots of water and food in metal jars down below. We can capture rainwater and fish for food. There are maps down below too. We looked at them last night, and there are some islands along the way—maybe just a week from here. We can stop there and find more food and water." He pointed proudly to a domed compass in front of the large wheel. "This boat has a compass, and there's even a clock. We have everything we need—so long as you don't tell anybody where we are."

"Don't worry, I'm not going to tell anybody."

"I know. Because we'd like you to come with us until we get to our first island."

It sounded like a friendly invitation, but I knew it wasn't. There was no reason for them to trust me. Very politely, Adam asked whether I'd mind going below while they got things ready to sail. I wasn't sure what would have happened had I refused, but after a few feeble complaints, I decided to comply.

Left alone down below, I immediately found the VHF radio. I turned it on, pressed the microphone button, and froze. I just couldn't bring myself to go through with it. First of all, it seemed unfair—I'm sure they didn't even know what a VHF was. And then if I did report them, they'd be up on kidnapping charges, which is a whole different ball game than breaking and entering. If I denied that I had been kidnapped, then I'd be up on charges of aiding and abetting. But I guess the real reason I turned the radio off was less altruistic: my life was missing something, and had been for many years. I didn't know where Adam and Mati would end up, but it certainly wasn't back to my office. I suppose if they hadn't insisted, I wouldn't have had the guts to volunteer to go with them, but the fact is, I really wanted to follow this thing through.

It took about twenty minutes before we were on our way, and another ten before Adam called down and invited me back on deck.

Chapter 42 _____

WE ARRIVED AT KIRITMATI almost two weeks after leaving Kona. The *t*'s are pronounced like *s*'s and the first and last *i*'s are silent, so, as strange as it sounds, Kiritmati is actually pronounced *Christmas*, which in past times has been adopted as an alternate spelling.

The trip was unspectacular but transformational. Our meals were sparse—in fact, without Adam's fishing skills, we would have nearly starved—but at the same time, I had never appreciated food more. Every day, every cloud, and every wave was as dreary as the one before, yet I was never bored. I had been kidnapped, held prisoner by a moat thousands of miles wide, yet I felt freer than I ever had. I would never have imagined, nor can I explain now, the bliss of whiling away the hours under sail. No stress, no appointments, no plans, and no noise. Just time. It was the first time in my life I could really say I was relaxed.

Back in my office, I'd kept a little sign above my desk reminding me of Shakespeare's famous words:

I wasteth time and now time wasteth me!

Though I'd stared at that sign every day, I had always misunderstood it: I had indeed wasted much of my life, but it wasn't by whiling it away in laziness; it was by not taking enough time to simply enjoy time itself.

We easily found the large protected lagoon that our maps indicated was on the northwest shore of Kiritmati. There was a collection of run-down shacks near the northern entrance to the lagoon, but that was about all. Kiritmati seemed to be the perfect compromise: large enough to offer stocks of food and water, yet backward enough that no one would be on the lookout for a pirated sailboat. Just to be safe, however, Adam anchored a good distance off shore—I admit, though, to wondering whether that was also to discourage me from making a break for it.

I had little reason for concern, however. Adam had been steadfast in renewing his promise to let me leave as soon as we reached landfall, and no sooner had we dropped anchor than Adam offered to row me ashore on a dingy tied to the front deck. With some hesitation, I lowered myself into the dingy with Adam and Mati, who were wearing their ever-present pareos, salvaged from the *Enterprise*.

It took a good fifteen minutes to paddle to the village. We were warmly greeted by a few villagers, no doubt anxious to sell us supplies. Evidently, we had found the largest town on Kiritmati, a metropolis of nearly two thousand people, ironically named *London*. As soon as we pulled our dingy to shore, I began asking locals about transportation from the island, and quickly learned that there were weekly flights to Honolulu, with the next one scheduled in two days. Unfortunately, while Adam had swum ashore to retrieve my clothing from the rocks of Kona, he had deemed my wallet and cell phone worthless and left them behind. Thus my most acute concern was how I'd get the money to buy my ticket home. It turns out there was a bank on the island, and it was surprisingly straightforward to call Kona and have money wired to Kiritmati.

Meanwhile, Adam and Mati quietly vanished in their dingy. I had really hoped to say good-bye properly and felt empty when I realized they had snuck away. Adam had never questioned how he would replenish the boat's supplies, and it wouldn't be by buying them; he'd just assumed he'd scavenge food from the native land, well away from London. I knew he would succeed, but only after a few days of hard work.

As I scanned the lagoon for their dingy, I realized I already missed them—or perhaps more accurately, I felt left out of the adventures they would undoubtedly find. I wanted to know what happened when they returned to Henderson. I wanted to see the others' reactions when they told them there was still a world out there. That's when it occurred to me that even though nothing grand or adventurous happened on the trip from Kona, it had somehow been the greatest adventure of my life. It also dawned on me that Mati and Adam could not possibly understand how risky it was to let me go. Did they really not understand how easily their escape could be cut short, even from here?

I can only imagine Mati's and Adam's reactions when they were awakened by the sound of a boat nudging up against theirs. Mati was the first up on deck. "Bill! You're back! What's all that stuff?"

It was wonderful to see her brilliant smile again, and made me even more glad that I had decided to surprise them like this. I had hired a skiff to take them more food and drink than they could possibly use in a month. Without asking, the pilot and I began to unload supplies onto deck. "Lots of things. Food that doesn't come from the ocean, for one. Real vegetables and fruit."

Adam came up then and seemed as happy to see me as Mati. "So, you found some of that money you were talking about?"

I became very serious. "Yep, but my gifts come with a condition."

Mati looked at me suspiciously. "Condition? What, we have to go back to that jail?"

"Nope, even worse. You have to take me with you."

"You want to go with us?" Mati laughed. "Why?"

"Well, for one thing, I want to meet all the people you've told me about, and I suppose I just want to see what Henderson is like. Besides, I've been hanging around that jail now for more than twenty years. I might not have been on the same side of the bars as you were, but I guess I was just as much its prisoner. It's time for a change."

Adam grinned widely. "So, you want to be a pirate now too?"

"Nope. I bought this thing—or at least I hope I did."

"What's that mean?" he asked.

"I called a friend of mine who's right now trying to find the rightful owner of this here boat, so he can negotiate its purchase. It's probably the first useful thing I've ever done with my money."

"So this is yours now?" Adam said. "Really?"

"Well, I hope so. Mine now, and yours when we get to Henderson. How's that for a deal?"

Chapter 43

WITH A WELL-STOCKED, LEGITIMATELY-OWNED boat, there was no reason to stop at Pitcairn or Mangareva, so we sailed straight through to Henderson, a trip we estimated would take almost two weeks, nearly all on a port tack. It was at the onset of the trip that I encouraged Adam to start writing a history of what had happened on Henderson, reflecting not only on his life, but also on what happened before he was born. I helped him with his grammar and spelling—and it needed a lot of help—and in exchange, he and Mati taught me to sail, fish, and, well, I guess they taught me to live. We were both slow learners, I suppose.

I also had some fun teaching Adam about the "modern" equipment on the boat, even though much of it was a decade old. Part of that was the boat's GPS system, which I demonstrated the first day out of Kiritmati. I suppose I should have shown it to him on the leg from Kona to Kiritmati, but he'd been so proud of his compass and clock, and was having so much fun learning to use them, I just didn't want to steal from his glory. In fact, he was disappointed once he saw how easy it was to find our position and track our progress with the GPS.

Not surprisingly, when we first pulled up the GPS map image, Henderson didn't show up, but of course if one wanted to hide an island, doctoring GPS databases would be critical. But it didn't really matter to us: since Pitcairn and Mangareva were on our charts, finding Henderson would be easy.

In addition, I showed them how to cook on the propane stove and even how to use the diesel engine to recharge our batteries and run the compressor for the fridge. I most enjoyed showing them ice forming in the freezer.

Though they were certainly entertained by all the gadgets, that's all these things were to them: amusing playthings rather than useful tools. Adam even insisted on using the clock to confirm the longitude readings on the GPS—he just wouldn't trust something he didn't understand, and I certainly couldn't explain to him how it worked. And as a matter of fact, why should he trust something that didn't even recognize that his home existed?

Adam and Mati spent much of the next two weeks speculating what they would find when we got back. Of course the others would have long considered Adam and Mati lost. Would Teiki have taken over control of the island? Would anybody have started to build a second boat to try again for Pitcairn? I found myself as engaged in the conjecture as they, and soon felt that I knew their fellow islanders as well as I knew anybody back on Hawaii. Of course, I would never get to meet Kimo, but I couldn't help wonder about him after hearing their stories. Whether he was just plain cruel or really thought he was saving the human race from extinction, one thing was certain: he had suffered from some form of schizophrenia.

As we got closer to our destination, my companions' moods darkened. Sure, they looked forward to meeting their friends and families, but there were some storm clouds on the horizon as well: Teiki for one, their own relationship for another, and then the big one—the truth they were bringing home. How would Michelle react, for example, when she learned that her kids were probably grown by now and might not even remember her? For all she knew, she could be a grandmother. And Don and Mary might possibly be great grandparents by now!

Their greatest fear, though, was that their two Kitchens would not approve of the intimate relationship they'd grown during their adventures. Mati and I had a conversation about it as we approached the island.

"I'm not sure how Adam's Kitchen will react," she told me, "but I know for sure that Teiki and Mom will absolutely forbid us from seeing each other."

"So what if they do? Can they really forbid you? I thought everybody elected Adam as some kind of island leader."

"I know, but it's not that simple. Sure, we can disobey them, but things were already almost at a breaking point between our Kitchens. If it gets any worse, I don't know what will happen. And now we've been away for so long, I'm sure they think we're dead. And if Teiki's the leader now—and he probably is—I don't think they'd pay attention to Adam. Then what's he supposed to do?"

"Come on, they're going to be so glad to see you, that's all they'll think about. Trust me."

"I hope you're right, but I'm not so sure. Maybe for a while, but … well, we'll see I guess."

"So why don't you two just get married and that'd be the end of it? They can't complain then, because it'll be a done deal."

"Married?"

"Let me guess: you don't know what marriage is either."

"Of course I know what it is, but I don't think it really means much. I think my dad was married to Adam's mom, but they both lived with other people—at least until my dad died. I guess David is married to Michelle, too, but they're not even in the same Kitchen. So what does it really mean anyway?"

"I'm the wrong person to ask. I never married. It's supposed to be an agreement between a man and a woman; that they'll always be together. It doesn't mean much in Hawaii either, to tell you the truth, but the idea is that you have a formal ceremony, invite friends and relatives, and declare your love and commitment in front of witnesses. It's also a legal contract, so it affects your taxes and … well, never mind that. The point is that it's a formal agreement to be together—or I guess *promise* is a better word."

"I don't think it would help, but it sounds nice. I kind of like the idea."

Adam wandered within earshot, put his arms around Mati, and looked at me firmly. "We're married already."

"You're married?"

"Maybe not like you think of it back in the Old World, but it's different where we are. Mom says that being married is a commitment to each other, not a ceremony or a legal contract. My mom and dad are married in every way that counts, and so are we." He looked at Mati.

Mati didn't seem completely satisfied with Adam's outburst, but let it drop. Knowing Mati, it was a safe assumption that, in time, they would have a ceremony of sorts. I couldn't help but wonder what it would be like. I also knew, though, that Adam was right: if ever there was a married couple, this was it. I had been with them day in and day out for so long, I had gotten to know them better than anybody I could remember, and what I knew about them more than anything was that if I ever there were a couple, this was it. They often seemed to communicate without speaking, as if reading each other's mind. They acted in concert, yet without a plan. My friends were often jealous of my lifestyle, singing praise for the single life, but for the first time, I began to really understand the completeness of a man and a woman.

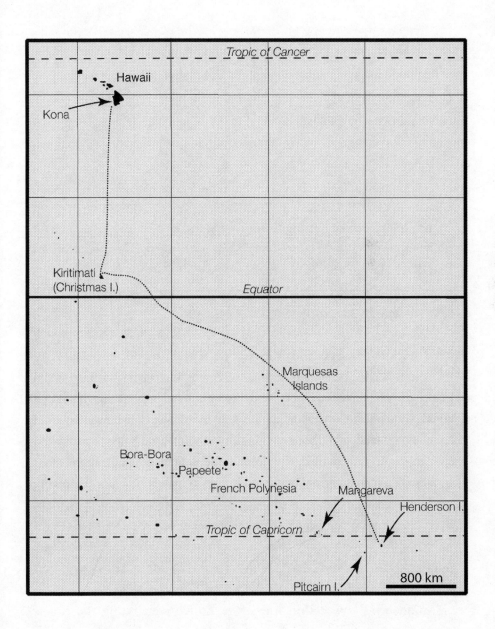

Chapter 44

IT WAS A BEAUTIFUL, sunny day when I first caught sight of Henderson Island. It looked like Kiritmati from a distance—although perhaps a bit higher and not quite as large—but it was nothing like the mountainous islands of Hawaii and Tahiti that I was used to. As we approached the island from the northwest, Adam told me we were sailing right over the spot where they found the *Sea Salva*'s anchor.

We tacked our way eastward along the north shore, trying to stay a few hundred yards outside the reef. Mati and Adam kept pointing to indistinguishable places along the way, discussing things I couldn't even begin to understand. When we were about halfway along the north coast, they pointed out the Point: a feature so distinctive even I would have recognized it without being shown. Not long after, I noticed a figure running away from the Point. Mati saw it too, claiming it must be Marco, even though we were too far off to make out a face. Knowing we had been seen, I began to imagine the excitement that must have been brewing on the island—and that was given the fact that they'd have had no way to know that the approaching boat was manned by none other Adam and Mati, about to make a triumphant return after nearly three months.

Suddenly, I saw a thin line of dark blue penetrating the reef—obviously the north beach channel. Without hesitation, Adam turned sharply right, calling for us to let out the sails all the way. At that point, people had begun collecting on the beach and were watching anxiously. As soon as they recognized Mati waving to them from the front of the boat, they started screaming and waving. Seconds later, there was a parade of people splashing their way into the lagoon. It looked like the start of a triathlon.

Meanwhile, Adam had already warned me that this would be the trickiest part of our trip. We had to coast through the channel, then almost immediately turn into the wind and drop anchor before we ran aground in the shallow lagoon. I handled the anchor, while Mati raced to get the sails down. To Adam's credit, he remained completely focused at the helm, never even looking up at his friends until the anchor was safely set.

In an instant, both Adam and Mati dove into the water and swam to meet their friends and families. They met the onslaught in about chest-deep water and erupted in an unrestrained party of celebratory hugs. I wanted to share in the excitement, but this was their moment, not mine, so I wandered over to the starboard side and sat on the gunnels, just watching. Though I was the outsider, I couldn't keep from bursting in sympathetic joy as I witnessed their reunion.

I remained unnoticed and forgotten for a good five minutes before Mati finally gestured for me to join them. I felt I knew these people on an intimate level by now, and they were people I really wanted to like me. I was as nervous as I imagine a girl might be meeting her fiancée's parents for the first time. But my unease was put to rest as Mati took me by the hand and introduced me to them one by one.

We started with David and Claire, who I knew were about my age. Their wrinkled, sun-baked skin made them look far older than I, but they were also obviously in much better shape. We then drifted over to Nani, who I had come to especially admire from their stories. Somehow the years had passed over her with little effect, at least so it seemed—she was a beautiful, magnetic woman. Next to her was Stan, tall, straight, and weathered, engaged in conversation with Adam while trying unsuccessfully to hide his tears.

Mati then turned to a tall, nearly emaciated woman that had arrived late on the scene and was still standing on the dry beach. She was so weak, another women was leading her around by the hand. From Mati's frozen stare, I knew who it had to be. But there was no need for words.

As Mati walked toward her, her mother fell sobbing into her arms. They held each other for several minutes, and I backed away to give them some space. After they finally broke their embrace, Mati, before saying anything to her mother, called me over and introduced us.

No sooner had Mati introduced us, though, than she looked around searchingly and asked, "Mom, where's Teiki?"

Stefani didn't answer, but embraced Mati again.

Mati pushed away and frowned. "Mom?"

Stefani still didn't respond. Finally, Nani wandered over and put her hand on Mati's shoulder. Then quietly, she said, "He's gone, Mati. We'll talk more about it later, okay?" Nani was nodding pleadingly toward Stefani as she spoke, but then turned to Mati. "Right now we're all just happy to see you and Adam."

Mati's high spirits were quenched instantly, but she understood that for some reason, this wasn't the time or place to discuss Teiki. For the next half hour, everybody dropped the subject of Teiki and chattered about a myriad of other topics that were meaningless to me: how the farm was doing, who'd caught what fish, who had been sick. The island gossip took priority over questions about the outside world; as near as I could tell, not a single person asked where Adam and Mati had been and what they had seen—it only seemed to matter that they were back.

After a while, however, it was clear that Mati and Adam were finding it difficult to stay focused, and Mati kept looking over the shoulders of others to find Nani, as if trying to keep track of her. Finally, Nani was able to wrangle a moment alone with them away from Stefani. Still in tow, I had a chance to hear the news along with them.

"Mati," Nani said softly, "your mom will be back in a second, but I need to tell you about Teiki." She looked at Adam. "Both of you. After you two sailed away, he kind of freaked out. He started to disappear a lot during the day—like Kimo used to."

Mati looked worried. "Disappeared? That's not like Teiki. He never did anything like that."

"Well, he did. We thought it was weird, too, but for the next two weeks, we saw him less and less at the village, and when he did show up, he avoided everybody, even his own Kitchen. Stef—your mom—was really worried and kept asking him what was wrong, but he just wouldn't talk to anybody. After a couple of weeks, we were all so worried about you two, we weren't paying much attention to Teiki, I guess. Mati, your mom was absolutely beside herself with fear for you—I guess I was too. Stan was the only person that kept saying you two were okay."

"I know," Adam cut in. "Sorry. We knew you guys were worried, but there wasn't anything we could do."

"No, I'm sure that's true. I didn't mean to say … but you can tell us your story later. Let me just finish this before Mati's mom gets back. After that third week—or I guess it was into the fourth week—Teiki headed out to the Point. Marco was out there fishing, so only he saw it, but he says that Teiki walked right up to the tip of the Point and jumped off."

I'd guessed that by then, Mati had realized the news wouldn't be good, but gauging from her reaction, that didn't seem to make it any easier. She grabbed Adam's arm for support. "He fell off the Point? What happened?"

Nani looked directly into Mati's eyes. "Mati, Teiki didn't fall, he jumped. I'm so sorry to have to tell you, but you need to know, so you can support your mother. She needs you now. She's hardly eaten or done anything since then. We've been so worried about her, but none of us have been able to help her. Seeing you changed everything. She thought she had lost both of you, but now that you're here, you're going to have to be the strong one and help her."

Mati was obviously struggling to keep herself composed. She turned to Adam, her eyes appealing for an answer. "But it's impossible. Why would he do that? It just …. " Mati froze, mouth still open.

"We don't know why," Nani continued. "We'll never know."

Adam started to say something, but Mati caught his attention with a subtle shake of her head, and he stopped.

Nani tried to change the subject with a deep breath. "Okay, so that's that and there's nothing to be done about it. So what about you? What happened, and what's the story with Bill here?"

Adam picked up the conversation. "There's so much to tell you, it's hard to know where to even begin."

Nani smiled warmly. "So then why don't we have a gathering tonight, and you and Mati tell us everything from the very beginning. Otherwise, you're going to end up telling the same story twenty times. Everybody is desperate to hear."

"Cool. But Mom, there's one thing I want to tell you first. Mati and I … we want … I mean we're … well, I think you were right, you know, about …"

Nani was grinning broadly as Adam stuttered to explain. Then, finally, with tears in her eyes, she interrupted him. "I know, Adam, I know. We all know. I think it was obvious to everybody but you. We all support you—even Stefani will. You'll see." She collected both of them in her arms and hugged them.

Seeing the happiness in Mati's and Adam's expressions was worth a million dollars, but suddenly I felt like an intruder. Down the beach I saw the woman that had helped Stefani, and took the opportunity to intercept her and introduce myself. I really just wanted to give Adam and Mati some much-needed privacy.

The woman was thin but not frail, and attractive, though weathered in the same way as the other Elders. I took a chance, hoping to surprise her. "You must be Michelle. Nice to meet you. I'm Bill."

"Yes, I heard. I suppose it's nice to meet you too." She seemed somewhat shy. "A stranger on the island—it's not exactly an everyday occurrence. I was just headed over to talk to Mati and Adam."

"Actually, they might want a little time alone just now. Nani just told them about Teiki, and … well, never mind, it's none of my business. Sorry, I shouldn't tell you what to do."

"No, you should, and you're probably right. I'll give them a bit of space. So what happened anyway? Everybody's dying to know where you're from and what it's like out there."

"Jeez, I don't even know where to begin. I'm sure Adam and Mati are anxious to tell everybody about their trip, and I don't want to steal their thunder. But I'm from Hawaii—I guess I can say that much."

"Hawaii? How'd they meet you?"

I smiled and shrugged.

"Okay, never mind. I guess I need to wait until the gathering like everybody else. I'm sure we're going to have a real party tonight. Want some food or something to hold you over? I feel like a terrible host asking questions and not offering you anything. You've probably been on the boat all day."

"Well, actually, much longer than a day—more like three weeks—but no thanks anyway. We ate really well on the boat, so I'm not hungry. What I'd really like, though, is to see a little of the island."

She grinned slightly, almost carefully. "Okay. What do you want to see?"

"Whatever you want to show me, I guess."

By the time Michelle brought me back, everyone was busy with preparations for the evening's gathering. Mati was spending the day close to her mother, and Adam told me he thought he should give them time together for a few days; it was important, he said, that Stefani understood he wasn't stealing Mati away from her. I suspected that Nani had helped him figure that out.

Adam also insisted on taking me on his own tour of the island, showing me some of the same things Michelle had, but from a different perspective, as well as features Michelle hadn't thought important. For example, he took me inside the bunker, which I found ordinary and anticlimactic. We wandered out on the Point and looked over Stan's Leap at the surf thundering against the rock wall; when I next saw Stan, I had an entirely new perspective of the gray-haired, wrinkled man that had once taken such a leap of love. Adam also took me on a swimming tour of the lagoon, which put even the pristine coves of Kona to shame.

The food that evening was spectacular, and surprisingly, nobody asked about me or about Adam and Mati's adventure. Then after we finished eating, suddenly, as if an alarm had rung, everybody fell silent, and Adam stepped in the middle of the three tables arranged in a triangle. I was more than a little curious to see how he would explain things and then to watch their reactions.

Seemingly in no hurry, Adam started with Stan's illness on the morning of their departure and the trip to Pitcairn. He carefully avoided discussing Mati's subterfuge in boarding the *Enterprise*, though I noticed Mati listening with downcast eyes, portraying remorse or even shame. At least Stefani wasn't making any accusations—at least not yet.

It was curious to watch the dichotomy of reactions to Adam's description of the metal roofs at Pitcairn. The Youngers were riveted to every word, while the Elders remained uninterested. When he explained why they decided to go on to Mangareva, the Elders stirred in confusion and disbelief, while the Youngers appeared not to even understand the issue. By that point in the story, Mati was chiming in often and enthusiastically, filling in bits of the story that Adam had omitted or failed to describe as colorfully as she thought appropriate.

When they came to the part about the demasting of the *Enterprise*, it was altogether obvious that Adam and Mati had found time that afternoon to rehearse. They said only that the forward mast had broken and they had managed to repair it using metal rope. There was no mention of Teiki's sabotage. I thought they were poor liars, but they got away with it. Perhaps it's the lawyer in me, but I didn't approve of the deception, even though I understood their motivation. The truth always emerges, and eventually, they'd be unable to shield Teiki from his role.

It must have been a full hour before the story progressed to their arrival in Hawaii. I could see the Elders fidgeting anxiously as the two described the house and the arrest. When Adam finally got around to telling them about typhoon Gita, and then implied that the Great Storm wasn't Armageddon after all, nearly all the Elders began to squirm. Finally David spoke up in protest.

"So then how do you explain why nobody ever came? Okay, I sort of understand that the Mangareva base was destroyed and that people thought that's where New Eden was, but it's been twenty years for God's sake! How can it be that no boat came by in twenty years?"

Adam tried to explain. "They have this thing called the Internet, and that's how they get all their information now. Somebody changed the Internet to make it look like there wasn't a Henderson Island, so no one even knows it exists."

"Impossible! I know what the Internet is, Adam, and it makes it more difficult to hide things, not easier."

Adam looked over at me, eyes pleading for my help. I stood and tried to explain the best that I could, but I'm not sure I was convincing.

David turned to Stan. "What do you think, Stan? You were a software developer. Is it possible?"

Stan was quiet a moment. "Yeah, I guess that part sounds possible. He's right. Everything back then, I mean all our information, was pretty much was accessed through Google or Yahoo, and I suppose that a worm like that could have been written that would target the big data centers. It wasn't really my field, and it's so long ago… " He shook his head and chuckled. "I had forgotten about Google and Yahoo—haven't heard those words in twenty years. But all that that doesn't explain why nobody came. What about the people that were here before us? Why didn't they tell others where the island really was?"

I handled this one as well. "Yeah, that bothered me too. I did a lot of reading about this storm Gita. First of all, you were only the third group of guests at the island, so not that many people had been here—only ten, in fact—but even more importantly, the news reports I saw were clear and adamant: the New Eden Resort was destroyed by the storm and everybody was lost. They didn't leave any room for doubt or question. There probably wasn't anything for the previous visitors to question."

David asked, "What about the lights in the sky? How else can you explain them? I can tell you, they were not normal or from any typhoon."

He had me on that one. I didn't want to say he was probably just exaggerating, but that was the only possible explanation. While I was thinking of a response, Stan asked, "What about the Polynesian Retrospective people? Chris Stetson was even on his way here in his boat. They told us that just as we left Mangareva. Why wouldn't he have said anything?"

"Chris Stetson's boat was lost at sea with everybody on board."

After a moment of silence, Claire asked, "During the storm? Do they know where?"

Since our short introduction, those were the first words I heard Claire say. I thought about her father. Later, I'd have to find the right words to tell her he was dead. "They think it was the night the storm hit Mangareva. They don't know exactly where they went down, but they were on their way to Tahiti."

"No, they were coming here," Claire mumbled. "They were flares."

We all turned to her.

"Flares," she said again. "Not solar flares, *distress* flares. What we saw were flares from his yacht, or maybe a lifeboat." She turned to Stan. "You remember when we flew out with Alan? Janice said Stetson was going to sail to Henderson, starting out the next day. If they sunk the night of the storm, I'll bet they were almost here—it would have been, what, two days of sailing?"

Stan nearly jumped up from his seat. "Right! They would have been fifty miles or so from here, and probably just to the west."

"And that's just where the red lights were," she said. "To the west."

The last piece had fallen into place. At least the last big piece. It still wasn't clear why Stetson had told Mangareva officials he was headed north to Tahiti, but then that seemed consistent with his secretive habits. They continued to challenge me, but after a while, I sensed they were arguing more with themselves than with me. They had lived the lie too long to shed it easily. Still, there I was, incontrovertible proof that there was a world out there.

At one point during the discussion, I noticed that David had become so distracted that he was no longer interested in arguing. He seemed to be watching my wrist, eyes averting every time I looked directly at him. Finally I realized what had caught his interest: my watch. With little thought, I removed my cheap Timex, mid-debate, and tossed it to him. It was like throwing a bone to a dog—he lost interest in everything we were saying and just fondled my gift.

Veering back to the others, I decided to take a different approach—the offensive. I turned the table, asking what in the world made them think the earth had been broiled by the sun. They stumbled for explanations, going through much of the same litany as Adam had: the strange lights, the lack of radio contact, and the appearance of the *Sea Salva*. I countered each one. In the end, they fell back on the same two central points: Kimo's certainty and the fact that nobody came.

Regardless of the details, the Youngers seemed not to care that there was another world out there—they were simply curious. On the other hand, the Elders were confused and emotional, seemingly at a loss for what to do about it all. Michelle was the only Elder who was clear: she was absolutely determined to go find her children as soon as possible. Even that night, she began pressuring Adam to take her to Mangareva. Adam didn't refuse but said he wouldn't be ready to go out again for a while. I think he knew Mati wouldn't leave her mother's side for some time, and he wanted to be there with her.

Michelle was my guide for the next two weeks. She showed me around and taught me about life on the island. She was a much better teacher than Adam because she was patient and understood my way of thinking. Those weeks were really a wonderful time for me, and I certainly wasn't anxious to leave, but inevitably, discussions about sailing to the Old World became regular fare. Feelings and reactions continued to be mixed, however: curiosity and fear from the Youngers and a surprising reluctance from the Elders. Obviously the prospect of a long ocean voyage was a fearsome one, but just as frightening was what they would find when the returned.

I had described some of the changes that occurred during the past twenty years, including the development of fusion power that had made electricity all but free, the attendant loss of interest in the Middle East's oil and ensuing rash of civil wars that nobody cared about anymore, and the progress in stem cell regenerative medicine, which had made death obsolete except by old age and accidents. The Elders would be almost as out of place in today's world as the Youngers would be, and I think the specter of learning how to live in yet another age was frightening to them—two were enough for any lifetime. I suppose as one ages, it's difficult to wander from the path of least resistance, and by now they were set in their ways.

After a great deal of vacillation, Mary decided that she would go with Michelle and I once Adam was ready to set sail. I supposed none of it mattered much anyway: as soon as the Old World learned the story of Henderson Island and put it back on the map, free of fictitious navigational hazards, communication would resume and other boats would come—maybe even a plane, once the airstrip was cleared.

So, at a gathering some three weeks after our return, Michelle again pressured Adam. "You only need to take us to Mangareva. I'm sure we can get help from there. Can't you at least take us that far?"

"Michelle, it's still almost two weeks to get there and back again, and you won't like it there anyway. Besides, I need to be here for a few more weeks at least." The situation between Mati and Stef was still driving his reluctance.

"I'll take you." I heard the words, but wasn't sure I had even said them. I certainly don't know what prompted them and was maybe more surprised to hear them than anybody. It was as if I were a ventriloquist's puppet. Everybody stared at me, until Adam broke the silence.

"Bill could do it. It's an easy sail. He even knows how to use all the electrical stuff."

Michelle turned to me. "You'll take me to Mangareva?"

There was no going back at that point. "Maybe Tahiti. I'm not sure you'll be able to get any help at Mangareva; there's not much there." I turned to Adam. "But I might cheat and use the engine a little, if you don't mind."

The next day we made preparations for our trip. The Elders made lists of what they wanted us to bring back, and we stocked the boat with fresh water and food. In a week or so, the world was about to learn that it had a new island population.

But then again, did the world really have to know?

Author's Note

Henderson Island is real, along with its reef, lagoon, the Point and beaches. The flora, and fauna are also generally as described herein, though the soil is poor and there are few trees other than coconut trees. I've also taken several liberties with respect to geological details, such as the moving the island's only fresh water spring and adding one of the channels through the reef. Polynesians briefly settled on Henderson Island more than five hundred years ago, but it is unclear what happened to their short-lived civilization—some believe they migrated on to Easter Island due to a lack of useful stone for making tools. There is no resort on the island—in fact, there are no structures or buildings of any kind, not even a bunker. In fact, the only sign that it has ever been inhabited are some scattered five-hundred-year-old bones in Lone Frigate Cave.

As described in the book, the Spanish discovered Henderson in 1606, but it wasn't seen again for another two hundred years—a testament to just how isolated it is. If you look at a globe and center your view on Henderson Island, you quickly appreciate why it often goes many years, even decades, without visitors (see figure below). There is a very rarely used shipping lane that passes about thirty miles from Henderson, but it is too far for visual contact. Even today, it almost never sees visitors except for rare side trips from Pitcairn or ambitious scientific expeditions. It is very likely the least visited bit of land on our planet.

Some twenty years ago, a retired American general tried to buy the island, purportedly with the intent of turning it into a vacation resort. British scientists objected and succeeded in protecting Henderson by making it a World Heritage Site.

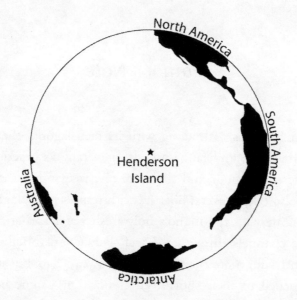

Pitcairn Island was also settled by Polynesians some five hundred years ago and likewise abandoned for unknown reasons. There is evidence, however, that that its civilization once flourished (at least relatively speaking).

After the Polynesians, the next people to set foot on Pitcairn were the Bounty mutineers in 1790, and there are close analogues between their true story and the fiction presented here. The men did indeed kill one another due to a combination of racial strife and sexual competition over each other's wives, leaving only John Adams alive amidst a somewhat unclear number of Tahitian women. The resulting "civilization" was briefly discovered eighteen years later, but the next physical presence on the island wasn't until twenty-five years later, in 1815, when Captain Folger of the Topaz finally stepped foot on land.

By then the civilization possessed a bimodal age distribution not unlike that described in the novel. The children had been taught a distorted version of Christianity by the domineering John Adams, who behaved almost like an emperor or chief—he was their Kimo. The only book on the island was a Bible, and they had no real knowledge of how it was to be interpreted or the context for its verses—the religious practices that resulted are in themselves worthy of study. The children also learned a strange language closely based on English but with some interesting twists. They also married absurdly young and with huge differences in ages, and they utterly refused to discuss their past (likely at the direction of John Adams, still afraid he would be returned to stand trial in England).

The initial conversation between the children of Pitcairn (approaching the whaling ship in their small canoe) and Captain Folger is indicative of how utterly out of touch the civilization was.

"Who are you?" [Asked by Captain Folger]

"We are Englishmen." [Answered by Thursday Christian, Fletcher Christian's son]

"Where were you born?"

"On that island which you see."

"How are you Englishmen, if you were born on that island, which the English do not own, and never possessed?"

"We are Englishmen because our father was an Englishman."

"Who was your father?"

With interesting simplicity, they answered, "Aleck." [Meaning Alex, John Adam's alias]

"Who is Aleck?"

"Don't you know Aleck?"

"How should I know Aleck?"

And later, when Captain Folger explained he was from the United States, they asked if that was in Ireland (John Adams' home country).[1]

---

1   Trevor Lummis, *Pitcairn Island: Life and Death in Eden*, (Ashgate Publishing) 1997.

It's also interesting to note that as small and isolated as Pitcairn is, the population has proven nearly impossible to uproot. In 1831, the entire population was moved to Tahiti, but unable to adjust, most soon returned to their island prison. Twenty years later, they again tried to relocate—this time to Norfolk Island—because the Pitcairn's resources were insufficient to support their burgeoning population. But again, most returned after just a few years. Today, the island remains isolated from the rest of the world, to the point of having nowhere to land a plane.

The idea that Stan and Nani could glide the Sea Salva into dock on Pitcairn is ludicrous. Even with the concrete pier now in place, bringing a boat safely ashore requires special boats guided with extreme precision, skill, and timing—and even now, the Pitcairners do not venture out except in ideal weather. To this day, no ship or even yacht has ever actually docked at Pitcairn.

The book does not attempt to capture the personality of the Pitcairn islanders, and in fact it does them a gross disservice. The Pitcairn islanders are noted to be extraordinarily friendly to the few visitors that are able to find their way there, and are a religious and conservative people (though these adjectives should be interpreted very freely). The legal issues discussed in the book regarding statutory rape on the island are, unfortunately, true. In order to survive, the islanders have had to adopt a unique social environment that is complicated, delicate; their customs are neither right nor wrong, but are certainly different and difficult for us to understand. Some simple math will highlight the difficulties of reproduction in a population of only fifty or sixty people. Still, the British brought criminal charges against their population.

There is also some truth to the thought that sustaining civilization on Pitcairn may soon be impossible. As ships become larger and more difficult to divert from established shipping lanes, the island grows increasingly remote and the island's population is dwindling. If the British courts continue to try to impose British law on this handful of unique people, it's all but certain that Pitcairn will again become uninhabited.

For more about the modern-day people of Pitcairn, I recommend reading Glynn Christian's book, Fragile Paradise (Long Riders' Guild Press) 2005, or the January 2008 article "Trouble in Paradise," featured in Vanity Fair magazine (no. 569, page 94, William Prochnau and Laura Parker).

The electronic "hiding" of Henderson Island is possible, though, of course, fictional. Worms and bombs do exist (including the example of miserable failure). Worms that are able to "leap" onto the data servers and modify targeted data presumably do not exist, but if our large data centers were to become infected by such fictitious worms, they could deliberately and carefully change data, and there is abundant evidence that the electronic fiction created by such antics would become universally perceived as truth.

As a side note, at the time of writing, if one looked in Google Maps for Pitcairn Island, the island that is identified was not Pitcairn, but Henderson Island. At the same time, Google Earth did not recognize that Henderson Island exists. The actual Pitcairn Island could be seen on satellite images, but was not recognized or labeled. At the time of final editing, Henderson had been found and correctly labeled.

Solar storms do exist. In fact, on September 2, 1859, such an event earned the name *The Great Geomagnetic Storm*. More specifically, there was a "white light" solar flare that resulted in a huge ejection of gamma radiation from the sun, dramatically enhancing the aurora phenomenon in earth's northern and southern hemispheres. In New York, the northern lights were so bright that one could read a newspaper from the light of the aurora! The gamma radiation's interaction with the earth's magnetic fields also produced an electrical field so intense that some telegraph lines cutting the electric field at the right angle could be operated without the use of a battery or external source of electrical power. Kimo's thought that such phenomenon can result in substantial heating of the earth's surface is, however, entirely without precedent or scientific foundation; in fact, most physicists would say it is theoretically impossible for the sun in its current phase. We should be safe for a billion years or so.

The name Kimo is the Hawaiian version of Jim. Nanihi is a Tahitian name meaning the complete woman, while Matahina means goddess eyes, and Teiki means king child.